"You shouldn't be kissing me like that,"

Johanna said, breaking his hold as she stepped back.

"We're married, Johanna," Tate said. He reached to tug her shawl over her shoulders.

"Not really." Her gaze fell from his, intent on the third button of his jacket.

"According to the law, we are."

"You know what I mean, Tate. We have a bargain."

He could barely stop his hands from fastening on her and hauling her into his arms. "I'm willing to make some changes in the deal we made."

She turned from him and ducked her head. "I'm not, Tate."

From the barn the noisy trumpet of the stallion sounded once more and Johanna's shoulders stiffened at the sound. "You'd best find a secure place to hold that animal for the next two weeks, Mr. Montgomery. One male creature on the loose around here is about all we need...!"

Dear Reader,

Carolyn Davidson, author of *Gerrity's Bride* and *Loving Katherine*, returns this month with a terrific new book, *The Forever Man*. This emotional story is about a reclusive spinster who, because of her past, has given up on love—until a marriage of convenience to a widower in search of a new life for himself and his two sons heals her broken heart and teaches her to trust in love again. Don't miss this exciting new tale from one of our up-and-coming authors.

Sharon Schulze, one of the authors in this year's March Madness Promotion, also returns this month with *To Tame a Warrior's Heart*, a stirring medieval tale about a former mercenary and a betrayed noblewoman who overcome their shadowed pasts with an unexpected love. And in *The Lieutenant's Lady*, her fourth book for Harlequin Historicals, author Rae Muir begins an exciting new Western series called THE WEDDING TRAIL. This month's story is about a hard-luck soldier who returns home determined to marry the town "princess," a woman who sees him as little more than a way out of an unwanted marriage.

USA Today bestselling author Ruth Langan is also out this month with *Ruby*, the next book in her ongoing series THE JEWELS OF TEXAS. *Ruby* is the delightful tale of a flirtatious young woman and the formidable town marshal who falls under her spell.

Whatever your tastes in reading, we hope you enjoy all four books, available wherever Harlequin Historicals are sold.

Sincerely,

Tracy Farrell,
Senior Editor

Please address questions and book requests to:
Harlequin Reader Service
U.S.: 3010 Walden Ave., P.O. Box 1325, Buffalo, NY 14269
Canadian: P.O. Box 609, Fort Erie, Ont. L2A 5X3

CAROLYN DAVIDSON

The FOREVER MAN

Harlequin Books

TORONTO • NEW YORK • LONDON
AMSTERDAM • PARIS • SYDNEY • HAMBURG
STOCKHOLM • ATHENS • TOKYO • MILAN
MADRID • WARSAW • BUDAPEST • AUCKLAND

ISBN 0-373-28985-5

THE FOREVER MAN

Copyright © 1997 by Carolyn Davidson

This edition published by arrangement with Harlequin Books S.A.

Printed in U.S.A.

Books by Carolyn Davidson

Harlequin Historicals

Gerrity's Bride #298
Loving Katherine #325
The Forever Man #385

CAROLYN DAVIDSON

lives in South Carolina, on the outskirts of Charleston, with her husband, her number-one fan. Working in a new/used bookstore is an ideal job for her, allowing her access to her favorite things: books and people. Readers' comments are more than welcome in her mailbox, P.O. Box 60626, North Charleston, SC 29419-0626.

To my sisters, Marion, Norma and Nancy.
They knew me "when"...and love me still!
And to my sister-in-law, Thelma, who is an unpaid but
much appreciated fount of information. What I don't
already know about horses, she does, not to mention
apple orchards and some other good stuff. Best of all,
she never laughs at my dumb questions!
But most of all, to my own "Forever Man,"
Mr. Ed, who loves me!

Chapter One

"I believe I have a solution to your problem, Miss Johanna." The Reverend Hughes folded his hands precisely and rubbed one thumb the length of the other, his eyes never leaving the young woman seated across the table from him.

Johanna nodded politely. Entertaining well-meaning townfolk had become a way of life over the past months. Seemingly, setting her life in order was the goal of every person who'd known Fred and Mary Patterson.

"When your daddy died, I knew it would seem like the end of the world to you, Johanna. That's why we've all been putting our heads together, trying to help you get settled."

She was about as settled as any old maid ever was, Johanna figured, but perhaps the preacher had a trick or two up his sleeve. If he could come up with a way to clean up the last of the garden, milk six cows and tend to a yardful of laying hens, besides lugging six bushels of apples into the fruit cellar during the next twelve hours, it would be a miracle fit for a sermon come Sunday morning.

"Are you listening to me, Miss Johanna?" Theodore Hughes leaned over the table, his eyes filled with concern as he sought to meet her gaze. "I feel the events of the

past months have sent you into a true decline. You almost
appear to be in the depths of despair this morning."

It was more she'd like to be in the depths of her feather
tick this morning, Johanna thought. Her every muscle aching, her eyes burning from lack of sleep and her empty
stomach growling were surely enough reason to feel despair. If she was the sort to fall into that trap.

"Perhaps I came too early in the day, my dear. However,
I felt it could never be too early to bring good tidings your
way." Leaning over the table in her direction, the preacher
smiled with kindly humor.

"Good tidings?" She'd heard nothing but foolishness
and claptrap from the steady stream of townspeople heading her way lately. Good tidings might be a relief.

"Your daddy left you a fine place, Miss Johanna. But if
you can't tend it properly, you won't be able to hold on to
it, what with the mortgage at the bank and your stock to
care for and the rest of the apple crop to get in."

She knew all that, Johanna thought glumly. She'd had
four solid offers from neighboring farmers wanting to buy
her place, one offer to teach school in the next county, and
a proposal from Neville Olson. Whether he wanted to
marry her or her farm, she hadn't quite determined before
she escorted him off the porch.

"You're a woman of means, Miss Johanna," the
preacher told her quietly. "I've been concerned that you
not be taken in by any scalawags or given poor advice,
even by well-meaning folks hereabouts. And late last night,
the good Lord sent the answer to your problem right to my
door."

Johanna resisted the urge to place her head on the table
and close her eyes. Whatever the man was nattering about,
she was too tired to care. Moving the big ladder from tree
to tree, then climbing it, to pick apples all day yesterday
had about done her in. As a matter of fact, if she didn't get

moving, chances were she just might not be able to resist taking a nap on the kitchen table, preacher or no.

"...one boy is about seven, the other just a little fella. Mr. Montgomery—Tate is his given name—is willing to come out here right away, this forenoon in fact, and talk it over with you." Face beaming, the preacher paused for breath. "I'm just delighted with this turn of events, Miss Johanna. I feel it's a real answer to your problem, one your daddy would have approved."

Johanna blinked. Somewhere along the way, she'd lost track of this conversation. Who in the dickens was this Mr. Montgomery? And what did two little boys have to do with her?

"I'm aware you must be awestruck by the providential aspects of such a happening," the preacher continued. "I felt the very same way when everything began to dovetail together last evening. Why, I almost drove right out here then, but it was almost sundown, and I knew you'd be ready to retire for the night."

Fat chance, thought Johanna. At sundown, she'd been separating the milk and getting ready to churn the butter for delivery to the general store in town today. A two-mile walk, one way. She lifted her hand to press against her middle. No wonder her stomach was grinding away beneath her palm. She'd gone without supper last night, and now the preacher had dragged her in from the barn before she had a chance to eat breakfast this morning.

"I'm sure you're at a loss for words, Miss Johanna. I understand that sometimes a heart is too full of thanksgiving to utter a sound." Rising from his chair, the young parson offered Johanna his hand. "I'll be back in a couple of hours, by noon at the latest, with Mr. Montgomery, my dear. God will surely bless this endeavor. You'll see."

The chicken feed sailed through the air with a *swish*, scattering over the hen yard. Clucking and pecking, the pullets moved about, sidestepping and nudging each other as they attended to their breakfast.

Johanna watched with pride as her white leghorns preened in the morning sun. She'd raised this year's batch from her own eggs, culling off the old hens and canning them up for the winter. Three young roosters still awaited the chopping block, the rest having become food for her table throughout the summer. Now her chicken coop held over thirty laying hens, their eggs providing her with a tidy sum every week at the general store, when she carried them in to Joseph Turner. That, with the butter she churned twice weekly, she was managing to keep her cupboards decently filled.

"Now to tend to filling my stomach," she told the hens clucking around her feet. "As if you care, so long as you get your breakfast." Edging them aside, she made her way to the gate of the chicken yard. One of the broody hens had escaped again, and was claiming a place for herself beneath the lilac bushes near the corncrib.

"You'll end up in the stew pot if you're not careful," she called to the clucking hen. "I don't have time to hunt down your eggs every day, and it's too late in the year to be sittin' on a clutch of eggs.

"I'm not up to chasing her today," she muttered to herself, scraping her soles on the metal bar she'd placed just outside the gate. After removing the layer of chicken droppings she'd managed to gather on her shoes, Johanna headed for the house.

A bowl of oatmeal was about as nourishing as you could get, she figured, watching the water as it came to a boil in her smallest kettle. She scattered a handful of oats from the box over the water and added a pinch of salt. In moments she'd sliced a thick slab of bread from the loaf on the tabletop and spread it with fresh butter. The oatmeal bubbled as she worked, and she stirred it, testing the thickness. Pa had always said she made oatmeal just right.

The spoon held in midair, Johanna considered the thought. In retrospect, it had been about the only thing she'd ever done that pleased him. Mama's bread had been lighter, her pie crust more tender. Even her chicken and dumplings had been ambrosia for the gods, if her father's memory was to be believed.

Johanna, on the other hand, had spent the past ten years being judged as somewhat imperfect by the father she'd tried so hard to please. "I picked six bushels of apples yesterday, Pa," she said into the silence of her kitchen. "If you hadn't sold the horse, I could haul them to the fruit cellar on the wagon. Now Mr. Turner will have to make a trip out if he wants them for the store."

Pa had done all sorts of strange things those last few months, as if his mind had slipped into another world. And perhaps it had. Selling the horse had been the final straw, to Johanna's way of thinking. Then staying in town to play poker with the hired hands from around the county on Friday night…something he'd never done before. He'd lost every penny in his pockets before he headed home. Johanna shook her head at the memory. Pa had never been much of a hand at cards of any kind. He'd walked home at midnight, two miles down the road from town, and stretched out on the porch to sleep.

She'd found him the next morning, all the life sucked out of him, like the west wind had taken what little zest for living he had left once Mama died. Three months he'd been gone, and she could still see him there, a faint, rare smile curling his lips, as if he saw something beautiful afar off.

The oatmeal was tasty, sweet as two spoonfuls of brown sugar could make it. The cream was rich, yellow and thick, and she poured it with a generous hand. Her jersey heifer was worth every red cent she'd paid for her, and more maybe, from the color of that cream. Pretty little thing, too, with those big eyes.

* * *

The sun was hot, shimmering on the hay field east of the house. Another week or so would make it ready for cutting, Johanna figured. Hardy Jones at the mill in town had made arrangements to come in and take care of it. Shares were better than nothing, and close to nothing was what she'd have if she did the arranging herself. Menfolk were afforded more respect than women, no matter how you sliced it. At least she'd have hay for the cows, enough to last till spring, after this last cutting.

She counted the wooden crates of apples as she neared the orchard, knowing the number even as she sounded them out aloud. Pure foolishness, Pa would say. Prideful behavior, thinking well of herself for such a simple task. She flexed the muscles in her calves as she bent to pick up the first crate. The muscles had been hard to come by. Climbing a ladder, moving it from one tree to the next as she went, was a far cry from a simple task, as far as she could see. At least for a woman alone.

Her lips tightened at the thought. She'd better get used to it. Either that or cut down the apple trees. And that she could never bring herself to do. The three acres she'd devoted to her apples was her favorite place to be, even if the work did about wear her down.

A "Hallo" from the house caught her ear as she straightened, crate held before her. Lowering it to the ground, she lifted one hand to her brow, shading from the sun's glare as she tried to make out the visitors waiting at her back door. She saw a wagon, filled to the brim, canvas stretched tight over the whole of it, the three figures on the seat looking at her. From the far side, the preacher waved from horseback.

"Yoo-hoo, Miss Johanna! I've brought Mr. Montgomery along, like I promised."

What the dickens had he promised? Johanna's brow furrowed as she struggled to remember the conversation she'd had so little part of. Whatever his plan, she'd apparently agreed to listen. She set off for the house, her long-skirted strides hampered by the tall grass between the orchard and the house.

The man had shifted on his perch atop the wagon seat to face her. His enigmatic look was measuring as she headed toward him, and his mouth was drawn tight. Looked like he'd swallowed a persimmon. Not a bit of friendly to him, if she had him pegged right.

And then her breath drew in sharply as she caught sight of the ridged scar that rode his high cheekbone. He lifted one hand to tilt back the brim of his hat, exposing his face to full sunlight as she watched. He lowered that broad, long-fingered hand to rest against his thigh, and his mouth twisted at one corner, as if he were daring her to react to his imperfection.

He wore the scar almost proudly, she thought, her gaze leaving it to sweep once more over the stern visage he presented her. Except for a faint tightening of his mouth, he was unmoving beneath her scrutiny. His shoulders were broad beneath the fine fabric of his coat, his trousers clung to the strong line of his thigh as he shifted after a moment, lifting one long leg, propping it against the front of the wagon.

He was a big man, a strong man, if the size of his hands, the flexing muscles in his thigh and the width of his upper body were anything to go by. Her gaze moved to tangle with his, meeting dark eyes that were narrowed just a bit against the sun's rays and held her own with unswerving intensity.

"What can I do for you, mister?" She drew to a halt several feet from the wagon, her irritation at the interruption vivid in her voice. The wind blew a lock of pale golden hair across her eyes, and she lifted an impatient hand to brush it back.

"From the looks of things, I'd say the question is what

can I do for you?" His words were harsh against her ear, and she bristled.

"You're the one comin' hat in hand, mister. Looks to me like you've got something to say. Spit it out or leave me to my work. I haven't time to do much entertainin' this mornin'."

"Miss Johanna! I've brought Mr. Montgomery here to do you a service." Reverend Hughes slid from his mount to hurry to her side. "If you can come to a mutual agreement, it will greatly benefit you both. I urge you to give him a few minutes of your time."

Johanna sighed. "I haven't got much time, Reverend. If Mr. Montgomery wants to sign on as a hired hand, he'll find the pickin' pretty poor here. Lots of work and not much pay to be found. And it looks like I'd be feedin' three more at my table."

"I've no experience as a hired hand, Miss Patterson." Tate Montgomery's voice vibrated with a multitude of impatience. "I thought we might come to an understanding, perhaps an agreement, but now I'm thinking your attitude would not be beneficial to my children." He turned in the wagon seat, speaking in a low voice to the young boys who were peering past him at Johanna.

"My attitude!" Her hands lifted to rest against her hips as she challenged his judgment. "I've been called from my work to speak to you, Mr. Montgomery, and you look me over like a side of beef at the general store. I've been judged and found lacking, and I don't even know what you're doin' on my property."

Looking down at her from his perch, he hesitated, then spoke quickly, in a voice that was pitched at a level she strained to hear. "I've been looking for a place to invest in, where my boys can live a peaceful life and I can build a future for them. But from the looks and sounds of things here, there wouldn't be much peace to be found." His eyes rested on her, darting to take in the telltale stance she'd taken, her hands propped belligerently against her hipbones.

His quiet words were chilling in their finality as he lifted the reins in one hand. "They've already lived through all the wrangling any soul should be obliged to contend with." Slapping the leather straps against the broad backs of his team of horses, he averted his gaze as the wagon creaked into motion.

Johanna bit at her lip, abashed by his scathing words, aware that his conclusions were fairly reached. She watched as the big wagon lumbered in a circle, heading back to the road. The two small boys had turned, looking back over their shoulders.

Maybe it was the quiet acceptance she recognized in their gaze, or perhaps the vulnerable curve of the smaller child's cheek as he flexed his jaw. A shadow of shame dulled the sunshine as Johanna watched. Those two young'ns looked like they could use a bite to eat and some shade to park in for a while, she thought, no matter how grim and ornery their daddy appeared to be.

"Mr. Montgomery!" Her voice was husky, but firm. "Come on back. Let those boys down to stretch their legs for a while."

The horses pulled the wagon another twelve feet or so before he drew it to a halt. His shoulders square, his head erect, he waited. Beside him, the two children wiggled, their whispers quiet, obviously urging him to consider the woman's offer. His glance downward encompassed both small faces, and he relented, nodding his agreement.

Needing no further permission, the boys edged to the wagon's side, the elder sliding to the ground and turning to help his young brother down. Tate Montgomery grasped the child beneath the arms and lifted him, lowering him to his brother's side. Then he turned the wagon once more, following the two boys back toward the house and the woman waiting there.

Chapter Two

Pete was the oldest boy's name. Seven years old, he'd said proudly—much older than his small brother, his uptilted chin had proclaimed. Timothy was four, Tate Montgomery had volunteered gruffly, even as four chubby fingers rose in silent affirmation of his father's words. Still carrying a vestige of baby roundness about his features, he'd smiled at her with innocent warmth, beguiling her with his blue eyes and rosy cheeks.

She'd offered them milk in thick china cups and a small plate of sugar cookies from her crock. Then she'd ushered them to sit on the back porch, where Timothy had grasped his cup with both hands to drink deeply of the cool milk. His smile had been white-rimmed above his upper lip, and she felt a strange warmth invade her as she remembered the sight.

Across the table, Tate Montgomery had removed his hat and unbuttoned his coat, the latter a concession to the warmth of her kitchen. He'd swept the wide-brimmed hat from his head as he bent to enter the door, holding it against his leg as he took the chair she offered him. His eyes had scanned the room, pausing as they reached the cookstove, where chicken simmered within her Dutch oven. She'd set it to cook before heading to the orchard, and now its aroma filled the room, a little garlic and onion combining to coax her appetite.

She watched him, unwilling to break the silence. The man had invaded her territory, so to speak. Let him make the first move. Yet a twinge of curiosity piqued her interest as she waited. What had he said? He was looking to invest in a piece of property. Probably wanting to buy her out. But no...that hadn't been it, either.

"Miss Johanna, would you be willing to listen to what this gentleman is here to speak of?" Theodore Hughes spoke anxiously from behind Mr. Montgomery, his own hat held before him, his fingers moving against the felt surface with barely concealed agitation.

Johanna nodded, her gaze moving from the parson to the man sitting at her kitchen table. "I can't see that it will do any harm," she allowed, clipping the words tightly. She felt invaded. The very moment he entered the room, she'd sensed his presence, inhaling his subtle scent, that musky, male, outdoor aroma some men carried. Unwillingly she'd been drawn by it, long-suppressed memories coming to life as she faced his imposing presence across the blue checked oilcloth.

"I'm Tate Montgomery, lately of southern Ohio. You've met my sons. They're the only family I have. My wife is dead." He paused, his gaze resting on her hands as she entwined her fingers on the table before her.

"I decided my sons needed a fresh start, away from some bad memories. We've been on the road for several weeks, stopping here and there, looking for the right place to settle."

Johanna watched his mouth as he spoke, catching a glimpse of white, even teeth between full lips. A faint white line touched his top lip, an old scar. Not nearly as noticeable as the newer one he wore. The one that should have detracted from his masculine appeal. But didn't.

"And you think this is the right place?" Spoken without inflection, her query reached his ears.

Tate sensed her reluctance, had made note of it from the first, when she trudged through tall grass from the orchard toward his wagon. Now it was in full bloom between them, that feminine need for self-preservation that kept her from accepting him at face value. He couldn't begrudge her the feeling. But the urge to press his advantage, now that he was inside the house, was uppermost in his mind.

There had been a feeling of homecoming as he drove up the lane toward the farmhouse. The two-story dwelling, shabby around the edges, but nevertheless graceful in its design, had drawn him with an urgency he'd not felt in any other place. The tall maple trees, towering over the house in a protective fashion, their leaves turning color, had bidden him welcome. Not like the woman, who had greeted him with little patience for his coming.

She'd scanned him and his belongings with a wary eye, only warming a bit when the two boys came under her gaze. She'd been more than generous with them, offering milk and sugar cookies, the sight of which had made his own mouth water. She was sturdy but slender around the middle, her apron emphasizing the narrow lines of her waist. Full-breasted. *Womanly*, might be the right word to describe her form. Johanna Patterson. A sensible name. He could only hope the woman would be as reasonable as a female in her circumstances should be.

Bristly and *faintly belligerent* described her attitude toward him, he decided with a wry twist of his mouth. Perhaps she wouldn't be the smallest bit receptive to his proposal. And that was the only word he could come up with for the bargain he was about to lay on the table before her.

"You grow apples, Miss Patterson," he began, nodding toward the brimming bowl on her cupboard. The ruddy skin of the snow variety glistened in the sunlight that cascaded through the window.

"I pick them," she corrected quietly. "They grow all by themselves, with a little help from the Lord."

His mouth moved, one corner twisting again, in amusement. "I agree. Most farmers consider themselves to be in partnership with the Almighty, I've found. Although sometimes he doesn't appear to tend to business, what with the dry spell we had this year."

"Farming's a gamble," Johanna answered. "Apples are a pretty sure thing. Provide them with a beehive in the vicinity and they pretty much tend to themselves, once the blossoms fall and the fruit starts to grow."

"You don't do much with crops?"

She shrugged. "The hay is about ready for a last cutting. Mr. Jones at the mill made arrangements for shares for me, last time around. I'll do the same this time, I expect. I've got eighty-six acres here, fifty acres of pasture for the cattle. I've been keeping some of them pretty close to the barn lately. My father fenced off a ten-acre piece, and I feel better having them close at hand, with winter coming on."

"How many head are you running?" he asked.

"Not many left in the far pasture, besides the bull. I sold off the young steers last month."

He shook his head. "'Not many' doesn't tell me much."

"I'm only milking six cows right now," she said, exasperation apparent in her tone. "There are more of them dry, with calves due in the spring. Why do you ask?"

"I want to offer you a proposition, Miss Patterson."

She waited, noting the faint furrow between his eyebrows, the twitch of his left eyelid as he leaned back in his chair. His arms folded across his chest in a gesture she sensed was automatic with him. As if he set up a guard around himself. She sat up straighter in her chair and nodded, unwilling to give him verbal encouragement.

"I've been on the lookout for a farm to invest in. It must

be a special situation in order for it to work to my advantage, though. I'd thought to hire a woman to live in, tend to my boys and run the house for me." He lifted one shoulder in a shrug that spoke of his lack of success thus far.

"When your minister told me of your place, I thought it would bear investigation. Then he told me you were not willing to move from here or sell out your interest in the farm."

Johanna nodded once. Apparently she'd finally gotten it across to folks in town that she was planning on living out her life here. At least the preacher had gotten the message, she thought. A chuckle rose within her, and she ducked her head, swallowing the sound before it could be born.

Tate Montgomery rose from his chair and paced to the cookstove, lifting the lid on the covered iron pan with Johanna's pot holder to peer within. Steam billowed up, and he inhaled quickly as the succulent scent of simmering chicken tempted his nostrils. He clapped the lid down and cast her a sidelong glance.

"You enjoy cookin'?" Not waiting for a reply, he paced to the doorway, looking out at his sons on the porch, then returned to where she sat.

His lips flattened, and he pushed the lower one forward a bit, as if he were considering what he would say next. "Have you thought of getting married, Miss Patterson?"

Her eyebrows lifted, and her eyes widened. If she'd thought herself immune to surprise, he'd just this minute effectively shot that theory all to small bits. "Not lately." It was an understatement, to say the least. Not at all might be more to the point. At least not in the past ten years.

"What I have in mind is a business arrangement," he said quietly, stepping back to where his chair was sitting at an angle to the table. He straightened it with one quick movement and planted himself on the seat, his hands braced against his thighs. "I would be willing to pay off your mortgage—"

"What makes you think I have one?" she asked, interrupting him.

He looked at her, noting the swift color staining her cheeks. "I'm sorry. I'm afraid I quizzed your minister last evening at great length. When he spoke of your place here, telling me of the situation you're in, I asked a lot of questions. Apparently, the townspeople are aware of your circumstances, the hardship caused by the death of your father and the need for help to run this place. There was no secret made of your father's—"

Her cheeks were bright with outrage and embarrassment, and she cut him off with a wave of her hand. "You had no right to pry into my business. You don't even know me." She swung to face the minister, who had taken up residence in the corner of the kitchen, near the window. "And you! You had no right to tell my problems to anyone. And especially not a total stranger! How could you be so...so..."

Her voice cracked, almost wobbling with her distress as she faced the man of the cloth who had betrayed her.

"My dear Miss Johanna! I only thought to help. Mr. Montgomery comes with letters of recommendation from bankers and ministers in his hometown. He is on a legitimate quest, and my only thought was to give aid where I could." The Reverend Hughes was distraught at her accusation, his dismay apparent on his youthful face.

"This is my fault, ma'am," Tate Montgomery said bluntly. "I should not have revealed my knowledge of your circumstances so quickly. I only thought to present my thoughts for your consideration. I am here to propose marriage, ma'am."

"Marriage! To you?" Johanna was aghast. The man was a stranger who in the course of fifteen minutes' time had suggested taking over her mortgage, and marrying her to boot.

Tate nodded. "It would be a business proposition. I need

someone to tend my boys and make a home for them. This would be much better in the long run than my hiring a housekeeper.''

She snorted inelegantly. "You mean I couldn't quit the job when I'd had a bellyful, don't you?"

He couldn't help the grin that escaped at her phrasing. "I guess you could put it that way, if you like," he said agreeably.

She shook her head. "This is ridiculous. I have no intention of marrying. Ever."

"You don't like men?" It was a simple question, he thought. And if the answer was not to his liking, he'd be on his way.

She was taken aback, her thoughts scattered. Like men? "What's to like about them? They're fond of making messes and being waited on and spending time in the saloon.''

"All of them?" His brow rose quizzically. "Perhaps you've been around the wrong breed of men, Miss Johanna.''

She backtracked a bit, silently acknowledging her haste in the judgment she'd spouted. "My father was not himself the past few years. Perhaps I had a bad example set for me in his recent behavior," she said grudgingly.

"There are good men to be found," Theodore Hughes ventured to say from the corner.

Johanna nodded in his direction. "I've met several in my time," she admitted. And then she looked at Tate Montgomery with a guarded glance. "I'll take the reverend's word as to your sterling reputation, but I'm not interested in marriage.''

He nodded politely. "Perhaps if I enlarge on my idea, you might consider it more carefully." He cast a look at the man who had brought him to this place. "Would you leave us for a few minutes, sir? I think this discussion merits some privacy.''

Theodore Hughes nodded agreeably, stepping to the doorway and out on the porch.

Tate leaned over the table and faced Johanna from a foot away. If she was unwilling to hear him out, he'd head on out. But it was worth giving it a shot. And the memory of his first sight of this house and the capable woman who was struggling to hold things together here provided the impetus he needed to speak his mind.

"We could have a good arrangement, Miss Johanna. I am willing to assume any financial burden you have, in return for a half ownership of the farm. You would take my boys in hand and tend to the house and whatever chores you want to assume outdoors. I'll make the place run. I'll make it run better than it's ever run before, and I'll do it well. You won't have cause to be ashamed of me. I don't drink and I don't chase women. I won't be expecting you to sleep in my bed, and I won't lay a hand on you in anger."

Her blue eyes blinked, widened, and blinked again. "Well!" Spoken with emphasis, the word was vibrant with meaning. Her thoughts were jumbled, stunned as she was by his list of rules and regulations regarding the marriage he proposed.

"What would you expect of a wife, Mr. Montgomery?" she asked finally. If the man didn't want a woman to take to his bed, he must be willing to settle for little more than a housekeeper, when all was said and done.

"I have sons, ma'am. I don't need more children. I just need these two fed and clothed and schooled properly."

"And nothing for yourself?"

A faint ridge of color rode his cheekbones, accenting the scar on the side of his face. "I'll need to have my meals provided and my clothes washed and ironed. I'm already well schooled."

She ducked her head. "You don't need a woman?"

"Not an unwilling one."

She lifted her gaze slowly, as if it pained her to face him but she recognized that she must. "I'm not willing. I don't think I'd ever be willing. I never intended to marry."

He nodded slowly. "All right. I can deal with that."

A vision of the apples awaiting her in the orchard, crates overflowing and needing to be carried, burst into her mind. She thought of the cows, impatient to be milked, morning and night. The hay field, awaiting the mowing machine, and the assessing looks she received from the men in town, recognizing her as a woman alone.

Images of Tate Montgomery, tall and robust, working the orchard, planting and sowing and dealing with the store-keeper and the mill owner cascaded through her mind in rapid profusion. Her gaze rested on his hands—heavily veined, broad and capable, fingernails clean, fingers long and straight. She would need to check out his letters of recommendation, but instinctively she knew him to be a man of honor. Why it should be so, she couldn't have said. But something about him, his innate dignity, his gentle-manly ways, his prideful look, his way with the small boys he'd handled with gentle touches, spoke of a man to be trusted.

"I'll give you my answer tomorrow."

It was more than he had bargained for. He'd been warned by the preacher that she was a hardheaded woman, that she'd turned down offers aplenty for her place, that she was considered to be a spinster by the townsfolk. He'd thought to find a dried-up specimen of womanhood. He'd been prepared to look her over and leave if the years of hard living she'd endured here had made her unappealing for his purposes.

Neither of those two things had come about. Instead, he'd found a slender, stalwart female who'd been bowed low by life's burdens and yet managed to rise above the problems she'd faced after her father's death. He'd found a woman of strength and courage, willing to work herself to a frazzle to keep her farm running. A woman who deserved better than what she'd been handed by fate.

"Tomorrow," he said firmly. "And in the meantime, can I make a bed for my boys and myself in your barn? It will save me taking the wagon back to town overnight."

She considered him for a moment, taking in the dark eyes that hid his emotions, allowing only a faint approval to shine forth as he met her gaze. His chestnut-colored hair was swept back from a broad forehead bronzed by the sun. Apparently the man didn't wear his hat all the time. His jaw was square and firm, his nose a bit crooked and prominent, but no larger than it should be, for such a big man. He could be considered handsome. Or at least appealing, she decided. If a woman was in the market for a husband, she supposed, he'd be a likely specimen.

"All right," she agreed. "The barn is available for the night. I'll tell you tomorrow what I decide."

His breath released on a silent sigh. "Thank you for your consideration," he said simply. "I'll tend to my boys now."

He rose from his chair, and she followed suit, standing across from the table from him, aware once again of his size, at least three inches over six foot, she'd venture to say. "I don't mind sharing my supper with you and your sons," she offered. He hesitated in the doorway, then turned to face her.

"That's kind of you, Miss Johanna. I'd be much obliged for the favor." He clapped his hat on his head and nodded abruptly. "I'll be in the barn."

Johanna followed him out on the porch, her hands reaching for the china cups the two boys had used. They gave them into her keeping with bashful looks and awkward murmurings of thanks at their father's urging, and she smiled at their childish gestures.

They romped across the yard at his side, and she leaned on the post at the corner of the porch to watch. They were like two young puppies, she thought, frisky and energetic. He spoke quietly to them as they walked and then, upon reaching the barn door, bent one knee to the ground to place an arm around each of them. His words set their heads nodding, and their faces looked earnest as he spoke. Apparently instructions for their behavior, Johanna decided as they walked with dignity through the barn doors into the shadowed interior.

If she married him... The thought spun crazily in her mind. If she married him, they would be hers, those two small boys with dark hair and straight, sturdy bodies. It would be a weighty argument in favor of his suit. The joy of caring for children had been denied her. Indeed, the thought of having a child of her own had been denied her for ten years. It would never be. But now, now she could tend these two young boys, perhaps earn their love.

A bitter wash of regret filled her to overflowing, and she stepped down from the porch. Better that she not expose herself to close scrutiny. Not now, not while old memories were bursting the seams of that hidden place where she'd long ago relegated them for eternity.

"I'll be leaving, Miss Johanna." The soft words of the minister broke into her thoughts, and she looked up quickly to see him astride his horse, reins in hand. "I'll be anxious to hear your decision, ma'am," he said. With a courtly gesture, he tipped his hat in her direction and turned his horse to leave.

Johanna watched him go, her thoughts in turmoil. Would tomorrow be time enough for her to decide her whole future? She lifted her gaze to the small rise beyond the house, where a low fence enclosed the family cemetery. Lifting her skirt a few inches, holding its hem above the grass, she made her way there, climbing the hill with ease, unlatching the wooden gate and leaving it open behind her as she knelt by the grave of her mother.

She reached out to pull a milkweed that had sprung up

in the past few days. Her fingers sticky from the stem, she rubbed them distractedly against her apron as she spoke. "Mama, a man wants to marry me." The words were soft, murmured under her breath. She'd spent a lot of time in these one-way conversations with the mother she'd helped bury over ten years ago. Sometimes she wondered if she didn't hear a faint voice within her that repeated some of her mother's favorite small sayings.

"He won't ever have to know, Mama. I won't tell him, and he says he doesn't want a real wife, just a cook and someone to keep his children clean and well fed. I can do that, can't I?" She rubbed her eyes, unwilling that the tears should fall, those tears she held in abeyance until the times she knelt here.

It was usually a lonely place, here where she'd buried the three humans most important to her, two of the graves tended carefully, the third marked only by a small rosebush. It was to that spot that she moved, shifting on the cool ground, mindful of grass stains marring her dress. She snapped two faded roses from the bush, the final flowers of summer, touched by an early-autumn frost during the past nights.

"Baby mine, your mama..." Her voice faltered as she spoke the words no other person had ever heard fall from her lips. And then the tears she shed only in this place fell once more, as she smoothed her palm over the grass that covered the grave where her baby lay.

Chapter Three

By the time she'd soaked her eyes in cool water, changed her dress and scooped up her hair into a respectable knot on the back of her head, Johanna had run out of time. Sure enough, she'd managed to get grass stains on her work dress, and she'd scrubbed at them, then left the dress to soak in a bucket.

Supper would have to be quick. Those two little boys were guaranteed to be hungry before long, with only sugar cookies and milk in their bellies since noontime. The image of Tate Montgomery popped unbidden into her mind, and she found herself imagining his big hands holding a knife and fork, eating at her table. She closed her eyes, nurturing the vision, leaning against the pantry door.

So real was the mental picture, she could almost catch his scent, that musky outdoor aroma she'd drawn into her lungs earlier. She inhaled deeply, and opened her eyes.

"Ma'am? I didn't mean to disturb you." Tate Montgomery stood at her back door, one hand lifted to rest against the frame, the other plunged deep in his pocket. Less than four feet away from the pantry door, he stood watching her, that intent, dark gaze focused on her face.

"Ma'am?" He shifted his weight from one foot to the other, and his gaze drifted from her face to slide in a slow, lazy fashion over her person. Not in a threatening manner, but as if he needed to see that all the parts were in place, almost as if he were assessing her womanly form.

She felt the flush rise from her breasts, up the length of her long neck, to settle deeply beneath the flesh covering her cheeks. "Do I suit you, Mr. Montgomery?" she asked tartly. "Do I look sturdy enough to be a housekeeper and cook and child-tender?"

His eyes focused once more on her face, the face she'd spent fifteen minutes bathing in order to hide the signs of her bout of tears earlier. She raised her left hand, brushing at a tendril of pale hair that had escaped her severe hairdo, allowing the pad of her index finger to sweep beneath her eye. There was no telltale swelling to be felt there, no evidence of her brief but shattering lapse. The relief inherent in that discovery put a measure of starch into her backbone, and she turned from his presence.

Her largest bowl in hand, she opened the pantry door and stepped within. On three sides, the shelves surrounded her, with their burden of food close at hand. The large bags of flour, sugar, coffee and salt were at waist level, easily reached for daily use. Above, where she must stretch a bit for a good handhold, were the glass quart jars she'd filled with the harvest from her kitchen garden during the past weeks. And to her right she'd arranged more canning jars, these filled with the boiled-up stewing hens she'd culled from the chicken yard once the young pullets began laying, come summer.

She grasped the bag of flour, bringing it to the edge of the shelf, where she opened it, tipping a good measure into the bowl she held. A scoop of lard came next, the dollop landing in a cloud of flour. Chicken potpie would be quick, once she rolled out a crust and put some vegetables on to parboil. She turned to leave the pantry, the familiar sense of satisfaction she found within its confines uplifting her spirits. There was something about seeing the work of your hands surrounding you, knowing you'd not have to worry about setting a table through the long months of winter. It was a pleasurable thing to be a woman, she decided.

"Can I help with something?" He was there, almost blocking her exit, and she blinked rapidly as her heart missed a beat.

"I didn't mean to insult you a few minutes ago," he said quietly. "And to answer your question, yes, you do look more than capable of doing all I've asked. You're a fine-looking woman, Miss Johanna."

For the first time, she saw a softening of his features, an easing of his closely held emotions, as he offered his apology. She nodded in acceptance of his words and carried the bowl to the table. Her fingers left it reluctantly. He'd said she was a fine-looking woman. She knew her teeth were straight and even. She brushed them every day with tooth powder. Her hair was a good color, golden from the summer sun, and thick, and her eyes were far apart, blue, like her mother's. If all that added up to fine-looking, then she could accept the small compliment as her due.

"Do you need the fire built up in the stove?" He'd stayed near the door, and she saw his glance out into the yard when a childish shriek sounded from near the barn. "Is the dog good with children?" he asked, his gaze leveled beyond her field of vision.

She turned quickly. "Sheba won't put up with any foolishness, but she doesn't bite. She's a herd dog, Mr. Montgomery, not a pet."

His smile was unexpected, and she savored its warmth for a moment. "Apparently she doesn't know that, ma'am. She's chasing a stick for Timmy."

Her lips tightened. They'd better get things squared away right off. "Animals are only as useful as you make them. I can't afford to feed a dog that doesn't serve a purpose. Sheba's no good to me if she attaches to the boys and forgets her duties."

His smile faded, and his eyes became guarded, the momentary pleasure she'd seen there replaced by a forbidding darkness. "I'll see to it." Abruptly the man who'd been at ease in her kitchen was transformed into the chilly stranger she'd first met earlier in the day.

"I'll tend the stove, Mr. Montgomery. If it's not too much trouble, you can open the back door of the barn. The cows will be wanting to come in to be milked before long." When she turned once more he was gone, and she watched surreptitiously from one side of the kitchen door as he made his way across her yard.

A pang of regret touched her, and not for the first time she rued her quick tongue. The boys weren't hurting anything, playing with Sheba. The dog was old enough to know her job, and even a dumb animal deserved a little attention once in a while. Almost, she called out to rescind her harsh words, hesitating but a few seconds. No, she might as well start out as she meant to continue.

And then she drew in a deep breath as she recognized that her decision had already been made. She would marry Tate Montgomery. She would take on his children as her own. She would be Mrs. Montgomery, a wife in name, at least. If he asked no more from her than that, she would never have to own up to the shame she carried as a great weight on her conscience. The shame of a fallen woman. A Jezebel, Pa had said.

"I'd see the letters you brought with you, Mr. Montgomery," she said, scooping a generous helping of chicken and vegetables onto his plate. She ladled a spoonful of steaming gravy over it all, then carefully placed the next piece of crusty topping over it and handed him his plate. She'd taken the first spoonful for herself, then served him, so that his crust would be unbroken and appetizing. It was a small gesture, one she'd seen her mother repeat often.

A man was the head of the house, given the best piece

of meat, the freshest bread. His coffee was poured first, his shirts ironed when the sadirons were cooled just enough not to scorch. Pa had expected it, the honor accorded him as a man.

Tate Montgomery, on the other hand, looked a bit amazed at the attention he'd been given by his hostess. She'd placed the fresh round of butter in front of his place, piled newly sliced bread on a plate and edged it with a jar of strawberry jam and a comb of honey. His cup was brimming with hot coffee as he sat and nodded his thanks with a raised eyebrow and a half smile signifying his surprise.

Timothy and Pete sat at the sides of the table, the three forming a setting she could not help but appreciate. They looked like a family, the four of them around the table, the kerosene lamp above, its glow circling them with a suggestion of warmth. The boys stretched their plates toward her, and she helped them to the food before taking up her napkin to spread across her lap.

Timothy watched her carefully, then removed his own napkin to follow her example. She caught his eye as he glanced at her again, and smiled her approval. His small, perfect teeth flashed for a moment between his lips as he allowed a crooked grin to touch his mouth. Then he ducked his head and tended to the business at hand.

"I'll bring you the letters after supper," Tate Montgomery offered as he swallowed his first bite of potpie. "You cook a fine meal, Miss Johanna," he said, as if compliments came easily to his lips. It was the second one he'd given her, and both in the space of a day. He was a gentleman, she decided. The fine woolen trousers had given way to farmer's overalls, and the coat he'd worn earlier had been replaced by a heavy flannel shirt, but he ate with clean hands and good table manners.

"Can I have jam on my bread, Pa?" Pete had made away with over half his dinner already. She'd been right. The boys had been more than hungry. She'd have to be sure to offer them apples in the afternoon from now on. Or maybe… Her mind swirled with thoughts of tending to three male creatures, the work implicit in their well-being, the extra washing to do, the meals to cook.

And where would they sleep? Once she married their father, the boys would move into the house, perhaps share her old bedroom with its big double bed and hand-hewn dresser.

Where would she sleep then? In the attic? In her mother's sewing room? Surely not in the big bedroom at the top of the stairs, where her parents had conducted a marriage for almost twenty years. That would be Tate Montgomery's room. He deserved it, as the head of the family.

"I said, I wouldn't mind another helping of that chicken pie, if you don't mind, Miss Johanna." His voice was quiet, sounding amused at her expense, as if he knew he'd caught her daydreaming. If such a thing could be, with night coming on. She'd done her share during daylight hours, that was for sure. But usually by this time of the day she was too tired to think of much else than setting the kitchen to rights and heading for her bed.

She spooned up another portion on his plate, and he murmured his thanks. His hands were deft as he spread jam on another slice of bread and handed it to Pete, then did the same for Timothy. He was used to looking out for them, she thought idly. It showed in his manner, in the way he watched them, unobtrusively but with vigilance, noting their behavior, nodding his head with approval or shaking it slightly as Timothy stuffed his mouth in his eagerness to eat the jam-laden bread.

"I'm glad your boys are good eaters," she said. "Will they like oatmeal for breakfast? Or would sausage and eggs be better?" Folding her napkin beside her plate, she lifted her glass to drink from its foaming depths. The milk was cool, fresh from this morning's milking. "Would you like more milk, Pete?" she asked, setting her glass on the table.

A glance at his father gained him permission, and Pete nodded his answer. He swallowed quickly and supported his unspoken request with a "Yes, ma'am."

Johanna rose from the table and lifted the pitcher from the cupboard, filling both boys' glasses, Timothy's not quite to the brim, in deference to his youth and his smaller hands.

"I'd take a small tumbler of that milk, if you don't mind," their father said as she straightened from her task.

"Would you rather not have coffee? I assumed... My father always liked coffee with his supper." She reached for another heavy glass from the shelf behind her and poured it full, placing it next to his plate as she spoke.

"I enjoy both sometimes. Coffee always, especially at breakfast. As for early morning, we take whatever's available. Oatmeal and the rest will do fine." he assured her. His gaze followed her as she moved across the kitchen. "Sit down, Miss Johanna. We need to speak for a few minutes."

She complied, bringing with her a bowl of cookies she'd taken from the crock where she kept them for freshness' sake. The boy's eyes brightened as they tilted their chins to better see within the dish, and Timothy was hasty in his movements as he finished up the last of his supper: He licked a stray crumb of crust from his upper lip and edged his hand across the table to where the bowl sat.

"Ask first, son." Though quietly spoken, it was a rebuke nonetheless, and the child nodded.

"Please, ma'am, may I?" he whispered, his dark gaze fixed on her face.

"You may have one of each, if your father says so," she offered, sensing his indecision.

His smile flashing, the child accepted her offer.

"Ma'am?" the older boy asked, his question implicit.

She tipped the bowl in the other direction, and the boy reached in.

Tate shoved his chair back from the table and stood. "I believe I'll make a trip to the barn, Miss Johanna. You boys can eat your cookies and then get on outside. Stay away from the back of the barn, like I told you."

They nodded simultaneously, their mouths full, Timmy's feet swinging beneath the table. Johanna felt the brush of his small boots against her skirt as he kept time to an unheard beat. It was a foolishly comforting touch, and she sat unmoving until he'd eaten every last crumb of his cookies and drunk the last drop of milk.

"Go along now, boys," she told them, gathering the plates and flatware. Intuitively she left the cup in front of Tate Montgomery's place. He'd not had any dessert yet. He might want more coffee to go with it.

Her hands were plunged in the dishwater when she heard him come back in the door. A quick glance over her shoulder proved her right. He'd taken the coffeepot to the table and filled his cup. At his right hand was an envelope, fat with folded papers. He gestured at it as she watched.

"Here are the letters of recommendation I spoke of. You'll find two from ministers in the town we lived in, and one from my banker, the owner of the general store, and my doctor."

She flushed, embarrassed for a moment as she anticipated reading personal things about this man. Surely she had the right to know all she could about him, but the thought of learning it in this way was almost like...maybe window-peeping, or reading another person's mail.

Drying her hands on the towel, she walked back to the table and sat across from him once more, then reached for the envelope.

"Go ahead," he told her. "It won't take you long. It's just information you'd expect to get from a doctor or banker. You'll find that I'm healthy and fit, I've got a decent bank account, and I paid my debts at the general store on time and in full. My minister even noted the amount I gave toward the building fund for the new church last year.'' His mouth was twisted wryly as he watched her, and she recognized his own slight embarrassment as he made light of the letters written in his behalf.

She held the envelope in her hand, squeezing the bulk of it and watching him closely. His eyes were dark, but not brown, as she'd thought at first. They were a deep, deep gray, with just a few blue flecks around the edges of the pupils. Sometimes they were flat, hard-looking, like when he'd gone to talk to the boys about the dog, earlier today. Now they were softer, more vulnerable, as if he were hesitant to lay his life out before her, all stuffed in a envelope and waiting for her perusal.

''I'd like to know a couple of things, Mr. Montgomery.'' She squeezed the papers, hearing the faint crackling of the crisp envelope.

''Do you think you could call me Tate after we're married?'' he asked quietly. ''In fact, maybe you could start now.''

She bit against her top lip. ''It's unseemly for me to use your given name.''

''Try.'' His eyes entreated her, and she looked away, settling her gaze on his folded hands instead. They were good hands. Strong and well formed, clean, with a tracing of soft curls across the back. She'd warrant his forearms were covered with the same brown hair. Her eyes closed as she recognized the drift of her thoughts. What was covered by his shirtsleeves was none of her business.

''Try, Miss Johanna,'' he repeated, and she sighed, aware that he wasn't about to give in on this matter.

''All right. I want to know how long your wife's been dead, Tate.''

''A year and a half. She drowned in a spring flood.''

It was more than she'd asked, and somehow the thought of the unknown woman being swept away by rushing waters made her want to cry. She gritted her teeth against the feeling and looked up at him. "It must have hard on your boys, losing their mother that way."

"They'd been staying with her sister for a few days when it happened. Didn't seem to cause much of a fuss over it, to tell the truth. But then, they were close to Bessie. That was her sister's name, and she kept them for another week after it happened."

Johanna felt a hollow spot in her middle expand and grow chill with his words. "Why were they with their aunt? Didn't their mother want them home with her?"

He unfolded his hands, and her eyes were drawn to the movement. He'd formed them into two fists, and his knuckles were whitened, so hard had he curled his fingers into his palms. "My wife hadn't been herself, hadn't been feeling well."

"She was sickly?"

He shook his head, and his gaze bored into her, impelling her eyes to sweep up the length of his chest, up his throat and chin, over his flared nostrils, and jam smack against the hard, cold look he offered her. "She had problems. She was unhappy with her life, and sometimes the boys bore the brunt of it. Her sister...well, her sister understood, and when things got touchy, she'd come and get Pete and Timmy and take them home with her."

"Was she mental?"

His mouth thinned, his teeth gritting together, and he moved his hands to the edge of the table, shoving his chair back and rising swiftly to his feet. "Do we need to discuss this now? I'd think it was sufficient for you to know that she wasn't herself sometimes."

Johanna shook her head. "No, I guess we don't have to talk about it any more. I just wondered..."

"I'm sorry, ma'am. I didn't mean to be rude. It's just not my favorite memory. It happened, and it changed our lives. My boys need a mother. To tell the truth, I decided when I first laid eyes on you that you were strong and had a clear mind and your eyes were honest and kind. And that's what I was looking for for my boys."

"You knew all that by seeing me out there by your wagon?"

He nodded. "I knew all that when I saw you come hot-footin' it across the field between here and your orchard. Any woman who planned on hauling all those apples to the house had to be strong. A woman who's been able to keep this place going obviously has a clear mind. And you've got the bluest, sharpest eyes I've ever seen on a person in my life. When you looked at my boys, the kindness just sort of shone through over your mad. Then, when you called me back, I knew it was because you'd seen how tired and antsy they were, riding on the wagon."

"I like your children, Tate." It had come easier this time, saying his name.

"You're a born mother, unless I miss my guess. You should have been married with a bunch of young ones of your own before now."

She stiffened, feeling the rigid length of her backbone as if it had been turned into ice within her. "I told you, I never planned on being married."

"I won't make you sorry you changed your mind, Miss Johanna."

The words were spoken like a promise. Almost as if they might be a preface to the wedding vows they'd be taking before long. "I'll not make you wait till tomorrow for my answer, Tate," she said, her voice coming out strained and harsh-sounding, as if it belonged to somebody else.

He stilled, reminding her of a deer at the edge of the woods. She heard his indrawn breath, and then he let it out in a silent sigh. "You haven't read the letters, Miss Johanna."

Her movements were abrupt as she handed the envelope back across the table. "I don't need to read them. Theodore Hughes read them and passed his approval. That's good enough for me. If we don't start this out with a measure of trust between us, we'll have a hard time later on. Maybe someday I'll want to read them, but I think the fact that you offered without holding back is good enough for me."

"You'll marry me?"

"You've got a strong body and clean hands, Tate. You treat your boys well, and you come highly recommended, if my minister is to be believed. You told me I'd have my own room to sleep in, and I'm not afraid of you." She took a deep breath and lifted her chin, eyeing him squarely. "I'm not afraid of hard work, either, but I'm mighty sick of it. I'll tell you right now, I've toted the last crate of apples I'm going to. You can unload that wagon of yours tomorrow and go out to the orchard and do the honors. It'll be fine to have a horse and wagon on the place again."

"When can we marry, Miss Johanna?" His words were harsh, as if he were holding back a measure of emotion he wasn't comfortable with.

"Sunday morning, after service, if that suits you." She bit at her lip, suddenly aware of the step she was taking.

His hand snaked across the table and grasped hers, enveloping it within his. It was warm and a bit rough, callused across the palm. She was still, her fingers touching his warm flesh, unmoving, as if she were fearful of brushing his skin with her own. It was the first time she'd touched a man's flesh in years. Except for when she'd helped to lay her Pa out in his Sunday suit for burying.

She felt the squeeze of his hand as he brushed his thumb over her knuckles, and she closed her eyes at the sensation of prickling heat the touch aroused within her.

"Miss Johanna, I'd ask that you treat me nicely when we're around other folks. You know, like we're really married. And if I touch you, or act friendly, you could…" He faltered as he searched for words.

"Act like this is a real love match? You don't want people to think we're not married in…in fact? Is that what you

mean?'' Her cheeks bore a faint flush as she provided the
words he'd sought. "That's fine with me, Tate. I don't
think it's anyone's business what we arrange between us.
I'll take your arm when we go into church.''

He nodded. "I won't ask for more than I told you this
afternoon." He released her hand and stood. "This is Friday night, Johanna. I'll ride to town in the morning and tell
your preacher he'll be having a wedding in his church come
day after tomorrow.''

"Good. You can take the eggs and butter into the general
store for me while you're at it, if you don't mind. It'd save
Mr. Turner a trip out if you'd take a couple crates of apples
along for him to sell over the counter, too.''

He nodded his assent and turned to the doorway. "I'll
go settle down in the barn, then. It's getting late enough
for those boys to be in bed. We'll wash up out back.''

She was halfway up the stairs when she heard a muted
shout of childish laughter. She'd crossed her bedroom to
the window when the sound reached her ears again. The
two boys were in front of the barn, Timothy on the ground
with the dog. Sheba's tail was wagging to beat the band,
and the boy's hands were buried deeply in her ruff.

Johanna's heart lurched in her chest as she watched, and
the doubts she'd entertained throughout the evening vanished with the setting sun. It would be worth it to move to
the sewing room, or even up to the attic. More than worth
it to scrub a man's work-soiled clothes again and cook three
full meals a day for his consumption. She'd have children;
finally, she'd know the feel of a soft, warm body and small
arms around her neck. Timothy was young enough to need
hugs.

Her gaze swung to the man who stepped through the barn
door. And for a moment, she wondered what it would feel
like to have that tall, muscular body close to hers, those
strong male arms holding her.

Her mouth tightened, and she turned from the window abruptly. "You've been that route, Johanna Patterson," she said aloud to herself, "and what did it get you but a lot of heartache? Settle for what the man offered, and count yourself lucky."

Chapter Four

"I surely didn't expect you'd be making your bedroom in the attic."

Johanna's breath caught in her throat as the deep voice cut into her thoughts. Her skirts swirling around her legs, she did an abrupt about-face, turning to seek out the man who was watching her. He was head and shoulders above floor level, his feet planted firmly on the attic stairs, one arm resting on the wide planking of the attic floor.

"Don't creep up on me that way!" Johanna's hand was at her throat, and her words were breathless, almost a whisper.

"I'm sorry," Tate said softly. "I thought you'd have heard me calling you from the back door."

"I didn't hear you come in," she answered, her hands sliding with measured nonchalance into her pockets.

His eyes slid from her to sweep the perimeters of the large, cluttered room, resting finally on the bedroom furniture that occupied one wall.

"What are you doing up here, Johanna?" he prodded, his forehead creasing into a frown.

"Moving things," she said abruptly.

She'd begun by shifting an old dresser, and then, snagged by bittersweet memories, she'd opened one of the drawers.

The clothing inside was neatly folded, just as she'd left it ten years ago, still smelling faintly of her mother's scented sachets. She'd lifted a soft, worn petticoat to her face and inhaled deeply, closing her eyes as they filled with unbidden tears, allowing the wistful thoughts to flood her being for just a moment.

Reluctantly she'd placed the garment back inside the drawer, her fingers lingering on the worn fabric as she set aside the remnants of her mother's clothing. Wiping her eyes and blowing her nose ferociously, she'd gently closed the drawer.

And then Tate had interrupted her pondering with his blunt query, startling her into a rude reply. It was time to backtrack.

"I'm deciding about this bed." She folded her arms about her waist, nodding toward the headboard she'd leaned against the dresser.

His eyes followed her direction. "What's the problem? It looks to me like it'll fit down that stairway just fine."

A spark of defiance lit her eyes. "You don't think the attic would be a proper bedroom for me?"

"I think I'd feel better about it if you slept downstairs with the rest of us." His frown had somehow vanished as he spoke, a glimmer of amusement taking its place, crinkling the corners of his dark eyes.

"It's just that it's my mother's sewing room I was thinking of using," she answered obliquely, her hackles rising to meet his arbitrary reasoning.

He tilted his head, his smile gentle. "Your mother's been gone a long time, Johanna. I doubt she'd want you to make a shrine out of her workroom." He climbed the remaining stairs and walked toward her. "I'll help you carry the headboard down if you'd like me to."

"I know exactly how long my mother's been dead, Mr. Montgomery. And if I want the bed taken down, I'll do it myself, the same way I got it up here." She'd stiffened at his approach, and now her head tilted back, allowing her gaze to clash with his.

He was stooped just a bit beneath the lowering eaves, a tall man, used to allowing for his height. Now he reached out to lay a warm hand on her shoulder, bending even closer, until she could see the shadows beneath his eyes. "You don't have to move furniture while I'm here, Johanna. If I'm to be the man of the house, I'll do the heavy work."

She held her ground, aware of his bulk, the masculine weight of his hand against her more fragile bones. Flexing the muscles beneath that pressure, she shrugged, as if to rid herself of his touch. It wasn't worth the fuss.

"Suit yourself," she said, dropping her gaze from his, her mind retaining the memory of his eyes and the shadows they contained. Perhaps he hadn't slept well out there in her barn. Maybe his nights, like hers, were occasionally prey to demons that stole sleep.

"Will you need help making room for us in the house today?" he asked, releasing her and reaching for the heavy wooden headboard. "The boys are anxious to see where they'll be sleeping. I think they've lost their appetite for roughing it."

"They'll be usin' my old bedroom. It has a big bed in it. I suppose they can bring in their belongings as soon as I empty my things from the dresser and the wardrobe."

"They're pretty easy young'ns," he said with a trace of pride. "They'll be happy most anywhere, long as there's something softer than the ground to sleep on."

Johanna stepped aside, watching him lift the headboard with ease, carrying it down the stairs as if it were no heavier than a length of two-by-four. She followed him, her steps light, her house shoes silent against the uncarpeted stairs.

"Which room am I headed for?" he asked over his shoulder, shifting his burden to accommodate the corner at the foot of the attic stairs.

"The end of the hallway, on the right," she told him, closing the attic door behind herself as she followed him down the wide corridor. She scurried past him quickly, opening the door to her mother's sewing room, making way for him to follow.

He halted in the doorway and whistled softly. "Not a whole lot of space, is there?"

A paisley shawl caught his eye, its folds draped gracefully over a sewing machine in one corner. The black iron treadle below was angled, as if a feminine foot had left it only moments ago.

A wardrobe filled another corner, its doors closed snugly. A small dresser was tight against the wall near the door, a daintily crocheted scarf centered on its surface. Beneath the window, a worktable lay empty, not so much as a pincushion remaining in view. Obviously Johanna had not made regular use of her mother's room. Either that or she was the neatest woman he'd ever met.

A faint scent, perhaps that of rose petals, caught his attention, and for a moment he felt another presence, as if the woman who had been the possessor of this space lingered still. And then the notion vanished as Johanna moved across the floor, her gaze measuring the walls and floor space.

"I think there will be room enough once the worktable and sewing machine are taken upstairs." She turned to him expectantly, as if she awaited his opinion.

"Whatever you think, Johanna." He'd already decided to be as obliging as he could. The house was her domain. The lines would be drawn soon enough when it came to the running of the farm.

"I'll move most everything upstairs." She spoke softly, one hand brushing at a speck of dust on the dresser. "This chest will be large enough for my things."

"I'll take care of the heavy stuff. Where do you want the bed to go?"

She started abruptly. "Oh! Here, put it against the wall. We'll have to move the sewing machine and the worktable out first, won't we?" Her fingers lingered on the surface of the dresser as she spoke. "I'll empty out these drawers after a while."

Tate leaned the heavy headboard against the wall and straightened. "Tell me how this table comes apart. I'll carry it upstairs and bring down the rest of the bed."

Johanna watched as he put one knee to the floor, leaning to peer beneath the table where long bolts held the legs in place. "My father built it for her," she told him, moving to his side and crouching next to him. "He made it just like the one her mother had, back in the city. Shall I get the tools from the kitchen for you to use?"

He'd shifted to both knees, his hands already busy with the heavy nuts holding the bolts in place. "Your pa did a good job, I'd say. These things are tighter than an old—"

Johanna's eyebrows lifted as he paused. "An old maid's pucker?" she asked.

He ducked his head, backing out from beneath the table, a grin twisting his mouth. "Yeah, that's what I was about to say. Then thought better of it."

"I am an old maid, Mr. Montgomery. And not ashamed of it."

"But not for long, Miss Patterson," he reminded her, his grin fading as he took note of her somber expression. His jaw tightened as he recognized the faint uneasiness she sought to hide. Her hands were buried in the folds of her apron, her fingers no doubt clenched tight. Johanna Patterson was taking a big chance marrying a stranger, and it would behoove him to treat her with kid gloves, at least till the deed was done.

"If you'll collect those tools for me, this won't take long," he said quietly. "I'll be taking that ride into town as soon as I move these things for you. I'm sure the preacher's looking for me to stop in to let him know what we've decided to do. It wouldn't look right for me to be staying here without making our arrangement legal.'' Rising, he reached one hand to where she crouched beside him, silently offering his assistance.

Deliberately, carefully, she placed her fingers across his, watching as he enclosed them in the warmth of his wide palm, then tugged her with gentle strength to stand before him.

"You haven't had second thoughts, have you?'' His grasp on her fingers had not lessened, and now he raised them to rest against his chest.

Her eyes widened at the gesture, her heartbeat quickening just a bit. Tate Montgomery was a tall man, a big man, standing head and shoulders over her. He could have been intimidating, had he chosen to do so, but the hand that held her own was gentle.

She shook her head. "No, no second thoughts. And yes, if we expect him to marry us tomorrow, I agree that you need to deliver a message to Reverend Hughes right away.'' Her mouth twisted wryly. "I don't want to have the town talking. Heaven knows we'll be giving them enough to gossip about tomorrow as it is. I'm not sure they'd even approve wholeheartedly of your staying here last night.''

"Well, I don't think my spending one more night in your barn will ruin you beyond redemption, ma'am. I suspect everyone in town knows I'm here, anyway.''

She winced. "Yes, you're probably right. They'll be looking you over in grand style come tomorrow morning, Mr. Montgomery. Not to mention whispering behind their hymnals when we march down the aisle before morning service.''

His hand exerted just the smallest amount of pressure on hers, his eyes assessing her quickly. Fine wisps of golden hair curled at her temple, a smudge of dust provided mute evidence of her foray into the attic, and her cheeks were

brushed with a delicate rosy hue that gave away the con-
flicting emotions she was struggling with. "I'll be with you,
Johanna. The boys and I will march down that aisle with
you, just like a real family."

"I'm counting on that, Mr. Montgomery." Her fingers
wiggled a bit, and he freed them readily from their captiv-
ity.

"Last night I was Tate," he reminded her. "What happened to turn me back into Mr. Montgomery?"

She turned to the door, resting her hand on the knob,
hesitating at his query. "Nothing, I suppose. Tate it is. I'll
go and get the wrench from the kitchen for you."

"I want to be in town by noon, Johanna. I'll take the
sewing machine upstairs now, and you can decide what else
you want moved after you find the tools. If you call out for
the boys, they'll help you get the eggs and butter ready for
me to take."

"Yes, all right." Her voice floated back to him from the
wide stairway as she hurried down to the first floor, and he
smiled at her words. He had a notion that Johanna Patterson
wouldn't always be so agreeable. In fact, if he had her
pegged right, she'd be a worthy opponent for any man. No
matter—he'd never backed off from a battle before. Settling
down to a marriage with Johanna might very well be a real
struggle, but it was one he was more than willing to wage.
She'd make a good mother for Pete and Timmy. As for
himself, he'd have the farm to run, and hot meals on the
table and clean clothes to wear every day.

He turned to where the sewing machine stood. It would
be awkward carrying it, but not more than he could handle.
Kind of like the agreement he'd made with Johanna Patterson, he thought with amusement. He might find things a
little awkward at times, but he'd warrant he could handle
her. Matter of fact, sorting out Johanna Patterson might
prove to be the most interesting part of the bargain.

* * *

"Blest be the tie that binds..." Voices soared around her as Johanna mouthed the words, her throat too dry to add sound. The hymnal she shared with the man next to her would have been impossible to read from, had she held it alone. Her hands were cold, her fingers trembling, and only Tate's sure strength kept the book from tumbling to the floor.

"...our hearts in Christian love..." he sang, his voice a pleasant rumble in her ear. At least he could carry a tune, she thought. That was one thing she knew about him now. No, she knew he liked cream in his coffee and he had a heavy hand with the sugar spoon, if this morning's meal was anything to go by. He'd eaten two bowls of oatmeal, laden with brown sugar and half a dozen biscuits, fresh from the oven, then been generous with his praise for her cooking.

His hand slid the songbook from her grasp, and she glanced up at him in surprise. The closing hymn was over, and he placed the book on the pew, then stepped a few inches closer to her. His pant leg brushed her skirt and his palm cupped her elbow as his head bent, the better for him to speak privately.

"You weren't singing."

Her breath caught, shivering in her chest, and she wished fervently—just for a moment—that she was at home, feeding the chickens or milking the cows or even carrying those dratted apples to the fruit cellar.

"Are you all right, Johanna?" The teasing note was gone, a worried tone taking its place.

She nodded, clearing her throat. "Yes, I'm fine. I'm just wondering what we do next."

He glanced over his shoulder to where the townsfolk were streaming down the aisle and out the door of the small church. Curious glances had warmed his back all through the service. Whispers of conjecture had accompanied the sound of the piano playing, and even now half a dozen women were gathering at the back door, their heads together. If he was half as smart as he'd always thought, he'd have arranged for himself and Johanna to show up at the parsonage after church.

"Pa? Are we goin' now?" Pete's loud whisper was impatient.

Tate bent past Johanna and spoke to the boy. "In a few minutes, Pete. Remember what I told you? Miss Johanna and I need to talk to the parson for a few minutes first."

The boy sat down on the wooden pew again, his hands hanging between his knees, his face dark with displeasure. Beside him, Timmy yawned widely and swatted at a lazy fly that had settled to rest on the pew in front of him. He waved his cap at it as the insect circled once over his head, and then cast his attention at the dust motes that floated in the brilliant sunlight from a nearby window.

"Have you told them?" Johanna asked quietly, shifting from one foot to the other as she waited for the church to empty.

Tate's nod was quick, his look a warning as three women made their way back up the aisle to where his family waited.

"Why, Johanna Patterson, it's sure good to see you here this morning," Esther Turner sang out loudly. "Thought you'd forgotten the way to church."

Selena Phillips turned an exasperated glare on the woman. "You know Johanna hasn't got a horse and wagon these days, Esther. It's bad enough she walks to town and back all week." She turned wise blue eyes on Johanna, and said quietly, "I'm so glad to see you today, Johanna. You've been a stranger lately."

Marjorie Jones adjusted her feathered hat, settling it a bit forward on her head and touched her top lip with the tip of her tongue. "I hear tell there's gonna be a wedding today. Anybody you folks know?" The look she threw at her friends was all but triumphant. That she'd stolen a march on them was obvious from the surprise they didn't even attempt to conceal.

"You're gettin' married?" Esther squeaked. "You and this gentleman here, Johanna?"

"Well, land sakes alive," Selena said breathlessly. "As I live and breathe, you couldn't have surprised me any more if you'd tried, child."

"We only just decided yesterday," Johanna said, aware of the warmth of Tate's hand on her elbow. And then that hand slid around her back and rested on the far side of her waist, allowing the whole length of his arm to press against her shoulder blades and ribs. She caught a quick breath and glanced at him. He was beaming at her, almost as if he were a genuine groom, anxious for his wedding to begin.

"Miss Johanna and I are just waiting our turn," he explained to the three ladies. "Soon as the preacher gets finished with his goodbyes out front, he's going to come back in here and marry me to this lady. Me and my two boys, that is. She's agreed to take on the three of us, and try to get us straightened out a bit." His smile was wide and his eyes were warm with humor as he offered his explanation.

"Well, I never..." Esther spouted. "You're going to marry up without any fuss at all, Johanna?"

Marjorie set her jaw. "Don't know why your friends can't be here, too."

Selena Phillips bent closer to where Johanna stood. "Perhaps you'd rather do this privately, Johanna. You've always been a quiet girl."

Johanna shook her head. "Yes... I mean, no, I don't mind if you want to be here for the wedding, Miss Marjorie. You too, Miss Esther. And you," she said finally, reaching to touch Selena's arm.

"Kinda sudden, isn't it?" Marjorie asked, her eyes narrowing as she turned to the man who'd set tongues wagging for the past hour or so.

"I'm Tate Montgomery, ma'am. And I've been known

to make quick decisions in my life. This one promises to be the best idea I've ever had. Miss Johanna has agreed to be my wife, and I'd like to invite you and your friends here to watch us do the deed.''

"You new in town, Mr. Montgomery?" Esther Turner chirped.

"Pretty much so, ma'am. But I'm well established already. The bank has my money, so I guess I'm on my way to being a solid citizen. I've got an account started at your husband's store, Mrs. Turner. And here I am in church. What more could you ask of a man?"

Behind them, boots clumped up the aisle, and an impatient voice heralded a new arrival to the group. "Mrs. Jones, I've got your boys in the wagon. If you don't want to walk home, you'd better be on your way."

Marjorie turned to face her husband. "There's to be a wedding, Hardy. Bring the boys back on in and wait, why don't you?"

His keen eyes scanned the small group. "You the groom?" he asked sharply, pinning Tate with his stare. "You marrying up with Fred Patterson's girl?"

At Tate's smile, he nodded vigorously. "About time she found herself a man. She's too young to be wearin' herself to a frazzle out there."

Tate swallowed a chuckle. If nothing else, Hardy Jones was blunt. "I'm honored to be marrying the lady. She's agreed to be a mother to my boys."

From her other side, Johanna heard a hushed sound that sounded dreadfully like words she'd never dared to allow past her lips. She darted a glance at Timmy and Pete. Timmy's head was nodding, and his one foot swinging several inches above the floor. Pete was glaring at the floor, his lower lip stuck out, his face flushed and darkened with anger.

"Pete?" she whispered. Surely Tate had told him the wedding would be today, hadn't he?

Dark eyes met hers and Pete's mouth twisted into a pout. "I don't need a mother," he whispered. "I got my pa."

"Oh, Pete!" She bit her lip. Whatever Tate had told him, it hadn't prepared him for this. "Can we talk about this after a while?" she asked softly, leaving the security of Tate's arm to bend closer to the boy.

"Won't do any good."

Johanna's heart beat faster as she lowered herself to the pew. Careful not to touch the child, she blocked him from view of the others. "Maybe we can be friends, Pete."

"I don't need any friends."

"I do." The words were faint, spoken on an indrawn breath. Johanna had let them slip from her mouth without thinking, and only after they had been uttered did she realize the truth they held. She didn't have a close friend to her name. Selena Phillips had always been kind to her. The other ladies in town had greeted her nicely and spoken to her politely. But never had she had a real friend.

From the far side of Pete's sturdy body, a small, warm hand crept to touch her palm as it rested on her lap. Timmy leaned forward, in peril of falling to the floor, balancing himself on the very edge of the seat, and smiled at her sleepily. "I'll be your friend, Miss Johanna."

Her heart skipped a beat. Her throat ached with unshed tears, and she blinked her eyes vigorously, lest she allow even one teardrop to fall. "I'd like that," she whispered.

Pete roughly pushed his brother's arm aside. "I'm your friend, Timmy."

Johanna smiled at the younger boy, and then the smile faded as she looked up at the children's father. His brow pulling into a frown, he bent to view the three of them.

"Everything all right, Johanna? The preacher's coming back in. Are you about ready?"

Was she ready? Heaven knew she needed a boost of strength from somewhere. She'd just been rejected by Tate's eldest boy, and that on top of the nervous stomach she'd been struggling with all morning. And now it didn't feel as if her legs were going to hold her upright.

Her lips curved into a shaky smile. "I'm fine, Tate." *Liar,* her heart cried.

His hand enclosed hers, and he tugged her gently to her feet, then led her to the altar where the minister waited.

"Last chance to back out, Johanna," he said so that no one else could hear.

Johanna thought of the cows he'd milked this morning, the hay he'd forked into the mangers. She remembered the easy way he'd carried furniture yesterday, his words of thanks as she served his supper. She envisioned the task of climbing a ladder to pick apples, imagined trying to tend to the herd of cattle all winter, when the west wind blew snow from the big lake. And then she swallowed her doubts as she accepted the hand he offered her.

His arm slid from around her waist, and he clasped her fingers within his own. It would be all right, she decided. It was a good bargain, this marriage she'd agreed to. Taking a deep breath, she fixed her gaze on Theodore Hughes, watching him open the small book he'd drawn from his pocket. His smile was encouraging as he lifted the cover and turned carefully to a page he'd marked beforehand. With one more long look at the couple facing him, he took a breath and began.

"Dearly beloved..."

Chapter Five

"I thought you'd told Pete we were going to be married today." She hadn't been able to look Tate fully in the face since the ceremony, and now she spoke with her back to him, her hands busy with stirring the gravy and tending the simmering kettle of beans. The vision of the small boy's sullen face had been in the forefront of her mind, a surprise she hadn't planned on.

"Pete's kinda hard to sort out sometimes," Tate said quietly. "He listened while I told him you and I were to be married, but it wasn't what he wanted to hear, and I suspect he just pretended to himself it wasn't going to happen."

"Did he think you were just going to stay here?"

Tate shook his head. "Who knows what a child thinks? He seemed happy enough with being here, I agree. I doubt he'd thought about my marrying again. We'd talked before about finding someone to watch after both boys." His voice softened. "To tell the truth, Johanna, till I caught sight of you, I hadn't worried too much about remarriage. I was willing to settle for a housekeeper."

"Until you saw me, or my farm?"

"Both, maybe. I just knew this was the place I was willing to put down roots. Don't ask me how I knew. I couldn't tell you. Any more than I could say why I knew you'd be a woman I could marry. I gave you a whole string of reasons why you appealed to me as a mother for my boys." He tilted his head and eyed her knowingly. "Maybe I just wanted to make it permanent, like you said, so you couldn't change your mind and skin out if the going got tough."

Johanna's spoon circled the skillet slowly, swirling the thickening gravy in a methodical fashion, a task she could manage without a whole lot of concentration. It was a good thing, too, because her thoughts had been in a swivet since the moment Tate Montgomery planted his mouth against hers, sealing their bargain before God and man.

She'd expected him to graze her cheek, or maybe the corner of her mouth. Just to make things look right. What she hadn't expected was the warmth of his lips, or the soft brush of them against her own before he found the spot he wanted to land on, or the impact of the male scent of him in her nostrils. She'd inhaled sharply when his mouth touched hers, thereby stamping the smell of his shaving soap and the aroma of freshly washed hair and skin on her mind.

It had only lasted a second or two, that kiss he'd given her with such ease and assurance, but the memory of it was still causing her to doubt her sanity.

She'd been kissed before, more thoroughly and at greater length. She'd been seduced by a man who was fairly knowledgable at the game. Her body had known the possession of that man, had shrunk from his greater strength at the end, had endured the rending of her flesh as her innocence surrendered to his taking.

Yet none of that had touched her inner heart as had the warm caress of Tate Montgomery's kiss. It had spoken to her of commitment, as if in that one gesture he'd taken on her problems, her debts, her worries and her woes. She'd felt, for that moment, safe and secure, with his hands clasping her forearms, his head bent low to salute her with the wedding kiss. She'd felt like a bride, almost.

Tate had held her arm in his grasp, guiding her past the women who would have gushed their well-wishes and words of advice in her ear, had he given them more of a chance. As it was, the two of them had made their way down the aisle and out the door within minutes of the short ceremony. Tate had gathered up his boys on the way and piled them into the back of the wagon with an economy of motion Johanna could not help but admire. The man knew how to make an exit, she'd give him that. As if he recognized her unwillingness to make small talk, he'd taken charge in grand style. They'd been on their way home before the preacher cleared the doorway, ushering the remnants of his flock before him.

"You going to stir that gravy all day, or are we going to get to put it on our potatoes?" Tate had left his seat at the table and walked up behind her.

"It's done." Her voice was downright normal, she was pleased to note. Her hands made all the right movements, picking up the pot holders, serving up the vegetables, pouring the perfectly smooth gravy into her mother's china gravy boat and then placing everything on the table. All without looking once at the man who watched her every movement as if he were trying to see beneath her skin.

"You're all upset about this, aren't you, Johanna? We need to be comfortable with each other. We can't live in this house like two strangers."

"I don't see how it can be any different, for now at least," she answered, pulling the oven door open, rescuing the biscuits in the nick of time. "We are strangers."

The woman who'd been dancing around in his mind for two days had taken to ignoring him ever since they repeated their vows, two hours ago. He'd thought to hear her making small talk while she cooked, maybe tell him about the people who'd hung around to watch the impromptu wedding.

She could even have told him about the farm. Hell, he hadn't even known how many head of cattle she had till he went looking for himself. Her "not many" had led him to think there were no more than a half-dozen young steers and milk cows in the pastures. The herd he'd tracked down in the far pasture last night numbered at least thirty or so. Accompanied by the rangiest, most worn-out bull he'd seen in a month of Sundays.

"We may be strangers, Johanna, but we're married. We need to talk about a few things." Beneath the genial words lay a tone of voice that had caused people to sit up and take notice over the years. He wasn't surprised to see her shoulders straighten and her spine stiffen. She'd gotten the message. Tate Montgomery was ready to set this marriage in motion. He would not suffer her silence any longer.

Johanna placed the pork roast on the table, careful to put it squarely on the hot pad that would protect her wooden tabletop. He watched as her gaze flicked over each bowl and plate, aware that she was assuring herself that her meal was ready for consumption and that each plate and fork and napkin was squarely in place.

And still that pair of blue eyes avoided his. Staring at the second button of his white shirt, she told him dinner was ready, her voice low and controlled, her unease apparent only in the pulse that fluttered in her throat.

He took pity on her. Johanna Patterson was having second thoughts, and his masculine presence in her kitchen had not helped matters any. His flat demand for a conversation had not set too well with her, either, if he was any judge. In fact, if he wasn't mistaken, she was about to bolt. And that he couldn't allow.

"Jo."

Her eyes widened, sweeping from the middle of his chest to his face, as if the diminutive of her given name had shocked her. She blinked, her attention on him fully for the first time since they'd left the church.

"I'm not pushing for any intimacies between us. I just want us to talk and act like families act within the walls of their home. Can't you just pretend I'm your brother or your uncle for the next hour or so? Talk to me like you would a man you've known for years, like you and your pa used to talk at mealtimes." He watched her closely, noting the faint flush that rose from her high-collared neckline.

"Pa and I didn't talk much, Tate. We didn't have a whole lot to say. Pa wasn't the same after my mother died." She spoke slowly, the words halting, as if she hesitated to admit the lack of closeness she'd felt with her father.

"You don't have any relations hereabouts? You didn't have folks in for Sunday dinner?"

She shook her head. "I fed the thrashers. Out in the yard, under the trees. Once Selena Phillips came out to see me, right after my mother died. Pa told her we didn't take to having folks hanging around. She didn't come back."

A wave of sympathy for the woman he'd married hit Tate with the force of an afternoon storm. She'd been alone here for years, living with her father, but as solitary as any human could be. Suddenly the wall of bristling, cutting words she'd thrown up between them at their first meeting made sense. Johanna Patterson was more than a lonely woman. She was hurting, and wary of any advances.

"Is it time to eat?" Timmy's treble voice through the screen door broke the silence that had fallen in the kitchen. His nose pushing up against the wire mesh, he squinted as his eyes adjusted to the dimmer light inside.

"Come in, boys." Johanna smiled at them, welcoming their presence. She could cope with them, talk with them, serve their food and get through this meal with a minimum of contact with their father. She watched as Pete pulled the door open, stretching the spring as far as he could, waiting for his brother to step inside, then allowing the door to slam behind him. His eyes lit with a degree of satisfaction as he darted a look in her direction.

"Don't let the door slam next time, Pete," his father said firmly.

"Yessir," the boy replied, ducking his head deliberately as he spoke.

"Your hands clean?" Tate asked, frowning at his eldest son.

"I washed mine, Pa," Timmy volunteered, holding up the items in question, his palms still wet and glistening.

"Pete?"

"They're clean, Pa," the boy mumbled. "We used the pump outside."

Johanna pulled out the chair to the right of her own. "Sit here, won't you, Timmy? Take the chair across from your brother, Pete." She clasped her hands before her, watching as the boys did her bidding, aware of the man who stood across the table, his own hands clasping the back of his chair. Finally she felt herself snagged by the strange warmth of his gray eyes.

"Sit down, Johanna. Everything looks fine. We need to eat before it gets cold." He waited for her to take her place, not allowing her to attempt retreat.

And the thought had passed fleetingly through her mind. Only the presence of the two children made it feasible for her to eat with any pretense of ease and affability. She waited while Tate bowed his head and asked a brief blessing on the food, then busied herself with fixing Timmy's plate, cutting his meat and watching as he took the first bite. As she'd noticed yesterday, his chin came only inches above the tabletop. Now he tilted it to ease the passage of his potato-laden fork as he aimed it toward his mouth.

"Would he do better with a pillow under him?" Johanna asked.

"I thought maybe a chunk or two of firewood would work," Tate said with a grin.

"I can kneel, Pa," Timmy volunteered cheerfully. Depositing his fork on the table, he scrambled to his knees and leaned back on his heels. "This will work good," he announced, setting to with renewed energy, now that he could reach his food more readily. "I was hungry, Miss Johanna."

For the first time in days, Johanna's mouth curled in genuine humor. The child's glee was infectious. "I'm glad you're hungry, Timmy. I like to cook for hungry men."

Across the table, Pete ate slowly, as if he begrudged every bite passing his lips. His eyes were downcast, his fork held in his fist like a weapon, his whole demeanor morose.

Johanna watched the older boy from beneath her lashes as she ate, wanting desperately to speak his name, to have him look up at her with open, cheerful good humor, yet knowing she must not infringe on his mood. His was about as far from a good mood as east was from west, and she wasn't about to get him in trouble with his father.

"Did you bring in everything from the barn, Pete?" Tate's query was pleasant, as if his son's ill will were not apparent.

"Yessir, it's on the porch like you told me." Green beans disappeared between his teeth, and he chewed diligently.

"Me too, Pa. I brung my stuff, my pillow and everything." Timmy's grin encompassed the table and all three of his companions. "When can we bring in the beds and stuff we brought?"

Johanna's head lifted, her gaze meeting Tate's abruptly. "You brought furniture with you?"

He nodded. "Some. I wasn't sure what we'd need. I didn't even know where we were going. I brought a supply of tools, too, some I didn't figure I'd want to have to replace. The boys wanted their beds and the feather ticks their aunt Bessie made for them, and some trunks I made them."

"You didn't tell me," she said, thinking of the big double bed she'd outfitted with clean sheets in her old bedroom. "We could have brought their things in last night."

"We had enough to do last night, what with getting your mother's room all fixed up for you."

"Well, I'm sure we can get the boys' things into the house after dinner and get them settled in. They'll want to put their clothes away in the wardrobe and dresser."

"Most of my stuff is dirty. Pa has to wash it," Pete said gruffly. "We didn't stop to do the washing for a long time."

Tate's smile was teasing. "I wasn't going to tell Miss Johanna about that till tomorrow, son. There wasn't any sense in scaring her off the first day. It'll take half the morning to scrub out the pile of things we've managed to accumulate."

"I'm used to laundry. My scrub board works real well," Johanna said obligingly. "Bring your things on in and put them in the washroom."

"You wash indoors year-round?" Tate asked.

"Pretty much. It gets cold here early on. We're not far from the big lake, and when that west wind blows, I don't enjoy being out in it, up to my elbows in wash water. My father built a washroom for Mama when he built this house. It's bad enough I have to hang things outside in the winter. Mama used to carry them up to the attic sometimes, when the weather got real bad, and string a line to put them on."

"What's wrong with a rack behind the stove?" Tate eyed the space between the cookstove and the wall, measuring it in his mind.

"I never thought of that. I didn't know they made such things," Johanna said.

"I can put one together for you. It won't hold everything at once, but things dry pretty good. Beats standing out in a cold wind, with a wet sheet flappin' in your face."

"Pa! Can we have pie now?" Timmy was plainly tired

of the talk of laundry day, and his voice was querulous as he attempted to change the subject. His plate was empty of food, his fork still held upright in his hand, and his eyes were glued to the apple pie sitting on Johanna's kitchen cupboard.

She scooted her chair back from the table. "Let me clear these things off first. Hold your fork tight, Timmy. You'll need it for the pie."

"I like mine in a bowl with cream over it," Tate said with a grin. "So does Pete."

"My aunt Bessie makes good pie," Pete offered stoutly.

Johanna's gaze met Tate's. It was easier this time. "Did you have apple trees on your place?"

He shook his head. "No, Bessie got them in town at the general store. She used to dry them to use in the winter. The boys spent some time with her.... She liked to fuss over them."

"We could have stayed there, Pa. Aunt Bessie said we could, remember?" Pete reminded him.

"It wasn't a good idea, son." Tate's firm words dismissed the idea, and the boy sighed loudly, eliciting another stern look from his father.

The wedding had changed him, Johanna thought sadly. The cheerful child of the night before had vanished, and she mourned his departure. It would take some doing to bring him back, she feared. Rising from the table, she quickly took up the plates, bringing the pie back with her. The pitcher of cream she'd poured for their coffee was still over half-full—probably enough for Tate's pie, too, she thought. She watched as he poured it over the slice she cut for him, watched as he lifted the first bite to his mouth, watched as his lips closed over the forkful of crust and filling. And felt a small bubble of rejoicing within her as his smile pronounced it good.

"It's as good as your aunt Bessie's, isn't it, Pete?"

The boy was silent, eating slowly, as if unwilling to allow any enthusiasm to creep forth.

Timmy had no qualms about expressing his approval. "You're a good cooker, Miss Johanna." It was high praise indeed, delivered with a flourish of his fork, crumbs surrounding his mouth, his eyes shining with glee.

"Yes, she is, isn't she?" his father agreed.

Johanna felt a blush paint her cheeks. She'd had more compliments during the past two days than she'd had in years. Tate Montgomery would fix himself a place in her life with his courtly manners and his gentle smiles, if nothing else.

The sun had gone down in a burst of splendor, leaving an autumn chill. Johanna had brought her shawl from the parlor, where it was usually draped over her mother's overstuffed chair, awaiting her use on cool evenings. Now she stood on the porch, watching warily as Tate carried another load of his things from the barn. He was truly moving into her house, and she felt a moment of apprehension as she considered that thought.

"This is the last of it," he said, resting one foot on the bottom step. He looked up at her, his eyes measuring. "What is it, Johanna? Are you fearful that I'll forget my bargain with you? That I'll forget which parts of the house I'm welcome in and which part is off-limits to me?"

She hadn't expected it, his ability to know her mind, and she clutched the shawl closer, as if the wind had sent a chill through her. "No, I'm not afraid of you, Tate. I told you that already. I've seen that you're a gentleman. I'm sure you'll hold up your end of the bargain."

He climbed the three steps to the porch. "Open the door for me, will you? I really loaded myself down this trip. I wanted to get all of it."

Johanna eyed the three boxes he carried. "Those look heavy. Can I help?"

"No." He shook his head. "They're mostly books. Some papers, too, and the contents of my desk. It's a big thing—probably foolish of me to pack it on the wagon, but I hated to leave it behind. I kept my records in it, and all the paperwork it takes to run a farm and family in one place, back in Ohio."

"There's a small room off the dining room you can have if you like," Johanna offered. Her face grew pensive as she thought of the evenings she'd spent by herself over the past ten years, wondering what her father did in that small room, while she sat by herself in the kitchen or in the parlor.

"Is it furnished?"

"Somewhat. You may as well bring those things on in here," Johanna said, leading the way. She went through the kitchen, into the formal dining room, which had been used so seldom that she kept the table and buffet covered with sheets. Across from the three wide windows was a door, and it was there that she headed. Turning the knob, she stepped within.

"It's dark in here," she called over her shoulder. "But there's not much to trip over. My father only kept a chair and ottoman by the window, and a table for his lamp and account books."

Tate looked around in the shadowed interior of the small room. An air of musty disuse assailed him, and he wrinkled his nose. "We need to open the windows in the morning and let in some fresh air and sunshine," he told her, bending to deposit his boxes on the floor against one wall.

"I haven't been in here since he died," Johanna admitted quietly. "It was his room. I guess I didn't feel welcome, even after he was gone."

"You'll be welcome, once it's mine." As a statement of fact, it couldn't have been any plainer. Tate would harbor no secrets from his wife. She doubted he would leave his bedroom door ajar for her to peek inside, but this room would be a part of the house once more.

Maybe she'd even remove the coverings from the dining room furniture and use the room for Sunday dining, as they had when her mother was alive. The thought cheered her.

"This is still your home, Johanna. When I pay off your mortgage this next week, it will be in my name along with yours, but the house is still whatever you want it to be."

She looked up at him, peering to make out his features in the dim light. "That all sounds well and good, Tate, but as a man, you have more rights than I'll ever have. I wouldn't have agreed to this if I wasn't pretty sure of you. As far as I know, a woman only has the rights her husband allows her, no matter what the deed says."

"It's a matter of trust, isn't it? When it comes to the bottom line, Johanna, you have to trust me. Can you do that?"

"Can I trust you? To keep up the place? I suppose so. Just don't expect more than that of me. I've learned to take care of myself over the years. I don't need anyone to do for me. I'll let you tend to the heavy work, gladly. But I'll not come to depend on you, Tate. I've learned that lesson well. I've allowed myself to…care about people. It won't happen again."

"You care already for my sons."

Spoken as a statement of fact, the words drew no argument from her. "Yes, you're right there. They're young and helpless. They need someone to tend them."

"And you don't?"

"Need someone? No, I've learned better." She folded her arms around her waist, a shiver passing through her slim shoulders beneath the warmth of the shawl.

His eyes caught the movement, even in the shadowed room. "You're cold, Johanna. Leave this for tonight. Tomorrow will be soon enough to set things to rights in here."

She walked out the door before him, her steps taking her into the hallway and toward the staircase. "I don't hear the boys. They must have gone to sleep." She looked up the stairway, then back at the man who watched her in the lamplight. "Good night, Tate. Will you turn out the lamp when you come up?"

He nodded, handing her the candlestick that waited on the hall table, lighting a match from the box she kept there. "Will you want the lamp lit in your room? Or will this be enough light for tonight?"

"This is fine. I only need to get ready for bed. I can do that in the dark," she said briskly, suddenly unwilling to feel his eyes on her any longer. "I get up early, Tate. Breakfast will be ready as soon as the cows get milked."

"I'll be milking them from now on," he reminded her. "I may not be as quick as you are at the job." His grin teased her. "I may need a refresher course."

She picked up her skirt to take the first step. "You'll do just fine, I think. No matter, we'll wait for you. And if you take too long, I'm still able to give you a hand."

"I'm teasing you, Johanna. I've done my share of milking. I won't make you wait meals for me. Just cook plenty. I plan on working up a good appetite in the barn."

"I've fed you the past two mornings. I have a good idea about your appetite, Mr. Montgomery," she said smartly.

He watched her climb the stairs, noting the slight sway of her hips beneath the muslin gown she wore. His eyes caught sight of her slim ankles above the low shoes she'd slipped into after church this morning. Limned in the candleglow, her form drew his gaze, her hair a fine halo in the gentle light, giving her an ethereal elegance.

"No, ma'am," he murmured beneath his breath. "You have no idea at all about my appetite. Matter of fact, till just this minute, I wasn't sure I had much left to speak of." And that was the truth, he thought, his grin rueful.

"Good night, Mrs. Montgomery," he said quietly, even as he heard the latch of her bedroom door shut.

Chapter Six

She'd survived two weeks of marriage. Johanna mentally marked the date on the calendar, and a sense of satisfaction curved her lips in a smile. It had been a busy two weeks, too, what with making several trips to town, facing the glances of the curious the first time out. After that, it had been easier.

Even in church on Sunday, they'd been greeted by one and all, with hardly a raised eyebrow to be seen among the congregation at Johanna Patterson's quick trip to the altar.

Tate was ambitious, she'd give him that, working from early till late. Today was no exception, breakfast barely swallowed before he hustled out the door. He'd lingered only long enough to place a warm hand on her shoulder, reminding her of a button he'd managed to lose from his shirt last evening. She'd agreed to replace it, her mind taken up with the touch of his hand, flustered by his nearness.

And then he'd been gone, leaving her to consider the strange awareness he aroused within her. He was a toucher; she'd noticed that with the boys, and he was given more and more to gaining her attention with a passing brush of those long fingers and broad palms against her arm or waist when the mood struck him.

From outdoors, a squeal of laughter and a shout from

Timmy commanding his brother to "Watch me now!" caught her attention, bringing a smile to Johanna's lips. Whatever the little scamps were up to, it sounded as if they were enjoying it mightily. Another whoop of glee caught her attention, and she left the sink, wiping her hands on the front of her apron.

From the doorway, she watched as Pete scampered from beyond the side of the barn. He carried handfuls of straw, tossing it in the air, blowing it vigorously, trying without much success to keep one piece afloat on the updraft his small lungs provided.

Johanna laughed, pleased at his carefree expression, relieved that the frown he'd worn like a favorite garment over the past weeks seemed to have disappeared.

"Watch me slide!" Timmy's high voice demanded attention once more, and Johanna halted midway to the stove.

Slide? What on earth could the child be doing? Where was he playing? The only thing around the corner of the barn was the big strawstack.

And in that moment, she knew.

Spinning on her heels, one hand outstretched to open the screen door, she ran. From the corner of the barn, Pete caught sight of her flying footsteps, dropping the remnants of straw he held, his eyes darkening as he watched her advance.

"Pete, have you been playing on the strawstack?" Her hands held the front of her dress from the ground as she hurried past him, not awaiting his reply, already certain of what she would see as she rounded the corner.

"Pete? Are you watchin' me?" Feet poking holes knee-deep as he climbed, Timmy was tackling the far side of the stack, gleefully chuckling as he plunged into the smoothly layered straw.

Johanna's hand lifted to cover her mouth as she watched, her aggravation at the ruin of the stack diluted by the child's pleasure. Once more down the slope wouldn't cause any more damage than he'd already done, she decided with a grimace.

Finally reaching the top, Timmy levered himself into place, and with a final *whoop* sailed down the smooth slope, landing in a pile of yellow straw. He lifted both hands to his face, brushing the floating wisps of straw from his eyes, catching sight of Johanna as he blinked.

"Did you see me, Miss Johanna?" Pride and laughter fought for supremacy in his chortled query as he knelt at the foot of her ruined strawstack.

"Yes, I saw you, Timmy." Her voice was a dead give-away, she knew, all harsh and breathless from her hurried trip across the yard. "You boys had no business climbing the strawstack. You've managed to make holes all over it for the rain to get in. It'll be ruined if we don't get it under cover before a shower comes up. Your pa has enough to do, without this kind of a mess to take care of."

Behind her, a snort of impatience announced Pete. "You just don't want us to have any fun. You think we should just work all the time on your old farm."

Johanna spun to face him. His jaw jutted forward as he completed his accusations, and his eyes squinted at her in the bright sunlight. Hands stuffed in his pockets, he stood spraddle-legged at the corner of the barn, defiance alive in his glare.

"Don't you know better than to play in the straw, Pete?" Living on a farm all his life as he had, surely his father had warned him about ruining a stack of straw. Canvas was hard to come by, but once the pile was disturbed, the rain would not slide from its surface, and only the heavy fabric would keep the stack dry and usable.

"My pa always let us have fun back home," the boy answered, his mouth drawn into a pout.

"I want you to have fun here," Johanna said quickly. "But not at the expense—" She drew a deep breath. It was no use scolding any longer. She'd only succeeded in making the child angry as it was, and poor Timmy was crouched in a pile of straw, looking as if he were about to be scalped.

"I'm sorry to have shouted at you. What's done is done." Johanna reached one hand to Timmy, taking several steps to where he squatted, almost in the cave where she'd pitched out straw from the side of the stack. "It's time for dinner. Come up to the house and get washed up," she told him, waiting for him to take her hand.

With a quick look at his brother, Timmy nodded, standing and accepting the hand she offered. "We was just climbing the mountain," he explained, his brow furrowing, his nose wrinkling as he sought to move a straw resting there.

Johanna swept her free hand through his dark hair, her fingers fluffing the stray yellow wisps from its silken length. Her heart went out to the child, his innocence shining from eyes so blue they reminded her of summer skies.

"We were just playin', and my pa won't like it that you yelled at us," Pete announced stoutly.

"Your pa will have to find a piece of canvas and top off this stack before the afternoon's over, and you'd better plan on helping him with the chore," Johanna told him quietly, her aggravation under control.

From the orchard, a shrill whistle caught her ear, and she spun to face the direction where her apple trees stood in neat rows. The tall figure of Tate Montgomery strode through the section where she'd planted several late-ripening northern spy trees, his head covered by a wide-brimmed hat. He lifted one arm in a wave, the other hand clasping a bucket laden with apples.

Her heartbeat quickened as she watched him stride through the tall grass, down the slope past the pasture fence and toward the house. His long legs carried him at a rapid pace, and a grin of satisfaction curled his mouth as he neared. So quickly he had found a place here on her farm.

Just as rapidly, he'd managed to plant himself right smack in the middle of her every waking thought.

She shook her head, willing the small trickle of pleasure she felt to be subdued. The man was a sight to behold, but she hadn't the right to…to what? Surely it did no harm to please herself by admiring his broad shoulders and long legged stride.

That she'd ever considered the young Joseph Brittles to be a likely candidate for her husband those ten long years ago was more than she could fathom now. Now that she'd met Tate Montgomery. Her eyes were fixed upon him as he brushed a path through the near meadow toward her, like a colossus making his way across a field of battle.

"Brought you a bucket of the first Baldwins, Johanna. Thought you could bake some for dinner. Sure would taste good with some brown sugar and cinnamon sprinkled over the top." He swung the heavy pail easily, as if the half bushel or so of apples weighed but a few ounces, instead of the twenty-five pounds she was certain it contained.

Tilting her head to one side as she considered his request, she nodded. "I can do that. Anybody who picks apples half the morning ought to get a little of the fruit of his labor, always figure."

His laugh was boyish in its cheerful exultation, as if he had not a care in the world. The bucket swung, the apples it held brimming over the top, and Johanna was struck by the masculine beauty of the man she'd married. His hair was blown by the breeze, probably tangled by apple branches while he'd poked amid them on the ladder. Sweat staining his shirt in a half circle beneath each arm and his hands soiled by the honest labor he'd done thus far today, he presented a picture she could only admire.

"I'll carry these to the kitchen for you, Mrs. Montgomery," he told her, a grin wreathing his face.

The somber man she first saw two weeks ago atop his wagon had been a far cry from the male specimen facing her now, she thought. Tate Montgomery thrived on hard work. Sunrise found him in the barn, milking and feeding the cows. Contrary to his joking appraisal of his skills, he was an accomplished farmer, she'd found. Whistling softly, cajoling the cows with gentle, coaxing praises, he made short work of the chores.

He'd taken to eating her food as if he hadn't sat at a decent table in years. His approval of her cooking was generous, and it pleased Johanna mightily that she could so provide for him. She plied him with food as a mother robin might tend her nestlings, proudly watching as her offerings were consumed. She'd never enjoyed her kitchen so much, gathering the final bounty from her summer garden to chop and peel and prepare for his approval.

Their noontime meals were hasty, Tate unwilling to keep from his work longer than was necessary to refuel his body for the afternoon's labor.

Supper was another matter entirely. Leaning back in his chair, he would watch her as she moved around her kitchen, ladling and pouring, readying the food for her table. His voice strong and vibrant, he'd tell of his day's accomplishments. Of the fences mended, the chores completed, the apples picked and sorted for storage, the last cutting of hay mowed and raked into neat rows.

His capacity for work astounded her. His cheerfulness in the face of such unending toil amazed her. His tenderness with the sons he'd fathered beguiled her. And the occasional look of assessment he cast in her direction piqued her curiosity. He'd made no advances; as he'd promised, he demanded nothing of her beyond what they'd bargained for. He bade her good-night at the foot of the stairway each evening and wished her a good day at the kitchen door every morning, after milking.

She walked behind him now as he strode to the porch, waited as he hoisted the apples easily to its wide planked surface. "Dinner's about ready," she told him, lifting her skirts to climb the three steps. "I just have to dish up."

"We'll wash at the pump. Looks like these boys have been rolling in the dirt." His big hands rested on young shoulders as he turned both children to where the iron pump stood.

Johanna heard the squeaks of Timmy's laughter as the cold water splashed over his hands and face. Her smile broadened as she imagined the three of them splashing water, clustered beneath the gushing flow, each of them taking a turn at wielding the long handle while the other two soaped and scrubbed.

How different her days were from the stern and staid life she'd led with her father for the past ten years. How quickly she'd welcomed the merriment two small boys and one tolerant father brought to this place.

This noontime, she feared, the smiles would be held in abeyance as she told Tate of the morning's small disaster.

Maybe the table laden with food would soften the blow she'd be obliged to deliver when Tate came in. He'd not be pleased to have to stop what he was doing to fuss with his sons' mischievousness. She'd have to soften the news, maybe wait until she served up the bread pudding she'd made for dessert. That Tate Montgomery enjoyed his sweets was a fact she'd come to appreciate.

Feet stomping across the porch alerted her, and she quickly carried the food to the table, gaining her seat just as the others found theirs. Timmy brushed off her offer of help, easing his way to kneel on the seat of his chair.

"For what we are about to receive, make us truly thankful," Tate prayed, elbows on the table, hands folded over his plate. She watched him through lowered lashes as his voice intoned the words, then quickly placed her napkin in her lap, lest he catch her peeking.

"Closing our eyes when we pray is a sign of respect," Tate said chidingly.

Johanna's head lifted quickly, her eyes seeking his. Surely he hadn't noticed!

"I always do, Pa," said Timmy earnestly, squeezing his eyelids shut, as if to demonstrate.

"Do you think God cares?" Pete's query was morose, as if he could not be concerned with what the Almighty deemed important. "I'd think he ought to worry more about other stuff."

"I've wondered about that myself," Johanna answered, dishing up potatoes on Timmy's plate before she served herself.

The older boy's head swung around, his eyes wide. "You have? You think he's got more important things to fuss over?"

Johanna nodded, doling out vegetables with a generous hand. "I used to wonder why he didn't look after my mother a little better, let her live a little longer. I prayed a lot about that, but she died anyway."

"Your mother died? How old were you?" His eyes were wide, and his somber, small face was expectant.

"Pretty old...sixteen. But I don't think you ever get old enough not to miss your mother when she's gone." Keeping her gaze deliberately away from Pete, Johanna dealt with Timmy's meat, cutting it into small pieces.

"Did she drown?"

It was a pitiful query, delivered in a wispy voice, and Johanna's heart melted, even as she shook her head. Perhaps she could let the matter of the strawstack go by the wayside until tomorrow. The thought of Pete being scolded by his father was more than she could cope with today. Suddenly, the loss of a pile of straw seemed trivial, next to the terrible deprivation suffered by the child when his mother had vanished from his life.

"Eat your dinner, Pete. We've got work to do this afternoon," his father said firmly.

"Yeah! We gotta clean up the mess we made in the

straw," Timmy volunteered brightly. "Miss Johanna hollered at us, Pa."

Dark eyes pierced her, bringing a flush to her cheeks as Tate wiped his mouth with the cloth napkin she'd provided for his use. "What happened?"

She evaded his gaze. "I'll handle it. The boys played in the strawstack this morning. I think I can take care of it, if Pete will help me."

"Pete?"

His father's look was stern, and Pete hunched his small shoulders, his fork held midair, laden with potatoes.

"We climbed the mountain, Pa," Timmy said brightly.

"And made holes in the straw?"

Pete nodded. "Yessir."

Tate took another bite of meat, chewing it forcefully. He swallowed and reached for his coffee. "I'll take care of it, Johanna. The boys know better than to play in the barnyard."

"Let me tend to it," she said quietly, aware that his temper had been riled.

"My boys made the problem. I'll clean it up."

Johanna folded her hands in her lap. Somehow she'd gone from being the bearer of bad news to the defender of the culprits. "I should have been watching them, Tate. They're my responsibility."

Pete shrank against the back of the chair, his dinner half-eaten, his eyes fearful as he listened to the two grown-ups.

"Is there canvas in the barn?" Tate speared the last piece of liver from the platter, carrying it to his plate.

"I'll have to look. Pa used to have some out there. Things got a bit unsettled over the past year or so. I may have to dig around for it."

"Unsettled?" Tate's eyebrows lifted, as if he disputed the word she had chosen to describe the state of her father's storage areas.

Johanna rose from the table, casting one glance at Pete, nodding at his plate in silent admonition.

Obediently he bent forward, fork in hand, and delivered a bite of food to his mouth.

"You'll help with the work, Pete. You too, Timmy," Tate announced. "I think we'd all better put our hand to it, in fact. It looked like a pile of clouds coming in from the west earlier. We can't afford to lose that straw."

"I thought we were going to have a real storm." Johanna looked toward the barn, across the yard where the thirsty ground was soaking up the showers as they fell to earth.

Tate nodded. "Look's like it's blowing over. Just as well, really. That hay we cut the other day is gonna need an extra day to dry before we bring it in."

"At least the straw..." She halted, aware that she'd managed to bring to his mind the very subject she'd been trying to avoid.

"I don't want you to pamper the boys."

"That sounds like an order." It was the first they'd spoken of the issue since the afternoon. Better to have it over with, let him have his say, she thought with a sigh of resignation.

He turned to look at her. "You'd have taken on the chore of cleaning up their mess this afternoon if I hadn't stepped in."

She nodded. "Probably. I'd already spouted off at them, Tate. I hurt Pete's feelings."

"They have to learn. Life isn't easy, and Pete tends to do as he pleases sometimes." He stepped back from the edge of the porch as a gust of wind blew the mist under the roof, dampening his shirt and pants. Leaning against the side of the house, he looked at her, barely able to make out her features in the light cast from the kitchen window.

"He misses his mother," Johanna said, uneasily awaiting his reaction.

Tate nodded. "Maybe. Or maybe he misses the idea of having a mother. Belinda wasn't one to cater to the boys. She left the mothering of them up to her sister, Bessie. Matter of fact, Belinda didn't enjoy much of anything about her life with me."

"She didn't like living on a farm?"

"No." He drew in a deep breath and rested his head against the bare siding of the house. "She was a city girl. Somehow I had the notion of making a farmer's wife out of her. Should have known better, I suppose. Her sister lived in town, and Belinda never got over resenting the fact that Bessie had neighbors around her and a store right down the road."

"Did you ever consider moving to town with her?" Johanna asked. She watched as Tate shoved his hands deep in his pockets, slouching a bit against the cool air, his shoulders lifting in a silent reply.

"Not really. I was born and raised on the place. It's all I knew." He looked at her in the dim light. "After we were married, I thought she'd come to like our life there. We had things pretty nice. I bought her a new stove and kitchen cabinets and had the water piped into the house."

"Do you miss her?" It was a brazen query, and she spoke it firmly, as if the issue were important to her. And she knew suddenly that it was. She couldn't bear it if Tate Montgomery was yearning for his first wife while he lived with the second one. If he thought of Belinda while he looked at Johanna... If he remembered his times with Belinda when he went to bed across the hall at night...

"Do I miss her?" He shook his head. "It was pretty bad between us, especially at the end." His hand slid from his pocket, rising to rest against the side of his face, his fingers tracing the scar on his cheekbone. As if it ached, he rubbed the raised tissue, his eyes narrowed, his lips tightly closed.

"What happened, Tate? How did you get the scar?"

His fingers left the ridged blemish, almost reluctantly,

his hand clenching as it hung at his side. "An accident with a knife."

Johanna's foot stopped its movement, and the rocker stood still. "You cut yourself?" She squinted up at him.

He shook his head, then, glancing down, took in her hunched shoulders and the fingers clutching her shawl. "You're cold, Johanna. We need to go in the house." He held out his hand to her and waited.

Her eyes lingered on his face, then moved to where his outstretched palm offered her his warmth. "Yes, I'm chilled from the wind," she agreed, allowing him to tug her from the chair. Beneath her fingers, the calluses he bore brushed against her skin, setting up a fine, tingling heat that invaded her flesh. She arose, aware of him as never before, and searched the shadows that hid his eyes.

His grip was firm, drawing her to where he stood. Turning, he sheltered her with his body against the wind as he opened the kitchen door. Then, inside the house, he kept her close, reaching behind himself to draw the latch.

"I think I need to go up to bed," Johanna said, her voice a whisper in the silence of the room. She tugged to free her hand, caught in the embrace of his fingers, but he would not allow her to escape so easily.

"Tate?" Risking a glance at his face once more, she was captured by the sober look of him, the straight line of his mouth, the taut clenching of his jaw, the piercing regard of his gaze.

For a moment, he watched her, as if he were weighing his words. And when they came, it was as if they were torn from him, raw and rasping in the silence of the room. "I don't miss Belinda, Johanna. I didn't love her for a long time before she died." His fingers squeezed hers in a painful grip. "I haven't made love to a woman in years." Tate's voice was low, and his words were harsh in their honesty, as he lifted her hand to rest against his chest.

She tugged at his grip, her heart beating rapidly, her

breathing audible as she drew in air with a shuddering gasp. "I don't want to hear this," she whispered harshly. "I don't want to know about the women in your life, Tate Montgomery!"

"You asked if I miss her, and I told you."

"You told me more than I wanted to know," she said, her eyes flashing her distress as she stepped back from him.

"Are you afraid of me, Johanna?" His words were soft, taunting, and as inflexible as his stance.

Once more she tried to free her hand, wincing at the careful pressure he exerted. It was no use, she decided, relaxing her grip, aware that she would not be released until he allowed her her freedom.

She closed her eyes. "Afraid? Until this moment, no, I've not feared you. Now..." She shook her head.

His lips twisted in a smile that held no trace of humor. "And now? I can't believe I frighten you. Have there been no other men in your life, Johanna Montgomery?" he asked, in a parody of her own words.

She felt the blood leave her cheeks, sensed a surging of shame through her flesh. Her eyes opened, and she shook her head. "Please, let me go, Tate. You've no right."

His grip softened, and then his hands moved, sliding behind her back and drawing her against him. "Oh, but I have, Mrs. Montgomery. I have every right. You're my wife, remember?"

He caught her close, her palms lifting to press against his chest, her lower body forming to his with only a few layers of fabric between them. Taking the weight of her easily, he held her, until the heat of his body reached her, permeating her very flesh.

It was an embrace she had not expected. But the warmth of him was tempting, and she leaned against him, her eyes closing.

She'd lied. Her fingers clutched his shirt as she admitted

the truth to herself. There was no fear in her heart for this man. Only a yearning to know his touch, his warmth.

"I won't hurt you, Johanna." His words were solemn, a vow, breathed against her forehead.

And then, as if in a dream, Johanna heard those same words repeated, in another voice, guttural, almost forgotten.

Thus Joseph Brittles had pleaded with her that night ten years ago, begged and coaxed her with his promises, until she gave in to his soft entreaties.

"Johanna?" Tate's mouth was pressed against her flesh, moving to her cheek, his lips open, his breath warm and coffee-scented.

With a shuddering breath, she turned her face from his seeking, and his mouth touched her ear. A shiver she could not suppress traveled from her body to his, and Tate laughed, a low chuckle that vibrated against her breasts. One hand rose to clasp her chin, and he turned her to face him once more.

She caught only a glimpse of his face, the ragged scar no longer a forbidding sight, as she sensed his gentleness.

And then his mouth touched hers, covering and warming her with soft, murmuring kisses. He spoke words against her flesh—broken, breathless sounds she could not comprehend. Johanna knew only a sense of wondering pleasure at the careful tasting of her, the gentle pressure of his lips against hers, the bold edge of his tongue that teased one side of her mouth and swept carefully across the surface of her lower lip to seek the other corner.

"Are you still frightened of me?" Tate asked, his mouth brushing hers as he spoke.

"No." The whispering admission was uttered on a shuddering breath, and he smiled at her honesty. Once more his mouth sought her smooth flesh, his lips opening against her cheek. He inhaled her scent, his groan of pleasure a low, urgent sound against her skin. Murmuring her name, he tasted her, the tip of his tongue brushing her silken flesh.

"Tate?" The whispered entreaty reached his ears, and he nuzzled her throat. Her head turned to one side, her neck seemingly unable to hold it erect. He grunted his satisfaction, and his lips moved to the curve of her jaw, then to where her pulse beat beneath the soft flesh of her throat.

"Johanna? Now do I frighten you?" As though he knew better, his words were laced with satisfaction.

"Yesss..." Once more, she lied, and fought the tears that surged within her, struggling with the untruth she uttered.

It was not what he had expected to hear. His arms loosened from their hold about her body, his head lifting, his mouth releasing the faint suction he'd held.

Johanna forced strength into her neck muscles, mourning the loss of his warmth, the comforting touch of his arms and hands, the muscular length of his body pressed against her softer parts. And in the mourning admitted to herself that she could never have what Tate Montgomery was offering her.

That he would be kind, she did not doubt. That his hands would woo her tenderly, she was most assured. That he would be expecting a virgin in his bed, she was certain.

And Johanna was not a virgin. Not even close. The thought of Tate Montgomery's scorn was more than she could face, and she held her eyes tightly closed against the brimming tears.

She had sealed her own fate on that night ten years ago. Jezebel, her father had called her. Perhaps that was the least of what Tate would label her if he knew the truth.

"Go, Johanna. Go to bed." His arms fell from around her, and she stepped back, blinking furiously, unwilling to meet his gaze.

Silently she turned from him. Aware of what might have been, woefully admitting to herself that it could never be, she climbed the stairs to her lonely bed.

Chapter Seven

"Will you drive the wagon for me this morning?" Tate stood in the kitchen doorway, his booted feet bearing traces of mud. "That sprinkle last night was just a teaser. We've got a storm coming, and that hay has to be under cover or we're going to lose it."

Johanna turned, wiping her hands hastily on the front of her apron. "Just let me change my shoes and get my shawl."

"Better wear your heavy coat, Johanna. The wind's pretty chilly this morning. Once the sun's out full, it won't be so bad." He watched as she bent to retrieve her outdoor boots from near the door, his gaze lingering on the lush curve of her hips. She'd whack him a good one if she knew he was taking advantage of the view she presented.

It was the first moment of humor he'd enjoyed since the failure of their encounter last evening. He'd spent a miserable night, aware that he'd overstepped his self-imposed boundaries, knowing full well the havoc he'd wreaked.

The kiss had been an impulse on his part. And once his hands contained her warmth, he'd been on a landslide to discovery. Only the knowledge of her innocence had kept him from carrying her to his room. She deserved better than an impromptu bedding, this prickly virgin he'd married.

And as wary as she was of him this morning, he'd probably best figure on months of solitude in that big bedroom.

He'd told her to start with that he wouldn't expect her to come to his bed, but that had been before he was exposed to her on a daily basis. Now he'd like to draw up a new bargain. Hell, he'd like to go back and redo the whole thing, from the word *go*.

Johanna Montgomery was a woman any man would desire, once he'd taken more than a cursory glance. Once he'd looked beyond the sharp tongue, to the quick wit that fed it. Once he'd grown to recognize the lonely woman, who was about as needy as any female he'd ever known. And needy didn't even begin describing his situation after last night. That Johanna hadn't brought it up this morning was a wonder.

She was ready. While he stood there gaping, she'd tied her boots and gathered up her heavy coat. Tate stepped back, holding the screen door open for her, then pulled the inside door shut behind them.

From her pockets, Johanna drew woolen mittens and tugged them on, tucking them inside her coat sleeves. She lifted her head, inhaling the morning air. "It's going to warm up before long," she predicted. "Where'd you get the mud, Tate? The yard's pretty well dried up."

He glanced down at his boots. "The wagon was in that low spot behind the barn. I had to hitch the horses up back there to haul it out. The field's pretty near dry, though. It shouldn't take us too long."

Rounding the corner of the barn, he turned to grin at her. "We'll put Pete on top to stomp down the pile as we go. He gets a big kick out of helping."

To Johanna's way of thinking, Pete hadn't gotten a big kick out of anything lately. He'd been subdued since yesterday afternoon, after the incident with the straw, and his smiles were few and far between anyway, as far as she could tell. Timmy, on the other hand, had behaved as usual, warming up to her without hesitation, even allowing her to help with tying his shoes and buttoning his coat.

"Where is Timmy?" Lifting her hand to shade her eyes, Johanna looked across the small meadow toward the orchard, then to the pasture behind the barn. "I haven't seen him since breakfast."

"He was playing in the haymow while I cleaned the stalls. I had him toss hay down to me for the cows a while ago. I suspect he's still up there."

"Will he ride on the wagon with me?" she asked. The thought of that small body pressed next to hers as they made the rounds of the hay field was an appealing one.

"Sure. It'll be a good place for him. Keep him out of the way."

Tate whistled a warbling three-note call and smiled once more at her. The second time he'd allowed that slow grin to slide into place in the past five minutes, she noted. The same grin he'd delivered last night, before he kissed her. She ducked her head at the remembrance.

"You callin' me, Pa?" From overhead, the small, shrill voice answered, and Johanna blinked, looking up quickly to where Timmy's head peeked over the edge of the window in the haymow.

"Hey, Miss Johanna, guess what?" he called, spying the woman below. "I found that old barn cat back in the corner, and he's got babies back there. Three of 'em."

"He has, has he?" Her laughter was spontaneous, Tate's own following as they digested the child's announcement. "They must be brand-new, Timmy," she said, tilting her head back to see him. "Tabby was still pretty round last night."

"You wanta come up and see, Miss Johanna?" Precariously, he leaned farther out the square hole in the side of the barn, and she drew in a quick breath.

"Tate?"

"Yeah, he'll be all right, Jo." Raising one hand, Tate

motioned the child away from the opening. "Back off, Timmy. You'll break your neck if you fall from there, and I'm too busy today to take you to town to the doctor."

"Oh, Pa! You're foolin' me," the boy chortled, scooting back readily at his father's bidding.

"Come on down, now," Tate told him firmly. "You can ride the wagon and help Johanna drive the team."

"Why can't I drive?" From behind them, Pete's voice was querulous.

His father turned and motioned to the boy. "Come here, Pete." One hand rubbed at the youngster's hair, smoothing it down where the wind had ruffled it. "I need you to keep the load even while I pitch the hay up to you. Can you do that?"

"I seen you doing it last summer," the boy said. "I'm big enough this year."

"You're growin' like a bad weed, son," Tate told him, his arm sliding down to grip the narrow shoulders. "It won't be long before you'll be able to pitch hay like a man."

The boy's eyes glowed at the words, and he sidled closer to his father. "Timmy's too little to help, isn't he?"

"No, I'm not," the smaller boy spouted, rounding the corner full tilt. "Pa said I can help drive the team." Attempting to clamber up the side of the wagon, he glanced back over his shoulder at Johanna. "Just wait till you see those babies. They're all squinty-eyed and runty-lookin'."

Tate reached to hoist his youngest son onto the wagon seat. "What color are they, son?"

"One's all different colors. The other two are black, mostly." Timmy bounced on the seat, his feet dangling. "Are we gonna keep 'em all? Aunt Bessie says one cat's enough to have around, doesn't she, Pa? But I'll bet we got enough room for more than one in the barn. It's a lot bigger than Aunt Bessie's shed."

"Yeah, but Aunt Bessie has a dog, too," Pete volunteered.

Johanna thought of the pleasure the two children had gained from Sheba over the past weeks. "You have a dog," she offered.

"She's yours, Miss Johanna. Pa said so." Pete's words were as sour as his expression.

Johanna shrugged. "She still manages to do her job, doesn't she, Tate?"

His grin when he heard the softening her words implied was welcome. "She's still a good herd dog, Jo, even though the boys have spoiled her a little." Tate tossed the pitchfork on the bed of the wagon and offered Johanna his hand as he helped her climb to the seat.

The wagon jostled over the ruts, the horses straining to pull it from the wet ground behind the barn. Soon it was free. Settling into a trot, the matched pair followed the lead of the woman holding the reins and the wagon turned toward the hayfield.

"It's going to be a late dinner, I'm afraid," Johanna said, slicing side pork with swift slashes of her butcher knife.

"That's all right. We'll all pitch in and help, seeing as how you spent your morning out in the field with us. What do you say, boys?" Tate's color was high, ruddy from the wind and the sun combined. He walked silently across the kitchen floor, his boots left outside the door. From behind her, Johanna felt his presence, even as he spoke in her ear.

"Can we have some eggs with that pork, ma'am? The ones from this morning are all wiped clean."

"I ought to use the older ones first," Johanna said, casting him a look over her shoulder.

"Let's have the fresh ones, Jo. I'll take the others to town to Mr. Turner. He won't know the difference, and wouldn't care if he did. He'll be tickled just to get your eggs. He told me he never gets an old egg from your basket. They're guaranteed fresh every time.''

Subduing the flush of pride she felt at his words of praise, she stepped away from him, reaching to take down the smaller skillet from its hook. She'd not been able to think of much else since last night, other than the man behind her, no matter how hard she tried to erase him from her thoughts. He just kept creeping back, insinuating himself into her every breathing moment. She clamped her lips together, shaking her head against the memory.

''You going to use that skillet, or bash me in the head with it?''

Startled, she whirled and caught a glimpse of him ducking the pan she held. It fell from her nerveless fingers, and she covered her mouth with the other hand. ''Oh, my word! Tate Montgomery! You almost made me—'' She halted abruptly as he swooped to pick up the skillet, his laughter in her ears.

''You need to keep your mind on your business, ma'am. We almost had eggs all over the floor.''

She'd come within inches of catching the blue speckled bowl with the edge of her skillet. The knowledge that he'd so easily managed to upset her concentration set her teeth on edge.

''Just move out of my way while I'm cooking.'' Her command was firm, and he bowed to her authority.

''You're the boss here, Johanna. I'll just sit myself down over here and keep an eye on things while you get my dinner on the table.''

She watched as he made his way on stocking feet to the chair at the head of her table. The place he deserved as head of the house. She thought how different he was from the man who'd last held that title.

Never could she remember her father passing out compliments or taking hold of things the way Tate Montgomery was doing. Or making cheerful small talk at meals. Or treating his child as a person worthy of love.

The eggs fried up quickly as soon as the side pork was finished. The pan of biscuits came out brown and broke apart fluffy, just the way her mother had taught her to make them. A bowl of fresh applesauce appeared from the pantry, and dinner was ready.

Timmy was glowing as he reported on the new kittens. Pete almost failed to hide his smile of satisfaction as Johanna complimented him on his work on the hay wagon. And Tate Montgomery sounded truly appreciative as he thanked his Maker for holding off on the storm until the hay was in the barn. In fact, so earnest was his gratitude, he almost forgot to mention the food he was supposed to be praying over, which resulted in a storm of laughter from the members of his family.

Deep inside, Tate Montgomery felt an explosion of warmth, spreading to encompass his whole being. Life was good indeed. No wonder he felt as if the sun were shining, even though the sound of rain was even now to be heard on the tin roof over the porch. His heart lifted as he caught Johanna's eye, again seeking the approval she had given him more often of late with her sidelong glances.

Yessir, things were looking up.

A shiny black buggy parked next to the house was her first warning of company as Johanna left the springhouse a few days later, carrying her basket of butter. On the buggy's seat, Marjorie Jones perched, one foot over the side as she reached for the step.

"Yoo-hoo, Johanna!" she warbled, attending to her footing.

"I'm out here," Johanna called, stepping briskly toward the buggy. "Is something wrong, Mrs. Jones?"

Marjorie's laughter was hearty. "My word, no," she said

brightly. "Can't a body come calling without a reason, Johanna? I just thought it was time to visit."

Since the lady had not done so in more years than Johanna could count, the theory had some holes in it, but she shrugged off that thought as she climbed the steps to the porch. "Come on in, won't you? I'll fix a cup of tea for us."

The kitchen was warm, the scent of dinner on the stove an inviting one. Marjorie settled on a kitchen chair, having refused the parlor in favor of the warmth to be found here.

"I declare, Johanna. It's been hard to imagine you as having a ready-made family these days," Marjorie warbled. "I was just saying the other day to Esther how glad I was for you, after you were so brokenhearted over that Brittles boy. Land sakes, that was a long time ago, wasn't it?"

Johanna brought the teapot to the table, placing it on the hot pad. "Ages ago. I'd almost forgotten him."

Marjorie darted a disbelieving look in her direction. "Really? I'd thought you were quite taken with him. Planning a wedding, weren't you?"

Johanna shrugged, her eyes intent on the spoon she held. Measuring a scant teaspoon of sugar, she stirred it into her tea. "We'd talked of it, but I was awfully young. Besides, my father needed me here."

"Well, it's just as well, I suppose, what with that nice Mr. Montgomery coming along and snatching you up. We've noticed he brings you to town with him right regularly. A lot of men wouldn't think of taking their woman along."

Johanna nodded agreeably. "He's a gentleman, all right. I'm very fortunate, I suppose."

Marjorie rambled on, her thoughts switching from one place to another, touching on the price of clothing and the hardship of being dependent on the farmers dealing at the mill.

Johanna hid her humor, knowing full well that Hardy

Jones was not stingy with his wife and that he had a captive clientele, being the only miller in this part of the county.

"Mr. Montgomery out in the barn?" Marjorie asked as she readied herself to leave, once the tea was gone and she'd managed to put away half a dozen of Johanna's cookies.

Johanna shook her head. "No, he's gone to town to see the blacksmith about something."

"I didn't see him on my way out," Marjorie offered, stuffing herself into the coat she'd worn as insurance against the cold weather.

Johanna opened the door and walked out on the porch, snatching up her shawl as she passed the coat hooks. She was working at being patient with the garrulous woman, anxious to get back to her chores. "He's due home soon," she said, hugging herself against the gust of wind blowing around the corner of the house.

Marjorie hoisted herself into the buggy and lifted the reins, turning the vehicle around before she raised a hand to wave a goodbye. "Why, looky there!" she exclaimed, pointing toward the road. "Isn't that your husband coming now? And will you look at that string of horses he's got!"

Johanna gaped at the sight. Tate, atop one of his mares, led three more horses behind, one of them a huge creature—a stallion, if her eyes weren't playing tricks.

"Yes, I see," she muttered, waving a farewell, even as she headed down the steps. If she hadn't waited till Marjorie was well on her way to the road, she'd have beaten him to the barn, but as it was, Tate reached there first.

If ever there were a thundercloud walking, Johanna was its name. Tate eyed the woman who stalked across the yard, heading for the barn as fast as her legs would carry her. Her skirts were swishing, her feet raising small clouds of dust with every step. Her mouth was pursed, and her eyes flashed signals that he was more than a little wary of.

This was Johanna Montgomery in a snit.

"Where did you get the idea we needed three more horses? We've got the two you brought with you, and it seems to me that's enough to be feeding for now. We can't use but two at a time to pull the wagon, anyway."

Framed in the barn door, Tate watched her approach, listened to her scolding, admiring the high color in her cheeks and the way her dress clung to the rise of her full bosom.

"I'm not plannin' on using them to pull the wagon, Johanna. Matter of fact, that stallion would be insulted if I tried to put him in harness." From the box stall within the barn came a trumpeting call from that very horse.

"What earthly good is a stallion, Tate Montgomery?"

His lifted eyebrow questioned her lack of knowledge. "Why, even a young lady like you ought to know the answer to that one, Jo."

Her quick blush made his grin widen. And her abrupt about-face earned her a muffled chuckle as he lifted a closed fist to his mouth, attempting to conceal his humor.

"I know what stallions are used for," she muttered darkly. "I just don't understand what makes you think we need one here."

He stepped closer to her and bent to whisper in her ear. "I'm planning on using him to make those two mares I just brought home into mamas. There's good money in raising horses, Jo." His breath was warm against her neck, and she shivered, which only increased his good humor.

She spun away, stamping her foot in a quick display of frustration. "You had no right to buy any animals without talking it over with me, Mr. Montgomery. I thought we were partners in this farm."

His hands settled at her waist, and he turned her to face him, his mouth drawn firmly, his eyes meeting hers with no trace of foolishness in their depths. "I was offered the mares at a good price from a man who'd stopped at the blacksmith's place. He was passing through town, heading back east and needing to make some money from his animals. He sold them at a loss, Jo, and I snatched them up. We'll need a riding horse for the boys to get to school by next fall. And as far as money's concerned, I'm gonna spend a little more this week. I've ordered us a two-seater surrey, for going to town and to church on Sundays.''

"A surrey?" Not to ride on the wagon any longer? That was a temptation she could barely resist. And she didn't even try. Johanna relaxed in his hold and took a deep breath. There was one more battle to be fought. "What about the stallion?"

His grin was back and, to her dismay, she welcomed it. "I borrowed him for a little while, just long enough to have the use of his services, and then I'll take him to his new owner. A fella the other side of town bought him, and he's lettin' me have the use of him. It was part of the deal, Johanna. He'll only be here for a week or two, at the most. Not much longer, anyway. Just till those two little ladies are ready for him."

Her blush deepened. "I don't think I want to hear about this, Tate. And make sure you keep the boys away from your shenanigans."

His hands rose to frame her face, and his head lowered until their noses were almost touching. "Is that what you call it? I'd have put a different word on it, but I guess we can settle for *shenanigans,* Mrs. Montgomery."

In a quick movement she couldn't have dodged, even had she wanted to, Tate planted a kiss on her open mouth. And then, after a second's hesitation, during which she could only stand and blink her surprise, he came back after another taste of her soft lips.

"The boys…" was all she could utter as he drew back the second time.

"…are up in the loft with the kittens," he managed between chuckles. "I explained to Timmy about boy cats and girl cats this morning, by the way."

"You did?" Her own laughter joined his, and Tate barely resisted the temptation she offered, her eyes shining, her lips smiling.

"Yes, ma'am. Now he wants to know who the daddy of those babies might be, and I had to admit my ignorance. Told him he'd have to talk to you about that part of it."

"Oh, my!" Her mouth formed a small O of distress as she considered that idea. "It was probably the Cooneys' old tom. He was hanging around for a week or so a couple of months ago. I guess that's when she... Well, you know."

He took pity on his bride, placing his hand loosely over her mouth, more to hide the temptation she offered than to quiet her explanations. "I know what you mean, Johanna. And all you have to tell Timmy and Pete, if they ask, is that the daddy lives at the Cooneys' place. They won't ask more than that." He lowered his hand, cupping her chin in its depths, and eyed her moist lips longingly.

"Don't you dare, Tate." Her eyes darted everywhere but to where he wanted them to focus, and he smiled at her innocence. So barely had he awakened her needs, so little had he shown her of his own masculine yearnings...so fresh and pure was the gaze of those blue eyes. The urge to wrap her in his embrace was almost overwhelming this morning, and only the thought of his two sons happening upon them kept his arms from the caress they longed to instigate.

Tate settled for one more brush of his lips across hers, one more taste of the sweetness she would have denied possessing, had he spoken his thoughts aloud. Like a prickly hedgehog, she'd bustled from the house—and now, like a hand-fed fawn, she looked at him, wary and hesitant.

"You shouldn't be kissing on me like that," Johanna said after a moment, breaking his hold as she stepped back.

"We're married, Johanna." He reached to tug her shawl over her shoulders, snuggling it around her throat.

"Not really." Her gaze fell from his, intent on the third button of his jacket.

"According to the law, we are."

"You know what I mean, Tate. We have a bargain."

He stuffed his big hands in his pockets, scrunching his jacket up in the doing. It was the only way he could stop them from fastening on her and hauling her into his arms. "I'm willing to make some changes in the deal we made."

She turned from him and ducked her head. Her steps were quick as she walked back toward the house. "I'm not, Tate."

From the barn, the noisy trumpet of the stallion sounded once more, and Johanna's shoulders stiffened at the sound. "You'd best find a secure place to hold that animal for the next two weeks, Mr. Montgomery. One male creature on the loose around here is about all we need."

Chapter Eight

The spanking-new two-seater surrey was a sight to behold, rolling into Belle Haven on Sunday morning. Selena, nodding and smiling, lifted one hand to wave a discreet greeting as it passed her by. Beneath her breath, she murmured her blessing. "He was worth waiting for, Johanna Patterson. I'll warrant he'll put a bloom in your cheeks and a baby in your belly before the winter's out."

She'd been the girl's stoutest defender when Neville Olson's suit was denied. Marjorie Jones had said "the Patterson girl should have snatched up the Olson boy, probably the best chance she'd ever have, at her age." Selena had secretly thought Neville's fascination was with the Patterson farm, not with the young woman who owned it.

Now, watching the surrey progress toward the church on this crisp late-autumn morning, Selena felt more than vindicated. If ever a fine figure of a man had existed in this town, Tate Montgomery was it. From the top of his head—each dark chestnut hair held firmly in place by a discreet application of pomade—to the tips of his shiny boots, he was a man worthy of respect.

She'd heard he'd ordered the surrey without Johanna's say-so, bought the mares on impulse and built a new corral in jig time, all in the first two months of his marriage to

he sharp-tongued young woman. What Johanna had to say
to all that was a mystery, since she'd never been known to
confide in anyone hereabouts.

The surrey pulled smartly into the churchyard, Tate lowering himself to the ground with an ease that spoke of physical strength. Fast on his heels, the two boys riding in the
back seat slid to the side and, with quick movements, he
lifted them down. Finally he turned to the woman he'd
married.

"Would you like a hand, Mrs. Montgomery?" His dark
gaze glittering with a silvery sheen, he held out his hand
to her, and Johanna slid across the black leather seat, aware
of more than just one pair of eyes focusing in her direction.

But it was the man before her who drew her attention.
The scar ridging his cheek should have detracted from his
male beauty. Indeed, the small white slash nicking the edge
of his lip might have been judged an imperfection, had
another man borne it. Instead, they only distinguished Tate
Montgomery with their silent message. This was a man not
to be underestimated. His face bore intriguing marks, from
the crooked bridge of his nose to the scars he wore with
self-assurance. She'd married a man to be reckoned with.

And unless she missed her guess, the day of reckoning
was fast approaching. Johanna gripped the wide palm he
offered, placing her feet carefully as she turned to climb
from the surrey. His hand at her waist took her unawares
as he guided her down, the other still grasping her fingers.

"I've got you." Steadying her as she got her bearings,
allowing his warmth to creep past the woolen cape she'd
worn, he pressed his advantage.

A habit he'd gotten into lately, Johanna thought ruefully.
Every chance he had, every time an opportunity arose, he
touched her. Like now, this very minute. By now she
should have gotten used to the pressure of his palm against
her back as he guided her up the path, toward the church

doors. They'd been observing this ritual for two months now, since their marriage in September.

But then, some things took a lot of getting used to. Like the way his gaze seared her with heat every time he took a slow survey of her form. Not in any way Johanna could make a big fuss over, not with the boys around, anyhow. And then there was the trick he had of telling her goodnight and watching her climb the stairs. Her cheeks burning with a mixture of unease and excitement, she would lift one foot, then the other, knowing without a shadow of a doubt that those gray eyes were marking every move she made.

One would have thought that the familiarity of the ritual would have eased her into a comfortable rut. Her mouth pinched as she considered the thought. There were no ruts in the life she'd chosen to share with Tate Montgomery, and not a lot of comfort, either, for that matter.

His hand shifted on her back, sliding up to center between her shoulder blades. It was a silent message, and she lifted her face to his, caught by the small smile he sent her. So well she knew this man already. And yet she knew him not at all. She'd washed his clothing, folding his stockings and undergarments into precise, neat piles for storage in his chest of drawers, leaving them on a hall table outside his door. She'd ironed the very shirt he was wearing, yet never touched the flesh it covered.

"Selena is waving at you." His head bent low as he delivered the message in a soft whisper.

Johanna peered past him. Selena hurried across the churchyard, skirting the muddy spots. One hand uplifted in an unmistakable signal, she silently bade Johanna wait.

The postmistress was past her prime. Johanna knew she had to be at least forty years old, and she certainly had lost the bloom of youth. But the firm flesh on her face and the golden hue of her curling hair allowed her the distinction of being one of the loveliest woman to inhabit Belle Haven.

Why she'd never married had long been a source of speculation, but over the past few years, she'd been accepted as just exactly what she was—a woman alone, beyond the age of marriage, a permanent fixture in the small post office that took up one corner of Joseph Turner's general store.

"Johanna! You didn't come to town yesterday." The words weren't an accusation but a statement of fact, and Selena accompanied them with a swift hug and a brushing of cheeks.

"We were in on Thursday," Johanna told her. "Twice a week, just like always."

"Well, I knew I could look for you tomorrow, but I wanted to let you know that there was a catalog at the post office for you, and a letter for your husband. I thought it might be important."

Tate halted before the double doors of the small church. "When did the letter come, ma'am?"

"It came yesterday morning. It may not be of importance, but I'd be willing to open the office and give it to you today, if you'd like, Mr. Montgomery." Without waiting for his reply, Selena's gaze flowed to rest on Johanna's face. "You're looking well, Johanna. I'd say marriage agrees with you, but I'm sure you've heard that from numerous others in town already, and I don't want to be a copycat."

"Thank you," Johanna answered, aware suddenly that a line of hopeful entrants to the church was gathering behind them on the path. "I think we're blocking the doorway, Tate. We'd better move along."

His hand slid to her waist as he opened the door and ushered her through the portal, motioning to the postmistress to follow his wife. As Selena passed him, he nodded. "I'll be most appreciative if you could make a Sunday delivery of the mail, Miss Phillips. We'll come by after church. Perhaps you'd like a ride in our new surrey, ma'am."

"Thank you, Mr. Montgomery." Sliding into her usual pew, Selena watched as the couple moved up the aisle. The Patterson family had always sat on the right side, in the fourth pew from the front of the church. Not that their name was attached to the polished oak seat, but by habit, the pew belonged to them. Now it was occupied by the newlyweds and their two small boys.

The service was joyous, a celebration of Thanksgiving, in honor of the holiday to come just four days hence. The congregation sang with vigor, the small choir adding considerable volume to the music. Theodore Hughes had gathered up all the scripture he could find that signified reasons to be thankful and presented them with gusto. Indeed, so long was his list that Johanna began sympathizing with the wiggles of Timmy and Pete long before the sermon was over.

"Let us pray!" The young minister bowed his head, amid sighs of relief from almost every young person in the congregation, and pronounced the benediction over the heads of his congregation. "...now and forever, amen."

The noonday sun was brilliant, unseasonably warm and more than welcome as the congregation flowed into the churchyard. "Good to see you, Mr. Montgomery," Esther Turner chirped. "You too, Johanna." Her keen eyes scanning the couple, she smiled her regard. "You two certainly make a fine pair. Haven't seen you look so good in a month of Sundays, Johanna."

Tate slid a proprietary hand to rest against the curve of his wife's waist and dipped his head in a nod of thanks. "I think she always presents a fine image, Mrs. Turner," he said politely, steering Johanna toward the surrey, parked amid a dozen others at the hitching rail.

Leah Ibsen, teacher at the schoolhouse, stepped before them. "I thought I might have your eldest boy in class, Mr. Montgomery," she said politely, her eyes fixed on the ruggedly handsome man.

His scar and crooked nose didn't seem to be a deterrent there, Johanna thought. Leah had obviously taken a shine to the new man in town. And then with a burst of charity taking hold of her accusing thoughts, she decided that the young woman was in good company. Certainly, the man's appeal wasn't dependent on perfection. The sparkle in his gray eyes and the cocky grin he was flashing right this minute were enough to set any young woman's heart to pounding.

Including her own. *And I'm the one he's married to,* she thought with a small degree of triumph.

"Next year, Leah," Johanna said, answering for Tate, who hadn't the faintest notion of the young woman's name. "Mr. Montgomery decided to letter Pete at home this winter. When he's a little older, we'll be putting him on a horse and sending him off to school."

From beside her, she caught the sharp sound of Pete's indrawn breath and the quick word that followed it. "Really?" His hand tugged at her dress. "Do you mean it, Miss Johanna? Will I really get to ride to school on one of the new mares?"

"That's what he got them for, Pete," she told him quietly, pleased by the pleasure painting his features.

"She won't be ready for you to ride for a while, son," his father told the boy.

That admonition had little effect on Pete's enthusiasm, so far as Johanna could tell. His eyes gleamed with anticipation as he bounced on the balls of his feet. "When I'm eight, Pa? That's when I can ride her?"

"When will you be eight?" Johanna asked him, basking in the warmth of his undiluted exuberance. For the first time in weeks, he was grinning at her with unhampered glee, his dimples exposing the pure happiness he exuded.

"Come next April," the boy told her without hesitation. "And that's only a little ways away."

"We've got the whole winter to get through first," Tate

reminded him. "And we haven't even had the first real snowfall. Next spring will come soon enough."

Pete scampered ahead of them, scrambling into the back seat of the surrey, his eyes bright, his color high, as he bounced up and down on the leather upholstery. "Will that lady be my teacher, Pa?" he asked, scooting over to make room.

"Looks that way." Tate plopped Timmy in place and looked around quickly. "Where's Selena Phillips? There's room for her with the boys."

"She's on her way now," Johanna said, climbing up to the front seat, Tate's arm firm beneath her fingers.

In seconds, Selena was settled in the surrey, one boy on either side, and they left the church. Twice up and down Main Street satisfied the requests of Timmy and Pete for a longer ride for the postmistress. Once would have been enough for Johanna, certain that the catalog was a copy of the new Sears and Roebuck. She'd read it all the way home, she determined, eager to open the cover, inhale the scent of fresh newsprint and then digest the myriad offerings its pages would spill before her.

Within minutes, Tate's letter in his pocket, the catalog in her lap, Selena's goodbyes in their ears, they headed down the road, a two-mile journey that could only be too short today, to Johanna's way of thinking.

"The letter was from my sister-in-law, Bessie."

Johanna had wondered yesterday, had known he must have read it privately and had decided to mind her own business. This morning had been rushed, what with loading the wagon for the Monday-morning trip to town, the most productive of the week, as far as Johanna was concerned.

She'd scurried around, getting breakfast out of the way, readying herself and the boys, doing her best to ignore Tate's withdrawal from his family over the past hours. He'd spoken to them, smiled at Timmy's foolishness and been unfailingly courteous. All that, but he just hadn't been there.

He'd had little to say, for the most part, since they finally headed out for town, covered baskets of butter and eggs safely tucked in the back of the wagon, both boys dangling their legs from the rear.

Johanna, though rarely impetuous, had had enough. She'd turned to face him, concern alive on her features. "Is something wrong?"

And then he'd told her. "The letter was from my sister-in-law, Bessie." He shook his head. "No, nothing's wrong. At least I don't think so. Guess it depends on your point of view." His gaze met hers, head-on. "Aren't you curious about how she knew where to send a letter, Jo?"

Her shoulders lifted in a shrug. "I guess I didn't think about it. I suppose I figured you'd let your family know where you were once you decided to stay here."

"I don't have any family," he said after a moment. "Bessie's about it, and now, legally, we're not really family anymore." He slapped the reins on the backs of his matched pair of horses and urged them into a trot. "Her husband died."

Johanna's indrawn breath signaled her surprise. "Thought you said there wasn't anything wrong? Seems to me that's a pretty big problem."

"You wouldn't think so if you'd known Herb Swenson. He was probably the crudest, rudest drunk in Fall River, Ohio. I never could figure out how Bessie got hooked up with him. Anyway, he went out hunting, half-lit before he started, and managed to fall on his gun, climbin' a fence."

"What will she do?" The vision of a woman alone didn't provoke feelings of despair in Johanna's mind. Being alone wasn't the worst thing that could happen, to her way of thinking. Although, if Bessie was a clinging-vine sort, it might be hard on her.

"She'll be all right. She's got the house, all paid for.

And she does sewing for ladies in town. Charges a fancy price for it, too. And I suspect Herb left her pretty well-off. He was a good worker when he wasn't drinking, and he saved his money. Anyway, she's thinking about taking a trip up here, down the line a bit, to see the boys and all.''

"Does she know you're married?"

He slapped the reins again, and the team obligingly stepped up their pace. "I told her I'd bought up your mortgage when I wrote to let her know where we were. I expect she knows we got married."

Johanna faced forward, folding her hands, rubbing her fingers together with a slow movement inside her woolen mittens. "I don't think you told her, did you?"

His scowl was threatening. "I wrote before we made up our minds. Right after we got here."

"When you took over the mortgage, we were already committed to it, Tate."

"Well, I told her I was going to pay off your debt and you were going to mind the boys and we'd share the farm. She should have known from that that we were gonna get married."

Gruff and *belligerent* were the only two words Johanna could think of to describe his attitude. Though she supposed she could add *embarrassed* to the list.

"Well, shoot! She thought it was a stupid idea, lookin' for a woman to watch the boys, when she'd been handy for so long. How was I supposed to tell her I didn't want to stay in Fall River, what with all the bad memories there? I'd have ended up scourin' the bushes for a mother for my boys and having all the eligible women in the county thrown at my head. I wanted to do it my own way.

"But most of all, I wanted to get a fresh start." His expression was dark, but the blustering attitude had disappeared, leaving only a man seeking approval.

"Do you think I was too old to be starting over, Johanna? That's what Bessie said when I left. She told me I was being childish, running away from the facts.''

"I don't think we're ever too old to make a new beginning, Tate. I've made a couple of them myself.'' Her fingers untangled slowly as she turned once more to face him. One hand lifted to present itself to him, palm upward, as if she were seeking his goodwill.

Without hesitation, he grasped it, lowering it to rest against the hard muscles of his thigh, his own covering it, easing her fingers to curl within his palm. "You can read the letter if you want to, Jo.''

She shook her head. "I don't need to. You've told me what it says.'' She drew in a breath of the cold air, noted the few snowflakes that swirled beneath the feet of the team and looked skyward. "We're in for a little snow, aren't we? Do you think it will amount to anything?''

"Just like that, Johanna?''

She regarded him steadily. "Just like that, Tate. Only make sure you send her my regards when you answer the letter. Tell her that you and your wife send their sincere sympathy in the loss of her husband.''

His mouth twisted in a reluctant grin, and his hand squeezed hers. "I'll do that. I'll do that very thing.''

Tuesday-morning breakfast was usually a time of doldrums after the excitement of Sunday and Monday, with their trips to town. But today was different. This morning she'd had no sense of foot-dragging reluctance to rise and make breakfast.

This morning, she planned to set about choosing from the new catalog, and the choices offered therein were beyond her wildest expectations.

"Do you know I've never had a Sears and Roebuck catalog before, Tate?''

"They've been sending them to just about every farmhouse in the country, Jo. I'd think you'd have been ordering from one all along."

She shook her head. "My pa wasn't one for buying things we didn't need. He said there was no sense in buying just to be buying."

Tate's brow rose quizzically. "He sure had you on a tight string, didn't he?"

"I guess." She rose from her seat at the kitchen table. "Are you ready for more coffee?"

"I'm about empty," he said, pushing his cup closer to the edge of the table.

"There's something in the catalog I want to show you, Tate," Johanna said, pouring his cup full.

"Were you waitin' to get me softened up first, Mrs. Montgomery? First pancakes with maple syrup, then a second cup of coffee, and now that I'm full and reasonably content, you'll slap me with buying you a— Doggone it, woman, give me back my coffee!" He'd leaned back in his chair to begin the teasing diatribe, then sat bolt upright as she snatched the cup of hot coffee from before him.

Rosy cheeks gave Johanna a strangely youthful look this morning, he decided, his grin in full view. There was no way around it. The woman had bloomed during the past months. The somber female he'd married had, right before his very eyes, become a shiny-eyed girl.

That he was responsible for the metamorphosis, that his teasing, tender attention had brought about the transformation was a fact he was willing to admit only to himself. That he'd thoroughly enjoyed the task of bringing a bloom to her cheeks and a smile to her lips was a bonus he was more than pleased to delight in.

His bride had almost reached the place toward which he'd been subtly steering her for over two months.

His bedroom. But probably not for a while yet, he admitted to himself. Hell, she hadn't even gotten past the door, except for changing his sheets once a week. And then, he'd be willing to bet, she only scooted in and snatched up the wrinkled specimens to exchange them for the clean ones in her arms and was back out the door, lickety-split. Probably closed her eyes while she was in there—as much as she could, anyway, and still do what she'd come for.

Johanna. He sighed, watching as she brought the new catalog to the table. Prickly and stubborn, she was far from the woman he'd married in Ohio over ten years ago. Back when he thought he knew what he wanted in a wife. *Thought*. That was the definitive word. Now he knew.

"I thought it would be a good idea to send for this," she told him, pointing to a hand-drawn picture of the latest in wringers. A Seroco ball bearing wringer, with tub clamp. For only two dollars and twenty-four cents. The picture was detailed, showing a hand-cranked pair of rollers between which a woman could insert wet clothing and, by dint of turning a handle, squeeze the excess water into a tub below.

"Makes sense to me," he said readily.

She glanced at him quickly. "You don't mind spending the money? I mean, it's not a necessity or anything. My hands are strong, and I've never had any problem wringing out things up to now. I just thought…"

"Johanna. I said it makes sense." As if that were the last word to be said on the subject, he slapped the book. "There's no point in you working any harder than you have to. Matter of fact, why don't you get a washing machine?"

His eyes searched the page as he muttered beneath his breath. "If you need something for the house, all you have to do is say so." His finger stabbed the middle of the next page. "Now look, here's a Fulton #1, there's an Acme combination, and they have a Sears model. Pick out one of them and put in the order. Whatever you need, we'll get. If I can buy two horses, you can certainly have a washing machine, and a wringer to go with it."

"My pa always—"

His big hand moved quickly, covering her mouth. "I'm

not your pa. I've come to believe that he and I wouldn't
have gotten along well. If you want a wringer or a washer,
or both, we'll order them for you. It's as simple as that.''

Her lips moved against the rough, callused palm. ''Thank
you.'' Above the edge of his hand, her eyes were darkened,
blue pools of confusion.

''Do that again.'' His voice was scratchy, raw and harsh,
and her eyes widened at the sound.

''Do what?'' she asked, her mouth tingling from the
brushing of her lips against his hard flesh.

''That. Kissing my hand when you talk.''

She blinked at him. ''I wasn't. I mean, I didn't mean to
be kissing...'' She drew back and eyed him warily. ''Are
you teasing me, Tate?''

He shook his head. ''You gave me goose bumps, Johanna. Haven't had those in years. Except for the night I
saw your pretty ankles for the first time.''

''You saw my— When did you see my ankles?'' In an
automatic gesture, her gaze flew to the hem of her skirt.

''When you climbed the stairs to go to bed.'' His grin
came into being, his eyes crinkling at the corners, and he
leaned back in his chair, aware of her giveaway glance.
''Sometimes, when you pull your skirt up a bit, I've gotten
a pretty good glimpse of your calf where it rounds out
and—''

''Stop that right now! What a way to talk!'' She grabbed
the catalog with both hands and with a quick movement,
brought it down smartly on the top of his head.

''Ow! Dang it, woman, you just raised a lump on my
skull!'' His protest was issued amid a burst of laughter,
which only served to aggravate her more.

''You just *thought* you were getting apple dumplings for
dinner, Mr. Montgomery. I don't believe I'm going to have
time to make them after all!'' Flouncing around the table,
she stowed the catalog beneath the kitchen cupboard and
returned to the table.

Struggling to hide his laughter, he coughed, almost choking in the effort. "Aw, Jo. You don't want to be nasty about this, do you? Think about Timmy and Pete. They heard you promise the dumplings before they went out to feed the chickens. Would you break your promise to a child?" Backing to the door, he snatched his hat from the hook, plopping it atop his head before he reached for his coat from beneath it.

Her hands full of plates and silverware, Johanna peered up at him. "Sometime I'll really let you have it, Tate Montgomery. Not just a little bash in the head with a book. One of these days…"

His fingers halted in their task of buttoning his coat, and he froze in place. "I'm waiting for that day to come, honey. One of these days, you'll trust me enough to let loose and give me what I want. And we both know what I'm talking about, don't we?"

The color drained from her face as she heard his words, his meaning unmistakable. "We made a bargain, Tate. If you can't hold to your word for longer than two months, you're not the man I thought you were."

He nodded. "I'll hold to my word, Jo. I've never gone back on a deal yet." He turned to the door. "Make out the order, and we'll mail it in town this morning. Anything else you want, add it on to the list. If we're payin' shipping charges, might as well make it worthwhile."

Chapter Nine

"I thought all the steers were gone. Mr. Cooney said he'd rounded up all of them in September." Johanna stood just inside the barn, a frown wrinkling her brow as she watched Tate pitch hay from the loft for the horses.

"Watch out, Jo," he called to her, dropping the pitchfork to the floor below, his aim sending the implement flat against the pile he'd accumulated in the middle of the aisle. He followed it down, his feet hitting every other rung on the ladder as he came. Swinging to face her, he slid his gaze idly over her closely wrapped form and smiled, his unspoken approval warming her from within.

"It's a good thing I scoured around back there in the woods," he told her. "Mr. Cooney was either in a hurry, or he didn't go far enough. I've found another fifteen head, and a couple of cows and calves with them."

Johanna's brow furrowed. "What will you do with them? It's almost Christmas, Tate. Isn't it too late to ship them off?" she asked, wrapping her arms around her waist, hugging the warmth of her coat against her dress.

Tate watched her, intrigued by the strength of this woman he'd married. She'd struggled single-handedly to run this place, and almost worn herself into the ground doing it. Even now, with a man at hand to tend to things, she willingly shared the worries and problems accompanying the job. His eyes settled on her troubled expression, and for a moment he was struck by the urge to smooth away the worry lines. She deserved more than life had dealt her in the past.

"Tate?" Impatience laced the single word. "Can we still sell them off, or do we need to wait till the spring?"

"I can't leave them in the swamp, Jo. They need to put on some weight or they won't bring much at all." For a moment he watched her, saw the frown draw down her brows as she fretted.

"Don't worry, Johanna," he told her, knowing even as he spoke the words that they were futile. "I'll take care of it. I'm more concerned with those cows and calves out there. I'll need to bring them up to the near pasture, once I get the steers settled. I don't like the idea of those young ones being so far from the barn when bad weather comes. And I need to do something about a couple of them, anyway. One of them is a heifer, but the other two... Well, they missed out on... They should have been..."

"I understand," Johanna put in hastily. "Mr. Cooney always helped my father with that job." And she'd always stayed far aloof from the proceedings, unaware of what was transpiring, unwilling to learn the secrets of that annual event, when the young bulls became steers by virtue of a nasty-looking instrument.

"I may have to call him in to give me a hand." Carrying the hay-laden pitchfork, Tate stepped to the nearest stall. From within, one of the new mares nickered, welcoming him.

"How are they settling in?" Johanna asked, walking behind him as he gathered up hay.

"They're doing all right. I think the chestnut is about ready for the stallion. He thinks so, too," he said, his mouth twisting into a wry grin. "He's been rousting around out there all day, blowin' and snortin' to beat the band."

"What about the bay?" Johanna had overcome her ret-
icence about discussing the business of breeding with her
father, but with Tate the subject presented a batch of problems. This breeding right up close to the house made her
most uncomfortable. Cows tended to the matter themselves,
it seemed. The bull had managed to take care of things
without anyone's help, somewhere out in the far pasture.
No one ever knew for sure which cows would drop a calf
come spring, but you could pretty well count on the good
old reliables to come up with a swollen belly every year.

"I bred the bay yesterday," Tate said, studiously avoiding her gaze. "I wasn't sure how much you wanted to know
about it, Johanna. She took him pretty well. It should be a
good breeding."

She turned away, looking out the barn door. "Will you
be taking the stallion back when you've finished with
him?"

"Yeah, I made arrangements for his new owner to meet
me at the livery stable next week, Monday."

"Will you need help? I can drive the team to town, if
you want to ride the stallion."

"I hadn't thought of that," he said. "Might be a good
idea. I'd thought to tie him to the back of the surrey. But
I think riding him will be better."

She nodded, anxious to see an end to the stallion's stay.
There was about him a danger, a risk, she felt vulnerable
to, and having him gone would not make her the least bit
unhappy.

Suddenly, across the yard, she caught sight of Timmy
approaching, carrying two kittens in his arms. "He's chosen those two to keep," she said quietly, relieved to change
the subject. "You don't mind, do you, Tate?"

His long arm draped across her shoulder as he moved to
her side. "Not as long as he keeps them outdoors. He's
hoping you'll let them in the house, you know."

Johanna's heart beat a little faster as she accepted his

nonchalant gesture. The warmth of that arm, the pressure of his fingers through the shoulder of her coat and the outdoor scent of his clothing all nudged her into an awareness of the pleasure of his presence beside her. She bit at her lower lip and lowered her head, looking from his scuffed barn boots to her own old black shoes. Like dusty companions, they stood side by side. Her mouth twisted at the absurdity of that thought.

"We make a good pair, Jo," he said, jarring her with his words. It was as if he'd caught hold of her meanderings and voiced them aloud. He tugged her against his side. "You're a good wife. You've been good to the boys."

"Pete..." She inhaled deeply, and his fingers tightened, sliding down to clasp her arm.

"He'll be all right. He's just feeling his way right now, testing you. I think he's coming along, though."

"Keep him away from here, will you, Tate? When you breed the mare, I mean."

His laugh was a rumble in his chest. "I'll have a long talk with him on my hands if he shows up. 'Course, maybe it's time. He's heading for eight, and farm boys grow up early."

"So do farm girls," she snapped. "But some things they're better off not knowin' right off the bat."

She'd gone rigid in his grasp, and he tugged at her, rocking her off balance. "Come on, Jo. I was just raggin' at you. I'll keep him busy somewhere else." He looked down at her, his eyes twinkling. "You wouldn't want to give me a hand with the job, would you?"

"Tate!" Properly scandalized by his proposal, she broke from his grip, stalking toward the house as his laughter rang out. And from deep within, her curiosity raged into being, consuming her with its tentacles of need as she considered the idea of standing by as the two magnificent animals mated. Her mind's eye caught a glimpse of the tall, mus-

cular stallion, rearing, mane tossing, hooves cutting the air
as the mare waited his attentions.

She stepped up her pace, her stride lengthening as she
neared the house. Flushed and breathing harder than the
slight exertion warranted, she reached the back porch.
Without a backward glance, she went in, hitching her shoes
off in the washroom. And then peeked from the edge of
the door frame to catch a last glimpse of the tall figure
watching from the barn door.

"Pa went out to check on the cattle he brought in from
the far pasture," Pete said darkly. "He said to tell you he
wouldn't be too far away when supper's ready." The boy's
lip was pooched forward as he spoke, and his toe was rubbing hard at a hole he'd managed to make in the dirt. "He
rode one of his old mares, but he wouldn't let me go
along."

Johanna resisted the urge to reach for the dark, silky
locks covering the boy's head. So badly she wanted to run
her fingers through his hair, caress him with a mother's
touch, that the impulse was almost overwhelming at times.
Only the knowledge that he would not welcome it kept her
from the deed.

"I'm sure your father had his reasons," she said quietly,
thinking of how Tate looked astride one of his mares. He
rode the docile animals he'd brought from Ohio bareback,
like a plowboy. Her father had had a small horse he used
for running down the loose cattle, usually calling in a couple of neighbors to give him a hand rounding them up.

"Maybe next time your pa will take you along, Pete. I
think he's only going to be gone a short while today."

"I'm gonna be able to ride pretty soon," the boy said
confidently. "I just need a little practice."

Johanna eyed him from where she stood, wrist-deep in
bread dough. Her hands turned the mass in a practiced
movement, pummeled it into shape and turned it again.

'He'll see to it you get on a horse before long," she told
him. "Your pa keeps his word."

The small shoulders slumped. "Not till spring, he
won't."

"Don't you have chores to do this afternoon, Pete?
Where's Timmy? I thought your pa said to shuck some corn
for the pigs today."

The glare he turned in her direction was dark, but his
shoulders straightened as he recognized the authority in her
quiet voice. "Timmy's out in the loft, watchin' those dumb
cats."

"Well, go find him and do what your pa said. It's warm
by the side of the corncrib, out of the wind."

The pile of corn was slowly being depleted, as Tate,
Johanna and the boys took their turns at shucking the ears
from the dry stalks. It was a tiresome task, done at odd
moments, but necessary before the snow came to cover the
rest of the stalks, which made the job even worse.

Johanna relented, swayed by the stubborn tilt of Pete's
dark head, the pouting movement of his mouth. "I'll come
give you a hand, once I've got this bread set to rise again.
I'll just get supper started first."

His shrug was no answer at all, she decided, watching
him do up the buttons on his coat as he started across the
yard. And then she set to work on the dough, dividing it
into loaves and placing them in the greased tins. They fit
neatly above the stove, and she gave them one last approv-
ing glance before covering them with a clean dish towel.

The meat was nicely browned within minutes, and she
sliced an onion over it and added bay leaves before covering it with water and putting on the lid to simmer.

The sight of Pete's unhappiness had nudged her into offering her help. Almost ruing the gesture, she slid into her
coat and wound a warm scarf over her head. She donned
her gloves then, knowing the damage cornstalks could do
to her hands.

From the back porch, she scanned the yard. Not a sign of the boys, but then all week Timmy had been spending his afternoons kitten-watching. Pete would have a hard time interesting him in chores. Even more reason for her to give him a hand. She set off for the far side of the corncrib, where the afternoon sun had long since melted the scant covering of snow that had fallen last night.

The cornstalks waited patiently, the sun shone brilliantly, but Pete was nowhere to be seen. "Pete? Where are you?" Lifting her hand to shade her eyes, she scanned the barn and beyond. There seemed to be no sign of life in that direction. Perhaps he'd gone around back.

The stallion. Her heart quickened as she thought of the beautiful chestnut stud occupying the corral, considered the temptation the animal offered to a young boy. Surely he wouldn't risk his father's displeasure.

But he had. As she rounded the corner of the barn, the small figure came into view, and Johanna caught her breath. Pete was high on the corral fence, straddling the topmost rail, leaning toward the huge stallion with one hand full of hay, tempting the animal closer.

The horse was prancing, showing off for his audience, his ears forward, his nostrils flaring. With a nipping gesture, he reached for the hay Pete offered, and the boy jerked back in surprise as the velvet muzzle touched his hand. He caught his balance quickly and dropped the hay, watching as the big horse bent his head to snatch up the scant handful.

"Here, boy." It was a tremulous command, Pete reaching into his pocket as he held fast with the other hand to the rail. From the depths of his coat pocket, he drew forth an apple, leaning again toward the stud to offer it on the palm of his hand. "Looky what I got for you," he coaxed, his knees tightening visibly as he stretched forth his arm toward the animal.

"I think you need to get down, Pete." Johanna's words

were quiet, and she watched, poised to move, only too aware of the danger the boy was in. The horse might very well take the treat with a gentle touch. Or those big teeth could just as easily nip at the small hand, drawing blood, frightening the child into falling. And it was common knowledge that a stallion could be mean, especially when he was riled up from having a mare just the other side of a barn wall.

"Pa won't care if I feed the horse an apple," Pete said stubbornly, maintaining his hold on the fruit. "I'm not gonna try to ride him or anything."

A vision of the boy leaping onto the back of the tall horse assailed Johanna's mind, and she closed her eyes, blinking it into oblivion.

It had been in his mind. As surely as she was alive and breathing, Pete had been considering the thought of riding the stallion in the corral.

Her voice strengthened by her concern for his well-being, she barked out an order. "You get down right this minute, Pete Montgomery. I don't want to hear another word, do you hear me?"

To the child's credit, he knew when he'd been outmaneuvered. Dropping the apple to the ground, he slid from the corral fence, his face a thundercloud of anger. He watched sullenly as the stallion snatched up the apple, chewing it between his strong teeth. A thread of juice hung in a glittering string from his muzzle as the big animal watched his audience. Then, with a snorting whinny, he tossed his head and galloped around the enclosure, tail high, hooves beating a quick cadence against the hard ground.

"Corn, Pete. Come on, I'll give you a hand."

"I don't need any help. I'll do it myself." He stalked away.

There was no need to further irritate the child, Johanna knew. That she'd halted his shenanigans with the stud was bad enough. She wouldn't make him spend the afternoon with her.

When she was back inside, the house held little charm, once she'd put the bread in the oven. The pot roast was simmering nicely, the kitchen redolent with its scent of onion and bay leaf. The sun pouring through the window was a temptation, and Johanna gave in to its beckoning.

Her shawl seemed warm enough, she decided, for a quick check on Timmy in the barn. He'd even slept away part of the day yesterday curled in the hay, watching over his kittens. Johanna walked slowly, soaking up the wintry sunlight.

From the other side of the barn, she heard Sheba's sharp warning bark, and her step quickened. Then Timmy's voice, high and shrill. Johanna's groan was heartfelt. Surely he wouldn't be fooling with the stallion.

Suddenly the child ran pell-mell around the corner, his eyes wide, his mouth open to yell her name. "Miss Johanna!" Skidding to a halt, he waved his hands in a frantic gesture. "Come quick! Pete's gonna— Come stop Pete." In garbled sentences, he sought her aid, and Johanna ran to him, crouching before him, holding his small hands within her own.

"Tell me, Timmy. What is it?"

He tore his hands from her grasp and clutched at her skirt. "He's gonna ride the cows! Pete's gonna practice."

"Oh, dear Lord, no!" Johanna's heart sank. Wandering the edge of the pasture was one thing. The steers Tate had put there were pretty placid animals. But the boys had been told to stay clear of them, and with good reason. Should Pete attempt to climb up on one of them, he could be terribly hurt.

She ran, aware as she did that the boy was indeed circling a wary steer, an animal who'd been roaming the woods and swamp for over a year. At the fence line, Sheba paced back and forth, barking her warning, dashing in to nip at the heels of the steer to send it from Pete's path.

"Pete! Stop it!" She bent as she neared the barbed wire fence to slip between the strands, dropping her shawl to the ground. Holding one strand as high as she could pull it, she hunched her shoulders, careful to evade the sharp barbs.

With a resounding snap the wire gave, pulling from its fasteners on the next post, coiling in a movement so rapid she could only catch a breath as it wound around her body. Stinging, fiery darts of pain surrounded her, and she jerked, knowing as she did that it was foolish. Yards of wire encircled her, the spaced barbs digging through her clothing, gouging and scratching her flesh as she drew away from them in automatic movements.

"Pete, come help!"

Timmy's shriek echoing in her ears, Johanna teetered, falling to the ground. She screamed—a high-pitched, painful cry that ended on a mournful note as she hugged her arms tightly against her body, seeking only to evade the piercing thrust of the barbed wire.

"Pa! Pa!" The boys' voices echoed in the clear air as they ran the length of the pasture fencing, one within the wire, the other outside. At the far corner, Pete slipped between the wires and raced full tilt, Timmy sobbing as he watched his brother go. Frightened, he retraced his steps, panting as he ran, murmuring beneath his breath.

"Pete went to get Pa!" he cried, his voice breaking as he knelt beside Johanna's still form. Tears ran in rivulets down his cheeks, and he rubbed at his eyes with chubby fingers. "I don't know what to do!" His words were anguished, his small face drawn into a mask of helplessness.

"Don't touch me." It was a gasping plea. She'd found that if she held her breath, forcing only shallow, small pants between her lips, she could bear the pain inflicted by the dozens of small wounds. The thought of being moved, of the wire pressing new lacerations into her tender flesh,

made her physically ill, and she swallowed the bile rising
in her throat.

The sun was mercifully warm, and in the outer reaches
of her mind she was thankful. Beneath her, the ground was
cold, and she cursed herself silently for not wearing her
heavy coat. The cuts would have been less severe, she
would not be as chilled, and she wouldn't have totally ruined her good house dress. That such a mundane thought
could occupy her mind in the midst of such pain brought
a grunt of aggravation to her lips, and Timmy bent over
her, brushing her cheek with his mouth.

"I wish I could kiss it and make it better, Miss Johanna.
You're bleedin' real bad on your arm. It's makin' your
dress all wet. And on your front, too."

She held her breath against the pain once more, and
squinted her eyes. The sun was dimmer, fading almost.
Surely it wasn't growing dark, not in the middle of the
afternoon. And then her eyes closed, and consciousness
slipped away.

"Get the wire nippers from the barn, Pete. Timmy, you
run to the house and get a dish towel and run some water
on it. Wring it out if you can and bring it here." Kneeling
beside Johanna's still figure, Tate called out orders, his
voice harsh. His hands clenching into fists, he forced himself to wait.

The wire had circled her several times, pressing its barbs
into her arms and body. Drops of blood stained her dress
in numerous places—one spot looked as though she'd
jerked against the wire, scratching a deep area on the fleshy
part of her upper arm. By some miracle, her face and head
had remained free of the lashing wire. He whispered his
gratitude, even as he sent forth a prayer in her behalf.

Surely the God she worshiped would be merciful. That
this good woman should be so badly wounded was unfair.
Though she was not in danger of bleeding to death, the

numerous wounds had brought her to a blessed state of unconsciousness. Her dried tearstains, silent evidence of despair, made him wince as he watched her. He longed to hold her close, knowing he could not touch her until the wire was cut and her body set free from its dreadful embrace.

"I got the nippers, Pa!" Pete was running wildly, his feet tripping over small hillocks as he plunged across the barnyard. Skidding to a stop, he handed the tool to his father, falling to his knees to watch the proceedings.

Fast on his heels, Timmy arrived, the dripping-wet towel in his outstretched hands. Tate took it and squeezed it quickly, then placed it on Johanna's forehead. Her lashes fluttered, and he gritted his teeth.

"Hold still, honey." His whisper was strained, and she shivered at the sound.

Transferring the nippers to his right hand, Tate slid the bottom pincer beneath the topmost wire and squeezed the handles. A soft moan of pain tore at him, and he clenched his jaw against the sound.

"Don't move, Johanna. Can you hear me? I'm cutting the wire." Again he manipulated the tool, careful lest he impress the barbs against her flesh. "Lay still, sweetheart. I'm going to have you free in just a minute."

His eyes narrowed as he shifted, loosening another loop, this one pressing across the fullness of her breasts. At the sound of her sob, he gritted his teeth, moving down another few inches.

"Just a few minutes more, Jo. Don't move, honey."

"Uhhh... Oh, God!" It was a beseeching whimper, spoken so low he scarcely could hear it, yet the sound of her fervent plea tore at his composure.

"Ah, damn it all, honey. Don't move, sweetheart! I'm tryin' so hard not to hurt you, baby."

As if he must bathe the wounds with tenderness, his words poured over her in a fervent litany. And she responded. Her breathing quieted, and only a small shiver each time he cut a wire revealed her awareness of his task.

Finally the wire lay spread on either side of Johanna, and Tate considered the problem of moving her from the grasping barbs that were still embedded in her clothing from beneath. Sliding his arms under her shoulders and knees, he half knelt beside her, ready to lift his burden.

"Now, when I pick her up Pete, very carefully pull down the wire that's caught in her clothes. Can you do that?" he asked, his eyes sending a message of strength to his young son.

"Yes, Pa." As if he knew his folly had brought them to this place, Pete bent low, his brow furrowing, his small hands ready to do the task his father had assigned. He bit at his lip, squinting through the tears that slid down his cheeks, and his hands grasped the wire, tugging it away as his father lifted Johanna from the ground.

Tate watched her face as he rose to his feet, his strong arms supporting her. Finally, as the last strand fell away, he held her close to his chest, his mouth open and warm against her forehead.

"Johanna, I'm so sorry. I'm so sorry. I should have had that fence in better shape. This is my fault. I'm so sorry." In a chorus of penitence, he moaned his regret, carrying her to the house.

Behind him, Pete dragged his feet. Timmy raced ahead, opening the kitchen door, holding it wide, allowing Tate to carry his wife into the house.

"Pete, find Johanna's scissors. They're somewhere in the kitchen, I think." Tate's voice floated back down the stairs as he climbed. "Timmy, fill the washpan full of warm water from the stove and have Pete carry it up here. Bring up a couple of towels with you."

Without hesitation, he pushed open his bedroom door and strode across the room. And for the first time, he placed his wife in the center of his bed. His mouth twisted as he absorbed the irony of it all and sat beside her, his fingers already busy with the buttons of her dress.

"I...hurt...so...bad." Her words were spaced, each one borne by a separate breath, and he bent to drop a quick kiss against her cheek.

"I know you do, honey. I know you do." The buttons were undone, and he drew back to consider the problem. "I think I'm going to have to cut your dress off, Jo. I hate to ruin it, but I don't want to move you until I find out how bad you're cut up."

"Bad." The one word, spoken in such a grumpy, sullen tone of voice, almost made him laugh. That she could be sassy was a good sign, he decided.

Through the doorway Pete appeared, carrying the pan of water, Timmy behind him, bearing the scissors. "Here, Pa. Where do you want this?" Towels were draped over his shoulder, and Tate took them from him, motioning to the bedside table. Depositing his responsibility there, Pete backed from the room. Timmy stepped closer to the bed, his gaze clinging to Johanna.

"Is she all right, Pa?" His words exposed the anxiety he felt, and Tate reached a hand to brush back the boy's hair.

"She will be, Timmy. Why don't you go on downstairs with your brother? Close the door behind you." Tate took the scissors and sent the child on his way, waiting only till the latch caught before he turned to the task at hand.

The scissor blade slit first one sleeve, then the other, slicing its way across the bodice of her dress to the front opening on either side. With a grim look at her closed eyes, he continued, opening the front of her clothing from top to bottom, splitting her petticoat and chemise, cutting through her underpants as he went.

Carefully, gently, he turned back the layers of fabric, exposing the pale flesh they covered, until only her stockings, held above her knees with store-bought garters, remained to cover her from his sight.

She was fair-skinned, this wife of his. Only her hands and lower arms were tanned from the summer sun, probably when she'd worked in her garden. Her breasts were full, rosy-tipped and firm. Across her left one, a long gouge angled from side to side, barely missing the puckered crest. His breath was a sigh of relief. How much worse that could have been, he thought. Her arms were riddled with numerous small punctures, the blood oozing anew from the removal of her dress tugging at the wounds.

He rolled her away from himself, noting each scratch, each small piercing of her flesh, down to where her hips rounded in a graceful curve and her buttocks showed evidence of more gouging. None of them looked to be serious, the long jagged cut on her arm the deepest.

Once more he brought her to lie on her back, and her sigh of relief was a shudder that swept over her small body. She'd looked so sturdy, so neatly put together, in her clothing. How could he have guessed the fragility beneath those cotton dresses, the slim length of her arms and legs that she'd hidden from his view?

Greedy for the sight of her, yet ashamed of his carnal desire for the woman he tended, he wrung out a towel in the water, careful in his ministrations as he bathed her cuts. Gently he cleaned the scratch across her breast, noting the automatic flinch of her flesh as he pressed his fingers against the plush surface.

"I'm sorry, Jo. I don't mean to hurt you." And he didn't. With all his heart, he wished he could take the pain he was inflicting on her and make it his own.

"It's all right." Finally, her words were clear, and his gaze swept to hers. Open and lucid, the blue eyes that looked at him were filled with pleading. "I don't want you to look at me, Tate."

He shook his head. "I know, but I have to, honey. I'm

just going to wash you off and then turn you over and do your back.''

"I can do it," she argued, her voice stronger now.

"No." It was a firm refusal, with no hint of compromise to be heard in its depths. "Just don't move now. We'll be done in no time, and then I'll put salve on your cuts."

The towel rinsed once more, he began at her waist, moving to the softly rounded flesh of her belly. And there his fingers slowed their movements, the towel hesitating in mid air as he lifted it from one spot to move to another.

Across the rounding of her hips, across the tender flesh above the thatch of pale, curling hair, were faint lines of white scarring.

"Jo?" His gaze flew to hers, even as the towel lowered to cover the evidence he'd discovered. "Jo?" How could it be? He shook his head, unbelieving, yet aware of the unmistakable signs he'd uncovered. His wife had borne two sons, had carried the same silvery scars across her belly and hips, mute evidence of her motherhood.

"Please, let me do this." Her whisper was a plea, and her gaze was fearful as her hands lifted to clutch at the towel he'd spread across her belly.

"It's all right. Hush, now," he said quietly, forcing the knowledge he'd gained in the past few moments to the back of his mind. Aware only that her need for his care must supersede all else, he continued with the bathing he'd begun. Her hands dropped to lie by her sides and her eyes closed as tears of mute misery spilled down her temples and into her hair.

And while he worked, bathing and applying salve, learning the curves of her body as he went, his mind dwelled on the silvered scars that betrayed her secret.

Johanna had had a child.

Chapter Ten

"I rescued the bread, Jo. And the pot roast is almost ready. I just cut up some vegetables and put them in with the meat. We'll have stew." As if he were reciting the letters of the alphabet, Tate listed his recent accomplishments.

He'd made matter-of-fact conversation. He'd cleaned up the mess of towels and the wash basin, disposed of her cut-up clothing and managed to find a nightgown to slip over her head. He'd lifted her, supporting her back against his broad chest, as he lowered the white cotton into place. His big fingers had buttoned up the bodice and tugged the material down to cover her, sliding the blanket back as he went, careful to keep her nakedness hidden from sight.

But he hadn't looked at her face. Not once in the hour or so he spent tending her, straightening the room, moving around the bed, had his eyes met hers. Even as he released her hair from its braid and combed through the golden length with his fingers, he'd carefully looked away, keeping himself from the intimacy of her gaze.

In one way, she was grateful. She'd feared reminders of those minutes when he'd tended her wounds, when the long-concealed secrets of her body had been revealed in the light of day to him. She'd seen his reaction, his eyes narrowing as he viewed her breasts. She'd shrunk from his fingers as they traced the scratch, embarrassed at the rush of heat that accompanied that callused touch.

Tate had only seen what most any husband would be more than familiar with. But not Johanna Patterson's husband. Not when she'd bargained to sleep alone in her lonely bed, lest he discover her lack of virginity and turn from her.

And now he knew. As he washed and tended her, he'd hesitated. His eyes had widened, his lips had parted for just a moment as he saw, recognized.

Johanna shivered, shrinking within the voluminous depths of her nightgown, painfully aware of the scratch across her breast, the deeper gouge in her upper arm. The rest of it was small potatoes. Just an irritating reminder of her own stupidity. Within a week, the scabs would form and fall and she'd be left with a series of small scars to mark the folly of her carelessness.

Tate Montgomery was another matter. The knowledge he'd gained this afternoon had managed to turn him into a silent, wary stranger. He'd been kind enough, his hands gentle as he moved her in the bed, his voice husky with concern as he bade her rest easy.

Now he stood in the doorway, as if unwilling to come closer, explaining the pan-rattling and stove-clanking she'd heard for the past hour.

"That sounds fine, Tate. I appreciate you taking hold this way." She rolled toward him, biting at her lip lest she allow the gasp of pain to escape, her skin protesting the shifting of muscle beneath it.

"Don't move, Johanna! I'll help you if you need to get up." In quick strides, he was at her side, his hands lifting the bedding to allow her movement beneath it.

"Before long," she muttered. The urge to make a trek to the outhouse was upon her, but she dreaded the ordeal, unsure her legs would carry her so far.

"I'll get the chamber pot from your room for you, if you need it. Just let me go get it, and I'll help you up."

She shook her head. "I can get into my own bed in a while. I'll use it then."

His silence was broken only by the sound of Timmy's laughter downstairs. Tate reached again to tug the blanket into place over her shoulder and said finally, "I don't think so, Johanna. You're going to stay here tonight. I'll help you sit up to eat in a little while. I'll help you get up to do whatever you need to do before bedtime. But I'm not going to let you sleep across the hall tonight."

"Where will you sleep?" It had been on her mind almost since he placed her in the middle of this big bed. The bed he'd once told her she wasn't obliged to occupy. But if the truth were known, she could think of nothing more appealing right now than having Tate Montgomery stretch out beside her and give her the warmth of his body.

"We'll talk about it after we eat, Jo. Don't stew over it. I'll be back in half an hour or so, and we'll sit you up. I'll bring the pillows from your bed."

There could be no doubt. He'd seen those telltale reminders of her pregnancy. She'd not even have known what they were, had she not tended her mother during those last days before she died.

She'd asked about the almost invisible marks her mother bore, and been astounded at the reason for their being. As for her own, she considered them a private matter. She'd never expected any other human being to see them, since she'd considered marriage to be out of the question.

But that had been before. Before Tate Montgomery came into her life, bringing new joy and purpose to every day. And now, what must he think? Surely he'd consider her life nothing but a lie, their marriage a union founded on deceit.

She'd owed it to him to be honest before they married,

to…what? To say, "Oh, by the way, Mr. Montgomery, I bore a child ten years ago."

Fat chance. He'd have been gone, lickety-split, down the lane and on his way to town.

She'd never have known his kindness and masculine strength. She'd have worn herself to a frazzle tending the stock. She'd have been toting apples all fall. She'd still be walking to town twice a week with eggs and butter.

She'd still be Johanna Patterson—spinster. And even though she wasn't really his wife, she was known as Johanna Montgomery.

He'd given her his name, and if there was any way to keep it she'd find it. Tate Montgomery was the best thing that had ever happened to her. She'd be danged if she gave up before—

"Pa's bringin' up our dinner," Timmy announced from the doorway. "Do you feel better yet, Miss Johanna?"

To banish this child's frown of distress, she'd have gladly lied about her pain till doomsday. "I'm a lot better, Timmy. I'll bet I could sit up if you helped me."

He approached, moving slowly, his mouth pulled down in a dubious manner, his head cocked to one side. "I don't think so," he ventured. "I'm not very big, you know."

"What are you trying to coax my son into, Johanna?" Humor laced Tate's words as he came through the doorway, both hands full with the kettle he carried. Behind him, Pete waited, a pail in one hand, a folded tablecloth in the other.

"I wanted him to help me sit up, Tate." Testing the movement of her arms, she pushed the bedcovers down.

"No need. I'm here to do that." He placed the covered stew pot on a braided rug next to the bed, motioning to Pete to come into the bedroom. "Bring those dishes on in, son. We need to have that small table from over by the window to put things on. Can you get it?"

Pete nodded, obeying his father's instructions, careful to

keep his gaze from Johanna, then busied himself lifting plates and silverware from the bucket, piling them on the table. "What do you want with the tablecloth, Pa?" he asked.

"Just you watch, son," Tate said. "First, we'll get Johanna ready to eat." He'd halted her attempts to rise by his very presence; now he reached to complete the task she'd begun. The blanket was pulled down, exposing her slim form, well encased in the white gown, only her bare feet showing beneath the hem.

"Fetch me the pillows from Johanna's room, Timmy." Tate bent, his arms sliding beneath Johanna's knees and shoulders, taking her weight easily, lifting her just inches above the mattress. "Now hold tight to my neck," he told her. "I'll slide you up to the headboard and prop pillows behind you."

She closed her eyes, gritting her teeth against the pain his movements brought about. The stabbing hurt was gone, but every shifting of her body caused fresh discomfort.

"There. Let me prop another one on this side, Jo. And then lift your knee and I'll put one under it to hold you, so you won't slide down in bed."

His hand lifted her leg, and she felt a flush rise from her breasts. He'd seen most all of her there was to see, she knew that for a fact. But the brush of those long fingers behind her knee, the warmth of the big palm against her thigh, was almost more personal than the lengthy perusal he'd made of her body earlier. That had been of necessity. This was a lingering touch, a careful movement of his hand, sliding her gown into place.

"Thank you," she whispered as he settled her against three plump pillows.

"Now we're going to feed you." Tate scooped a big helping of stew into a heavy crockery bowl. One-handedly opening a dish towel across her lap with a flourish, he placed the bowl there, gave her a spoon and stood erect.

"Let's have that tablecloth, Pete. We need to set up our picnic." Snapping his fingers in a bantering gesture, he motioned to the boys to draw closer. He opened the cloth on the floor and instructed the two boys to take their places, then filled their bowls. Thick slices of fresh bread, generously covered with jam, came next.

"Pray, Pete," Tate told his son. And they all waited while the boy stumbled through a short blessing. "Thank you, son." Tate shot a glance of amusement at Johanna, and she blinked her surprise.

He'd been so careful to steer clear of her, except for the lifting and propping, that she'd begun to think he would ignore her for the rest of the day. And now he'd made her a part of the picnic, with that one glance.

She lifted the bowl, holding it close to her chest, and tasted the stew he'd concocted. "It's good, Tate. I didn't know you could cook."

Serving himself from the kettle, he settled on the end of the bed and grinned. "I'm not real fond of the process, but I can do it in a pinch."

She nodded, relieved at his attempt at humor. "I'll have to bear that in mind."

They ate quickly, Timmy gleeful at the impromptu picnic atmosphere, Pete quiet but obviously relieved at Johanna's well-being.

The dirty dishes went back in the bucket, the tablecloth was folded and placed on top, and the kettle was carried downstairs. Johanna heard the dishes rattling, and then the sound of Tate's footsteps on the stairs once more.

"We need to talk." He closed the door behind him and approached the bed. "Look at me, Johanna."

"I thought you were the one not lookin' *my* way," she said quietly. "You've pretty much been avoiding looking at me since this afternoon."

"I didn't mean to be rude. I just had some things to think

about,'' he told her. His gray eyes had lost their sparkle.
''I think there's something you need to tell me, Jo.''

''Now?'' She looked around the room, as if seeking an
escape. ''The boys...''

''The boys are getting ready for bed. I'll tend to them a
little later. Right now, it's just you and me, Mrs. Montgomery.'' Sitting down on the side of the bed, he reached for
her hand, holding it within the cradle of his palm. ''I may
be going about this the wrong way, Johanna, but I think
we need to—''

''Please...'' Her heart felt as though it would burst. She
drew up her legs. It was a painful process, and her eyes
closed tight at the hurt she dealt herself with the movement.
Her head bowed to cradle against her knees, and her hair,
unbound and free, fell to cover the sides of her face.

''Ah, damn it, Jo. I'm not tryin' to cause you any more
pain than you've already had to bear.'' He scooted closer
to her, his big palm cupping the back of her head, ruffling
her hair awkwardly in comfort. ''I didn't mean to be so
ornery to you earlier. I was just sort of in a snit, I guess.''
His voice softened, and he bent nearer, his face resting
against her head. ''Come on, Jo. Don't take on this way.
We'll talk tonight, if that's what you want.''

She nodded, moving her head against her knees, willing
him to hold her against his chest. But it was not to be.

He cleared his throat. ''Do you need to get up now?''

She nodded, only too aware of the misery she'd tried to
ignore for the past hour. This was the part she'd been
dreading, when he would be privy to her most private tasks.

''Here, sit on the side of the bed, while I get your chamber pot.'' He pulled her to the edge of the mattress and
eased her legs to the floor. His hands cupped her shoulders
then, holding her upright until he seemed to be sure she
was balanced and able to hold herself erect. ''Will you be
all right for a minute?''

She nodded once more, and lifted her head to snatch a

glimpse of him as he walked away from her. The sheer size of the man had struck her more than once today. He'd rescued her, carried her, comforted her—all of which had fed the terrible hunger she'd lived with for so long. To belong to someone. To have a human being in her life who would not turn away from her.

Her mother's death had left her bereft. Joseph Brittles had turned his back and walked away, denying his love for her. Her father had chosen death over living, even knowing he left her alone. And the greatest hurt of all had been the loss of her child, a tiny scrap of humanity who might have been the one bright spot in her life. Perhaps it had been God's will that she be punished for her terrible sin. Perhaps he'd taken the child in vengeance, taken the small life before he could draw breath.

It might be that she was doomed to be alone and lonely.

"Johanna?" Tate stood before her, hand outheld to her. "Let me help you up."

She nodded, extending her fingers to clasp his wrists, allowing him to lift her from the bed. He drew her up until her body was pressed against his, her breasts flattened against his chest, her fingers grasping to clutch at his shoulders.

He held her there, as if he understood her need for solace, his arms sliding into place around her back, taking her weight, lifting her to ease the strain of standing. "All right now? Can you walk over to the screen?"

He'd placed the chamber pot behind the folding screen her mother had used to dress behind for all the years of her marriage, and it was there that he led her, one arm around her middle, the other holding her hand in a firm grip.

"I can do this," she told him. "I can, Tate."

He frowned, unwilling to trust her strength.

"Please, just go check the boys. I'll be fine," she told him, tightening her jaw. This was where she must draw the line. And her glare from stormy blue eyes reinforced her words.

He left her there, one hand holding to the back of a rocking chair, the other brushing at her hair. "I'll be back after a while. If you need me, call out." It was a firm commitment, and she nodded her agreement.

She'd made it back to the bed. He'd given her an hour and spent the time well, working in the barn, where the six milking cows had waited impatiently.

Now it was fully dark, and he entered the room quietly, latching the door behind himself. Beneath the covers, only the pale gleam of her hair was visible in the moonlight.

"Johanna? Are you asleep?" Unwilling to startle her, he called her name softly. The movement on the bed was response enough, and he lifted the lamp chimney to light the wick.

"We don't need the lamp, Tate. Unless you..."

Sensing her reluctance, he replaced the chimney. "All right. No lamp, but enough light for me to see you," he said firmly. He lit the short, squat candle on her dresser. Then, lowering his suspenders, he hesitated, hands set to undo the heavy work pants he wore. "You might want to close your eyes for this part," he said teasingly.

"Yes." She turned her head to face the window, and he slid quickly from his clothing, leaving only his short drawers and undershirt on. The bed gave to his weight, and he pulled the covers over himself.

"Are you warm enough? I could have put on an extra quilt."

She shifted, turning back to face him, her fingers twining in the edge of the quilt. "I'm fine. The register brings up the heat from the kitchen."

"We'll need to start the fire in the parlor evenings. That part of the house is pretty cold tonight." He turned to his side and reached for her hand, his fingers gentle as he loosened the grip she'd taken on the covers. "Your hands are cold, Johanna. Let me warm them."

"Don't be so nice to me."

For the first time, he caught an edge of petulance in her voice, and his smile was quick. "Why shouldn't I be? You're my wife. I guess I don't know you as well as I thought, but then, we all have secrets, don't we? I was thinkin' while I was out milking the cows. There's some things I haven't told you, Jo. I don't know if they're important or not, and sometime I'll probably..."

Her fingers squeezed his hand, and he heard the sob in her voice as she inhaled sharply. "Don't, Tate. I can't stand for you to be so good to me, when I've deceived you from the beginning."

He nodded. "Maybe you did. But then again, maybe it wasn't time for me to hear some things. We didn't know each other well enough then, Jo."

"And now we do?" She sounded hopeful, to his way of thinking. In the dim light, she'd shed her prickly ways and her pride. Tomorrow she'd probably be the old Johanna, but for tonight she was willing to soften to his touch.

He lifted her hand to his mouth and kissed the back of it, his lips open against her flesh. "We're gonna know each other better before morning."

She was silent for a moment, and he ventured another kiss, moving his mouth across her fingers, then tucking them against his cheek. His hand moved to her shoulder, pulling the quilts higher against the back of her neck. His fingers pressed against her back, and he shifted in the bed, moving closer to where she lay, until his shins felt the cold pressure of her feet.

"I'll get you warm, Johanna, if you let me." Somehow his voice had lost its even tenor, had developed an urgency of its own.

She drew in an audible breath, harsh and rasping. "You're not going to...do that, are you, Tate?"

"No, honey." Without hesitation, he allayed her fear. "I only want to share my body heat with you. You're cold, Johanna."

Her whisper was a harsh confession. "I've been cold for years, Tate Montgomery. Even in the summer, sometimes I'm cold inside and out."

"Well, Mrs. Montgomery, you don't have to be cold now."

"I think it's time for me to tell you something, Tate." Seeking his gaze, she took a deep breath. "I think I knew it would come to this one day, and I was going to show you instead. But maybe it's better to prepare you first." She peered at him in the dim light, her eyes anxious. "There are three graves up on the hill. My mother and father, and—"

His whisper cut in smoothly. "Your baby, Johanna?"

"Yes." It was a hissing sound, her confession, and he moved closer, until his face was just inches away.

"Who was it, Jo? Who gave you a child and left you on your own?"

Her shoulder lifted in a shrug. "His name was Joseph Brittles. He lived in town and worked at the mill." She touched her upper lip with the tip of her tongue, and his eyes caught the gesture. "My mother had just died. She was sick for a long time, and by the time she died, it was almost…almost a relief, I suppose." Her laugh was rasping. "I think I felt guilty, because I was…"

Tate moved his hand from her back, lifting it to rest against her face. "Sometimes it's harder to be the one left behind, Johanna." Her skin was soft to his touch, and his fingers cherished it, brushing back stray wisps of hair as he traced the line of her cheek and the furling edge of her ear.

Her eyes closed, as if she relished the comfort he offered. "Joseph had been keeping company with me, and he talked about getting married and setting up our own place. He was a big comfort to me, Tate. I think I felt I owed him some-

thing for taking up so much of his time, after Mama died.''
She closed her eyes for a moment, and he waited, his hand
moving in a slow, comforting caress.

''He persuaded you to make love with him?'' The words
were difficult for him to utter, emerging in a harsh tone.

''I didn't want to. I told him we should wait, but he said
he couldn't, he loved me too much. And even then...''

''He took advantage of you, honey.'' As if he must give
her some particle of comfort, he leaned to kiss her forehead,
his fingers buried in her hair, holding her in place for his
touch.

''It was horrible, Tate. He hurt me, and I was ashamed
that I'd allowed it to happen.'' She drew a shuddering
breath. ''When I knew I was going to have a child, I went
to see him. He'd stayed away from the farm for weeks. He
told me he was busy at the mill, working as many hours
as he could to save money for us. But when I told him I
needed to be married right away, he pushed me away. He
said he wasn't ready for that yet.''

''How old were you, Jo?'' The thought of her begging
for what should have been hers by right was repugnant to
him, and he sensed an enormous hatred for the man that
filled him almost to overflowing.

''Sixteen. Old enough to know better.'' Her laugh was a
bitter sound, and he shook his head.

''You were a child. Just a child, Jo.'' Carefully, he raised
the covers, his arm sliding beneath them, lifting her with
gentle hands, holding her closer, till her shivering flesh was
comforted by his warmth.

She rested her head in the bend of his shoulder. ''He left
town, Tate. When I went in the next week with the butter
and eggs, I stopped by to see him, and Hardy Jones said
he'd quit his job and gone.''

''What did your father do about that?'' Had she been his
daughter, he'd have chased the coward down and strung

him up, Tate thought vengefully. But apparently, Fred Patterson had been a milder man than he.

She laughed again, softly—a mirthless sound. "When I finally had to tell him, Pa said I'd tempted Joseph. He called me a Jezebel." The word took on the sound of a curse as she spoke it. "And then the baby came early. He never breathed. He was so small and blue. I never saw his eyes."

Tate's arms tightened around her, and she stiffened in his embrace. He muttered a curse word beneath his breath and relaxed his hold. "I'm sorry, Jo. I didn't mean to squeeze you. Did I hurt you?"

She shook her head. "Just a little. I'm stiff and sore, mostly. The parts that hurt worst are on the front of me."

The vision of her pale, rounded breast, its smooth surface marred by the shallow, slashing wound, pierced Tate's mind, and he stifled the urge to expose it to his view once more, even as he yearned to caress its rounded softness. His mind visualized the scar she would sustain, and he swallowed the need to purge the hurt she'd borne with the pressure of his lips. His whisper was rough and rasping as he fought the yearnings roiling within himself. "The cuts aren't deep, Jo. They'll be healed in no time."

"I know." She nodded her head, her hair brushing his lips. "I can reckon with those kind of scars. It's the ones that don't show on the outside that are the hardest to deal with."

"Johanna? Who cared for you, when you had the baby? Did your father help you bury him?" For one reason or another, he had to hear it all. Even knowing the hurt he inflicted on her as she recounted the ordeal, he must hear each detail, must live out with her the final days of her torment.

Shaking her head, she whispered the saddest words of all. "No one helped me. I was alone. I wrapped him in a flannel blanket I'd hemmed from one of my mother's nightgowns and put him in the box my shoes had come in. It's a good thing it was summer. I had to dig a long time to make sure he was deep enough in the ground. And then I buried him. I knew I couldn't mark the grave, but I thought maybe... Anyway, the next spring I planted a rosebush there.'' She shivered once more in his embrace and buried her head against his chest. ''It was a horrible night, Tate. It was the darkest night of my life.''

He'd heard it all. She'd stripped her soul bare of its sad secret and placed it before him. It was a gift of sorts, he supposed. That she could bring herself to trust him so readily was more than he'd hoped for.

For a moment, he faced his own hurt. That he had wanted her to be virgin, that he had hoped to be the only man to lay hand upon those soft curves, was a fact he must face. And, to his shame, he felt a sense of bitter disappointment that she had lain in another man's arms before this night. That she had given her love to another.

''I'll understand if you want to divorce me, Tate.'' Her words were brave, uttered firmly, but the tremors that shook her body lent little substance to her offer.

He eased her closer, and his kiss against her forehead was tender. ''I'm not going to divorce you, Jo. I said all the same vows you did, about for better and for worse, remember? I think maybe the worst is behind us now.''

His arms enclosed her, his body lent her its warmth and on the dresser, the candle flame guttered and flamed its last. And for the first time in more years than he wanted to count, Tate Montgomery was at peace.

Chapter Eleven

"I brought you your shawl, Miss Johanna."

Before her, head lowered, Pete waited. Her damp, dirty shawl clutched in his hands, he shifted from one foot to the other.

"Why, thank you. I'd forgotten I left it outdoors, Pete." Her feet on the small footstool, Johanna sat propped in her mother's rocking chair, awaiting the summons to supper. Tate had covered her with a quilt and left her there, even though she'd assured him she was more than able to fix a meal.

"Do you want me to wash it for you, ma'am? It got pretty dirty out there overnight." His voice cracked on the words he spoke, and he risked a glance at her, not quite meeting her eyes.

"Why don't you put it over the edge of the washtub, Pete? I'll take care of it tomorrow or the next day."

He nodded and turned away, as if relieved to be released from her presence. His back to her, his spine stiff, he cleared his throat. "I'm sorry, Miss Johanna. I didn't mean for you to get hurt. I wouldn't do that." The words came out in a rush, one fast on the heels of the next.

Johanna's mouth twisted in a smile, and she struggled to

suppress the tears that filled her eyes. "I know that, Pete. You aren't a mean boy."

"I was mad at you." It was a hard admission, delivered in a whisper, and his shoulders slumped as he paused halfway to the parlor door.

"Pete, look at me," she bade him quietly, and as he turned to obey, she stretched out one hand.

He approached hesitantly, as if loath to accept her forgiveness, unwilling to abandon his hair shirt of penance. His gaze drifted over her warmly clad body, draped in a pieced quilt and propped in comfort in a rocking chair. And then his eyes met hers and she saw the terrible need he tried to hide behind his belligerence.

"I'm not angry with you, Pete. You disobeyed and you were being naughty. I'm sure you're sorry for what you did, though, and I don't think we need to ever talk about it again, do you?"

He shook his head. "I have to tell my pa what happened. He's gonna be mad at me, but it was all my fault."

"I think it could be just between you and me, Pete." That Tate had already figured out the general sequence of events of the day before, she was pretty sure. What he chose to do about his son's involvement in her accident was a topic they'd not discussed.

"Pa knows. He always knows stuff like that." Pete's sigh was resigned. "But he's probably waitin' for me to tell him myself. He says we have to own up to things we do."

Johanna nodded. "Your pa's probably right about owning up and such, Pete. Just remember, he loves you."

"Yeah." Clutching her shawl to his chest, the boy flashed her a look so filled with yearning, she could scarcely bear it.

"Come here, Pete," she coaxed, once more holding out her hand.

And he responded, his feet fairly flying as he catapulted

into her arms. His head against her bosom, he shuddered, taking long indrawn breaths, his small hands fiercely clutching at the quilt. She held his wiry, slim body in her arms, pressing silent kisses against his dark, silky hair.

For long seconds, gripping her with a silent desperation, he clung to the comfort she offered. Then, as if he'd thought better of his actions, he straightened, rubbing at his nose with the back of his hand.

Johanna pulled her handkerchief from the depths of her pocket and handed it to him. And over his head she caught sight of Tate, just beyond the doorway, taking in the scene before him. She shook her head—a small, almost imperceptible movement—and he nodded in reluctant response.

"Run along, Pete," she said softly. "Put the shawl in the washroom and get ready for supper. I'm sure it's almost ready by now."

Tate was gone, his footsteps silent, and Johanna watched as Pete obeyed her order. There would be a confrontation, of that she was sure. Tate would be fair, but his sense of right and wrong was strict, and somehow Pete would make reparations for his wrongdoing.

"I thought you meant just for a couple of nights." Johanna's protest was whispered in the darkness of the hallway, midway between her room and the large bedroom Tate occupied. Held against his body by the strength of his left arm, she sensed the futility of her argument as he turned her in the direction he intended her to take.

"You're my wife, Jo. From now on you'll sleep in my bed."

That was simple enough for any idiot to understand, she figured glumly. He'd spoken his piece, and now he expected her to obey. Dragging her feet as he led her through the doorway, she watched as he closed and latched the heavy door behind them. She'd not felt this awkward in a month of Sundays, not since she refused Neville Olson's proposal of marriage several months past, shaking her head as he stumbled through his offer.

Tate wasn't giving her a chance to refuse his decision, for it couldn't be called an offer. He was hustling her to his bed, his hands careful of her healing wounds, yet firm in their intent. Stripping her of her robe, he sat her on the mattress and removed her house shoes, then lifted her legs to the bed.

She sat there, wide-eyed and watchful, wondering what she should do next. It seemed he'd accomplished his purpose and, having placed her where she belonged, was going about his own preparations for bed.

He was undressing, stripping out of his trousers, hanging them on the bedpost, placing his shirt atop them till morning. His stockings were next, a matter quickly dealt with, and then he'd climbed into the big bed.

And still she sat, upright and chilled, aware only of the steady gaze he turned in her direction.

"You've slept in my arms for the last three nights," he reminded her gently, his fingers lifting to tug at a stray lock of hair, tangling in the waving remnants of her braid. "I think it's time for you to be my wife, Johanna."

She nodded, as if speech were beyond her. As surely as the sun would rise tomorrow, she knew he'd drawn a line and she must step over it, if they were to move beyond this moment.

"I want to be your wife, Tate. I just don't know how to do this." She whispered the words reluctantly, wishing he would reach for her, yearning for him to pull her down to his embrace. If only to receive the warmth he offered, the tenderness of his touch, she was more than willing to accept his body into her own.

There was within her a terrible need, and suddenly she recognized it as being akin to the need that had painted young Pete's face with such dreadful yearning. As the flowers needed the sunlight in order to thrive, she needed what Tate was offering her now, the warmth of his embrace.

"I'll show you, Johanna." Offered in a gruff undertone, his words coaxed her, and she bent to him, leaning back on one elbow, turning to her side, her other hand fumbling as she sought his fingers, clasping them tightly as she lowered herself to lie beside him. Her movements were careful, for the scratches she'd received were more tender than she'd expected.

Their faces were mere inches apart, and she allowed her eyes to move to the scar ridging his cheekbone. Her fingers were careful, tracing the raised flesh. She closed her eyes for a moment, imagining the pain he must have suffered.

"Does it bother you?" he asked. "I know I'm not a handsome man, Jo. My nose is bent out of shape, and my—"

"Shhh...don't say that," she whispered, her fingers moving to still his words. "You're a strong man, Tate. You've been hurt, more than once, but the scars don't take from your looks. I only hurt for the pain you felt."

His grin was crooked as he kissed her fingertips. "There's no pain tonight, Jo. Not for me." His mouth sobered, and he rolled to hover over her, easing her to her back. "I'll be careful," he vowed. "I wouldn't knowingly cause you harm."

"Will you turn out the lamp?" Her glance skittered to the bright flame. Its brilliance was harsh against her eyes.

"I've already seen you, Jo," he reminded her gently. "We don't need any more secrets between us, do we?"

"It's not a matter of keeping secrets, Tate."

Her eyes wide, she watched as he lowered his head, allowing his mouth to meld with her own. His lips opened, his teeth tugging against her lower lip, holding the plump prize in a gentle grip, drawing it into his mouth. And there his tongue bathed the sensitive flesh with a caress that coaxed a moan from her throat. Her eyes closed once more as she savored the shivering sensation.

She tingled throughout her body, gooseflesh erupting upon her arms and legs. She shifted beneath him, her aching muscles and numerous cuts forgotten for the moment as she concentrated on the shimmering delight of his touch.

And then his mouth moved, releasing her slowly, as if he were reluctant to forfeit the small territory he'd conquered so easily. His lips were agile, seizing the lobe of her ear, his teeth measuring its size, then moving to explore the soft, vulnerable skin of her throat.

Whispering against her flesh, he spoke broken phrases and hushed messages that she blushed to hear. "Soft... You're so warm and...smell so sweet, here...and here."

His hands were gentle, his fingers careful, as he freed the small buttons on her gown from their moorings. And then moved the fabric aside, allowing the lamp to illuminate her flesh with a golden glow. Slowly, he bent his head, his mouth brushing against the rounding firmness, his fingers circling beneath to caress with tender care, even as he lifted and held the fullness in his palm.

So careful was his touch, so gentle his caress, she forgot the wound marring her skin, until his tongue laved across its healing surface. She'd cleaned it this morning, washing the salve from the scabbing flesh, leaving it without a covering bandage, to heal. Now, in a tender bathing, as if he would take the hurt of her injury, he ministered to her, finally tracing it with his lips, taking the last vestige of moisture with his mouth and then blowing against the damaged skin to dry it.

Johanna felt the puckering of her nipple, the drawing of her flesh as his warm breath flowed over her skin, and she shivered. Tate's chuckle was a low sound, as if he were pleased by her response, and she opened her eyes. He was watching her, lifting to his elbows, his gaze intent on the changes his touch had wrought on her tender flesh.

"Tate?" Wary of this loveplay, she whispered his name.

"Ah, Jo, you're such a prize," he said softly, his gaze moving to capture hers. "Don't stop me, sweetheart. I feel as if I've waited forever for this."

She could not resist his plea, could not resist this man who had crept into her heart with such ease. She, who had determined never to be a bride, had in these few moments discovered that she was ready to be a wife. So quickly, Tate Montgomery, with all his own secrets intact, had eased his way into her life and taken his place there.

"I just don't know what you want me to do," she told him in a hushed whisper.

His smile was crooked, and his eyes glowed with a warmth she reveled in. "Just let me love you, Jo," he said. "I won't hurt you. I'll be careful."

She nodded, giving herself over to his care, willing herself to relax beneath him as he lowered his head to the skin he'd left untouched until now. His mouth was firmer in its pursuit here, his tongue brushing against the crest that rose to meet his caress. And then he captured that small nubbin of flesh, took it between his lips and suckled it against the roof of his mouth, his tongue holding it captive.

She squirmed beneath him, breathless, caught by the web of piercing pleasure he wrapped about her. Her mouth opened on a moan of protest, as though she could not withstand such a concentration of feeling.

As if he sensed her need, he released her from his mouth, his lips moving to brush reassurance against her skin as he quieted her trembling. He tended her, his fingers cradling her, his breath warm on her skin, spending countless kisses across the surface of her breasts. Ever aware of the scarred surface, skirting it, murmuring soft phrases of comfort, he touched either end of the long scratch with his lips, as if it would shrink and heal at his loving.

And then he rolled onto his side, leaning up on his elbow and pulling the covers from her, lowering them until only her gown kept her from his sight. His hand tugged at it, lifting it, easing it up her legs, and she caught her breath at the brushing of his callused fingers against her skin.

Feeling the pressure of his touch easing between her thighs, she moved, whispering a protest, tightening the muscles that would keep him from his goal. "Tate...please cover me. I'll be cold."

His head dropped, his forehead meeting hers, brushing back and forth in a mute refusal. Then he meshed their mouths in a kiss that was different from the others, a hot, damp blending of lips and tongue that smothered her objection, urging her to a new exploration. She allowed it, giving in readily to the invasion of his tongue, intrigued by the path it traveled as he forged new ground, coaxing her into a fusion that sent shivers of delight down her spine.

So sweetly he pleasured her, so careful was he in his tender movements, that she was almost unaware of the brush of his hand over the thatch of curls he'd claimed as his own. Until his fingertips foraged farther and a glittering surge of pleasure brought a piercing cry from her throat. His mouth muffled the sound, capturing her once more in the hot, wet embrace of his lips.

With a groan of surrender, she lifted her arm, easing it around his shoulder, her fingers sliding into his hair as she held him to her. She moved to his pace, her body giving way to his clever fingers, her legs relaxing at his bidding, ever aware of the gentle pressure of his hand against her flesh.

He lifted his head, calling her name, his whisper hoarse in the silence. "Johanna! Look at me, sweetheart."

"No..." Shaking her head, she frowned, unwilling to leave the haven of pleasure he'd offered her, unable to control the hushed sounds that breathed between her lips. Still, he persisted, whispering his bidding once more.

Her eyelids fluttering, she murmured a protest. But he would not be denied. Coaxing her, his lips urgent against her cheek, he nudged her to obey, and her eyes opened reluctantly, then widened at the expression of tenderness on his face.

"Jo, sweetheart…"

Tate urged her to the brink of discovery, the edge of ecstasy. And then watched the wonder unfold as she catapulted to pleasure, her mouth opening in a silent cry, her eyes closing tightly against the tears that trickled from beneath her lids.

He drew her against himself, rocking her carefully, lest he hurt her arm, his face buried in her fragrant hair. And then, as the spasms eased, as she quieted in his embrace, he lifted himself over her. She encouraged him, enclosing him, her knees hugging him, even as she felt the gentle thrust of his invasion of her body.

It was welcome, this coming into her most secret part, this careful taking of her womanhood that he had set about with such certainty. For a moment, the painful past reared, and she forced it from her mind. Tate bore no resemblance to Joseph Brittles, at whose hands she'd known only shame and despair.

He'd wooed and won her with care and concern, and she gave him the homage due his tenderness. She lifted to him, uncaring of the pain she dealt herself with the movement. She held him in a full embrace, her torn flesh forgotten in the knowledge of this most intimate act of marriage. Clinging to him, she gathered the sum and substance of his whole being within herself, sheltering against his big body, willing him to lay claim to her as he would, withholding nothing from his surging power.

He shuddered against her, gasping a guttural cry of completion, and his groan was magnified by her own. He dropped his head to rest beside hers, his breathing harsh against her ear.

"Ah…Johanna…" As if he could say no more, he shook his head, then brushed a series of warm kisses over her face, across her throat, tipping her head back with the urging of his mouth.

She clung, her needy spirit given sustenance by the silent adulation he spent on her so lavishly. Her arm slid to the bed, the throbbing of her wound finally catching her attention, but she pushed it to the back of her mind, brushing the unwanted reminder aside.

"Jo? Did I hurt your arm?" His voice was hushed, worry taking hold as he sought her reassurance.

She shook her head. "No...I just..."

He groaned and turned to his side, taking her with him, easing the weight of her arm, careful as he lifted and held it in place. "I tried to be careful, sweetheart. Here, let me see."

He slid the bodice down until the bandage was in sight. "It's not bleeding," he muttered, his fingers testing the flesh around the injury. "It's not swollen, Jo, not even red or angry-looking. Do you think I hurt it?"

Johanna shook her head, the pain settling to a dull ache once she relaxed the muscles, pleased by his solicitude, allowing him to pamper her as he would.

Easing himself down on the pillow, Tate cradled her head against his shoulder. "Are you all right now?"

She nodded, unwilling to speak, afraid of the words that would reveal the message of her heart. Surely, if she allowed her voice to give reply, it would give sound to the words she feared to utter.

For as well as easing his way into her life, tonight he'd laid claim to her heart. As surely as Tate Montgomery had taken her body, filling her with the gift of his own splendid manhood, he'd captured the essence of her being. And with it the boundless bounty of love she'd hoarded for so long.

"It's a lot harder gettin' the chicken poop off my boots than it was gettin' it on 'em, Miss Johanna." Pete's grumble was halfhearted at best, his small face glowing with accomplishment as he scraped industriously at the soles of his boots.

"Your pa gave you a hard job to do, didn't he?" Johanna used her left foot as a lever, pushing the porch swing once more. The stench of Pete's boots, wafting to her nostrils, almost convinced her to send him farther from the porch to continue his task, but she'd be missing his company if she did. And the simple joy of watching his face as he worked was worth the odor of chicken droppings in her nostrils, she figured.

"Aw, it wasn't too bad." Pete's offhand dismissal of the severity of his punishment was a sure sign that he was reveling in his father's good graces. He'd paid the price for his behavior, and Tate Montgomery had inspected the chicken coop and pronounced it fit for the chickens to inhabit. And, in the process, had once more deemed his son's punishment complete.

"Cleaning the chicken coop is a nasty job." Johanna's opinion of the chore was obvious. The wrinkling of her nose and her shudder of distaste were not a display for Pete's benefit. Too well, the scent of his boot scrapings brought back the memory of mornings she'd spent at the task.

"Yeah, well, I guess Pa gave me the awfullest chore he could think of," Pete said, his voice taking on a hint of pride as he considered his accomplishment. He shot a glance at Johanna, his eyes speculative. "He was madder at me than you were, wasn't he?"

Johanna nodded. "I expect he was, Pete."

"But it was you that got hurt." He leaned to peer down at the pile of droppings he'd scraped from his footwear. "If I leave this mess here, it's gonna smell something terrible, isn't it?"

"Probably," she said agreeably, shoving her foot against the floor of the porch again, sending the swing once more into motion.

"I guess mothers don't get as mad about stuff, do they?" Pete's attention was absorbed by his task as he scraped his mess into a pile. Had she not been watching closely, Johanna might have missed his furtive look in her direction.

"I don't know, Pete. I've never been a mother." She was astonished at her calmness, given the pounding of her heart. Unless she was mistaken, he'd just placed her in that category. In a roundabout way, he'd given her his stamp of approval, and the occasion called for a celebration of sorts.

Holding the wide shovel in place, Pete loaded it with the results of his boot-cleaning, scraping the top layer of dirt with it. "I guess you catch on pretty quick, Miss Johanna. You'd be pretty good at it. If you had kids, I mean." Rising from his crouch, he lifted the shovel, holding it firmly, lest the contents spill.

"I'm gonna dump this on the manure pile," he said, setting off toward the barn. "Then I gotta go help Pa with the pasture fence."

Johanna pushed herself upright, wincing only a little as she gripped the swing with her left hand. Her muscles were tender, but the cut was healing well. She watched as Pete set off, and her heart went out to the boy. So small, yet so knowledgeable.

"Pete!" She waited till he halted, then turned his head. "Maybe I could practice on you and Timmy."

He nodded agreeably, his mouth twitching as he attempted to hide his obvious approval of her notion. "I guess that would be all right, ma'am. Timmy won't care." He turned away, his attention riveted on keeping the shovel level, his load intact. And not until he was sure Johanna could only see his back did he allow a smile of satisfaction to curve his lips.

Apple dumplings ought to be in order, Johanna decided. It seemed like something all three male members of her

family would enjoy. Her heart singing, ignoring the stiff-
ness of her sore muscles, she went into the house.

"Thank you, God!" It was a fervent whisper, delivered
with open eyes and a joyful spirit, a far cry from the doleful
messages her father had been prone to deliver to the Almighty. Probably not at all the sort of prayer Theodore
Hughes would approve of, she thought with a smile.

Although perhaps, of all people, Reverend Hughes would
appreciate her heartfelt surge of thankfulness this morning.

Chapter Twelve

As if winter had only been waiting for some hidden signal before it officially began, the snow had arrived. With a four-inch fall late one evening, the ground had been covered, presenting a pure and pristine welcome to Pete and Timmy the next morning.

They were ecstatic. Bundled in mittens and scarves, booted and capped with care, they indulged in a romp such as Johanna had never before seen take place in her yard. Sheba forsook her dignity to chase first one boy, then the other, barking and frolicking as if her life revolved around the entertainment of these two small humans.

A snowman appeared quickly, Pete instructing Timmy in the proper construction, even lifting the smaller child to place a withered carrot where a nose must be. Tate had refrained from mentioning chores, and indeed, Johanna had had a difficult time tending to her own, what with standing at the window to watch the shenanigans taking place outdoors.

By the time dinner was on the table, the boys were soaked through and red-cheeked, and more than ready for the hearty stew Johanna had prepared. The yard was a sight. No longer was there a lush carpet of white to beguile the eye, only a bedraggled patchwork of dried grass and trampled snow remained.

Another blizzard of more major proportions exploded within days, drifting snow before the barn door, causing Tate to grumble as he shoveled it from his path before dawn. Johanna was reduced to drying clothes in the house, the rack behind the stove in almost constant use, with wet mittens and trousers draped over its length.

Then the sun came out, melting the wintry show of force, and for over a week they puddled through mud and rutted roads. Johanna suspected this was the final spell of moderate weather they would get until spring, and a lowering sky proved her right.

It was a mere scattering of snow, compared to the past extravaganzas nature had provided, but enough to cause her to leave a trail behind, her footprints clear in the moonlight, as she stepped from the silent house to the porch, and then across the yard.

She was gone. Acclimated to her presence in his bed, he sensed her absence. So quickly, in a matter of days and weeks, she had become part of his sleeping habits. Now, half-awake, Tate reached beside him, patting the quilt. "Jo? Johanna?" His voice was rusty, heavy with sleep, and, stilling the movement of his hand, he closed his eyes, listening. From the parlor below, he heard the chiming of the clock, announcing the hour.

Three in the morning. He rubbed his eyes and sat upright in the bed. Perhaps she'd gone downstairs. Before the thought had time to be born, his long legs were swinging over the side of the bed and he was reaching for his trousers. He slid into them quickly, his ears alert for a sound from below.

Noiselessly Tate moved through the hallway and down the stairs, his bare feet chilled by the cold floor. Inside the parlor, the moonlight splashed a path across the floor all the way to the wide double doors where he stood. The room was empty, the couch holding only a rumpled afghan, left there at bedtime. The rocking chair stood unmoving in the shadows, and outside the lace curtains the silvery moonlight cast an unearthly glow over the snow.

Tate's brow furrowed into a frown as he headed for the kitchen. He'd not expected her to be there, either, for some reason, and a twinge of concern had him biting his lip as he looked out the window toward the barn and the scattering of outbuildings across the yard.

The chicken coop and the springhouse were illuminated by the full moon, as were the corncrib and the outhouse behind it. But not a sign of Johanna.

He turned to the washroom, bending low to where their boots sat in a row. And found that only an empty space existed where Johanna's small work boots should be.

Above the kitchen table, the kerosene lamp swung from his touch, and he reached out to grasp it firmly, lifting the chimney as he struck a match. It flared and caught quickly, the bright glow causing him to blink and narrow his eyes. The pegs on the wall were heavily laden with his sheepskin-lined coat and the boy's jackets. Johanna's heavy woolen coat was missing. He shook his head as he headed for the back door.

He looked out across the yard, toward the lane. Beyond it was the rise of land where the small burying ground had been established with the death of Mary Patterson, and it was there that his seeking ended.

Atop the hill, illuminated by the full moon, stood a figure, wrapped in a bulky coat, unmistakably Johanna. Head bent, arms curling around her body, she was immobile, as if cast from metal, to his eye resembling a portrait of mute sorrow.

"Johanna!" It was a whisper breathed from his lungs, a yearning cry as he sensed her grief, there on the hill where three graves marked the resting place of her family.

He spun from the door's window, snatching his coat from the peg, stuffing his feet into his boots and hurrying from the house.

Following the path her smaller footprints had made through the scattering of snowflakes, he climbed to where she stood, then waited, sensing her need for solitude. She was unmoving, only the wind teasing her scarf giving proof that he was watching flesh and blood, and not a graven image.

Then she lifted one hand to brush at a lock of hair, and that slender member trembled as he watched. Her fingers curled in on themselves, and she wiped her cheek with the back of her fist.

It was more than he could bear, and he wondered, with a moment of insight, how many other nights she had come to this place, silent and alone with her grief. Surely, now that she was no longer alone, now that he and his sons were sharing her life, she could find solace within the new family that had been formed. Yet she had left his bed to climb the hill in the chill of the winter night to keep vigil in this place where only restless spirits kept her company. Had she come other nights, had he not known when she made silent journeys in the dark, had he slept, unaware of her absence? Surely not, for he'd have sensed the empty space next to him, as he had tonight.

"Johanna." The sound of her name fell between them, and her shoulders stiffened. Her fist opened and her fingers swept again over her cheek, as if she must dismiss the evidence of her tears from his sight. And then she turned to face him.

"Did I wake you? I'm sorry. I tried to be quiet." She whispered, barely disturbing the silence, her hands clutching the front of her coat, where buttons and buttonholes had not been paired. Beneath it, her white nightgown was scant covering against the cold, and she shivered, as if she had just noticed the wind that came from the west.

Tate swept his arms around her, moving his hand against her head as he held it beneath his chin. Her ear was cold against his palm, and he bent to her, roughly pushing her head back until he could see her face. Then his mouth was there, his lips taking possession with a force he had not spent on her before now.

As if he were angry, distraught over her venturing from his bed, his mouth plundered the depths of hers, his tongue taking liberties he had not sought on other nights. He lifted from her, his eyes caught by the wide-eyed surprise she made no effort to hide.

"You frightened me. I didn't know where you were." His voice was hoarse, and his scowl was accusing. Against her arms, his grip tightened, holding her with bruising strength.

Unafraid of his anger, perhaps drawn by his concern, she leaned against him, as if she sought the warmth his broad form offered. Her head tilted back, the better to gaze into his shadowed face. The tip of her tongue touched the inner tissue of her upper lip, traveling the path his own lips had taken only moments earlier, and he watched the movement from narrowed eyes.

"I'm sorry." Stretching upward on tiptoe, she offered her mouth, her hands releasing the front of her coat to snatch at his, instead, as though fearful he might put her from him. A rising excitement quickened her heartbeat, flaring her nostrils as she inhaled sharply, pressing against his solid form. Accepting her surrender, he slid his hands to her hips, holding her there as he eased the fullness of his loins against her belly.

Deep within her, she sensed a primitive response, and welcomed the burgeoning evidence of his need. His hands rough, his mouth demanding, he drew her headlong into deep water, and willingly she took the plunge.

"Tate?" She whispered his name, a Lorelei in the night,

and he bent to her, seduced by the innocence of her swollen mouth and the clutching of her fingers against his chest.

His mouth was gentler now, coaxing her to respond. His tongue met no resistance as she parted her teeth, and welcomed it with her own. His curling and coaxing, hers tempting and teasing, they sparred.

Until, breathless and wide-eyed, she tilted her head back, gasping for a breath of air, exposing the slim line of her throat to his view. As a dominant male accepts the surrender of his mate in the wild, so Tate Montgomery took the offering she gave, his mouth finding new flesh upon which to leave his mark of possession.

He suckled at her throat, just above the line of her collarbone, pushing the flannel nightgown to one side, his hand moving in a familiar touch between their bodies to release the top buttons. His tongue touched the skin of her throat, tasting the faint salt flavor. His grin was feral against her flesh as he thought of the perspiration that had come to that surface earlier in the night. As always, she had accepted his loving, reveling in his possession, her body slick against his as he claimed her for his own.

Nowhere in his past had he yearned so to possess a woman. Not just in the intimacies of their coming together, but in the everyday drudgeries of their lives. The urge to stamp her as his mate, to know that she was his, even as she washed his clothing, cooked his meals, tended his children, consumed him.

And she was allowing it. His desire surged to a new, painful edge as he recognized her willingness to be subdued by his greater strength. She clung, her arms slipping around his neck. She leaned, her softness meshing with the muscular lines of his frame. She warmed, her shivering absorbed by his heat. And in the midst of it, she groaned her need in a wordless sound, a yielding, yearning cry for his possession.

He scooped her up, her gown and coat twisting around

her legs, exposing them from the knees down, where her heavy boots hung like the exaggerated fetlocks on a work-horse.

In strides that pounded his heels into the ground, he walked down the hill, leaving the graves behind. Past the house, across the yard to where the barn sat, colorless in the moonlight, its red boards washed gray by the silvering of the moon. With the fingers of his right hand he tugged at the door, sliding it open far enough for him to enter. The warm scent of animals, their big bodies creating a haven in the cold, met him full force, and he sensed for a moment a kinship with them.

As if he, too, were driven by a force not controlled by his human mind, he carried his wife through the door, down the aisle and into an empty stall. Filled with straw, ready for occupancy, it waited. And he blessed his forethought, as he'd cleaned and prepared it earlier for the animal it would contain on the morrow.

Now the bedding was awaiting the female creature he held in his arms. He lowered her to the thick layers of straw, following her to the ground as he straightened her body to match the lines of his own. Knowing he was heavy, his weight burdensome, yet yearning to conquer with the force of his masculine strength, he covered her.

And with a crooning acceptance, she tightened the grip she'd maintained, shifting only her hands as she drew him closer, her arms circling his neck. As though she could not be crushed by his weight, she lifted herself to him. As if she craved the possession his thrusting loins promised, she moved against him. And in the darkness of the barn, surrounded by the animals that made up a part of their lives, they came together.

His hands were trembling as he lifted her gown, spreading her coat to either side, his fingers fumbling as he undid the front of his trousers, releasing his manhood to the cold air. And his groan was heartfelt as he meshed their bodies in a surging whirlwind of passion.

There was no light to guide their hands, only the darkness that made each movement a grasping, needy urgency. Their fingers meshed, his holding hers against the straw as he lifted and fell, time and again, against the softness of her smaller frame. There was only need, desire, and an overwhelming passion that sparked a response neither could deny.

Sensing her coiling urgency, he drew her into the web he wove with each movement, pulling her with him to that glittering promise of delight that hovered just beyond her reach. And then, with a guttural groan, he thrust her beyond the boundaries of her own yearning, into a shimmering knowledge of pleasure.

In the silence of the barn, Johanna caught huge, gasping breaths, her lungs straining to fill as she compensated for the overwhelming breathlessness that had seized her body. Tate was heavy, crushing her, and she held him tight, unwilling to lessen by one inch the intimacy of their coming together. But he withdrew from her, a gradual lessening of his embrace signaling his own return to the lucidity demanded by the cold night air.

"Johanna? Are you all right, sweetheart?" Husky and deep with concern, his words enthralled her. That his first concern was for her well-being brought a quiet joy to her heart, and she responded to his plea.

"Yes...I think I'm about as all right as I've ever dreamed of being, Tate." She sensed a moment of reluctance, an unwillingness to end this moment of unadulterated bliss at his hands. And then he levered to his knees and tugged her coat together, covering the flesh he'd exposed to his touch. She heard his clothing rustle, felt the movement of his body as he shifted and arranged his trousers and buttoned his coat.

He rose and bent to her, lifting her to her feet, giving

her only a moment to gain her balance before he swept her into his arms once more.

"Still got your boots on?" he asked, a trace of humor evident in the query.

She nodded against his shoulder.

"Can you pull the door shut?" He'd managed to slip through the opening he'd left, and he turned, allowing her to shove the door into place.

With a sigh of contentment, she slid her arm around his neck, biting back the urge to make her own way to the house. She was perfectly capable of walking, but the sense of security she was reveling in at this moment precluded her need for independence.

Tomorrow she could walk. Tomorrow she could tend to herself. In the morning she would arise, clothed once more in the skin she had worn for so long, that of a strong, able female, capable of tackling any chore that crossed her horizon.

For now, for the few blessed minutes left of this night, she would be only what Tate Montgomery asked her to be. And if part of that was his urging her to be compliant, to rest in his embrace as he carried her to his bed, she would be the most willing of women.

The burden of grief she had carried with her to the hillside earlier was gone, vanquished by the storm of his loving. She'd left it amid the fallen leaves of autumn, beneath the scattering of winter snow that covered three graves. She'd buried it beneath the frozen ground that held prisoner the body of the baby boy she'd borne and buried by herself. And in the shedding of that terrible cloak of sorrow, she'd donned a new garment, woven of love, knit with the care and concern of a generous soul, stitched and fitted to her precise measurements by the fervent embrace of the man she had married.

As he carried her up the stairs, she clung unashamedly to his greater strength. As he pulled her worn boots from her feet and placed them by the bedside, she bent to kiss the crown of his head. And as he drew her into his embrace, she gifted him with the secrets of her heart.

"I had to let him go, Tate." It was an offering she was willing to give, this admission of hers. "I'd held his memory in my heart for so long, I feared there would never be room for anyone else."

"You've grieved over that baby long enough, Johanna. It was time." His hand rubbed slow circles against her back as she nestled against him.

She nodded. "There wasn't room for all that sorrow anymore. Not since you came. But I had to tell him goodbye. I had to go up there and explain that I couldn't let him hold me back from loving your boys. Or you."

His arms tightened, and his breath caught in his throat. "Me?"

"I love you, Tate. I've needed to tell you." Her confession muffled against his chest, she sighed, as if relieved to be rid of its weight. "I thought you must know, but I want to say the words."

He brushed his mouth against her forehead. And she waited as his warm breath bathed her flesh. Until she could wait no longer.

"Tate?" It was a small sound in the darkness.

"I care about you, honey. You must know that." Evenly spaced, soft as the whisper of a dove in the springtime, his words spread comfort throughout her being.

"Yes, I know that. I know you wanted to…" She hesitated, brave in the darkness, but unwilling to put words to the moments of loving.

"I want you more than I can tell you, honey." The sound of his laugh was strained, and there was a reserve in the words he spoke. "I still do. I need you for my wife, I need the comfort you give me." His kiss against her brow emphasized the admission. "You ease my pain, Johanna. Your body takes my manhood, and somehow, you heal me. You draw all the bad memories and leave me clean and fresh and feeling like a man who could conquer the world.'' His laugh was short, tinged with embarrassment, as if he rued the poetry of the words he spoke.

''You'll think I've gone soft in the head, Jo.'' He rocked her in his embrace, dropping kisses against the pure line of her forehead as he spoke.

''No.'' It was a softly uttered denial of his fear. ''No, I wouldn't think that. I guess I just don't understand why you can't bring yourself to speak about your life with Belinda. Maybe I need to know what happened then, so I can understand what you feel.''

''I feel…mixed up sometimes.'' He shook his head, as if he were struggling to express himself for her benefit. ''I need you, Jo…but I don't know if I have any love left to give you. I've had to put everything I have and all I am as a man into those boys of mine for a long time. I was mother and father both a good share of the time—all the time, lately. Until we came here. There just doesn't seem to be much love left in me for anyone else, once I've poured it out on them.''

Her throat was dry at his denial of the emotion she craved. Her hands closed into fists, mute evidence of the tensing that surged throughout her slender body.

''But what happened back then, Tate?'' She touched the scar on his upper lip, her fingers gentle against his mouth. ''Were you hurt in an accident?'' Her hand moved upward, resting against his cheek, her fingertips marking the ridged scar he bore, and she hesitated at the indrawn breath he could not hide from her hearing.

''What happened here?'' she persisted, once more caressing the ragged reminder of injury. She rose on one elbow and leaned closer, her mouth against his cheek, as if she would place a kiss of healing upon the blemish he wore.

''Stop it, Johanna. I don't want to discuss this right now.'' Gruff and terse, his words halted her, and she lifted her head, her eyes seeking his in the darkness. But it was no use. They were closed against her, effectively barring her from his thoughts.

So she turned, sensing the ruin of the unity they'd shared during those minutes in the stall, unable to look any longer into the stern visage he presented. Easing her way, she turned to lie with her back to him, allowing only the firm line of her spine to touch the front of his body.

"I need to sleep, Tate," she whispered. "Morning's almost here."

If he sensed her withdrawal, he hid it well. His arm encircled her waist, his big hand sliding up to capture the full measure of her breast, enclosing it in the embrace of his hand, plumping it to fit the palm, his fingers spread to contain the whole of it. It was as if her turning away had erased his mood, as though he would mend the distance he'd brought about between them. And then his head dipped, allowing his mouth to touch the side of her throat, leaving a last kiss there before he curled his big body around her.

Yet even as he slept, his soft snoring a hum in her ear, she lay unmoving, her eyes wide in the darkness, her yearning heart hungry for the words he was unable to speak.

In the light of day, Johanna recalled the almost-quarrel they'd conducted in their bed, remembering the words she'd fretted over through the hours of the night, and decided she'd best leave well enough alone. She hadn't bargained for the man's love when she married him. That she'd fallen into that trap was her problem, and she'd manage to live with it. She lifted her shoulders in a gesture of resolve.

Whether or not Tate Montgomery had any love to spend on her, he was generous, more than willing to give her full advantage of his bank account, and that was a bonus she could not help but appreciate.

Turning the crank that operated her new Fulton #1

washing machine, Johanna listened to the sound of a load of undergarments and shirts being agitated. It was like music to her ears. The water splashed and sloshed in a most satisfying manner, and she couldn't help the small smile of satisfaction that would not be denied.

The scrub board hung on the wall, dry as a bone, unused for well over a month, ever since the day Tate had brought the new washer home on the wagon. Some washdays it made her feel downright lazy, Johanna thought with just a flicker of guilt—guilt she suppressed with hardly a twinge of effort. Yet the new machine still required a considerable amount of muscle to run, given the instructions that came with it.

She must turn the crank ten or twelve minutes for each load, which was a deterrent to doing the breakfast dishes or gathering the eggs. But she'd found a woman could do a powerful lot of thinking during a ten minute period.

Like wondering how she'd come to be so attached to a man in such a short time.

That Tate was a good husband could not be denied. That she was fast becoming addicted to his brand of loving was also true, and her mouth curled at the thought. He'd managed to coax her and beguile her in ways she'd never imagined in her wildest dreams. That those dreams had been limited by her lack of knowledge was a fact. But that was no longer the case, she admitted to herself, aware of the warmth she'd generated by her industrious cranking, not to mention the memories stirred by her thoughts of Tate.

Rising from the low stool he'd made for her to use, she opened the washing machine and viewed her load of laundry. Suds rode the top of the water like a flotilla of sailing ships, and she burst a series of bubbles as she reached beneath the surface for the clean clothes. The Seroco ball bearing wringer Tate had clamped on the rim of the washer accepted a small pair of drawers, nudged by her gradual turn of the handle, and she watched with satisfaction as the soapy water was wrung from the cotton fabric, running back into the machine.

She'd filled her washtub with cold water and within minutes it contained the contents of the new washing machine. Johanna loaded the new appliance with Tate's shirts and her own dresses and turned the crank several times to churn them into the depths of the soapy water. She'd let them soak for a few minutes, while she rinsed and readied the underwear for the clothes rack.

On a graduated series of wooden rungs, it held a considerable amount of washing, one layer hung only inches from the next. The heat from the stove dried it readily, a vast improvement over the lines Johanna had strung in the washroom and across the kitchen in other years.

"You've left your mark on my house, Tate Montgomery," she whispered, spreading the small pieces across the wooden dowel rods. *And in my heart,* she added silently. In a matter of a few months, he'd taken over the Patterson farm and turned it into the Montgomery place.

The banker in Belle Haven, August Shrader, even tipped his hat in a most gratifying manner when he caught sight of Johanna on the street these days. Always polite, he had become almost friendly since Tate Montgomery placed his affairs in the hands of the Belle Haven Bank.

That she had no notion of the state of Tate's bank account was immaterial to Johanna. He had paid off the mortgage and given her free rein at the general store, not to mention a generous hand when it came to the Sears catalog.

She headed back to the washing machine with a light step, pausing only a moment to stir the thick soup she was cooking for the noon meal.

"Miss Johanna?" Timmy's call from the porch nudged her from her daydreams, and she hastened her pace.

"What is it, Timmy?" The chill air had her reaching for her shawl as she opened the door.

"We're leavin' for town. Pa wants to know if you need

anything at the store.'' Shifting from one foot to another, the child cast a worried glance at the wagon in the yard, where his father and brother waited.

''They won't leave without you, Timmy,'' she assured him, reaching to tug his cap over his ears for greater warmth.

His earnest look accompanied by a quick nod, he agreed. ''I know. Pa said he'd wait while you make up a list.''

Atop the wagon, Tate's steady gaze lured her, and she stepped onto the porch, disregarding the cold wind whipping around the corner of the house.

Half running, she headed in his direction, Timmy scampering ahead. ''Maybe my order from the catalog is in, Tate,'' she said breathlessly, her eyes seeking his, her hair a glittering golden circlet atop her head in the wintry sunshine. And once more, she met his eyes, caught in the dark, silent seduction of his allure.

''You'll take a chill, Jo.'' His frown encompassed her, and she grinned, willing its disappearance.

''I come from sturdy stock.'' But her shiver denied the claim, and he swung down from the wagon.

''Hold the reins, Pete. I'll be right back.'' Reaching her side in several long strides, Tate turned her around, leading her back to the shelter of the house. One long arm around her shoulder, he hustled her along, her feet fairly flying over the frozen ground.

On the porch, he opened the back door, stepping inside, pushing her ahead of himself. There he halted, only to tug her nearer, lifting her chin with his gloved finger.

''I ought to give you a good talkin'-to, Johanna Montgomery,'' he growled, his eyes narrowed to steely gray slits as they slid from her face to the rounded lines of her bosom. ''You're some fine example to those young'ns out there, running around without your coat on, getting chilled to the bone. Look how cold you are!'' His hand moved to cup

and lift one breast, emphasizing the effect that lured hi
gaze.

She laughed—a low, seductive sound—and his eye
made a slow journey to her mouth. Even as he watched,
formed a pouting moue, and then his head dipped, his col
lips taking abrupt possession. "You are the most distractin
female I've ever encountered."

"Complaining?" she asked, her eyes opening slowly a
she caught her breath.

He shook his head. "After last night? Hardly, sweet
heart."

Her blush was immediate, and he grinned his delight. "
can't believe you still get all hot and bothered when I..."

"Tate!" she wailed, punching at his chest with her fists
"Go on now. Get those eggs to town before they freeze
Did you get the last of the spies out of the fruit cellar fo
Mr. Turner? They're pretty well wrinkled, but he said h
wanted them anyway. People are still asking for apples."

"I've got everything under control, Mrs. Montgomery
Except my wife, it appears."

Johanna laughed aloud. "Her, most of all, it seems t
me. Up to her elbows in wash water, while you go galli
vanting off to town."

"I asked you at the breakfast table if you wanted to go,"
he reminded her, "and you said you had too much to do."

She nodded. "Just check the catalog order, and don'
forget the coffee and lard. That's all I need."

His hands releasing her reluctantly, he nodded. "W
won't be long, Jo. That soup smells good. We'll be hungr
when we get back."

She watched as he crossed the yard. He climbed to hi
seat, lifted the reins from Pete's hands and slapped then
against the backs of his team of mares. They were gon
quickly, as if the promise of dinner urged their pace.

She closed the door, returning her shawl to the peg i
the washroom before she settled down on her stool onc

nore. Her hand clutching the handle, she resumed the steady motion required by her new washing machine. Still aware of the damp remnants of Tate's kiss, she touched her tongue to her lip, as if she could taste his coffee-scented breath.

And smiled when she found just a trace of him there.

Chapter Thirteen

There was an underlying current of seduction these days in every encounter between Johanna and him, Tate decided. Whether it be his decision that she should sit next to him at the kitchen table from now on, instead of across the wide bleached boards that made up that piece of furniture, or the casual placement of her hand on his shoulder as she poured his coffee at the supper table. Or the hasty decision he'd made one wintry day last week, hustling her into the house for an intimate farewell kiss, while his sons waited for him on the wagon seat.

Or even the meeting of their eyes now, as they rode in companionable silence to church this wintry Sunday morning.

They'd reached for and grasped intimacy with both hands. That thought pleased him. A tingling warmth invaded his body as he considered the woman he'd married.

She was as prim and proper as could be, all gussied up in her Sunday-go-to-meeting dress, covered head to toe in a hooded cape of fine alpaca, lined with wool from more common animals than those found in South America. He'd sent for it from a catalog at the general store, one Esther Turner had received from New York. She'd kept his secret from Johanna, her cheeks rosy as she shared his pleasure over the purchase.

It had been Johanna's Christmas gift, and his heart lifted as he remembered her sigh of delight as he'd placed it around her, wrapping her in its voluminous folds. He'd bent to kiss her, lifting the hood to rest upon her golden hair, still spread over her shoulders in early-morning disarray. She'd blushed, still unused to such displays of affection.

Now those pale tresses were properly plaited and pinned into place, but the memory of that day was one he'd tucked away. Their first Christmas—a series of small celebrations. The tree he'd found and dragged to the house, where they'd decorated it with ribbons and strings of popcorn and candles on the tips of each branch.

The gifts they'd ordered from the Sears catalog for the boys and wrapped late in the evening, hiding them beneath their bed, lest small eyes should seek out the Christmas surprises too soon. And, best of all, the late-night giving of that most precious gift, the loving they'd shared in the darkness, the soft whispers, the muffled laughter, the sighs of satisfaction and repletion.

Tate cleared his throat, aware suddenly of a telltale pressure in his groin, his thoughts running rampant as he savored the remembrance of bedding the woman he'd married.

"Tate?" She was watching him warily, sensitive to his shifting about on the seat. "Is something wrong?"

He slapped the reins against the backs of his team, aware he'd allowed them to slow to a walk as his mind wandered. "Nope! Everything's right as rain," he announced, his grin of delight a bewitchment in itself.

She responded with a faint smile, a blush rushing to color her cheeks. "Tate Montgomery! You're on your way to church. You might consider thinking about subjects more conducive to worship."

"Now how do you know what I've got in mind, Mrs.

Montgomery?" he asked, his eyes twinkling. "I'm just enjoyin' this fine winter morning, riding to town with my family."

"I know that look," she announced primly, eyes once more on the road ahead, ever aware of the two small boys in the seat behind.

"Pa looks like that a lot, Miss Johanna," Pete offered innocently.

Johanna ducked her head, hiding the flush of pleasure the child's words gave her.

"Yeah, Miss Johanna," Tate whispered, reaching to take her hand. The gloves they wore were heavy, warm against the winter air, bulky covering for their fingers. Yet he sensed a yearning to communicate his need for her in this small way, their hands joining.

She shifted in the seat, easing closer, her skirt brushing against his warmly clad thigh, her shoulder pressing against his.

"Cold?" He slanted her a glance, taking in the warm, rosy hue of her cheeks, the half smile curving her lips.

She shook her head. "No."

"Thinking about things more conducive to worship?" he asked, his drawl stretching out the words as he teased her.

She jabbed him with her elbow. And then lifted her chin, her delight in the wintry sunshine, the man at her side and the memories he'd given her all awash in her mind.

"If being thankful for what I've got and dwelling on the blessings instead of the bad times is worshipful, then I suppose I'm about as ready for Sunday-morning church as I'll ever be."

Tate squeezed her hand, his throat full with a rush of emotion he could not put name to. "I'm not much of a praying man, Johanna. Never have been. But I'm thankful for what I have, most of all for what you've given me."

"Me? You've done most of the giving, Tate."

He shrugged. "Think so? Reckon I'd better give you a chance to catch up, then, hadn't I?" Releasing her hand, he placed it on his thigh and snapped the reins, the sharp crack ringing in the air. The mares responded, their shod hooves digging into the snow that had fallen during the night, the bells on their harness jingling apace.

Ahead, the church bells rang, and below the steeple a steady line of townspeople filed through the wide double doors. Tate Montgomery drew his surrey up to the hitching rail and tied his team in place. Then, quickly, lest they be late for the first hymn, he lifted Johanna to the ground and hustled his family through the fresh-fallen snow toward the church doors. Scooping his hat from his head, he felt the sun's rays warm him, and he glanced up at the blue January sky.

There was no doubt about it. Belle Haven on a Sunday morning was a fine place to be.

February brought a series of dark days and cold nights, sending Johanna on a trip to the attic to seek out extra quilts for the beds. She'd always dreaded this shortest month of the year, simply because it usually carried the nastiest weather with it. This year had been different, she realized. Life with Tate and the boys brought with it a share of happiness that no longer allowed the dreary days of winter to impinge on her spirits.

A sparse ray of February sunshine cast its beam across the kitchen floor as she ironed before the cookstove, and she moved the ironing board to catch the warmth. Through the window she caught a glimpse of the wagon, then heard Sheba's welcoming bark and the jingling of the bells Tate had put on the team's harness.

In less than a minute, fresh from town, where he'd left Johanna's eggs and butter at the general store, Tate burst through the back door, bringing a draft of cold air with him.

Waving an envelope in his hand, he stamped his feet, checking his boots for clinging snow. "Bessie wants to come visit. She says she's lonesome for the boys." Empty egg basket in hand, he opened the pantry door, depositing the basket on the shelf before he sat down at the table, Bessie's letter in his hand.

Johanna stepped to the stove, exchanging her cooling iron for another from the hot surface, carefully transferring the flannel pad she held it with.

"Did you hear me, Jo? We got a letter from Bessie."

"Yes. She wants to come for a visit, you said." Her face was not visible from where he sat, but he'd warrant it was as sober as that of a hanging judge, if her tone of voice was any indication.

"Jo? Is something wrong?" His eyes swept her form—the straight back, where her apron was tied in a precise bow in the center of her spine, her narrow shoulders, squared and stiff. She hadn't even offered him a kiss in welcome. In fact, once she caught sight of Bessie's letter, she'd turned back to her ironing, quick as a wink. And now she was ignoring him, putting her weight behind the movement of her sadiron and shaking out his shirt with crisp movements as she shifted it on the board.

Something was wrong. And he'd be jiggered if he let her say any different. He stood, shedding his coat on the chair he'd vacated and took three steps to stand behind her.

Her head bent lower, and her iron took on a burst of speed. He bent and touched her cheek with cold lips.

"Hey, Mrs. Montgomery. Don't I get a kiss hello? After I sold your eggs and butter and brought you the latest news from town, and even remembered your green tea?"

Her sigh was almost silent as she nodded. Then, deliberately, she placed the iron on the stove and dropped her flannel cloth on the ironing board. Turning to face him, her arms lifted to curve around his neck.

"Of course you get a kiss, Mr. Montgomery. My mind

was a million miles away, I guess.'' She rose on her toes and placed a damp salute upon his mouth. ''That's for the green tea.'' Another kiss followed the first, and he was ready for this one.

He drew it out, teasing her with small, biting caresses, holding her against himself, lifting her with both arms around her waist. ''What was that one for?'' he asked, releasing her mouth with a loud smacking sound.

''Ummm...the safe delivery of my butter-and-egg money, I guess.''

''You don't have it yet,'' he reminded her, lifting his eyebrow in a suggestive manner. ''Let's try another little bribe here.'' Inhaling her sweetness, he bent his head to her again. It held him captive, this scent of freshness she wore. Like a blending of starch and soap, a savory mix of apple-blossom cologne and beef stew, it filled his senses and drew him into her orbit.

She laughed, her fit of pique almost forgotten, knowing and reveling in the power she held over this man. Her eyes half-closed, she tilted her head, willing the moment of unease to pass from her. His mention of a letter from Bessie had hit her the wrong way. That the woman missed the boys was probably true. That she was coming here for more than that obvious reason was also more than likely.

It had been her opinion from the first that Bessie Swenson had been unwilling for Tate and the boys to leave Ohio. Not only because of missing her sister's children, but because of the man who had fathered them. And now that her own husband was gone—and good riddance, from what Tate had said—Bessie was about to make an appearance.

''What about the news from town? You got a haircut. Did you talk to Jacob Nelson? Did he ask Leah to the church social?'' The new barber in town had been obvious in his looks of longing toward the young schoolteacher during Sunday-morning church service. And that young lady was in dire need of a suitor, if her sidelong glances at several of the handsomer menfolk was any indication.

Tate shook his head. "I didn't hear anything about Jacob, but Esther Turner said Mr. Shrader from the bank was calling at the store twice a day last week, once to check his mail from the morning train and again in the afternoon to pick up groceries for his supper."

"He has a housekeeper to do that," Johanna said, her brow furrowing as she considered Tate's news.

He grinned. "He even asked me if I thought Selena would be agreeable to his company on a regular basis. Esther thinks Mr. Shrader is looking to court Selena. She said he spends an awful lot of time looking over his mail every noontime."

"Selena?" Johanna's eyes widened with surprise. "She's too young for him. Why, he must be almost sixty years old."

"Selena's no spring chicken, honey."

"I'll bet she's barely forty," Johanna said, denying his words.

He nodded sagely. "That's what I mean. She's beyond the age where she'd be looking for a husband."

"I think she's lovely!" Johanna cried, as if to deny Tate's assertion. "I'm just not sure August Shrader isn't too old for her." She considered the matter for a moment. "What else did he say to you?" Her brow furrowed. "When did you talk to him, Tate?"

"I stopped at the bank for a few minutes on business, Jo." Backing from her, he snagged a coffee cup from the cabinet, reaching to fill it from the pot on the stove.

She watched him, sensing a reluctance in his reply. He eased into his chair at the table and blew on the surface of his hot coffee, then turned his attention back to her.

"Anyway, I doubt Selena will be asking for advice, from what Esther said." Tate leaned back in his chair, his mouth curving in a satisfied grin, as if he relished his bit of news.

"They're going to the social together. Esther overheard him asking and saw Selena nod him an answer."

"He's courting her! Sure enough." And suddenly the age difference disappeared from Johanna's mind, dissipating like a puff of smoke as she thought of the slender postmistress and the lonely life she led. A tender smile graced her lips as she looked across the kitchen at Tate. Even the thought of a visit from Bessie could not mar her joy as she basked in a vision of Selena wearing a wedding gown.

"Looks that way," Tate agreed. "Why don't you check out that stew and see if it isn't ready to eat, honey? Those boys of mine complained of empty stomachs all the way home from town. They'll be headin' in the back door before you know it."

"Yes..." She drew out the word, still caught up in the excitement Tate's news had engendered. "Perhaps they'll have a spring wedding, Tate."

"Maybe," he said agreeably, and then pounced, deciding to prevail on her good mood. "You want to drop Bessie a line and issue the invitation to come visit, Jo? Maybe she'd feel more welcome if it came from you."

There it was again, that faint reluctance as he spoke her name. But she brushed it aside and nodded. "Yes, I can do that. Do you think she'll wait till the weather breaks?"

"Don't know. Sounded like she was anxious to come. Trains run winter and summer, honey. No reason why she couldn't be here in a week or so, once she gets your say-so."

But the reply from Ohio was a surprise to Tate. When Bessie's letter arrived after the first of March, he found that she would not be making the trip until early April.

"That's all right," he said, watching while Johanna read the words Bessie had penned to him. "It'll give me time to make a trip to Chicago this month."

Johanna looked up quickly. "Why do you need to go to Chicago, Tate?"

"I'll be wanting to arrange sending that bunch of steers to the stockyards pretty soon. They've fattened up good over the winter."

Her brow furrowed. "But can't you do that without making a trip there? My father—" She paused, aware she was questioning his authority in the matter, unwilling to step on his toes. The cattle were his concern. He'd taken on their care, lifting the load from her shoulders. Now was no time to be shifting the burden. She was too glad to be shed of it.

"It will only be for a couple of days, Johanna. You and the boys will be fine here." He turned away from her, looking out the kitchen window, and a sense of disquiet seized her.

"Tate? I don't mean to interfere. I know the cattle are your concern, but..."

"Jo! Trust me in this, will you?" Unwilling or unable to meet her gaze, he offered her his back, and she heard his request with disbelief. "Johanna?"

It was a nudge for her to accept his decision, and she nodded. "Yes, I... You know I trust you, Tate." Indignation tinged her words, as if he had somehow insulted her by his asking for a verbal acknowledgment of faith.

He turned, and she was struck by the tenderness of his gaze. "I had no right to insinuate otherwise," he said quietly. Stepping from the window, he gained her side, reaching to clasp her hand, turning her to face him. "Anything I do is for you and my boys, Jo."

She bit at her lip, for once unsure of the direction in which he expected her to go. Life with Tate had been without surprises, except for that of finding herself in his bed. And that particular gift she was willing to accept without second thoughts. But today there was about him an air of secrecy, a quiet urgency she could not digest. As if he intended something she was not allowed access to. As if there were plans in the making that didn't concern her.

"Johanna, don't look so serious. This is something I've been meaning to do for quite a while. Now just seems to be the best time for the trip. Don't fuss, sweetheart. You'll be safe here. Sheba is a fine watchdog. And I'll ask Jonas Cooney to stop in and check on you if you like."

"No! That isn't necessary. We'll be all right." She bit at her lip again, hating the almost foreign sense of insecurity that was overwhelming her.

"I want you to write to Bessie again while I'm gone. Tell her to wire us the date she'll arrive. And I think we'd better not mention it to the boys until it's about time for her to get here."

Once he made up his mind about something, it appeared, Tate Montgomery felt no reason to waste time. Johanna felt she'd barely heard his plan to take the evening train to Grand Rapids and there board the early-morning Chicago express before he was packed and ready.

A faint sense of being shuffled about was blackening her disposition as he lifted her to the front seat of the surrey late on Monday afternoon.

"I think I need to take the reins, Tate," she announced as he climbed in next to her. Behind them the boys bounced on the second seat, excited at the prospect of watching the train arrive, thrilled at the prospect of what their father would bring them on his return from this trip.

"If you like." Amiable to a fault today, Tate handed her the leathers and leaned back, his arm riding the back of the seat as he turned his genial smile on her.

"I haven't driven your team but in the fields and down the street in town once or twice," she said, "and then it was with the wagon."

"You'll find a little difference with them pulling the surrey. It weighs less, and they tend to kick up their heels a bit."

Her eyes flashed a challenge. "I can handle them." She snapped the reins and clicked her tongue, and the team obeyed, settling quickly into a fast trot. Tails held high, hooves reaching forward eagerly, they headed for town. As if they sensed a different pair of hands on the reins, they behaved skittishly, heads bobbing, then tossing back, delighting Johanna with their antics.

"It seems I didn't need any practice with them after all," she announced, her chin tilting, her smile filled with satisfaction. The reins laced through her fingers, her feet braced against the floorboards, she controlled the prancing horses with ease.

Behind her, the boys urged her on, Timmy chortling his glee while Pete watched with a trace of envy. "When can I learn to drive the team, Pa?" he asked, leaning against his father's arm, peering between the two in the front seat.

"Won't be long, Pete," Tate answered. "We'll let you take a shot at it come spring, when we cut hay."

"Is that when I'm gonna get to ride one of the new mares?"

"Want to hear about a surprise, son?" his father asked, drawing out the query, as if there were some doubt as to the boy's answer.

"Sure!" Pete fairly danced on the floorboards, leaning to touch his chin on Tate's shoulder.

"I've ordered you a small saddle for your birthday. Thought it might be better than trying to learn on mine."

Pete's dark eyes lit with a blend of wonder and enthusiasm as he considered that idea. "Will I be riding the littlest mare, Pa? The red one?"

"That red is called chestnut, son," Tate told him. "She's going to be Johanna's to ride, but I'm sure she'll share her with you."

"Mine?" Johanna blinked at Tate's casual statement. "I don't ride, Tate. Pa never let me on his horse."

"Well, then, it's past time you learned, Jo. I think your pa—" He hesitated, wary of the disparaging remark he had almost uttered, fearful of tarnishing whatever small amount of good memories she held of her parent.

"I've been up on both of them. The bay is a little skittish, but the chestnut is quite a lady. They need to be ridden more before I trust Pete on a saddle, but before you know it, he'll be riding off to school."

The outskirts of Belle Haven surrounded them, and Johanna pulled back on the reins, holding the team to a more sedate pace as the shiny surrey rolled past the schoolhouse.

"It will be full dark by the time you get home," Tate said quietly. "I lit the lamp in the kitchen, so you won't have to go into a dark house."

Johanna sighed. Just when she was about to feel set adrift by his departure, he gave her reason to feel secure. No matter that she had been alone in the dark more nights than she wanted to remember over the past year or so. Tate was concerned that she not arrive at the farm with no light other than that of the moon and stars.

"If you don't wait for the train to leave, you can get back to the farm before nightfall," he said, leaning to speak close to her ear.

She shook her head. "I can't do that. We promised the boys they could see the train, and wave goodbye to you."

"I'll be back on Thursday morning, early, Jo." As though he recognized her unease at his going, he reminded her once more of his return. "I put the last two bushels of the snow apples on the wagon and covered them up good so they won't freeze in the barn. You can bring them along to town Thursday along with your butter and eggs."

"Thank you." She'd not looked forward to the chore of loading the last of her crop from the underground fruit cellar. She'd canned up all she wanted of them and dried more than she'd use till summer. It was time to be rid of the leftovers.

"I'm going to miss you." Her whisper had barely been given voice when she felt his hand rub against her shoulder and he bent closer to brush his mouth against her ear.

"I'll bring you a present too, sweetheart." The words were breathed against her flesh, bringing a shiver of delight, and she ducked her head.

"I'll just bet you will, Mr. Montgomery."

The general store was on the right, and Johanna pulled the team to a halt in front of the hitching rail. Tate climbed down, the boys on his heels and tied the short line, holding the horses close to the rail. He bent to scoot beneath the long pole and approached Johanna, raising his arms to her, his hands grasping her around the waist as he lifted her down.

"I'll get the eggs, Jo. You can carry the butter." He handed her the wicker basket she'd packed the golden rounds in, each of them about a pound and marked with the sign of a daisy pressed into the surface. The flower designated them as coming from the Patterson farm, and Johanna felt a sense of pride as she carried the heavily laden basket.

Tate held the door open, and she stepped inside the general store, Esther Turner's wave and smile greeting her from behind the far counter.

"Yoo-hoo! Johanna! It's good to see you. And you, too, of course, Tate." Beaming, she reached for the butter basket and placed it before her on the countertop. "We never have a bit of trouble selling this," she proclaimed, patting the handle. She opened the lid and counted the rounds within. "Twelve, as I see it, Johanna."

"Yes, and six dozen eggs, Mrs. Turner." Johanna motioned to Tate, and he placed the egg basket close at hand.

"I'll just put them in the crock," Esther said, her hands

quick as she transferred them, four at a time. "I declare, you do have the largest eggs of anyone around, Johanna."

"I kept the double yolks at home," Johanna said, willing her voice to be devoid of the rightful pride she felt at the storekeeper's praise.

"I could get a good price for them." Esther's words were coaxing. "The hotel likes serving them, and my Joseph thinks they're something special."

"So does my Tate," Johanna answered flippantly, and then flushed when she heard his laughter.

"You'll not get the best of her, Mrs. Turner." His tone was confidential as he leaned across the counter. "She's got a sharp wit about her."

"Johanna!" From the far corner of the store Selena Phillips called her name, and Johanna turned quickly.

"It's good to see you! I've wanted to talk to you, but I didn't get a chance after church yesterday." Hurrying to where the postmistress sat behind her desk, Johanna smiled her pleasure. "I heard you're going to the social with Mr. Shrader on Saturday."

Selena flushed a becoming pink and brushed at her hair with the back of her hand. "News travels fast." She leaned forward. "But I wanted you to know, Johanna. I'm not sure it's the right thing to do, but I couldn't say no when he asked me. He's...he's a kind man."

"Is that important, Selena?" Johanna's hand reached to cover the other woman's, and she squeezed gently at the slender fingers. And then answered her own query. "Of course it is. Kindness is a fine quality in a man." She glanced to where Tate stood at the counter, and her eyes softened.

"You were very fortunate, Johanna," Selena said softly. "I only hope I can be so lucky."

"With August Shrader? Do you care so much already, Selena? You've only—"

"I've been thinking about him for quite a while, Johanna," Selena said quietly. "We've passed the time of day, and he's dropped by my home of an evening several times."

Johanna's eyes blinked. "I didn't know that. I hadn't thought about the two of you till Tate told me about Mr. Shrader asking you to the social."

"We kept it very quiet. It really wasn't proper for him to call on me, with no chaperone present, but I felt beyond the stage of having to account for my actions. I'm forty-two years old, and if I want to entertain a gentleman caller, I think I'm within my rights."

"Yes...of course you are," Johanna agreed quickly, seeing the gentle woman with new vision. "You shouldn't be alone, Selena."

Selena looked down at her hands, folded in a graceful fashion before her. "Sometimes there are things in our lives we don't like to think about, or talk about, for that matter. It takes a special sort of man to understand those things, don't you think, Johanna?"

Johanna's breathing quickened, her heart pounding unevenly as she digested the oblique statement. Selena knew. Somehow, the secret Johanna had thought hidden from the world was known to this woman. "Yes," she whispered between dry lips. "Sometimes it takes a special man."

"I'm so glad you have Mr. Montgomery. I knew he was right for you. Just as I know Mr. Shrader is right for me." Selena smiled, a strange, sad little twist of her mouth. "We're very alike, my dear. Not in all things, but in some ways we're amazingly similar."

The door of the store opened, the bell sounding the entrance of another customer, and Johanna looked up. August Shrader stepped inside, hat in hand, and wiped his feet on the mat provided.

"There you are, Mr. Montgomery," he said, walking toward the counter where Tate stood. "Thought I'd save you a trip to the bank when I saw your surrey outside."

Tate moved quickly across the floor, grasping the bank-er's arm and turning back to the door. "Let's go outdoors and talk, August."

Johanna's brows lifted as the bell rang again, the door closing behind the two men. What could all that be about? Tate hadn't mentioned stopping at the bank today. She took one step toward the door, but was halted by Selena's low voice.

"Just men's business, I'm sure, Johanna."

Johanna hesitated, strangely uneasy. "Yes, I'm sure you're right," she said, her eyes still focused on the tall figure of Tate Montgomery outside the door.

The train station was just ahead, and Johanna eased back on the reins, pulling the team to a slow walk as they neared the red building.

"Will the train scare the horses, Pa?" Pete asked, wide-eyed, as he looked up the track, northward, where even now the iron monster was making its way toward Belle Haven.

"I don't know, Pete. Guess I'd better hold the harness when the engine lets loose with a blast, hadn't I?"

Timmy hugged the seat, only his head showing over the back. "Maybe I'll stay here in the surrey, Pa." His eyes huge with awe, he cast a wary glance at the chugging beast that neared the station.

Tate jumped down, striding to stand before the horses, holding their heads, but they needed no reassurance, giving scant notice to the noisy engine. He patted the satin noses of his team and turned to the surrey, snatching his sachel from the back before he looked at Johanna.

"Will you wave from here?"

She nodded. "I think so. Pete wants to get closer, though. Timmy and I will be happy to watch from the sur-rey."

Tate leaned over the side to snatch a kiss from his youn-gest son and whisper a word in the boy's ear. Then he reached to hold Johanna's chin in his palm and drew her face closer for his farewell, glancing around first, lest his action draw the notice of onlookers.

She kissed him, aware of a sense of loss, as if his leaving were causing a rift. Struggling with sadness, she accepted his caress and his whispered words of goodbye.

Within minutes, the train was heading south, Pete was trudging back to the surrey and she'd picked up the reins, turning the horses around for the trip home.

"How long is Thursday, Miss Johanna?" Pete wanted to know as he settled in the seat next to her.

"Three days," she answered.

"That's this many," Timmy said from behind her, waving his fingers beside her head. "Can I come up there and sit with you, too, Miss Johanna?"

"Yes, of course," she told him, pulling the team to a halt and lifting him over the back of the seat.

He settled next to her and, reaching up, took the ends of the reins in his hands, mimicking her movements as she urged the horses into motion.

"When I'm big as you, I'll be able to drive the team too, won't I?" His grin was infectious, and she answered it with one of her own.

"You can help me drive now," she told him, and then lifted him to sit in her lap, needful of the warmth of his small body against her own.

The surrey moved quickly, but not as rapidly as the setting sun, darkness overtaking the trio long before they reached the farm. Still a good distance away, from her kitchen window, a beam of light beckoned, and Johanna's heart was stirred.

Even in his absence, Tate had managed to remind her of his concern and caring. With determination, she set aside the unease that had plagued her this day.

Chapter Fourteen

The bed was terribly empty without Tate's warm body next to hers. Johanna punched her pillow, then brought his closer, hugging it against herself, doubting she'd be able to sleep. Yet even as she inhaled the scent of his shaving soap from the pillowcase that had known his head only that morning, she found her eyes closing.

For two days she lived with the memories of her lonely existence before Tate Montgomery had entered her life, and the process was enlightening. The boys were good company, and good help, for that matter. But the absence of their father was a blight on their days. Scarcely an hour passed when one or the other of them didn't mention Tate's absence. Johanna didn't have the heart to be impatient, for her own thoughts never strayed far afield from him, either.

Mr. Cooney had been there when they arrived home from the train station. He'd taken on the milking and much of the caring for the stock, trudging about with goodwill. That Tate had planned for this, asking the neighbor to lend a hand, was but another reminder of his thoughtfulness.

She'd told him once that her heart was full of love for him and his boys. Once, she'd said those words. And not again. The thought of his inability to feel that same deep emotion for her had somehow prohibited her from releasing her spoken avowal into his keeping.

So foolish she'd been. What did it matter if he never dealt in the rituals of courtship? Tate Montgomery had shown his caring in numerous ways over the months, had spilled his tender concern upon her from the first day. And she was stewing over his lack of love?

On Tuesday, Johanna churned butter and washed the eggs, sorting them into baskets, holding the largest for Tate's consumption. She fed the new mares and the heavier draft horses, enjoying the companionship of the big animals, talking to them in the same low, crooning fashion as had Tate. And in every task, every moment of those two days, she missed the man she'd married with a ferocious intensity.

Tuesday night found Timmy at her bedside, dragging his quilt behind him. She sat upright, startled by his appearance in the middle of the night, and reached for him.

"Timmy! Are you all right? What's the matter?"

He leaned against her, warm and soft and smelling like a little boy, a mixture she could not have described if she tried. She only knew it was a special aroma, peculiar to the children who lived in her house.

"I'm awake, Miss Johanna," he said through a yawn.

"So I see." She hugged him close, tugging him up onto the mattress beside her.

"Can I sleep with you?" he asked plaintively.

Arranging the covers over him, she tucked him next to her, just as Pete trailed through the doorway.

"Where's Timmy?" he growled.

"I'm sleepin' with Miss Johanna," Timmy piped up from his vantage point on his father's pillow.

"You can climb in, too, if you want to," Johanna said, pleased by the company the presence of the boys offered.

"Gimme the quilt, Timmy," Pete ordered, his tone bossy. He snatched up the heavy covering and climbed up to curl himself at the foot of the bed. Mumbling beneath his breath, he pulled the quilt around himself until all that could be seen was a blurred lump near Johanna's feet.

"Is today the day? Is this Thursday?" Timmy's question preceded him into the kitchen as he clambered down the staircase, his high-pitched voice bringing a smile to Johanna's lips.

Turning to the doorway, she welcomed the child with open arms, and he leaped into her embrace with vigor. "Yes, today's Thursday," she told him, her lips pressing kisses against his dark hair. How she loved this little bundle, this wiggling, chattering boy.

She looked up to see Pete leaning against the doorway. "When are we going to town?" he asked, stifling a yawn as he scratched his nose.

"As soon as breakfast is done and the chores finished." Johanna deposited Timmy on the floor and turned back to the stove. "The oatmeal is about done, Pete. Why don't you and Timmy put your coats on and feed the chickens, so Mr. Cooney won't have to? I'll need the eggs gathered, too."

"I don't like the chickens," Timmy offered. "They squawk at me."

"That's 'cause you chase 'em," Pete told him with a scowl.

"You don't like 'em, either." Timmy made a face at his brother as he tugged his coat from the peg by the door.

"That's 'cause they try to pick at me when I steal their eggs." Pete scowled at the younger boy, wrapping Timmy's scarf around his neck before donning his own heavy jacket.

"Put on gloves first, Pete. They can't hurt you that way." Johanna covered the oatmeal with a lid and opened the oven to check on the leftover biscuits she was warming, calling after the boys distractedly. "Hurry now! Breakfast is almost ready."

Still wrangling good-naturedly, the two boys left the house, and she glanced out the window to watch them crossing the yard. The sun was up, the eastern sky washed with its glory, and she closed her eyes for a moment. It was almost too much, this joy, this inner exuberance she felt sometimes.

Mr. Cooney was making his way from the barn, laden with milk pails, and she hurried to the door. "Yoo-hoo! Mr. Cooney! Would you like some breakfast? The biscuits are warming, and the sausage is ready."

Depositing his double burden by the springhouse, he opened the door. "I'll just take a couple with me, missus. My woman will be waiting breakfast for me at home."

The boys were inside the chicken house, and Johanna watched as the hens tottered down the ramp from the small entrance they used. They scurried around the fenced-in area, heads to the ground as they fed on the scattered corn Pete had provided. Timmy appeared, holding the door for his brother, and Pete emerged, carrying the blue-speckled pan full of eggs, his tongue tucked neatly into the corner of his mouth.

They made their way across the yard, then, with a great stamping of feet, came into the kitchen. "Here's your eggs, Miss Johanna." Pete carried his burden proudly. "We got almost two dozen this morning."

"That's more than all my fingers," Timmy announced, shedding his coat and scarf just inside the door.

"We gotta wash in here. It's too cold by the pump." Depositing the eggs on the cupboard, Pete made for the sink.

"I left you a pan of warm water," Johanna told him, her hands full of food as she carried sausage and the pan of oatmeal to the table.

"Hurry, Pete. We're gonna get Pa." Timmy rinsed his

hands, standing on tiptoe to reach the water, and dried them ineffectually on his shirt.

Breakfast was quick, the food disappearing rapidly, and then they were ready. Johanna headed for the barn, stopping by to pick up the butter she'd left, wrapped and in the basket, in the springhouse. Pete carried the basket of eggs, and Timmy ran ahead to open the barn door.

In a matter of minutes, she'd harnessed the horses and loaded the wagon, her fingers fairly flying as she fastened buckles, performing the familiar chore. In the full light of day, they set off for Belle Haven, Johanna's reticule containing the letter she'd written at Tate's request, assuring Bessie Swenson of her welcome come April.

And this morning, even that approaching event could not quell the happiness that rose within her.

There he was, waiting for the train to come to a full stop, one hand holding the pole, one foot already on the step, his satchel behind him. As the puffing engine passed, Johanna waited impatiently. The rail cars slowed, until finally, with a screeching of brakes, the iron wheels skidded on the tracks and the whole shebang rocked back and forth.

''Pa! We been waitin'!'' Timmy's shriek carried to the stationmaster, and beyond him, to the assortment of townsfolk who waited for the variety of goods to be delivered from the city. Mr. Turner's helper sat aboard an empty wagon. Selena Phillips stood in the doorway of the station house, empty mailbag in hand, waiting to exchange it for this morning's delivery.

And from the passenger coach, Tate Montgomery stepped to the platform, reaching back to swing his satchel from the train. Two small boys approached at breakneck speed, and he braced himself for their assault, bending to catch their bodies as they hurled themselves into his arms.

Johanna's tears came close to overflowing as she watched. Such fatherly love was beyond her imagining.

And then the big man on the platform lifted his gaze to where she stood, and she saw a change sweep over his features. His eyes narrowing against the rays of the sun, he scanned her motionless form. His mouth tilting up at one corner, he gave each portion of her anatomy a slow, thorough inspection that pleased her enormously, even as she blushed at his scrutiny.

With one boy in each arm, hat askew and face drawn by weariness, he approached. "Ma'am? Do you know these two scallywags?" he asked, squeezing the small bodies tightly.

"Pa! She knows us real good!" Timmy hollered, loudly enough to make his father wince and tilt his head away from the excited child.

"He's teasin' us, Timmy." Pete's scornful set-down went unheeded as Timmy wiggled to be lowered to the ground.

Running back to where the brown satchel had been abandoned on the platform, Timmy struggled to lift it, both hands wrapped around the handle. "Pa's got our presents in here, I'll betcha."

Tate bent, lowering Pete to the ground. "Help your brother with that, son," he said, his gaze still on Johanna.

And then he reached her, his hands circumspect as they rested on her shoulders, only the force of his fingers revealing the depth of his need. His kiss was brief, a mere brush of lips, but the breath he expelled against her cheek told her of his restraint. Never would Tate be less than a gentleman in public, but the effort was costly.

"Just wait till I get you alone." If it was meant to be a threat, he'd missed the mark, Johanna decided. Delivered in a growling, guttural tone against her ear, the words sent a thrill of anticipation down her spine.

"Did you bring me something?" she asked, sweetly and innocently, her eyes blinking a teasing message.

"A couple of somethings. But one of them will have to

wait,'' he told her, releasing her from his grip and turning back to where a boxcar was being unloaded.

A ramp was lowered to the platform, and from within the dark interior, a bellowing creature of enormous proportions was being led by a very sturdy-looking man. ''That's a red-and-white purebred shorthorn bull you're looking at, Mrs. Montgomery.'' He'd turned her to view the proceedings, and his hands were on her shoulders, his lips near her ear. ''How do you like your present, honey?''

''My present?'' She was bewildered, to say the least. Instead of getting rid of fifteen head of cattle, it seemed, they were about to take possession of a bull.

''How do you like him? Isn't he a dandy?'' Tate's enthusiasm was overcoming his weariness, if his excitement was any indication.

''We already have a bull.'' She hadn't seen the creature lately, but if the swollen bellies of the cows in the near pasture was any indication, the animal had done his job last year. Johanna didn't have to be close up to believe in the animal's prowess. She'd as soon he stayed out in the far corners of the farm. Bulls were worrisome.

Now Tate had announced that this beast was a gift meant for her benefit.

''I meant it as a surprise, Jo.'' Releasing her from his touch, he walked to where the stockman held fast to the bull's rope. The other end was looped through a ring piercing the animal's nose, and Tate gripped the rope tightly, controlling the bull with a knowledgeable grip.

''I'll tie him to the back of the wagon,'' he told her, leading his prize past where she stood.

Johanna followed him at a safe distance, her teeth biting at one corner of her mouth. ''He looks expensive,'' she ventured quietly.

Tate shot her a knowing grin. ''I'll say! I had to bid high for this one. But he'll be worth it, Jo.''

''I didn't know you were that rich, Tate.'' She'd seen

the ads for this kind of creature in the farm magazine her
father bought on occasion. A purebred shorthorn must have
cost a fortune. Well, perhaps not that much, but at least a
whole lot more than Johanna had in the bank.

"It would have taken everything I had left, Johanna."

"Would have?" She wrinkled her brow, not understanding his statement.

"Can we talk about this later, honey?" Tate tugged at
the rope, making sure of its knots as he tied the bull to the
back of the wagon.

"No, I don't think so," she said slowly. The thought of
riding home with that animal behind her gave her a feeling
of unease she could not have described. But she was even
more apprehensive about the eerie sensation that had seized
her at Tate's announcement. If he hadn't spent his bank
account on the bull, where had he gotten the money? She
doubted the men in Chicago had given him credit.

"Johanna? We need to hurry. We'll have to drop off the
apples, along with the butter and eggs, and I don't want to
have this bull in town any longer than we need to."

Butter and eggs and four bushels of apples were the least
of her worries right now, Johanna thought, her insides
twisting into an aching mass as she faced her husband.
"Where did you get the money?" She felt the blood leave
her face, felt it pooling somewhere deep within her, felt the
cold chill of disbelief sweep over her.

Across the width of the wagon, his mouth tightened, and
his gaze pierced her with steel-gray strength. "I took out a
small mortgage on the farm. Now climb in the wagon, Jo,
so we can get going."

Her feet felt made of stone, so heavy and huge inside
her boots, she feared she could not move one in front of
the other. But she did, turning from him to make her way
across the platform to where the wooden sidewalk led to
the center of town. Ahead of her, on either side of the road,
were the buildings making up the town of Belle Haven.

The bank, the livery stable, the general store and the hotel. Assorted shops and businesses touched, side by side, shop-keepers and early customers visible without and within.

She made her way, slowly at first, then more quickly as she heard the bells on the harnesses of Tate's horses approaching behind her. He slowed, keeping to her pace.

"Get in, Johanna."

She shook her head. "I'll walk, thank you." Chin high, she stepped quickly, her feet lighter now, her gait fueled by the flame of her anger. He'd mortgaged her farm. Without one word, without the suggestion of a consultation with her, he'd put her farm in jeopardy. And he'd dared to do it without a mention of it in her presence.

The appearance of August Shrader in the general store on Monday took on new meaning now. And the way Tate had hustled him out the door to conduct his business only proved his intent to deceive her.

A mortgage. Like the sword of Damocles, the word hung over her head, and she was threatened by it. The man she had trusted with her property, her livelihood, her very self, had betrayed her. And then expected her to be overjoyed with the resulting proof of that betrayal!

Her feet stomped harder as she traveled the wooden sidewalk. Beside her, the front door of the Belle Haven Hotel was a glittering expanse of beveled glass and mahogany, but she gave it not a moment's notice. The barbershop, marked by a peppermint-striped pole out front, barely caught her eye as she stepped firmly past its entrance. Even the newspaper office, home of the *Belle Haven Gazette*, was ignored.

Not until she reached the door of the general store did she pause, and only then, as if she'd been aware all along of the wagon keeping pace with her rapid footsteps, did she acknowledge its presence. Her gaze took in the mammoth creature standing meekly at its rear, the nose ring almost a guarantee of his compliance. And just inches from where his lead rope was attached to the wagon were her baskets of eggs and butter.

"Will you be so good as to hand me my baskets and then unload the apples?" Though her words had resounded warm and cheery in his ears fifteen minutes ago, her request now smacked of icebergs and icicles.

Tate leaned forward, his elbows resting on his knees, the reins between his hands, and observed his wife glumly. "I reckon I could do that, Johanna." Behind him, the two boys huddled together next to the apples, looking for all the world as if they needed a blanket to cover them, more than did the fruit. Their faces were pinched and wary, their eyes bleak, as if their existence hovered on the edge of disaster.

And even that terrible sight could not pierce the flaming fury that drove her. She recognized their panic-stricken mood. It was one she'd survived only minutes past. When she saw the bull and first became aware of Tate's ownership of it.

Her gaze went beyond the two children, to where Tate was lifting the fruits of her labor from the wagon. She'd been in partnership with her chickens and cows for years, and considered their contribution to her existence to be a given. She fed the hens, and they in return gave her their eggs, albeit not with any amount of grace on some occasions. The cows were another matter. They were more than happy to rid themselves of the milk swelling their udders twice daily. In all, a most satisfactory method of earning money, to Johanna's way of thinking.

She took her baskets from Tate's grip, not allowing him the courtesy of carrying them into the store for her, and he gave in to her without argument. And then she stood in front of the door, both hands full, and suffered the indignity of waiting for him to turn the knob, allowing her to pass through the portals of the store.

"Mrs. Montgomery!" Joseph Turner approached from behind the counter, hands outstretched, his wary glance bouncing from Tate, empty-handed in the doorway, to Johanna, heavily laden as she stomped across the floor in his direction. "Let me take those from you!"

It seemed his every word was emphasized this morning, Johanna thought, her smile strained as she gave over the weighty burden she bore. Not that she hadn't carried heavier in other times, but between the thumping of her heart and the throbbing at her temples, she was becoming suddenly weary.

Tate stalked back to the wagon and, with not a backward glance, Johanna followed the storekeeper to the far counter. Mr. Turner began unloading her eggs and butter, with a considerable amount of his attention on Tate's silent figure, transferring the crates of apples to the sidewalk. She watched stoically as Mr. Turner counted the rounds of golden butter, marking the number on a piece of brown wrapping paper. The eggs he transferred to a crock. She counted with him, noting that his larger hands each held six at a time.

His pencil stub calculated swiftly, and he drew his account book forward, thumbing through the pages until he came to the one with her name on the first line. "Adding in the apples, your credit's good for another good bit, ma'am," he said quickly. "What can I get you today?"

Johanna thought of the short list she'd committed to memory that morning and shook her head. "Nothing today, Mr. Turner." Not for a moment longer than necessary would she stand here, with Tate's brooding gaze drilling a hole in her back. Better that she survive the next few days without a supply of tea and vanilla and the rest of her needs.

Besides, the road to the farm was two long miles, and she intended to walk every step. The less she had to carry, the better-off she'd be.

Mr. Turner's head bobbed his farewell as she turned from him and headed back to the double door, her eyes focusing on the sidewalk beyond, hardly noting the grip her husband took on her elbow as she passed him.

"Get in the wagon, Johanna." It was an order, delivered in a voice that brooked no argument on her part. His fingers gripped her elbow firmly, holding her through the fabric of her coat. Even in her anger, she knew a moment of pride as she looked up at the dark-haired splendor of her husband. His nostrils flaring, his lips narrowed and firm, the scar on his face white against the ruddy anger painting his cheeks, he was a magnificent specimen of manhood.

And yet she defied him. Digging in her heels, she stopped, gritting her teeth at the pain in her arm as he continued on his way, unaware in his own wrath that she had failed to keep up with his lengthy strides. And then he released her, turning on his heel as he recognized her defiance. He faced her with both hands propped on his hips, great puffs of air pushed from his lungs by the force of his breathing.

"Just what the hell do you think you're doing?" He challenged his wife, uncaring of the townsfolk who had stopped their everyday doings to watch the small melodrama being played out before their very eyes.

She lifted her chin just the faintest bit higher, wondering if her neck would take the strain as she met his gaze. Her lips twisted in a caricature of a smile as she tilted her head to one side. "Why, I'm going to walk home, Mr. Montgomery."

"Ma'am!" The doors of the general store opened behind her, and Mr. Turner burst through, waving Johanna's baskets in his hands. "You forgot your butter and egg baskets, Mrs. Montgomery." His eyes were avid as he neared. "Can I put them in the wagon for you?" For the first time, he caught sight of the enormous bull tethered to the rear of the vehicle, and his steps slowed.

"You get a new bull?" he asked Tate.

Tate's glance was condescending. "Yeah, you might say

that,'' he drawled, moving a few steps in order to relieve the shopkeeper of the baskets he was gripping.

"Sure is a big one."

Selena Phillips's appearance at the door of the store caught Tate's attention, and he moved another few feet to speak to her. "Can you talk to Johanna?" A small note of desperation tinged his request.

She shook her head. "I don't think she'd listen to me right now, Tate." Her look was pitying as she faced him, meeting his gaze head-on. "She's quite angry, isn't she?"

He nodded, his flush deepening. "You could say that."

"I think you're the one needs to talk to her." Selena turned and went back inside the store, pulling her shawl tightly around herself, as if the chill in Tate's eyes had totally negated the warmth of the sunshine.

Johanna was several hundred feet ahead of him by the time Tate lifted the reins and cracked them in midair over the backs of his team of horses. The wagon rolled down the street, the bull keeping pace behind, and Tate held the reins in one hand, aware of the glances he was accumulating as he followed the woman he'd married.

She moved along at a smart pace until she came to the end of the sidewalk. Then the going was a little tougher, the choice between staying in the ruts or moving to walk in the stubble beside the road. Johanna chose the easier route, her boots stomping their way over the bumpy ground, still covered with a scattering of snow. She stumbled once or twice, almost going to her knees, and Tate caught his breath when she tripped.

If the blasted woman would only watch where she was going, he wouldn't be so worried. But her head was high and her eyes were straight ahead, never veering to check out the bumpy ground she traveled. He drove his team at a slow pace, their lumbering walk a travesty of the usual quick trot he demanded of them. But nothing would make him drive on home, leaving Johanna to follow. Only the thought of a physical confrontation in front of his sons kept him from climbing from the seat and forcing her to ride beside him.

It was going to be a long two miles, he decided. The acquisition of the bull had seemed to be a highlight of his life, one short day ago. The thought of Johanna's pleasure in the purchase had filled him with anticipation on the long, tiresome train ride. He'd sat up all night in the coach, striving for a few hours' sleep amid the noise of clanking rails and the total discomfort of the seat he struggled to fit his big body into.

And then he'd found that his wife did not share his long-range view of prosperity, guaranteed by the purchase of a bull who would over the next few years fill their pastures with a finer breed of cattle than had ever graced the Patterson farm. He'd dreamed of improving her herd. He'd planned this trip, on which he'd thought to show her his blueprint for success. Damn, the farm was theirs, not hers. He'd paid the not-inconsiderable mortgage her father had taken, two years ago.

He'd brought new life to the orchard, pruning and planting. He'd mended fences, hunted down recalcitrant cattle with the aid of Sheba, gathering her herd into a manageable group for the winter. He'd repaired and mended and attended to a farm that had been well on its way to collapse.

And for what? The very first time he asserted his share of ownership, taking out a small mortgage, instead of using the dwindling capital he'd banked in a savings account, she blew sky-high. Her anger was monumental, her fit of rage far out of proportion, as far as he could tell.

Let the woman walk! Maybe she'd get shed of some of her high-handedness by the time she made it home. It would serve her right if he just drove on past with the wagon and left her follow at her own pace.

His hands lifted, his muscles poised to snap the reins

once more, touching the backs of his team to urge them to a faster pace.

"Miss Johanna sure is mad, Pa," Pete whispered in his ear.

"Don't she love us anymore?" Timmy wailed from his spot behind Tate.

"Of course she does," Tate growled beneath his breath, relaxing his hold on the reins, his jaw tightening as he recognized his inability to leave her to fend for herself on the frozen ground with his sons fretting over the quarrel.

Certainly she was able to make it home by herself. She'd walked it alone before. But not lately. Not since her name was Montgomery, and he'd be jiggered if she'd ever walk it alone again. With a weary tilt to his shoulders, he drew his team to a halt, tying the reins to the post and jumping from the seat to the ground.

From the corner of his eye, he caught sight of her stiffened spine as she stepped up her pace, tripping again over a tuft of frozen weeds. And then he walked forward, grasping the harness of his gentle mares, leading them with his hand gripping the leather.

Just ahead, Johanna moved to the road, choosing to walk the fairly even path between the ruts. Behind her, he followed, walking apace, leading his mares, the bull behind.

Chapter Fifteen

❧

She'd planned to cook a big meal, welcoming Tate home. Instead, she'd put together a pitiful excuse for dinner that almost made her ashamed of herself. Cold leftovers from Wednesday night's supper, along with a pot of potato soup, had made up the meal, and Tate's look of disbelief had almost done her in. He'd managed to wrap pieces of yesterday's pot roast in a slice of bread and eat it, along with a bowl of applesauce and one of soup, before he excused himself to head for the barn.

Probably out there building a fancy place to stick his bull, she thought angrily. And if what Timmy had to say held any water, he had been. Not satisfied with a corral built from poles, he'd reinforced it with barbed wire, then added a lean-to, protecting his purchase from the weather.

She'd cooked up another pot of oatmeal for supper, opening a can of peaches and frying a panful of apples. Tate had cheerfully explained to the boys about fruit and oatmeal, coaxing them to sample both peaches and fried apples atop their bowls of oatmeal. Timmy had complained that oatmeal was for breakfast, but subsided when his father's glance of disapproval was aimed in his direction.

Tate had filled up on bread, once his bowl of oatmeal had disappeared, and for a moment she'd felt an overwhelming sense of shame as she repented her foolish stubbornness. She should have made him a meal. The man had worked hard all day, and she'd offered him a kettle of porridge.

To his credit, he hadn't made any noises she could classify as an objection. Just tucked into his supper and put away every living bite of food he could find. Her hands stilled in the dishwater. She might be mad, but she was obliged to uphold the terms of their bargain. And part of that included cooking good meals.

Tomorrow would be another story, she determined.

Her feet were heavy as she trudged up the stairs. Shod in stockings, she made no noise against the worn treads, but the weariness that had struck her following the walk home this forenoon had not left in the hours since. His disappointment in her weighed heavily on her shoulders, and only the knowledge that she had been right sustained her anger.

He'd brought that big red-and-white-spotted creature here and built him a fortress out back. Without so much as a by-your-leave, he'd decided to breed her cows this year to a highfalutin big-city bull bought on money borrowed against her farm. The insult was too great to be borne.

Her feet stomped on the top step, jarring her slender frame, but she ignored the soreness of aching muscles. He'd left her to run the place for three days—make that two, a sense of fairness amended. For this angry moment, she ignored the help he'd arranged for her. She'd cared for his boys and washed his clothes. In the washing machine he'd bought, without a murmur of reproach for the money spent, her honest heart reminded her silently.

She opened the door of her mother's sewing room. Even in the weeks she slept there, she had not claimed it as her own. She'd spent hours, wide awake and aware of the man just across the hallway, there in that bed. She'd looked out the window her mother had gazed from, stored her clothing in the small chest her mother had cherished.

It was still her mother's sewing room, no matter how many nights she'd spent there. And tonight would add to that number. No more would she curl against that masculine frame and soak up the warmth of his body. No more would those long arms enclose her in their embrace, holding the darkness at bay, easing her into a dreamless sleep as his hands touched her with the knowledgeable skill she'd come to crave.

She shook her head, closing the sewing room door behind her. Such nonsense. She'd slept alone for years. In no time, she'd have forgotten those nights in his bed. Johanna jerked her nightgown from its hook inside the wardrobe and spread it on the bed. Her fingers flew as she unbuttoned and untied the fastenings on her dress and underthings. The gown enveloped her as she shed her clothing beneath its folds and kicked them to one side.

Tomorrow was soon enough to be neat. Tonight, she was cold, and the quilts beckoned. With one swoop, she threw back the covers and slid between the cold sheets. Shivering, she pulled the quilts over her, burrowing beneath their weight.

Soon she heard him coming up the stairs and toward his room, his feet sounding heavy against the hallway runner. His voice rumbled as he opened the third bedroom door and spoke his good-nights to the boys, admonishing them to go right to sleep. And then he opened the door across the hall from where she lay.

Her ears strained in the silence, her eyes closing as she sought to catch any sound he might utter, any step he might take.

The doorknob turned, and the door opened. Even with her eyes closed, she could sense the light from the big bedroom against her lids. And then she felt his hand, covering her own where it clutched at the quilts beneath her chin.

"Johanna. I'm only going to say this once. You will sleep in my bed. You're gonna get up and march your little butt across the hall to my room and get yourself into that bed. I don't give a damn how mad you are or how high you tilt that sassy chin of yours, you're still my wife, and you will not sleep anywhere else but with me."

His fingers gripped the quilts, and he tugged them from her grasp, throwing them back, exposing her huddled form to his view. He lifted her upright in a series of movements that brought her to sit before him in a matter of seconds.

"Now get up." It was an order from a man who would tolerate no quibbling to a woman who had found new food for her anger.

That he dared to invade her bedroom, putting his hands on her person and ordering her about as if he had a right was more than she would tolerate.

Her mouth opened to tell him so. And then closed abruptly as she thought of the two little boys, awake and probably listening, just one room removed from where she was confronting this man of huge proportions. Any dispute, verbal or physical, would be sure to be overheard, and causing those boys any more distress was the last thing Johanna wanted to do.

She struggled to rise, at a disadvantage with Tate right in front of her. He solved the problem neatly, as if he had only been waiting for her to show a semblance of obedience. His arms scooped her up, holding her to his chest, giving her no option but to cling to his greater strength as he carried her across the hallway, into his room.

There he placed her on his bed. Then he turned his back to turn out the lamp and undress. By the time he was down to his underwear, she was curled up at the very edge of the bed, covered and tucked tidily beneath the quilts.

His grunt of disapproval was accompanied by one long

arm, snagging her and dragging her across the expanse of clean sheet until she was exactly where he wanted her—her bottom nestling against his loins, her back warmed by his chest and belly, her breast cradled by the palm of his hand.

Johanna took a shuddering breath.

"Don't say one word, Mrs. Montgomery. Just shut your mouth and close your eyes and go to sleep. I'm too tired and hungry to argue with you tonight."

The words he muttered in her ear were strangely comforting, she decided. He'd solved the problem neatly. Tomorrow she could be angry, when she was better fortified for the battle. For tonight she'd just let him think he'd settled her hash.

The darkness was filled with familiar sounds, his breathing, his small murmurs of satisfaction as he relaxed and shifted position, readying himself for sleep. And then the soft, subtle sounds of his snoring, the warm breath he expelled against her as he slept and the gentle squeezing of his hand against her breast.

It was going to be very difficult to hold her anger, she decided. In fact, for right now, she wouldn't even try.

Breakfast was a meal of monstrous proportions. Angry or not, she'd vowed to stick to her part of the bargain and she was determined to give him no more room to quibble over it. If Tate felt any amusement at Johanna's display of foodstuffs on the table, he hid it well. Murmuring a brief few words of grace over the meal, he set to with a calm purpose.

He ate four eggs, half a plate of bacon and six biscuits, covering them with two ladles of pale gravy before he settled down to his meal. There was a single biscuit left in the basket, and he took it, without even offering it in her direction.

"Any jam?" They were the first words he'd spoken to

her since the night before. She jerked in her chair as he spit
the question in her direction.

"Yes, of course." She felt Tate's eyes on her as she
opened a fresh jar of raspberry preserves from the pantry
shelf. Placing it before him, she backed away, conscious of
his gaze resting on her. Aware that his need of her body
had not been sated for several days, recognizing the flush
that rode his cheekbones, the steely glint in those gray eyes
that scanned her form, she trembled.

It didn't seem to matter to him that she was angry with
him. And if she knew anything at all about the matter, he
was not too happy with her, either. Still he watched her,
his mouth biting into the biscuit, his tongue swiping at a
bit of jam on his lip, his eyes never leaving her for a moment. He made a production of eating the two halves, finally licking a red dab from his thumb, his tongue again
darting out to catch the last particle of sweetness.

"I'd like chicken for dinner," he announced, shoving
back from the table.

Her mouth agape, she formed a protest. That he could
think to order her to cook to his specifications was an insult
not to be borne.

"Wow! Chicken? Fried chicken, Pa?" Timmy's awed
response to his father's decree was spontaneous.

"We haven't had fried chicken for a long time," Pete
added woefully, his eyes mournful as he aimed a look at
Johanna.

"We had fried chicken for dinner on Sunday." Gathering up the plates, she set her mouth primly, her movements
crisp and a bit more forceful than was usual. The heavy
china clunked noisily in her hands, the silverware clattering
to the tabletop.

"We'll have it again today," Tate said, rising and towering over her.

Pete and Timmy slid from their chairs, aware once more

that the two adults in their lives were not behaving in their usual manner.

"Miss Johanna? Did you wash my old hat like you were gonna?" Timmy tugged at her skirt, his words quietly catching her attention.

Johanna looked down, her fit of pique set aside for the moment. "It's behind the stove, on the rack, Timmy. I rinsed it out yesterday morning."

He ducked his head, a gesture of thanks, and she rested her hand on him, aware of the distress she'd placed on that small, sloping shoulder. "I'll get it for you," she offered, lifting the plates she'd piled on the table and carrying them to the sink. Quickly she reached behind the stove, where assorted items of clothing hung across the wooden rack, and snatched up Timmy's hat. Knit of coarse wool, it showed signs of wear, and she determined to spend the next evening or so in making him a new one. Carrying it to where he waited, she met his gaze and smiled.

"How would you like a new hat? Maybe red, so I can see you easier out in the yard?" Her fingers were gentle as she tugged the cap into place on his dark head, tucking his hair beneath the edge.

"A new hat? This one is still good, Miss Johanna." As if the lessons of practicality had been taught him at an early age—and he barely four years old—he protested his need.

"A red one would be better," she countered, leaning to brush a quick kiss across his forehead.

Pete watched the proceedings from across the room, shoving his arms into his coat, searching in his pocket for the cap he'd thrust there the day before. He jerked it into place atop his head and glared at Timmy. "Mine has a hole in it, and I don't complain," he said angrily.

"Timmy didn't complain," Johanna told him. "And if you want a new hat, just say so and I'll knit one for you."

"My aunt Bessie made this one, and it's good enough."

As if that were the last word on the subject, Pete turned, heading for the door.

"Don't be rude, Pete," his father reprimanded softly.

"Beg your pardon, ma'am," he muttered, his eyes averted as he obeyed Tate's unspoken order.

"I'd really like to make you a new hat, Pete," Johanna said quietly. "I have blue and green yarn left over. Would you like a striped one?"

The boy cast a glance at his father and pressed his lips together for a moment. "Yes, ma'am, that would be fine," he allowed, easing his way out the door.

Tate paused, drawing on his gloves, hunching his shoulders beneath the heavy coat he'd donned. "Do you want me to catch a chicken and kill it before I go out back?"

Her look was far from benevolent as she slanted it in his direction. The softness she'd bestowed on Timmy, the understanding she'd offered Pete, had disappeared. Left for Tate Montgomery was the scornful look of a woman thwarted in her revenge. He'd hauled her from her chosen place last night, forcing her into his bed, and she'd found the process far from punishing. There was no other method whereby she could silently state her position.

Her mouth pinched, her eyes flashing, she faced him. "I caught and killed chickens before you ever set foot on my farm, Tate Montgomery. Just go out there and take care of your bull, and I'll tend to fixing the dinner you ordered."

A shutter seemed to fall behind his eyes, darkening the gray to a steely black, and his jaw clenched, a visible response to her smarting reply. "You just do that very thing, Mrs. Montgomery," he told her coldly. "I'll be back in at noon. Have it ready."

She closed her eyes, hearing the door shut quietly. He was too angry with her to even relieve some of the pressure by slamming the door, she thought. She'd never seen quite that degree of icy calm in Tate before. Perhaps she'd gone too far. He'd been willing to make amends of a sort, if her instincts were to be relied upon. He'd enjoyed his breakfast. If only he hadn't ordered up his dinner as if he were eating at the hotel dining room in town.

She dumped hot water from the stove on the dishes, adding a handful of soap from beneath the sink, sloshing it around to form suds. The silverware followed, disappearing beneath the surface. She poured the residue of coffee from her cup and then lifted Tate's to her mouth, sipping the last of the cooled coffee into her mouth. She imagined it bore the faintest trace of the taste of his mouth—utter foolishness, she decided, plopping the empty cup into the dishpan.

Snatching her hatchet from the pantry, where she kept it hung between two nails, she headed for the back door. The air was cold, but the sun was warm against her back as she stalked to the henhouse. There were two young roosters left from last spring's hatchings, and they needed to be caught up and gotten out of the way before she readied the brooding area for spring.

Today would take care of them, and with a vengeance fired by her confrontation with Tate she headed for the two unwary creatures she'd settled upon, her hatchet at the ready.

"Did you mail the letter to Bessie?" Tate wiped his mouth with his napkin and leaned back. The chicken had been fried to a fare-thee-well, the potatoes creamy, the vegetables flavored with bacon grease and onions and cooked all morning on the back of the stove. He'd enjoyed every bite, savoring the crisp coating Johanna used on her chicken, relishing the pale gravy she'd placed before his plate. Now came the moment of truth. He'd told her to write the letter, given her three days to accomplish the deed.

"I took it along to town yesterday, but I forgot to mail it," she said, only now remembering the presence of the envelope in her reticule. "We can do it Monday."

He nodded, aware that the anger between them had no doubt chased all thought of the letter from her mind. Johanna was an honest woman. If she said she'd forgotten, then that was what had happened. Devious, she was not.

"The chicken was good, Johanna. Thank you." His gaze traveled to the countertop. "Is that a pie?"

"Yes." She pushed back from the table, leaving her plate half-full of food, eyeing it with distaste. That Tate had so thoroughly enjoyed her cooking, while it stuck in her craw like so many bites of dry bread, was a fact that irked her mightily. The sense of disquiet she'd lived with all day had blunted the edge of her appetite, and even the dried-apple pie she'd baked held little appeal.

Her knife was quick as she sliced it into eight equal pieces, lifting one to place on a small plate for Tate. She served it, her left hand taking his dinner plate, even as she substituted the pie for it. The apples oozed from the crust, the thick juice dripping to settle on the plate, the spicy scent of cinnamon rising to tempt her nostrils.

A spasm of nausea rose in her throat, and she swallowed against it, blinking as she recognized its recurrence. The same thing had happened yesterday, and one day last week. Sweets simply were not agreeing with her these days, and she frowned at the thought. Apple pie was her favorite, and suddenly she had no appetite for it.

"Pete? Timmy? Do you want pie, too?" Turning away from Tate, she made her offer, and the boys responded with nodding heads, Timmy still chewing on a chicken leg as he craned his neck to catch sight of the pie.

"Yes, ma'am," Pete said quickly, as if he remembered the chastisement earlier and was intent on a polite reply before his father should take note.

Johanna brought them their dessert and then picked up the coffeepot. "Tate?"

He held his cup toward her. "Yes, please." Then watched as she filled it. "Are you feeling all right?"

Her look in his direction was quick. "Yes, of course."
But she wasn't, and the falsehood made her blush. She
fussed at the stove, moving the coffeepot about, lifting a
burner lid to check on the fire inside, her fingers testing the
temperature of the water in the reservoir. Hot to the touch,
it gave her an excuse, and she took it, reaching for a pan
and filling it. She carried it to the sink, splashing it in the
dishpan, adding soap and readying for the dishwashing.

Tate came to stand behind her, his footsteps almost silent, only the warmth of his body behind her making her
aware of his nearness. "Jo?" One large hand rested on her
shoulder, and he pressed his fingers against her, their movement sending a cascading shiver down her spine.

Her eyes closed and she gritted her teeth against the unwanted reaction. So easily he was able to affect her, her
body so ready to lean to his bidding that she was barely
able to resist turning to him.

"Jo! Look at me." Reaching past her, he took the pan
from her hand, dropping it with a clatter on the drainboard.
His hands turned her to face him and she was pinned
against the sink, her heart thumping in the her throat. Sliding from her shoulder to her face, his palm cupped her chin,
lifting and coaxing until she bent to his will.

"I'm fine, I'm fine!" Like puffs of wind blown by a
spring breeze, the words burst from her lips. She bit the
inside of her cheek, fighting to keep from shedding the tears
that had formed without her knowing. If only his hands
were not so warm, his eyes not so filled with concern. If
only...

Tate's voice was low and carefully controlled. "Boys?
Pete, take your brother into the parlor. Find your books and
tell Timmy about the pictures, will you?"

"Yes, Pa." His tones subdued, Pete eyed the last bite of
pie on his plate and scooped it onto his fork. "Come on,
Timmy." Tugging at his young brother's arm, he set off
for the parlor.

"Tate, let me go." Johanna lifted her hands to push against his broad chest. But he would not be moved. Blinking rapidly, she looked at his shirt, focusing on the fourth button, unwilling to meet his gaze. "Please, Tate." She tried again, testing his strength, and finally, with a groan of despair, allowed her head to drop against his chest.

"Jo…" It was a whisper, a pleading, needful sound that was almost her undoing. "Jo? I can't stand to see you this way. I know you're angry with me, but I need to set things right between us."

"You put a mortgage on my farm. It doesn't matter what you say to me, Tate. You can't deny what you've already done. Paying off my land and my house…those were the terms of our marriage. And now you've gone behind my back and…"

"You don't trust me to pay it off?" His whisper was harsh, unbelieving, in her ear. "You think I'm not capable of making the payment when it's due?" He shook her, firmly and quickly, and she looked up, startled.

"Do you have any idea what a new bull will do for your herd? Have you any idea how much that purebred shorthorn will be worth to this place?"

"No! Of course I haven't! How could I know? You went off to Chicago… Or is that where you really went? Anyway, wherever you went, you bought a bull and brought him back and never even talked to me about it first!"

He was stunned, his eyes registering the disbelief he felt. "It was a surprise! And beyond that, handling the stock and the buying and selling is my end of the bargain. I wouldn't think of questioning you about your share of this deal. You do as you please about the house, the buying at the general store, the use of your butter-and-egg money. Not once have I asked you to account for anything, have I?"

She shook her head. "No, you haven't. But then, I

haven't taken it upon myself to borrow money at the bank to finance my plans, either.''

''Mr. Shrader wouldn't lend it to you, anyway.'' His voice was grumpy, almost sullen, as he stared at her, exasperated by her reply.

''That's why I married you, Tate. Because a woman alone has nothing. No security, no clout in financial matters, no say-so when it comes to the bank or the mill or the stockyards.'' Her frustration had reached its peak, and she jerked her arms from his grip, uncaring of the bruises she would wear tomorrow or the stunned expression on his face.

''And that's all I mean to you? Security? Clout? A man to do your bidding and mind your orders? I'm not to make any decisions of my own?'' He waited, unwilling to release her, holding her with the force of his body, his hands clenched at his sides.

She paused, absorbing the words he spoke, listening to his angry questions, realizing for the first time the unfair advantage she'd held. Her breathing was ragged, her mouth was dry, her lips were open as she caught her breath, vainly seeking release from his presence. She needed to think, she needed to consider what he had done, perhaps look at it from another point of view.

Most of all, she needed to catch a deep breath.

''Damn!'' His hands slid beneath her arms, holding her erect. She'd gone all limp against him. He recognized the shuddering breaths she took, the way her head lolled to one side; Johanna was about to faint in his arms.

Quickly, he lifted her, carrying her to the table where he dropped into a chair, holding her on his lap. ''Johanna!'' It was a strained whisper, his mouth brushing over her forehead. She drew a shuddering breath, then another. ''Here, take a swallow of my coffee,'' he said, holding the cup to her mouth. She obeyed, gulping the tepid brew.

"I'm all right," she said softly, struggling to rise from his lap.

But he held her fast. "Sit still! I mean it. You're upset and shaky. Just stay right here for a minute." He pressed the cup to her lips again, and she swallowed another mouthful.

"We're not going to talk about this anymore today," he told her firmly. "You're going to go up and take a rest, hear me? I want you on my bed, and I want you to stay there for at least an hour."

One arm held her, his fingers pressing against her hipbone, the other hand gripping hers, supporting and half lifting her as they climbed the stairs. In seconds, she was on his bed and he'd slid her shoes from her. Then, tossing the quilt over her, he tucked it beneath her feet. Her face was pinched, her lips colorless and her eyes wary.

"Stay here for a while, hear?" At her nod, he bent low to brush a kiss across her forehead. "I know you're still mad at me, and that's all right. But for now, just forget it and sleep awhile."

"Supper…" she began, but halted as he shook his head.

"You cooked enough chicken for a small army. We'll eat it cold, and between us we'll find enough to make a meal."

And if she didn't eat any more at supper than she had at the noon meal, he didn't think they'd have to scrape up much for her benefit. Johanna was pining, or ailing, or just off her feed for some reason. Whatever the reason, he didn't like the looks of her, all pale and shaky as she was.

Anyone would think she was in the throes of morning sickness or something.

His mind stopped its forward progress and beat a hasty retreat. Her reaction to the pie, her easy tears—for he'd seen the struggle she'd gone through to hide the evidence of her distress. The crankiness he'd never before associated with the woman he'd married.

Tate Montgomery looked down at his wife, and his eyes were thoughtful. Could it be? Of course, his sensible self replied. He'd been making love to her with regularity for over three months. If his seed hadn't taken root by this time, he'd have been surprised, now that he thought about it.

And yet, she didn't seem to have considered the idea. He tried to remember the past weeks. Had she had a monthly flow? His mind searched in vain. Not for at least two months, she hadn't. Maybe longer. And that pretty much solved the puzzle as far as he was concerned.

He looked down at her, noting the faint flush on her cheeks, her mouth, open just a little, the edges of her teeth showing, and the regular rise and fall of her breasts as she gave in to the weariness that had overtaken her. She was a sturdy little thing, his Johanna. His Johanna.

His Johanna was likely carrying his child.

It was more than he could contain, the sudden joy that swelled within his breast, and he turned from the bed, lest he allow a whoop of delight to awaken the woman sleeping on his pillow.

Chapter Sixteen

He'd been true to his word, working beside her as they put together a meal. She'd slept much longer than an hour, to find the sun fast heading for the horizon as she awoke. Tate and the boys were on their way in, hungry and ready for a meal, as she entered the kitchen and reached for the lamp.

By the time they gathered beneath the golden glow it cast, she'd gotten her wits together and tied her apron in place. A jar of green beans put on to heat and a pan of corn bread, mixed quickly and placed in the oven, were her contribution. Tate set the table and uncovered the plate of chicken left from dinner.

"I sure am glad you fried two chickens, Miss Johanna." Pete was willing to be amiable tonight, and for that she was grateful. He waited at the table, barely able to keep his eyes from the food as she found one thing, then another, to add to the assortment.

Do we have any syrup, Jo?" Tate asked from the pantry.

"Yes, of course." She dried her hands hurriedly and joined him in the narrow space, squinting in the dim light, seeking the metal tin. "It's here somewhere. We had some on pancakes while you were gone."

"Pancakes, without me?" he teased carefully, his dark gaze intent on her face.

"The boys asked for them." Her words were a mumble as she scooped the tin from the lower shelf and backed into the kitchen.

He followed, sensing her retreat. She wasn't ready yet for a truce, and he sat down at the table, watching her as she moved around the kitchen. She was more like herself, it seemed, her color back to normal, the circles beneath her eyes gone for now. Maybe tonight…maybe they could come to an understanding.

But it was not to be, for when Tate finally left his desk and climbed the stairs to his room, it was to find Johanna sound asleep. He undressed and crawled beneath the covers in the dark, and his hands were gentle as he gathered her in his arms.

She mumbled a few words, his name interspersed among them, then settled against him with a sigh that smacked of contentment, if he was any judge. Perhaps in sleep she was able to be purged of the anger that had made her so unhappy during the past days. Maybe tomorrow would find them on better terms, with Johanna seeking him out, as was her wont. He'd missed her company all day, but at least she'd stopped glaring at him. And for that he would be grateful, he decided.

She'd been tolerant of him today. Tomorrow he'd try for friendly.

By the end of a week, he'd decided that tolerant was as good as it was going to get. He was horny as hell, and even though he enjoyed her cuddling against him while she slept, he wasn't sure how much longer he could keep his hands to himself.

And Johanna was giving him no encouragement.

He moved his milking stool to the next cow, the pride of Johanna's herd, a small, gentle jersey. He'd done a powerful lot of thinking in his day, working with animals. Today was not any different. The rustling of hay in the manger, the swishing of the Jersey's tail and the warm scent of milk rising to his nostrils surrounded him as he worked, and he was comforted by the familiarity of the chore.

His eyes closed as he thought about Johanna. She'd kept to her part of their bargain. In fact, if anything, the meals she'd been cooking for the past days had surpassed his expectations. As if she were trying to make up for that one day of rebellion, she'd done her best to keep him well fed.

She was pleasant in front of the boys, sweet as pie to Esther Turner at the general store, and downright enthusiastic when she spoke to Selena Phillips.

She'd agreed, a bit grudgingly, to go to the social at the church hall on Saturday, and then spent the evening with the womenfolk. He'd asked her to join in a square with him when the fiddles tuned up and the caller got set up on the platform. She'd politely excused herself and helped with setting up the food tables instead.

He'd watched her for a while, then spent the rest of the time with the older ladies, dancing up a storm. Selena Phillips had accepted his invitation with good humor, and from there he'd gone on to Marjorie Jones and Esther Turner, swinging them with enthusiasm, sending their skirts flying.

Lifting his forehead from where he'd rested it against a brown flank while he milked the last cow, he drew a deep breath. They needed to talk. Not just "Pass the milk," and "Is it warmer out today?" It was time for Johanna to have her eyes opened to a few things. She needed to know his reasons for what he had done.

He was about ready to sit his wife down and give her a quick tour through her father's desk. He'd never seen such a mishmash of record-keeping as Fred Patterson had left behind. Tate's evenings spent trying to make head or tails of the mess had been most frustrating. The old man had about reached the end of his financial rope by the time he died, as far as Tate could tell.

The herd of cows had been let go almost beyond redemption, except for the new milkers Johanna had apparently insisted on, the Jersey and a spotted guernsey. There was no way to tell just how old that scrawny bull out there in the far pasture was, but it was for sure that he was past his prime. Not worth much, no matter how you sliced it. He'd decided right off that new blood was in order, and to his way of thinking, the purchase of the shorthorn was the best move he'd made yet. Within a couple of years, the calves that bull produced would bring in more money than Tate had spent on the animal. The steers he sired would be heavier, the heifers would produce more milk, and the calves would be stronger.

And that was worth a heap, Tate decided, carrying the last pails of milk across the yard toward the springhouse. The door was propped open, Sheba sitting just outside, as if she were standing guard over her mistress. Within, he caught sight of Johanna, the churn between her knees as she lifted the lid, checking out her progress. The early-morning sun was caught and reflected by her golden hair. She'd twisted it atop her head, not taking time to braid it, then haphazardly pierced the gleaming mass with large bone hairpins to keep it out of her way.

"You're churning early. Is it done?" Pausing in the doorway, he rested for a moment.

She nodded. "Yes. I thought it felt about right." She pushed the churn aside and rose from her chair. Reaching for an empty pail, she tilted the churn, ready to drain off the skim.

"I'll take that out to the pigs for you," Tate offered, depositing his burden on the low table. He bent to where she worked and took the weight of the churn from her, careful to hold the lid in place, so as not to lose any of the butter.

She looked up at him, her eyes wide at his nearness. "I can take care of it, Tate."

He shrugged. "I know you can. I just wanted to help. I'd as soon you didn't lift the heavy pails, anyway."

Her laugh was strained. "I've been lugging heavier than this for years. Getting married didn't take away any of my strength. I'm a strong farm woman, Tate."

His gaze swept over her, easing its way from her face down the length of her body; his lips thin, and his nostrils flaring. Her dress was snug across her breasts, outlining them for his viewing, and he paused there in his survey. The woman did have a fine figure, and unless he missed his guess, she was filling out that dress even more than usual.

How could she not know? He swung his gaze back to her face and smiled. "Yeah, you sure do look strong and healthy to me, ma'am. Fact is, I'd say you're a prime piece of womanhood."

Her flush was instantaneous, sweeping up from her throat to cover her cheeks with a rosy hue. Her eyes sparkled— perhaps with aggravation, he thought, but shiny and tempting nevertheless. It was more than he could resist, the privacy gained by the small building, the look of her, dampened curls at her temples from the hard work she'd accomplished, and the neat, rounded figure so near.

He lowered the churn to the floor and wiped his palms against his pant legs, his eyes never leaving her face. And then he reached for her, his hands at her waist, lifting her against him until they were eye-to-eye.

"Tate! Put me down!" She reached to balance herself, her hands gripping his shoulders.

"I need you, Johanna." It was a primitive response to her nearness, his body reacting quickly, his thighs taut with the tension of his arousal, his feet apart as he braced himself. The scar on his face was livid against the ruddy hue of his cheekbones, his eyes darkening as he spoke the challenge aloud.

"Tate! Put me down!" she repeated, whispering now, as if she sensed the tension he could no longer suppress. Her eyes were frantic as she looked past him at the open doorway. "The boys will see you, Tate."

"Kiss me, Johanna." As if her words had gone unheard, he growled the command, his fingers tightening against her resilient flesh.

A shiver passed through her body, and she shook her head. "No, not here."

"Just a kiss." He nudged her, his mouth hot against her cheek as she turned her face from him.

Her breath was indrawn, a shuddering sound as she inhaled through her mouth. "Put me down first."

His muscles quivered as he lowered her to the floor, and his hands slid to cover her back. "Now." Giving her no quarter, he bent to her, his mouth opening over hers, claiming the caress he'd demanded as his due.

She was stiff in his embrace, but only for a moment, and then she softened, leaning against him, tilting her head to better receive him. Her woman's need rose within her, the temptation of his arms and hands, the heated, damp pressure of his mouth adding to her yearning. She'd learned well the lessons he'd taught through the long night hours, and her body responded to the familiarity of his touch.

"Johanna!" It was a soft cry of torment, and he buried his face in her throat, as if the temptation of her mouth were more than he'd bargained for. And then he released her, his fingers sliding reluctantly from her back.

He reached down for the pail of skim milk, afloat with small globules of butter. "I'll take this out to the pigpen," he said, his voice roughened by emotion.

"Breakfast is ready, Tate. I left it warming in the oven before I came out here."

His nod accepted her announcement, and he turned from

her. "We need to talk, Johanna. There's a lot you need to understand, about the farm and your father's way of doing things."

"After breakfast?"

He shook his head. "I've got too much to do this morning. Let's make it tonight, after supper, when the boys go to bed."

"All right. After supper."

"We need to settle this between us." Tate sat at the desk, Johanna beside him in a chair he'd brought from the dining room. "Have you ever gone through your father's records? Looked through his books?"

She shook her head. "No. He took care of the money. I only knew that his bankbook was in the drawer, and when I saw how little he had in his savings account, I figured the farm hadn't done well for a while."

Tate nodded. "He'd run his herd into the ground, Jo. That bull out there is about petered out. He should have gotten rid of him a long time ago. The cattle he was selling to the stockyards weren't bringing in enough to support the place. That's why he got a mortgage a couple years back. He'd been getting along on the money ever since, and not making any headway."

Her frown deepened. "What can we do?" The knowledge that her father had neglected the farm came as no surprise. She'd known that the fences and outbuildings had fallen into disrepair, but maintaining the house and garden had kept her busy. Besides, Fred Patterson had not welcomed anyone else's ideas about his place, least of all those of the daughter he'd almost totally ignored over the past ten years.

"I've already done it, Johanna. That bull was about the best idea I could come up with. The herd needs new blood. He'll produce bigger steers, and the new heifers will make better milkers. You need to get rid of four of your old ones, anyway. They'd be better off producing calves after we get some new milkers out of the shorthorn.''

"So, why didn't you talk to me about it first?" Her mouth was set in a stubborn line and she glared at him, the old argument still unsettled, as far as she was concerned.

"We've already had this conversation, Johanna. I did what I thought was best, and I'll not apologize for that."

She rose from the chair, hands rising to rest against her hips. "What conversation? The one where I ask for an answer and you give me the same old story? It's down to what you decide, isn't it? Like I'm not supposed to have anything to say about this place."

He looked up at her and gave a sigh that bespoke extreme tolerance. "Look, I know you're not feeling well, but there's no need for you to get so unreasonable."

"Unreasonable! You think it's unreasonable for me to express an interest in your spendthrift ideas?"

"Now, hold on for just a minute," he blurted out, rising to his feet as if he must be on equal ground.

She stepped back, tripping over a wrinkle in the carpet and losing her balance. His hand came out swiftly, automatically, grasping her arm, holding her until she caught her balance. And then she cast his help aside, her look scornful.

"Don't touch me, Tate. You think you can coax me by your sweet talk and your niceties, but it isn't going to work. I just can't believe you'd go behind my back and put my farm in jeopardy. I lived with not knowing whether I was about to lose this place or not after my father died. The whole reason we got married was so I'd never have to worry about such a thing happening again."

"And you don't trust me to make the payments?"

She drew in a shuddering breath. "So what! You can't even trust me enough to tell me about—" Her lips clamped shut, forming a mutinous line.

"Tell you about what?" he roared.

"About that scar you've got! About what happened with your wife!"

"You're my wife! Belinda is in the past," he growled, lowering his tone as he cast a glance toward the open door.

"You know what I'm talking about, Tate!" She gritted her teeth at his bullheadedness. "Then I guess there isn't much else to say, is there?" she said quietly. "You've got an answer for everything. I told you all there was to know about me and...and—" Her voice broke as she groped for words, and she shook her head, unwilling to continue.

"I'm going up to bed, Tate," she told him, turning away.

"I'll be up in a minute," he said. "Leave the chair. I'll put it away when I'm done."

Sensing his eyes upon her, she escaped the small room he'd made his own over the winter months. She climbed the stairs, thinking of his presence in that room of her father's. Tate's account book was neatly placed in the center of the desk, accessible should she care to open the cover. His pens and pencils were in the desk drawer, the spectacles he used when he did close work in a leather case beside them.

His books were lined up between heavy brass bookends. Books dealing with the care of animals, periodicals from far-off places with pictures of cows and bulls gracing their pages. Her Sears catalog had been brought to his desk, and she'd seen it open tonight to a page of women's clothing, catching only a glimpse before he swept it from her view, placing it on the far corner of the desk. The room was clean—she'd swept the carpet herself this morning and dusted the desk, careful not to disturb his papers.

Her days of being denied entry to that male sanctuary were gone. The door remained open now, Tate frequently leaning back in his chair to hold one or the other of his sons on his lap while they told him of their day's doings. It was a different household since Tate Montgomery had come into her life. A better place to be.

She climbed the stairs slowly, her thoughts confused as she sought vainly to sustain the anger she'd felt for the past week. Perhaps he'd been right to buy the bull. If only he'd told her first, asked her about the new mortgage. But would she have told him to go ahead with it?

She paused at the doorway to their bedroom. No, she probably would have backed from the suggestion, her fear of being indebted to the bank a strong deterrent to such an idea. But he should have told her. Stubbornly she clung to the thought. He'd gone behind her back and mortgaged the farm. Once more she was at the mercy of the bank.

She undressed slowly and crawled beneath the quilts, her pillow drawn as close to the side of the bed as she could get it. She'd been awakening every morning in his arms, and for the life of her she could never figure out how she'd gotten there. He made no excuses, releasing her reluctantly as she pushed away from his warmth in the early-morning darkness, and she shivered as she thought of the promise of pleasure those strong arms held.

His footsteps were almost silent as he came up the stairs and down the hallway. She'd left the lamp burning, a low flame that sputtered as it struggled to stay lit. In the faint glow, she watched from beneath lowered eyelids as Tate slid his suspenders from his shoulders and opened the front of his trousers. As if he welcomed her scrutiny, he undressed in front of her, sitting to remove his stockings, shedding his shirt to the floor and stripping off his trousers with one swift movement.

She knew he'd seen her watching, had caught the quick flicker of his eyelids as he glanced toward the bed. And yet she could not look away. He went to the dresser and turned the wick on the lamp, until only the moonlight from the window lit the room. Then, clothed in his underwear, he walked from her view, to the foot of the bed and around behind her.

The mattress gave when he sat on it, the cool air rushing

beneath the covers when he lifted them. His big body filled the other side of the bed as he stretched his long legs to press against the foot board.

As surely as if she were facing him, she could see him there, looking up at the ceiling, arms bent, his hands stacked beneath his head. And then she turned over, tugging impatiently at her nightgown as it twisted about her legs.

He tilted his head, looking at her, his eyes barely discernible in the darkness, and the need for his touch rose within her like the bubbles in a kettle coming to a full boil.

She swallowed, her throat constricting. "Tate? I'm sorry I've—" Her voice failed her, the words she had thought to say seeming to be lodged in her chest.

"Sorry?" His movement was rapid and almost overwhelming as he turned onto his side, blocking the light from the window behind him.

She tried again, moistening her lips and closing her eyes, as if not seeing him loom over her might make it easier to speak. "I mean...I haven't been a wife to you for a while, since before you went to Chicago."

"Well, that's true enough," he said dryly. He shifted, lifting himself to his elbow, leaning closer. "Are you offering to make love with me, Jo? 'Cause if you are, I won't refuse. And if you're not, you'd better scoot back over and hug that mattress before I get any more ideas than I've already got about the matter."

"You've got ideas?" Her voice trembled, and her eyes opened wide, as she grasped the last thing he'd said, repeating it as if at a loss to speak a thought of her own. Her brain befuddled at his nearness, her only thought was to reach out, to touch him, to feel those big, strong hands against her flesh.

She was close to weeping as she considered a future without Tate Montgomery. Even one more day without him holding her and giving her the gift of himself was almost more than she could bear.

"Johanna? If you don't want me to do this, you'd better back off right now, because I've stayed clear of you about as long as I can."

His hoarse whisper was a warning, one she could not heed. Her heart was beating with a strange thumping rhythm, her ears were ringing, her eyes were blurring with tears that would not be denied, no matter how hard she blinked.

Her body was limber, forming to his as she rolled against him, her arms clutching him in a frenzy of despair. "I need you, Tate," she cried against his shoulder, unknowingly echoing his own urgent cry in the springhouse in the early-morning hours. Her sobs were harsh as she clung to him, her fingers digging without mercy into his shoulders, sliding to his arms, then reaching for a frantic hold against his back.

"Tate?" Her cry muffled against his throat, she thrust her body upward against him, seeking the union of flesh, only to be frustrated by the layers of clothing that separated them.

"Johanna... Here, baby, sit up for me." He spoke in her ear, his voice harsh, as he tugged at her nightgown, pulling it up and over her head. It caught, the buttons half-undone, and his big fingers struggled to work at them. He finally tore at the fabric before he managed to free her from the voluminous garment.

Kneeling beside her, he lifted her to face him and she knelt, too, swaying as his head bent to her breasts. He cupped them in his hands, holding them before him as if he would feast on their bounty, his mouth open against the firm flesh. Whimpering, she stroked his fingers, the backs of his hands, squeezing with her lesser strength as he molded her to suit his purpose. His lips were hot and hungry against her, and his tongue was urgent as he suckled, and she cried out, a high, keening sound, her head falling back, her eyes closing.

The tears ran in a steady stream, her choked sobs accompanied by the sound of his name, spoken in breathless murmurs and yearning whispers. "Tate! Tate!" She twisted against him, her whispers urging him with frantic wooings. "Yes, please...there...there." Her hands left his and pressed the back of his head, as if she were fearful that he would move from her. She leaned over him, her mouth brushing countless kisses across his hair, his temple, wherever she could find a place to press her lips. As though she were cradling a child to her breasts, she rocked, pleasuring him with mouth and hands, her fingers tangling in his hair, her lips speaking garbled phrases.

And then he was gone. He'd eased his way from her grasp, stripping the undershirt he wore from his body. His hands were swift, tossing it to the floor, then returning to undo his drawers and push them down his thighs. Quickly he stood, shedding the garment, and her breath caught in her throat at the sight.

Limned in the moonlight, he was framed by the window behind him, like a mythical giant of yore, bent on conquering the woman before him. His broad shoulders and narrow waist were a symphony of power, his arms and hands, reaching for her, an extension of that strength. And when he lifted her to himself, she groaned her exultation.

The touch of his warm flesh against her own beguiled her, the crisp curls on his chest brushing her breasts coaxed her to move against him. His arms tightened, one hand spread over the curve of her bottom, pressing the urgent need of his manhood against the soft flesh of her belly. Rigid and pulsing, it wedged between them, searing and seducing her with its promise.

The long nights in his arms had only served to ready her for this moment. The memory of hours spent in the circle of his embrace surrounded her, enticing her with a sensual

promise she could not resist. A willing captive, she surren
dered, clinging, sobbing, her hands frantic against him a
she groaned her need.

He fell with her to the bed, catching his weight on hi
forearms, lest he crush her against the mattress, and sh
was fluid beneath him, forming her body to his. Tate ben
to her, his mouth seeking, taking her cries and multiplyin
them with his own.

And then he could wait no longer, the days and night
of abstinence pushing him beyond his limits of control. Hi
knees pressed between her thighs, and she moved to hi
bidding. Surging against her softness, he held her fast, im
prisoning her by the force of his male strength. As if h
must lay claim to his woman with no preliminaries, n
coaxing phrases or pleas for her favors. Only the primitiv
urgency of a man left bereft by the absence of his mate fo
too long a time.

And yet it was more than that, for he could exist withou
the relief her body offered. Even as he took possession o
her, he knew that the force driving him required more tha
ease from the passion possessing him in these moments—
more than release from his physical urgency.

The impetus was that of a man's powerful sense of com
pletion. Without this woman, he was less than he could be
Without Johanna at his side, he was fated to forever see
the elusive unity they had only begun to forge betwee
them over the past weeks.

Lifting to meet his powerful thrust, Johanna caught he
breath, her body stretching to conform to him, her hear
pounding against her ribs. She twisted beneath him, sob
bing as she sought to accommodate his manhood withi
herself, clutching at him, lest he withdraw from her an
take that nourishing presence from her grasp.

"Johanna!" His muted cry was that of a man too long
denied, a man who had sought and in the seeking had fi
nally found the satisfaction he yearned for. And with

shuddering spasm that rocked them both, he surged against her.

She cried out, her face buried against his shoulder, her teeth against his flesh, her being held in the clasp of a pleasure so pure, it seemed she might die from the pain of possessing it. And for a moment, she rested in it, closing her eyes and absorbing the waves of shivering ecstasy it afforded her.

He was heavy against her, and she reveled in his weight. His lips were soft against hers, and she suckled them, carefully, tenderly. His hands were lax, fingers tangled in her hair. She rubbed her head against them, seeking the possession of his touch.

Tate rolled onto his side, taking her with him, folding her in his embrace and pulling the covers over them to keep out the chill of the night air.

"Tate..." Her whisper was his name, but he hushed her with a single word.

"No."

He could not bear to speak. He could not bear to listen. He could only hold her, seek the comfort of her flesh for the rest of the night, storing up the ardor she had spent upon him as a buffer against the silent woman she might be on the morrow.

For although they had met and shared the passion each had offered the other tonight, the reason for their estrangement had only been put aside for this short time. And he dreaded the dawn, when the woman in his arms would take on the armor of mistrust and wear it as a shield against him.

She must learn in her own time, and nothing he did would bring that to pass any sooner. Almost, he rued the moments just past. He'd behaved like the stallion he'd bred to his mares, taking and conquering without the wooing and coaxing a woman deserved.

He hugged Johanna to himself, knowing that he would

do the same again if he could live over those minutes of possession. That small space of time when they'd become one in the fullest sense of the biblical term. When each small part of them had been in complete accord with the other, when their bodies had found completion in the molding and meshing of male and female. When, for that small instant of time, he had sought for, and found, a taste of what heaven must be.

Chapter Seventeen

"Looks like spring out there." Pulling on his coat, Tate turned from the window, his gaze seeking Johanna. "Won't be long before we hear robins in the mornings."

"I saw a pair last week." Johanna answered from the pantry.

"They're probably already nesting back home. I'd have had my land about plowed by now in Ohio. I used to like watching the robins follow me along the rows, looking for worms." He crossed the room as he spoke and peered into the pantry. "You suppose we could have pancakes this morning?" Johanna glanced up from where she was filling a bowl from the sack of flour on the shelf. "I suppose," she answered quietly.

He'd watched her all morning, from the time she left their bed to dress. She'd been aware of him, there on the bed, his dark eyes on her, as she stepped behind the screen to don the dress she'd worn the day before, unwilling to wear her Sunday dress to cook in.

He'd risen then, following her example, pulling on his trousers and heavy shirt, and he'd been right behind her as she came down the stairs. Now, readying himself for the milking, he dallied, his attention still focused in her direction.

She squeezed past him, carrying her heavy crockery bowl in front of her, her eyes unwilling to meet his gaze. "Breakfast will be ready by the time you finish milking."

It sure sounded like an invitation to leave, as far as Tate could tell, and his mouth twisted into a grin as he followed her across the kitchen.

"Johanna?" His fingers working at the buttons and buttonholes of his coat, he came toward her, and she looked up from the egg she was cracking into the bowl.

It was hard to face him this morning. She'd known from the first that the memory of last night would lie between them. And Tate was not willing to leave it dormant. She bit at her lip, wiping her hands on the front of her apron.

"I don't think I want to talk about this, Tate." Their conversation had been of robins and pancakes, but her mind had been on another subject entirely, and she was well aware that his own thoughts had shared the same topic.

He bent to kiss her forehead, a brush of his lips that spoke of understanding. "Just one thing, Jo, and then I'll not say any more about it."

She drew in a deep breath. "All right. What is it?"

"I don't want you fretting about what happened last night."

She glanced up at him and then away, as if the warmth of his gaze could not be tolerated. "I'm... I just..." She turned her head aside.

His hand touched her cheek, and he spread his fingers to cradle her jaw, tilting her head back. "Don't ever be ashamed of what you feel, Jo. What we have between us is private. What we share is sacred to our marriage."

"What I said—" Her voice choked on the words.

He leaned closer. "You said you needed me. I'd already told you the same thing earlier. Nothing you said or did should cause you shame, Johanna. We're married, and our coming together is always right and proper. And last night was about as right as it's ever gonna get, as far as I'm concerned.'' He grinned down at her, his lazy, lopsided smile begging her response.

"I don't know how I could…be that way with you." Her gaze anguished, she dared another look, her eyes pleading for his understanding. "I'm still feeling…confused, Tate. I'm still angry with you." She blurted the words harshly.

He nodded. "I know that. It'll work out, Jo. We'll make it work."

Once more he bent, his mouth warm against hers in a brief kiss. As if he bound a bargain between them with that gesture, his hands settled on her shoulders and he squeezed firmly.

Johanna's head ducked, her tongue touching her upper lip in a tentative movement, and she backed from him. "You'd better get on with the milking. I'll send the boys out to feed the hens and gather eggs."

Tate turned to the door, fishing in his pocket for the gloves he'd left there. "I think I'm going to put Pete up on the mare today, maybe after dinner," he said. "That'll put a shine on his Sunday, won't it?"

Johanna looked up, her eyes alight as she imagined the boy's reaction. "He'll be tickled pink. I'll tell him."

He glanced toward the doorway and into the hall, where the stairs climbed to the second floor. "They need to be up. Want me to call them before I go out?"

Johanna shook her head. "Just go on now and get the milking done. We'll never get to church if we don't hurry."

He nodded and turned from her, reaching for his hat as he passed the peg by the door where it hung.

It had been a mistake to tell the boy before church, Johanna decided, watching as Pete fidgeted throughout the sermon. Reverend Hughes's words were passing right over his head as he swung his feet, gripping his fingers on the edge of the pew beside her. The sermon about springtime and renewal and all the wonder of Easter coming up in a couple of weeks were wasted on Pete Montgomery, as far as Johanna could tell. In fact, if she knew anything about it at all, his head was filled with visions of a chestnut mare, himself on her back.

She placed her hand on his knee, stilling the swinging of his foot, and he glanced up at her, blinking as if she had roused him from a delightful daydream. Her barely noticeable nod was enough to make him grin and duck his head.

Tate leaned close, his whisper low in her ear. "He's thinkin' about that mare."

She nodded again. "I know." She breathed the words, aware of a glance sent their way by Marjorie Jones. With a voiceless apology, she bit her lip and nodded at the woman, catching sight of a smile as Marjorie turned away.

Once more Pete's leg swung, and his heel brushed against Johanna's dress. She sighed, accepting that he was lost in his own world this morning. Her hand moved from her lap to rest against his knee once more, and she patted it softly, smiling when he looked up guiltily. Her fingers squeezed gently and her mouth formed a smile. He accepted her touch with a tolerant grin of acknowledgment, nudging her calf with the toe of his boot.

Theodore Hughes wrapped up his message with an admonition to his congregation to take time from their duties to pay heed to the beauty of the earth, the advent of spring and the renewal of life. Then, bidding them rise, he led them in a booming rendition of a hymn, the pianist banging out the melody with more passion than skill.

No matter that the stationmaster's wife was not an accomplished player, Johanna thought, her soul soaring with the music. The words alone, sung from memory, her voice blending with Tate's deeper baritone, were enough to fill her heart with the joy of the new season.

"Lord of all, to thee we raise, this our hymn of grateful praise!"

* * *

It seemed that teaching Pete to ride required the whole family in attendance. The dinner dishes were left to soak, Pete's face pressing against the screen door as he urged Johanna to hurry. Timmy was at the barn already, perched on a nail keg, watching as his father prepared the sleek mare for riding.

Johanna's heart thumped with anticipation as she accompanied Pete across the yard, her shawl hanging from one shoulder. She'd snatched it from the back of her chair as she passed, tossing it in place as she stepped from the porch. The March sunshine had remained, a harbinger of the summer days to come, and she basked in the welcome warmth of it.

Tate led the mare from the barn, his hand grasping the bridle firmly. "Think you can get into the saddle, son?"

Pete nodded, swallowing hard, as he walked past his father.

"Should I give him a leg up?" Johanna asked, wary of the small boy struggling to reach the stirrup.

Tate shook his head, leading the mare to where a large log had been placed. "Left foot in the stirrup, Pete." The chestnut stood quietly, soothed by the soft sounds of her master, untroubled by the slight weight of the child who climbed quickly into the saddle.

"Lift the reins, son." Spoken in the same soft tones, Tate's command was simply a part of the wooing process he'd undertaken with the horse. As he walked with her, he spoke in an undertone, constantly aware of the child in the saddle, his attention attuned to the mood of the animal he controlled.

Pete looked lost in the saddle, to Johanna's way of thinking. Perhaps she would feel better when the smaller one Tate had ordered arrived. But Pete seemed to have no qualms about the ride he'd undertaken. His legs hung down, his toes barely touching the stirrups, and his face glowed with an eagerness she'd seldom seen expressed by the boy.

He held the reins in his hand, unaware that he was only a figurehead, that his father was the guiding hand in this endeavor.

"Pa, can I ride, too?" Timmy squeaked, bouncing on his toes as he watched his brother's triumph.

"In a while, Timmy," Tate promised. "I'll let you sit in front of me later on. But not by yourself yet."

"Come here, Timmy." Johanna held out her hand, and the boy ran to her. "Let me pick you up so you can see better."

Tate brought the mare in a circle, gripping the reins beneath her chin, stepping up his pace until she broke into a slow trot. In the saddle, Pete bounced in time to the gait, his knees gripping in vain for purchase.

"I can't make my butt stay where it belongs, Pa!"

Tate grinned. "You'll learn to ride with it, Pete. It takes time. Don't squeeze with your knees. Hang on this way." He paced beside the boy for a moment, his hands pressing on Pete's lower leg, showing him what he meant. "That's right, son. Now, just hold the reins easy, don't pull on them."

He slowed the mare and halted before Johanna, the dark muzzle just inches from Timmy's hand. "You can touch her, Timmy, if you want to." Tate watched as the small boy reached a tentative hand to press against the long face, his fingers stretching to brush against the stiff hair. Then his hand slid, touching the velvety muzzle, and he laughed aloud.

"She's soft, like the kittens, Pa." Bending forward, he breathed deeply of the horse's scent. "She doesn't smell like the kittens, though, does she?"

Tate's laughter rang, and Johanna relished the sound, her arms hugging Timmy close. Tate shook his head, still chuckling. "No, she smells like a horse, son."

"I like her, Pa." Timmy leaned forward, his cheek

brushing against the mare's jaw, as if he found bravery in Johanna's arms.

Tate reached out, taking some of the child's weight, his arm beneath Johanna's, and his eyes swept the woman who held his son. "I like her, too, Timmy," he said softly, his gaze tender. "But I think you're kinda heavy for Johanna to hold for so long. You need to get down."

"All right." Sliding to the ground, Timmy maintained his hold on Johanna's hand and backed off a step. "That horse looks bigger from down here, Pa."

Pete's hand reached forward, and he stroked the mare's neck, his look impatient as he glanced at his small brother. "Can we ride some more now?"

"I need to tell you a few things first, Pete," Tate said. Releasing the reins, he snapped a lead rope onto the bridle, then handed it to Johanna. "Here, Jo. Hold this for me, will you? I think she's pretty well settled down. She seems to take to kids like a champ."

Johanna held the rope, Timmy reaching up to grasp the end of it, his face glowing. Together they watched as Tate instructed Pete in the holding of the reins and the movement of them to one side or the other.

"I'm going to let you go in a circle around me, Pete." Tate took the lead from Johanna's hand and motioned her to stand closer to the barn.

She watched as Tate moved out across the yard, feeding the rope through his fingers, controlling each movement of boy and mare with softly spoken words of instruction. The sun shone with brilliant splendor on the scene before her, and the sky was so blue it seemed to stretch farther than her mind could fathom.

It was a moment of perfection, a space in time to be cherished in memory, and she watched as if mesmerized, as if compelled by the grace and strength of man and beast, the youthful beauty of the child, his face shining with the joy of this moment.

"Miss Johanna? When does it get to be your turn?" Timmy tugged at her hand, his small face earnest as he peered up at her.

Johanna smiled at the boy's query. "Not today, sweetie. One at a time is enough for your father to handle."

"I heard that, Jo," Tate called out. Wrapping the rope into a coil, he drew the mare in a tighter circle, finally reaching to grasp the bridle and bringing her to a halt. "When you want her to stop, you must pull back gently on the reins, Pete, and say, 'Whoa.'"

Pete nodded, his look solemn; he was quite taken with the responsibility he'd gained today.

"I'm going to let you slide down now, and then we'll let Johanna have a turn." Tate watched as the boy easily gained the ground and took a tottering step.

"My legs feel funny, Pa." Pete frowned and then grinned as he gained his balance. "I feel like I'm still up there."

Timmy was tugging at Johanna's hand. "I knew it would be your turn next," he chortled. "Come on, Miss Johanna!"

She dragged her feet, unwilling to be exposed as less than courageous. "Pete's young and spry, Tate. I think I'm a little old to be learning how to ride," she protested.

His look was sober. "You might need to ride someday, Jo. I can't believe your father never put you up on a horse when you were a child. Besides, you might enjoy it once you get the hang of things. I'll give you a hand up."

She frowned, looking down at her dress. "I'm not sure this will work."

"Trust me." His hand was beckoning, his nod urging her compliance. And then he hesitated, his mouth twisting, his eyes measuring, as if he had reconsidered.

Now that the prospect of sitting astride the animal was upon her, the chestnut mare had assumed gigantic proportions, and Johanna swallowed a moment's terror, determined not to appear a coward before her audience. "How do we do this?"

"Maybe...maybe we won't, just now," Tate said slowly. Taking a chance with Johanna wouldn't be a smart move, he thought. There was no sense in courting trouble, should she truly be carrying a child. "We'll let you have a turn another time, Jo," he said glibly.

"All right." She backed off, relieved not to be tested today. "Another time."

"Is it my turn, Pa?" Timmy clambered from his spot by the barn door. He was bouncing on his toes as he watched, and Tate took pity on his impatience.

"Now it's your turn, Timmy. Come on over here and talk to the mare." Tate pulled the animal's head down, closer to the boy's level, and the child approached.

"She likes me, doesn't she, Pa?" he asked, his eyes round, as he reached to pat the patient creature.

"Sure she does," Tate assured him. "Now let me lift you up on the saddle, and then I'll get on behind you." He unfastened the lead rope and tossed it to Johanna, then, with an easy motion, swung from the ground, mounting the mare and lifting Timmy to sit on his thighs. One arm around the boy's waist, the other hand on the reins, he turned the mare in a tight circle and headed down the lane toward the road, his feet hanging free, the stirrups too high for him to use.

"Oh, boy! Oh, boy! Lookit me, Miss Johanna!" Timmy's cry of triumph resounded, and Johanna laughed aloud as she shared his enjoyment.

Pete sidled up next to her. "I'll be able to ride by myself pretty soon, won't I?"

"I'm sure you will," she assured him, one hand rising to rest on his shoulder. "I wouldn't be a bit surprised if your father doesn't put you back up on the mare when he comes back from taking Timmy for a ride. He said he was going to work with you for a while."

"I was thinking we need to have a name for her. It'd be

easier when I'm riding her if I knew what to call her, don't
you think?'' Pete's small face was screwed up with concern
as he voiced his thoughts.

"Why don't you and Timmy talk about it after a while?
I think your father would like you to name her," Johanna
said, hoping silently that Tate would agree with her.

"Yeah, we could do that!" Pete agreed, his enthusiasm
doubling as he watched the mare turn around and head back
in his direction. "I'll bet it'll be my turn again now."

Johanna dared to squeeze her fingers gently against the
boy's shoulder, and then lifted her hand to smooth his hair,
her fingers relishing the dark, silken locks that were so
much like his father's. She met Tate's gaze as he brought
the mare to a stop before her, and her eyes delivered a silent
message even as she spoke.

"Pete's probably ready for a longer lesson, if you've got
time." *Agree with me,* her eyes told him.

"I planned on it, as a matter of fact," Tate said
smoothly. "We've got all afternoon. I thought maybe I'd
put a bridle on the bay later on and ride with Pete. I used
to be pretty good riding bareback when I was a kid."

The song of a robin caught her ear as Johanna headed
for the house, and she lifted her hand to shield her eyes
from the sun's rays, searching the sky for the bird.

"Over by the house, in the maple tree," Tate said, pointing high to where a solitary bird perched on a bare branch.
"He's calling his mate."

"How can you tell, Pa?" Pete asked, peering to where
his father pointed.

Tate shrugged. "I know the words to that song, son."
And then, with a final glance at Johanna, whose mouth was
resisting the urge to curve in a smile, he lifted the boy into
the saddle once more.

"It was a good day, wasn't it, Jo?" In his usual position,
Tate cradled his head on his open palms, looking up at the

bedroom ceiling as his wife undressed for bed. Had she not been behind the screen, he'd have been watching her. As it was, he was depending on his memory to provide the details his mind could only imagine.

"Yes. Pete was still working on a name when you sent him to bed." Her voice was muffled beneath layers of fabric as she lifted her skirts over her head, and Tate grinned to himself, imagining the maneuvering she was doing behind the screen.

"I'd be glad to help you with that if you came over here," he offered.

"I can manage, thank you. I've been undressing by myself for twenty-six years now." She tossed the dress over the top of the screen, the arms dangling in his view.

"Your nightgown's out here, Jo." He'd filched it from the hook on the wall before he crawled into bed, concealing it beneath the covers, and now he dragged it from hiding.

She peeked around the corner of the screen, shoulders bare except for the narrow straps of her chemise. Her brow furrowed in a frown as she eyed the garment he held. "I thought I'd left it here." And then she glanced down at herself quickly, apparently deeming her attire fit for his viewing. She stepped from the concealment of the screen and approached him, her hand outstretched.

He sat up in bed, holding the gown from her grasp, his eyes making a slow survey of her form, from the drawers that were tied below her knees to the chemise that provided a scant covering of her upper body. "You're a fine figure of a woman, Mrs. Montgomery," he told her with unmistakable candor.

She blushed, evading his gaze, snatching for the gown he taunted her with.

But it was not to be. His hand reached out, grasping her arm and tugging at her with a steady pull, bringing her to the side of the bed.

"Tate!" It was a warning, half in jest, half in earnest and her head tilted to one side as she offered it.

"I don't think you need this nightgown tonight, Mrs. Montgomery." The object in question fell to the floor, and his free hand rose to loosen the tie at her waist, allowing the drawers to fall to her hips.

She reached to grab for them, clutching the cotton fabric in her fist, holding it against her belly. "Tate!"

"I'll keep you warm." His mouth whispered the words, a seductive promise she could not fail to recognize, and she shook her head.

"I can't do this, Tate. I want my nightgown."

"I'll turn out the lamp, Jo," he said, his smile willing her to comply, coaxing her gently.

She looked down at him, and her flush deepened. Her fingers twined in the material she clutched, and she bit at her lip.

Tate swung his legs over the side of the bed and settled her between his knees. He leaned forward, his face pressed against her waist, and he lifted the edge of her chemise, allowing his mouth to touch the bare skin beneath it. His breath was warm, and she shivered, shifting against his legs.

"Reach over to the table and turn out the lamp, Johanna." He'd released her wrist, allowing both of his hands access to her body, and he held her close as he gently pushed the loosened drawers down over her hips.

Recognizing the precarious threat to her modesty, she reached quickly to twist the knob on the kerosene lamp, turning down the wick and casting the room into darkness.

"Feel better now?" His words teased her as his hands swept the white garment down her legs, his fingers agile as he loosened her stockings and pushed them to her ankles.

"Lift your foot, sweetheart," he told her, easing the stocking from one foot as she obeyed. And then the other, as she complied with his nudging fingers.

His mouth was on her again, following the hem of her chemise as he lifted it, over the fullness of her breasts and to her armpits. "Raise your arms. Let's get this off you."

Obediently she did as he asked, aware only of the male strength of the man before her, her senses attuned to him, knowing he was set on a course with only one possible destination.

And she could not refuse him. It had been a day of pure happiness. From dawn till dusk, Tate had given her his attention, gifting her with smiles and sidelong glances, sharing with her the simple pleasure he found with his children. The quarrel between them held in abeyance, they had allowed the tension of their dissent to be forgotten for this moment. By mutual consent, they had put it aside from their time together as a family.

And now he asked for this, seeking her compliance. Not without recompense, though, for she knew what route this path would take. His arms would cradle her, and his hands would be gentle against her skin. The brush of his mouth against her breast was a promise of pleasures to come and his whispers were breathless vows he would fulfill, should she bend to his wooing.

Lowering her arms, she watched her chemise fall to the floor at her feet. Her hands on Tate's shoulders, she bent her head forward, resting her cheek against his dark hair. His mouth on her skin was gentle, his lips nuzzling at her flesh, and she shivered as he suckled, paying homage to her with tender touches.

"Lie down with me, Jo, please." He tilted his head back, his words offering her the choice, and she responded, her arms circling his neck, bending to find his mouth with her own.

Chapter Eighteen

The letter from Bessie arrived less than a week before the lady herself stepped off the train in Belle Haven. The usual cluster of townsfolk waited for the Tuesday-morning express out of Grand Rapids, among them Selena Phillips, with mailbag in hand, talking with Mr. Turner at the end of the platform.

Jacob Nelson, the barber, had been notified that his second chair would be arriving this morning, and his excitement was contagious, spreading to include Leah Ibsen and her group of schoolchildren. They were to be allowed inside the mail car for ten minutes, each of them having chosen someone far off with whom to correspond. Those who had no relatives or friends outside of Belle Haven had been given names of schoolchildren in Miss Ibsen's hometown of Dearborn, a town near the city of Detroit. Already, the youngest were estimating the time they must allow before their reply would be brought by this very train.

Jacob Nelson's interest in Miss Ibsen was apparent this morning as he inspected himself in the streaked window of the railroad station. His collar was stiff, his tie straight and every hair on his head pomaded into place as he sidled into her group.

Johanna watched the goings-on from the surrey, feeling

detached, as if she were waiting for a fatal blow to befall her. Her mind had been filled with the advent of Bessie's visit for seven days, and with good reason. Pete and Timmy had spoken of little else for the past week, their excitement reaching fever pitch by this morning.

Racing through their chores and breakfast, they'd been waiting on the porch an hour before Tate was ready to leave. And he was little better, Johanna thought miserably. The woman must be a saint, what with all the talk of Aunt Bessie this and Aunt Bessie that.

Johanna had decided Bessie must be the most comfort-able example of womanhood on the North American con-tinent, what with all the variety of cookies and cakes she had baked and served to Pete and Timmy. She'd imagined her as Belinda's older sister, probably stout and graying and grandmotherly. The boys truly loved their aunt, and Johanna was trying hard to be thankful for the good wom-an's concern for her nephews.

Tate had been no better. He'd hoped Bessie would be comfortable in the sewing room, since she was used to a larger bed. Johanna had set her jaw and refused to comment on that remark, which she considered a veiled criticism of her home.

Now, waiting for the woman to arrive, only the hopeful thought that she was younger and probably slimmer—in most places, anyway—than the wonderful Bessie Swenson, kept her from setting off for the farm afoot.

The train tracks ran in an absolutely straight line, and by standing on the platform and looking due south a person could see the engine and the smoke it produced from sev-eral miles away. Pete was the first to spy the cowcatcher gleaming in the distance this morning. His call to attention brought Tate from the station house door to stand near his sons on the platform.

August Shrader appeared at the far corner of the station, making a beeline for Selena, doffing his hat and standing

as close to her as etiquette would allow. Selena's face took
on a rosy hue, and even from where she sat in the surrey,
Johanna could see the postmistress flutter her eyelashes at
the banker. A wedding was likely in the near future, Johanna thought, chagrined as she realized she had spent little
time of late with Selena.

Timmy was barely able to keep his feet on the ground
by the time the train came to a screeching halt. Pete
bounded back and forth, peering in the windows of the
coach and almost running full tilt into the conductor as he
placed a stool on the platform for his passengers' use. A
lady took his hand as she departed the train, carefully placing her black side-buttoned shoes so as not to mar their
gleaming finish.

Johanna's heart missed a beat. Surely this was not the
Aunt Bessie she'd heard about for the past seven days without ceasing. This tall, slender, dark-haired woman, fashion-
ably garbed in a striped taffeta dress, carrying a parasol that
looked to be straight from New York City. Her hair, done
up in a series of ringlets and piled upon her head, was
adorned with a hat consisting of feathers and veiling that
had to have cost a small fortune.

Johanna's mouth fell open in stunned surprise. Herb
Swenson was dead a matter of weeks, and his widow was
dressed like an illustration from a Chicago newspaper.
She'd seen only a few such ads from the big-city stores,
but she was certain that what Bessie wore could in no way
be construed as mourning.

The woman's smile was warm and her arms were outstretched as two small boys vaulted in her direction. She
scooped them up, straightening and hugging them to her
bosom, accepting their cries of welcome and adding her
own soft words to their greetings. Even Tate was included
in the joyous reunion, being saluted with a brush of her
cheek against his as he bent to place his hand on her shoulder.

Johanna looked down at her plain everyday muslin dress. It was not only not striped taffeta, it wasn't even flowered dimity. It was a common, ordinary farm woman's go-to-town dress, bought from the shelves of the general store three years ago come summer. Neat and tidy was about all she could offer, Johanna thought glumly, lifting one hand to smooth a wispy lock that had slipped from her carefully pinned braids. Wound in a circle atop her head, they were prim and presentable, a far cry from gleaming dark curls beneath a fancy milliner's delight.

She slid from the seat of the surrey, recognizing her duty as Tate's wife, and walked toward the reunion taking place in front of a good dozen of the townsfolk. Selena, obviously curious about the new arrival, cast Johanna a look of wary sympathy.

"Johanna! Come here and meet Bessie." Beckoning her forward, Tate held out his hand to her, a welcome sight if she'd ever seen one. Having his broad palm enclose her fingers would be a comfort as she endeavored to be polite and cheerful.

"I'm so pleased to meet you Bessie," Johanna said, looking up several inches in order to meet the other woman's gaze. This was the woman she'd thought to comfort, perhaps, in the death of her husband. Had Tate been the one buried so recently, Johanna suspected, she would still be swathed in black linen and wailing to beat the band.

But the marvelous Bessie was not. Smiling, the visitor leaned forward, deposited the two boys on their feet and extended a hand to Johanna. "I wondered what sort of woman would take Tate Montgomery's eye. And now I know."

Sultry was the word that jumped into Johanna's mind as Bessie greeted her. Soft, drawling words, accompanied by an all-encompassing glance, made her feel that she had surely left a button undone or split a seam on her bodice. Never in her life had Johanna felt so inadequate.

How could Tate have chosen to marry her, when thi beautiful creature was living at the other end of the train tracks, in southern Ohio? But Bessie hadn't been availabl then. When Tate set out to find a place to settle, Bessie ha been the wife of Herb Swenson.

Now Herb Swenson was dead and buried.

Tate was shepherding his group into the surrey, having picked up Bessie's tapestry satchel from the platform. H gave Johanna his hand and helped her into the front seat Bessie was prevailed upon to sit between the boys on the back seat, and her satchel was deposited in the rear.

Thankfully, Johanna wasn't required to add much to the conversation as the surrey rolled toward the farm. Tate kep his team at a fast clip, and as if they, too, must make an impression, the sturdy mares swished their tails, tossing their manes in great style.

Bessie *ooh*ed and *aah*ed over the cows pastured next to the road they traveled, and was properly impressed when she caught sight of the new shorthorn bull at a distance Tate had set him loose in the near pasture, where the bull had immediately taken stock of his new harem and staked his territory.

"I'm planning on at least three dozen calves from him next spring," Tate said over his shoulder to Bessie, who appeared awed by the huge creature.

"Pa? What's that big black cow doing out there?" Pete asked, pointing into the area where the red-and-white-spotted shorthorn had set up court.

Tate squinted, following the direction Pete indicated, finally raising his hand to shade his eyes from the sun. "Looks like the old bull to me. What do you think, Johanna?"

"I haven't seen him in years. Pa always kept him out closer to the swamp." Sensing Tate's apprehension, she looked up at him. "Shouldn't he be there, Tate?"

Tate shook his head. "I didn't want the two of them

aving a tussle for the herd. Bulls don't do well in the same pasture." He lifted the reins and snapped them over the backs of his team. "I think I'd better hustle on home and get things sorted out."

Johanna was left to escort Bessie into her home and up the stairs, Tate making hasty excuses as he headed for the barn. In minutes, he'd saddled the chestnut mare and set off for the pasture at a gallop, his rifle in one hand as he rode.

"We'll have dinner in an hour or so, Bessie," Johanna said, opening the door to the sewing room and showing her guest in. Small and compact at best, the room seemed cramped today, Johanna thought, settling Bessie's bag next to the small chest.

Bessie looked around quickly. "What a charming room. I'm so glad you were able to find a place for me to stay. I hope I haven't put you out too much, Johanna."

Lack of mourning clothes notwithstanding, she couldn't fault the woman's manners, Johanna thought, nodding and smiling her best. But it was for sure that Bessie was as far from what she'd expected as any creature could be. Comfortable and stout, indeed!

Dinner was ready and being held on the back of the stove when Tate came back, stomping his boots noisily on the porch. "Johanna! Can you come out here?" Tate's voice was harsh, and Johanna hurried to open the door, drying her hands on her apron.

"What's wrong, Tate?" she asked, stepping onto the porch. From the barn, the boys ran toward the house, Timmy clutching a half-grown kitten in his arms.

"Damn bull! Those animals never do what you expect them to. The old one got into the near pasture and challenged my shorthorn and got himself gored for his trouble. I had to put him down."

"Is your new bull all right?" Johanna's heart trembled within her chest as she thought of the money invested in the red-and-white creature who had caused such an uproar already.

"He's dug up a little. Nothing I can't take care of with some salve. I need your long butcher knife now, Johanna. I'll have to gut that miserable animal right away, so the meat will be good. Not that it'll be anything but tough, anyway." He gestured to his rifle, on the porch. "Put that gun away, will you?"

She picked up the gun and held it uneasily, her mind still on the slaughtered bull. "What will we do with him?" The thought of having the meat to tend to, with all the other distractions she faced right now, held little appeal.

"I'll think of something." Tate was glowering darkly, in no mood to answer questions from the looks and sounds of him, and Johanna stepped back in the kitchen to find her knife, leaving the rifle in the pantry until later.

"Make me a sandwich out of that meat loaf, will you? I won't have time for dinner," Tate said from the other side of the screen door. "I'll take it with me."

"I'll do it, Tate." From behind her, Bessie's melodious voice offered help, and Johanna swallowed her thoughts.

"Thanks, Bessie." Tate grinned at his sister-in-law and then peered through the screen. "Johanna, where are you with that knife?"

"I'm sharpening it!" Using the edge of her egg crock, Johanna honed the blade, careful to mind the edge as she swept it over the stone. Bessie got the smile and she got the sharp side of Tate's tongue, Johanna thought acidly, swiping the blade once more to ensure the edge.

Tate stuck his head in the door. "I'm goin' out to the barn to get a rope to haul the carcass back to the house. I'll be right back. That sandwich about ready, Bessie?"

Bessie slapped the two slices of bread around a generous helping of meatloaf and, reaching for a clean dishtowel from the cupboard, wrapped it securely. "It's ready when you are, Tate."

"Can I go, Pa?" Pete watched, wide-eyed, as his father strode toward the barn, keeping pace, skipping to match Tate's longer steps.

"You go on back to the house and have dinner with your Aunt Bessie, son." Tate's mind was filled with the job ahead, and his answer was short, and Pete turned away, starting back to the porch, kicking at a clod of dirt.

Timmy was on the porch, the young cat beside him, telling Bessie about the litter, now down to the last two, since a family in town had taken one. Going down the steps, Johanna eyed them darkly, butcher knife in hand.

"Wash up for dinner, Timmy. You too, Pete," she added as the older boy scuffled his way toward her.

"My hands aren't dirty," he argued, scowling at his father's reproof.

"Don't argue, Pete!" Johanna was in no mood for a sulky child, and she sailed past him as she spoke.

Tate came from the barn, rolling up a length of rope and slinging it over his shoulder. He paused for only a moment, taking the knife from Johanna, and then went onto the porch, leaving her to follow.

Bessie waited near the steps, handing him the wrapped sandwich and speaking in a low voice, just beyond Johanna's hearing. Slowing her steps, unwilling to seem nosy, Johanna watched as Tate nodded, then turned to where his horse waited at the hitching post. Without a backward glance, he mounted and pulled the chestnut mare around, heading at a quick trot toward the pasture beyond the barn.

It had been a miserable day all around, Johanna decided. Tate had gone to the Cooney place to offer Jonas the dead bull and, accompanied by Jonas, had hoisted the creature onto the Cooneys' buckboard. By the time she'd heard gruesome details from both boys about the bull's bloody remains, she felt she'd never want to cook another meal of beef in her life.

Supper was late, Tate having had to do chores in the twilight, and if it hadn't been for Bessie being so cheerful, the meal would probably have been silent. What with Pete still upset at his father and Johanna's stomach in an uproar and Tate in a foul mood after killing the bull, things had gone rapidly downhill all day.

"I'll be glad to clean up the kitchen, Johanna," Bessie offered after dessert. "Why don't you go into the parlor and sit for a while? You're looking a mite peaked."

Disgruntled with the day's events, Johanna took her up on her offer, only to hear the three males of the household laughing and teasing as they assisted in the cleanup, an unheard-of event, in Johanna's experience. It was more than she could tolerate. Bessie was not only practically a raving beauty, she was efficient and capable of sorting out Johanna's kitchen without once asking a question.

And on top of that, she had won today's battle, hands down.

Battle? The word stuck in Johanna's mind. Why on earth did the advent of Bessie Swenson seem to have all the earmarks of a war? The woman had been pleasant and affable, offering to mend Timmy's favorite quilt, admiring Pete's book of letters and praising Tate to the skies as she looked over the improvements to the barn and his new mares.

She'd nodded knowingly as Tate explained his theory of improving the herd, hugged Timmy with enthusiasm after he complimented her on her pretty dress, and even coaxed Pete into allowing her to cut his hair before supper.

"How'd you let his hair get so ragged-looking, Tate?" she'd trilled, casting a sidelong glance at Johanna as she spoke. "He never looked so shaggy when..." She'd stopped, smiling apologetically at Johanna and shrugging daintily.

Johanna had been itching to get at the boy's dark hair for months, but he'd been adamant that only his father could lay hands on his head. Today it had taken Bessie less than a minute to have him wrapped in a towel and sitting on a chair while she clipped and combed.

The rocker had never had such a workout. Johanna, wrapped in her shawl, unwilling to lay a fire, even though the air had grown cold with the setting sun, sat in solitary splendor in the dark room, her foot pushing the chair into a steady rhythm.

"Jo? What are you doin', sitting in the dark?" Tate stood in the doorway, and she scowled in his direction, glad of the dim light.

"Just enjoying the peace and quiet," she said, modifying the speed of her rocker.

"Come on out and join us. We're going to play a game of spoons."

She shook her head. "I think I'll go up to bed early. I've had a long day."

A burst of laughter from the kitchen drew his attention, and he hesitated, then looked back at her. "Are you sure, honey? You looked tired at supper, but I hate to have you miss the fun."

"I'm sure you'll get along fine without me," she said, rising and walking toward him. He stepped aside to let her pass, and she headed for the stairway.

"I'll be up shortly, Jo. The boys need to get settled down before long, and I'm sure Bessie'll be ready to have a good night's sleep, too. She had a long trip."

"Take your time, Tate." She started up the steps, lifting her skirt, her feet feeling as though they weighed a ton apiece. Suddenly weary to the bone, she clutched the banister to ease her way, ignoring the man who watched from below.

By the time the week was past, Johanna had retreated into a mood she could not seem to escape. Feeling out of sorts and more like a scullery maid than the owner of a prosperous farm, she found herself making more work for herself than was necessary.

Chasing Bessie out with the boys after breakfast, she scrubbed the kitchen to a fare-thee-well. Bessie'd mentioned the old open shelves in passing, telling of her own newly refurbished kitchen. Complete with fresh wallpaper and a new cabinet, outfitted to hold grocery staples in assorted nooks and crannies, it sounded like a marvel of modern design.

On Friday, Johanna washed the curtains, turning the crank on the new washing machine with a vengeance, then rinsing and starching them before hanging them outdoors to dry. She'd sprinkled them down and ironed them before supper, only to be disgruntled when Tate didn't even notice the clean curtains and sparkling windows.

Bessie had watched her idly for a while as she turned the crank on the washing machine. "I bought the Acme combination washer in the Sears catalog for myself last month. They tell me it's got your Fulton #1 there beat all to pieces."

"Is that so?" Johanna'd replied, determined to avert a head-on fuss with the woman. Apparently, once Bessie got her husband buried, she'd had a field day. In fact, if her recitation of facts was to be believed, the house she lived in in Ohio was literally full to the brim with all sorts of work-saving devices. Not the least of these was a brand-new Singer treadle machine, with which she had made the new shirts she'd brought along for Timmy and Pete.

And Johanna, having learned long ago that sewing was not her finest skill, had been forced to admire the woman's handwork with a semblance of enthusiasm. "Don't you think every woman owes it to her husband to save money on clothing?" Bessie had asked Johanna over the supper table. "I used to sew for these boys quite regularly when I had them nearby."

"I'm sure you did," Johanna had muttered darkly, ignoring Tate's look of reproof.

One noontime, Bessie regaled the boys with tales of her new bicycle, which they could certainly ride, should they come to visit. Apparently, Herb Swenson, for all his boozing, had left her well provided for, if all her tales could be believed. If Tate had waited around awhile, he'd have had a soft berth there, Johanna thought mutinously.

Not only would the boys have had their wondrous aunt Bessie to tend to their every want and wish, but Tate could have had her hovering over him every day. As it was, she'd made all sorts of fancy pies and cakes in Johanna's kitchen, shaping cookies by the score for the boy's enjoyment.

"Nothing wrong with a plain, ordinary apple pie," Johanna muttered as she set a pan of dried apples to soak on Saturday afternoon. At least she had Bessie beat when it came to solid food. Desserts were her specialty, the woman had said cheerfully. She had a part-time cook and housekeeper to do the drudgery.

Johanna swallowed her ire as best she could, determined to put on a cheerful face. It was hard today, though. Her breakfast had been stuck in her craw all morning, and she'd been swallowing against a sour taste for the past hour.

It was no use. As much as she hated to admit it, she was about to lose the meal she'd eaten so grudgingly, and she scooted into the washroom as the nausea rose in waves, making her dizzy.

An empty slop pail, rinsed and ready to be filled with scraps for the pigs, was in one corner, and she fell on her knees next to it, a cold sweat breaking out on her forehead. With a retching that stretched to the pit of her stomach, she lost it all—her breakfast, the final shreds of good humor she'd managed to cling to, and her appetite.

"Johanna? Are you all right?" It was Bessie, coming in from the yard, where she'd been teaching the boys how to play croquet, having bought a game from Mr. Turner at the general store on Thursday.

"I'm fine," Johanna lied, wiping her forehead on her sleeve. She settled back on her haunches and took a deep breath. "Something didn't settle right, I'm afraid."

Bessie looked at her knowingly. "Are you sure that's all it is?"

Johanna nodded crossly. "Of course I'm sure. What else would it be?"

Bessie leaned against the wall, inspecting her fingernails and looking down at Johanna with a half smile. "I've heard Tate say he wasn't interested in having any more children."

Johanna's eyes widened as she turned to face the woman. "What does that have to do with anything...and how would you know what Tate wants?"

Bessie shrugged. "I've known him for years. He was married to my sister." As if that relationship had given her privileged information, she smiled.

"I don't think he was the happiest man on earth while he was married to Belinda," Johanna said quietly, only too aware of her position on the floor, in front of the remains of her last meal.

"Well, Belinda wasn't any too overjoyed, either, having to live on that godforsaken farm. I've always thought I'd have had better luck talking Tate into living in town. Belinda didn't know how to handle him. And her going after him with a knife certainly left him with a bad taste in his mouth."

"A knife?" Johanna repeated the words, unbelievingly.

"Of course, Tate's told you about their final battle, hasn't he? The poor man was lucky to come out of it alive. And then there was all the talk after he left about how Belinda died, falling in the river and all, with no witnesses. And Tate with his face all cut up."

"I don't think I want to hear this, Bessie," Johanna said firmly. "Tate can——"

Bessie cut in. "Tate doesn't talk about it. Besides, I never for a minute believed the things some people said. But for sure they'd had a fight, and when all's said and done, Belinda was the one who ended up dead."

Johanna shook her head. "Tate would never hurt any woman, Bessie. I can't believe you'd repeat such tales."

Bessie stepped back, allowing her to pass, and Johanna went to the sink, rinsing a cloth to wipe her face, her hands trembling within the folds of the fabric she pressed against her cheeks. The nausea was past, but a weakness unlike any she'd ever known had gripped her, and she clung to the drainboard.

"I'm sorry if I upset you, Johanna," Bessie said from the doorway. "I thought you'd have known all about Tate's marriage. To tell you the truth, I'd hoped he would see the light of day and quit his wandering around and come back home where he belongs before this." She smiled with barely concealed glee as she watched Johanna's distress. "The talk has about died out, anyway, back home."

Stepping closer, Bessie spoke in a lower voice, as though confiding in Johanna. "You know, I was amazed that he found it necessary to marry a woman to get the piece of property he wanted." Her laugh was crisp and glittering, like a glass shattering against a stone. "I'd have been glad to buy him a hundred acres to play with. It's too bad he didn't hang around a few more months, till Mr. Swenson passed out of the picture. I'd have been happy to raise the boys for him."

Johanna gaped at the crass words spoken by the genteel woman before her. "Why didn't you have children of your own, Bessie?" she asked quietly. "You truly love Pete and Timmy."

Bessie's jaw tightened, her laughter a thing of the past, and she tilted her chin, whispering. "If I couldn't have Tate Montgomery's children, I didn't want any at all. Belinda snagged him first, right out from under my nose, and I watched her make his life a misery.'' She sniffed, dismissing her sister as of little account. "She never knew how to handle him. I'd have had him working at the bank or running the hotel in no time, if I'd married him.''

"Tate's a farmer, through and through.'' With all her heart, Johanna believed those words, and yet there was a niggling doubt as she considered Bessie's words.

Tate Montgomery looked like a true gentleman in his suit. With his shoes polished and his hair trimmed and his nails squared off, he was the picture of elegance, and no woman in her right mind would turn her back on him once she'd had a chance to have him as her own. Maybe Bessie could have coaxed him into working in town. He certainly wouldn't have the worry of crops failing and hail punishing a field of wheat or calves freezing in a late spring sleet storm if he was working in a suit and tie.

"Aunt Bessie! Come on out! What're you doin' in there, anyway?'' Pete called from the porch. "I hit Timmy's ball clear over by the garden, and he says I cheated.''

Bessie's eyes were dark with speculation as she looked at Johanna. "Have you ever heard such a fuss? You'd think I was their favorite person in the whole world, wouldn't you now?''

Johanna nodded, a sense of defeat catching her broadside. "Yes, Bessie, I guess you could say that.''

Night had settled, bringing a spring rain that splattered through the window onto the bedroom floor. Johanna roused from her sleep as the wind blew across the room, twisting the white curtains and spraying the bed with a fine mist.

Rolling from the mattress, she pushed the curtains to one side and lowered the window, reluctant to lose the fresh breeze, but aware that a west wind always blew hardest in this bedroom. The boy's room would be dry, the window only cracked for a breath of air, and facing east as it was.

She looked out over the yard, barely able to catch a glimpse of the trees through the slanting rain, and her heart was filled with a strange sadness. The hopes for happiness she'd harbored over the past months had been scattered by Bessie's words. That the woman could be so cunning and yet have Tate so completely enthralled by her sweetness and the boys wrapped so securely around her little finger was a conundrum she was not able to solve.

And to say such things about Tate—insinuating that he'd had something to do with his wife's death. Why, anyone who knew the man, would know…

Johanna closed her eyes. If she could trust Tate in this, why couldn't she trust him to do what was right when it came to her farm, when it came to buying a new bull? And then, amid all of the turmoil in her mind, she found a small kernel of truth. She did trust him. With her farm, with her very life, with her love.

Yet she remained at the window, her thoughts turning to the niggling notion Bessie had nudged into the forefront of her mind this morning. This puzzle had been much easier to reason out, once she had it pointed out to her so clearly. Bessie's words had set her thinking, and within minutes she'd been able to sort out the solution. Her monthly flow had not come around since December. Why she hadn't paid it any more mind than that, she'd never know. Perhaps the newness of marriage, once Tate had taken her to his bed, maybe the fun of Christmas and then the issue of the bull. At any rate, she'd successfully ignored the signs that were there to be seen, if only she paid attention. And now it could no longer be ignored.

"Johanna?" His voice muffled, Tate called her name, and she turned back to the bed, assured of the darkness hiding the tears she shed.

"Yes, Tate. I just had to close the window. It was raining in." Her feet were damp from the wet floor, and she sat on the edge of the bed, wiping them on the rug. "It's a good rain, a real soaker."

He grunted, turning to his side. "We needed it. It'll make the plowing go easier next week."

"Plowing already?" She covered her legs with the quilts and curled on her side.

"Yeah, we're having an early spring. I think I'll get the corn in before the first of the month." He stretched his arm across to where she lay, catching her around the waist and tugging her snugly against him. "Sleepy, Jo?"

Ducking her head, she wiggled in his hold. "Don't, Tate. Not with Bessie right across the hall."

"For crying out loud, honey! She can't see us in here." He leaned to nuzzle her neck. "You haven't wanted me to touch you since she got here. What's wrong, sweetheart?"

"I'm just tired, I suppose." She closed her eyes, aggravated by the effect his mouth was having on her. Tate Montgomery could have her in a loving mood faster than a spark could light tinder. "Please don't, Tate." She stiffened in his embrace, and knew a moment's regret as he backed away.

"All right, honey. I know you've had a hard week. You're doing too much lately."

"I'm not complaining," she said, pulling the covers over her shoulder, strangely chilled as Tate turned from her.

"Go to sleep, Jo," he told her, yawning widely and reaching to pat her shoulder in a gesture of comfort.

"Yes..." She closed her eyes. But, caught between Tate's soft snores and the certain knowledge of a child growing within her, she lay silent and unmoving, unable to relax. Finally aware that she would not sleep again, she watched the rain against the window, until the last sprinkling drops were chased from the sky by the westerly wind and the rising sun.

Chapter Nineteen

"Aunt Bessie's gonna stay another week," Pete announced, the screen door slamming behind him as he tore through the kitchen. "I gotta find my string. We're gonna make a kite."

He was gone, his feet fairly flying up the stairs as his words sailed back to ring ominously in Johanna's ears. The wonderful Bessie was once more proving to be innovative and charming. Kites, indeed! Fixing pot roast for supper was more the order of the day, as far as Johanna was concerned.

Playing games and entertaining the children was all well and good, but when it came right down to it, small stomachs needed nourishment three times a day, and somebody had better be in the kitchen.

Not fair! Johanna's heartfelt cry was no less poignant for its silence, and her tears dripped steadily as she tended her meal.

She'd never been so childish and foolish, she thought, swiping at her cheek with the pot holder she held. Imagine being jealous of a poor old widow who had no children of her own and had come for a visit. Even to her own mind, that statement smacked of insincerity, and she laughed aloud as she attempted to relate the sumptuous Bessie to the vision of a ''poor old widow.''

Admittedly, Tate's attention to Bessie had waned, his work taking him farther from the house during the past couple of days. The first week of Bessie's visit, he'd pretty much stuck close to home, playing the part of host. But Monday morning had found him impatient to ready the fields for planting, and the visit to town had produced bags of seed corn from the mill.

''It's a new breed of corn I'd like to try,'' he'd said as Johanna questioned the purchase.

''Pa always used his own crop for seed the next year,'' she'd told him stubbornly, thinking of the money he was spending.

''I told you before, I'm not your father, Johanna.'' Tight-lipped, he'd refused to defend his theory, and they'd spent the ride home in near silence. Except for the giggling of two small boys in the back of the surrey as Bessie regaled them with stories.

Selena had been cautiously sympathetic when Johanna stepped to her desk to pick up the mail.

''Will she be staying long?'' Her fingers were deft as Selena sorted through envelopes and periodicals, her query casual yet pointed.

Johanna had groaned. ''It's been too long already,'' she confided, leaning forward so as not to be overheard.

Bessie had emptied her small leather purse of change, spending it on penny candy during that shopping trip, and Johanna had been at her wit's end, dealing with Timmy's stomachache throughout the night hours.

''The boys aren't used to eating a lot of sweets, Bessie,'' Tate had told her at the breakfast table, his smile an apology for the statement.

Bessie had sniffed and shared a secret smile with her two coconspirators. ''Nonsense! A little candy never hurt these boys before. I think Johanna's been a bad influence on you,

Tate. You never used to be so stingy with your sugar!'' An arch look of fond remembrance had accompanied her remarks, and Tate had subsided after a quick glance in Johanna's direction.

Now Johanna chewed on that last bit of suggestive reasoning Bessie had offered. Just what sort of ''sugar'' had the woman been speaking of? Surely Tate had not been involved in that direction? No, Tate Montgomery would never stray beyond the boundaries set up by marriage vows, be they his or someone else's. That was one thing Johanna would stake her very life upon.

''Jo?'' Soft and cajoling, his calling of her name jarred her from the reverie in which he had played so large a part.

He stood behind her. His smile was tentative, as if he doubted her approval of his appearance there, and she wondered at that. Tate was not usually dubious about his welcome in her kitchen.

''I've been thinking about something, honey, but I want to make sure you'll like the idea before I do it.''

She was right. He was here, asking her to pass judgment on his next project, and she frowned. ''You're not about to buy another bull, are you, Tate?''

His laughter was subdued, as if he were not willing to call attention to his presence. ''No, even though time will prove me right, I did enough damage with that deal to last a long time, Jo.'' His gaze was tender, almost yearning, as he reached for her.

The hand clutching the pot holder moved to his shoulder, and she brushed there at wisps of hay that had tangled in the fibers of his shirt. ''I think we're about past that point, Tate,'' she said, her eyes fastened to the worn collar of his work shirt, needing to assure him, needing to put their quarrel to rest finally.

''Lord in heaven, I hope so,'' he said feverently. Bending, he touched his mouth to her forehead. ''This is something else, Jo. I've got something to show you.'' He drew her across the kitchen floor, pushing the screen door open, tugging at her hand, pulling her to the porch.

"I found an old fallen hickory-nut tree down at the edge of the woods, and I thought to cut it for firewood. Take a look at this, Jo." He bent to where he'd placed a slab of wood perhaps four inches thick, an elongated oval, cut against the grain. "This'll sand down real nice. Just look at the lines in the wood, honey."

Johanna frowned, puzzled by his fascination. Wood was good for burning in the stove or building furniture with. Perhaps Tate was intent on making a table from his find. "What will you do with it, Tate?"

"I've been thinking…"

From the field to the east of the house, Sheba barked shrilly, and a cry rose, catching his attention as Tate broke off in midsentence.

"Pa! Pa! Look at our kite!" Pete was shouting as he ran, his words punctuated by the squeals of Timmy, whose short legs could not keep up with those of his older brother. Over their heads, caught by the wind, a magnificent kite with a tail of fluttering white bows sailed at the end of Pete's string.

"Bessie knows how to make kites," Johanna offered, her tone neutral as she stuffed her hands into her apron pockets.

Tate chuckled. "She's amazing, isn't she? You'd think she was just a young sprout herself, the way she carries on with them. Too bad she's not much use for anything else."

Johanna stiffened at that telling remark, and turned to the door. "My potatoes will be boiling dry if I don't watch out, Tate. Supper will be ready in fifteen minutes. If those boys want to eat, they'd better haul that kite down and wash up." Her skirts swishing smartly, she turned from him.

"Jo?" His lips tightened as he watched her go, the project forgotten. At least on her part. Tate picked up the slab of wood, carrying it to the barn, and there he wrapped it in an old burlap sack, placing it on his workbench. He'd wait until he was finished before he showed it to her again, he decided. If she didn't approve of his decision, so be it.

Now to call in the boys. He didn't look forward to seeing their long faces at the interruption to their kite-flying. But Bessie would talk them out of their pout.

"Spoons ain't nearly so much fun without you, Pa," Pete declared glumly. Tate pulled the door shut behind himself and latched it for the night, his gaze taking in the game in progress around the kitchen table.

"You seem to be doin' all right. I had a chore to work on," he said, scrubbing at his hands over the washbasin in the sink.

"I thought the chores were finished a long time ago," Bessie said, her chin propped prettily on her folded hands.

Tate shrugged. "They were. This is just something I'm doing for Johanna." He looked beyond the kitchen doorway to the dark hallway. "Where is she, anyway?"

"Gone to bed, Pa," Timmy offered. "She looked sleepy."

"It's about time for you boys to follow her, I'm thinking," Tate told them. "Tomorrow's another day."

Used to following orders, Pete slid from his chair, albeit reluctantly, and nodded at his brother. "Come on, Timmy. Let's go."

"I'll go up with you," Tate offered. "You'll need a light."

"Miss Johanna said she'd light the lamp in the hall upstairs, Pa. We can see all right by that," Pete said.

Tate nodded. "I'll come up a little later, then."

"Sit down and talk for a few minutes, why don't you?" Bessie asked Tate, her fingers wiggling a good-night message to the boys as she spoke.

Tate filled a cup with coffee from the back of the stove and pulled his chair from the table. "Might do that. I'm just afraid once I sit down, though, I won't want to get up.''

Bessie leaned toward him, her mouth pulled into a sympathetic moue. "Have you ever thought about going into business for yourself, Tate? Maybe someplace in town, where you won't have to work from morning till night, the way you do now?"

He shook his head. "Nope. Farming's what I do, Bessie. You know that."

She smiled knowingly. "As smart as you are, you could succeed at anything you set your hand to, Tate Montgomery. I'll warrant you could give any merchant in town a run for his money if you wanted to."

"Maybe," Tate answered agreeably. "But walkin' around in a stiff collar and being inside all day sure wouldn't set right with my soul." He lifted his cup and sipped at the strong black brew, then eyed it cautiously. "This stuff sure has a kick. Johanna must have added an extra handful of grounds."

Bessie's smile was strained. "She's quite a switch from Belinda, isn't she? Rather down-to-earth, and all that."

Tate's mouth twisted, his eyes narrowing as he considered her words. "Down to earth? I guess that's a good way to describe her, Bessie."

"She doesn't do much with the boys, does she?"

Tate considered that idea. "I don't know. She works with Pete with his letters and numbers. She's teachin' him to read, you know. And she helps with the chores and keeps their clothes clean and cooks their meals. I guess she manages to put a lot of time in on them, all around."

Bessie's voice softened. "They need more than physical care, Tate. They need love!"

His head lifted abruptly, and his eyes darkened. "Love's more than playin' games, Bessie. Don't you doubt for a minute that Johanna loves my boys."

She laughed—a trilling sound, guaranteed to travel the distance from the kitchen to the bedrooms overhead.

Johanna pulled the quilt over her ear. The rumble of Tate's voice had sounded through the register in the floor, followed by Bessie's softer words, all incomprehensible, each one a barb in her battered feelings.

"They sure have a lot to talk about," Johanna muttered, pulling up her legs, tucking her nightgown down around her feet. She'd claimed to be sleepy. The truth was she'd had about all she could take of Bessie and her games. Not just the hilarity of spoons being grabbed and tussled over at the kitchen table, but the continual reminders of another life Tate had led. The game of placing Johanna in the nether regions, while Bessie endeared herself to the males in this household.

Another burst of tinkling laughter from the kitchen added fuel to the fire of resentment that burned in Johanna's heart, and she pulled the quilt all the way over her head as she closed her eyes, grimly determined to shut out the reminder of the woman's presence in her kitchen.

"I need to get to bed," Tate told Bessie in the room below.

"You haven't told me how you came to buy those new horses, Tate," Bessie said, her mouth pouting prettily.

His eyes lit as he recalled that particular day, and he leaned back in his chair.

The Monday-evening train would be picking up a passenger at the depot in Belle Haven. Bessie would be leaving tomorrow, and Johanna's heart lifted at the thought. The Sunday-dinner dishes done and the kitchen clean, she looked out the door. The yard was empty, the barn door stood open, and within she caught a glimpse of Timmy as he played with his half-grown cats. They'd be having babies of their own before the year was out, Johanna thought.

From beyond the barn, she heard the sound of Tate's

voice and the laughter of Pete and Bessie as they worked with the horses. Surprisingly, Bessie had turned out to be fond of the creatures, a good rider herself and the owner of a split riding skirt.

They were probably heading out for a ride, Pete on the chestnut. He'd become more than attached to the animal in the past weeks, and Tate was proud of his progress.

"Maybe I'll take a walk," Johanna said aloud, and then laughed as she recognized her old habit of speaking to herself, in lieu of constant silence.

Snatching up her shawl, she slipped out the back door, casting a quick glance at the sky. It was warm for an April day, but the clouds to the west promised rain by nightfall, and the air would cool in a hurry in a couple of hours.

"I'll bet there are trilliums along the ditch," she said to herself, hastening her steps as she thought of the wildflowers she'd not taken time to look for during the past weeks. Spring was her favorite season, but Bessie's visit had kept her busier than usual, as if she must prove her worth to the woman from Ohio.

Not today! Johanna vowed. *I'm taking a walk, and I'm not coming back until I find a handful of violets and a better mood.* She set out across the side yard, taking a shortcut to the road, bending as she came across a patch of lily of the valley beneath the maples. She plucked one stem and held it to her nose, inhaling the sweet scent.

Then, tucking it into her top buttonhole, she sauntered on. The road was dry, and she walked through patches of shade and sunshine, where pine trees edged the road, stopping to watch as she caught a glimpse of a shy bluebird on a stump.

"Mr. Bluebird, I'll warrant you'll be looking for a place to nest," she said, grinning at her own foolishness. Playing hooky was good for the soul, she decided, and ambled on.

The sun was warm, even though the breeze was cool, tugging at her hair. She removed the pins holding her braids ecurely around her head. Fingers combing through the ресses, she let them hang loose over her shoulders.

She felt free, unfettered, and her footsteps quickened as he considered the adventure she'd set out upon. "I believe 'll let the wonderful Bessie fix them their supper tonight," he told a rabbit that peered at her from behind a clump of weeds.

A spot of purple caught her eye, and she ventured from he road to where a patch of violets bloomed amid dark green leaves, begging her attention. Bending to them, she quickly gathered a handful, holding them to her nose. "I'll vet Selena would enjoy these," she whispered, closing her eyes as she savored the scent. They'd hurried home from church, and she'd only waved at her friend.

Turning, she looked back, but the farm was too far away o be seen, and somehow it didn't even matter. For the first ime in months, Johanna found herself thinking only of the pleasure of the moment. A somewhat selfish, exceedingly satisfying sensation of hedonism made her giggle, and she heard herself as if listening to another person. Johanna Pat-terson never in her life had giggled. She'd never walked into town just to spend a few minutes with a friend either.

"But I'm not Johanna Patterson any more," she re-minded herself aloud. "And I'm going visiting."

Her stride lengthened as she walked back to the road, heading for Belle Haven, violets in hand.

"Pa, Miss Johanna isn't in the house, and the stove's gone pretty near cold." Pete stood in the barn door, watch-ing as his father rubbed down the bay mare. Timmy was curled up in the corner, weary from his long ride, perched in front of his father on one of the old mares.

"Is she upstairs, son?" Tate asked, intent on drying the mare thoroughly before he put her in her stall. "Maybe she's taking a nap in the bedroom."

Pete shook his head. "No, I called her, and I even went

up and looked in your room. She's not in the attic either
I climbed the stairs and looked around.''

Tate thought a moment. ''Could be she's in the springhouse. She might have decided to churn today, instead of
in the morning.''

Pete looked disbelievingly at his father. ''It's Sunday,
Pa. Miss Johanna says it's a day of rest.''

Bessie laughed, sitting on a milking stool, near the tack
room door. ''Maybe she ran off, Tate. You don't seem to
have much luck with your wives, do you?''

''That wasn't funny, Bessie.'' He shot her a look guaranteed to give her pause. ''Johanna doesn't bear any resemblance to your sister, and you know it. Besides, we have
an audience, and I'd just as soon not discuss the past.''

''They'll know one of these days, anyway,'' she said,
shrugging off his remark with a smile.

Somehow Bessie's company had become cloying of late,
Tate decided, his gaze sweeping over her slender form.
True, she was wonderful with his sons, always had been,
for that matter. But she didn't wear well. Belinda had called
her shallow, and he hadn't tended to agree back then. Now
he was beginning to see for himself that the woman was
all surface.

His strokes across the flank of the bay mare slowed as
he thought of the female who shared his life these days.
Where on earth could Johanna have gone to? It wasn't like
her to abandon her kitchen in the middle of the afternoon.

Pete's voice called from beyond the barn door. ''She's
not in the springhouse, either, Pa.'' Skidding to a stop in
the wide doorway, his small face darkened by concern, the
boy faced his father. ''You don't think she left us, do you,
Pa?''

''No! You know better than that, Pete.'' Tate shook his
head at the idea.

Timmy sat up abruptly, horror painting his features. ''We
need to find her, Pa. She's gotta cook my supper.''

Tate frowned in his direction. "Miss Johanna doesn't gotta do any such thing, Timmy. She takes care of us because she wants to."

"'Cause she loves us, Timmy," Pete chimed in.

Bessie stood, stretching and easing her shoulders forward. "My, my, what a testimony to Miss Johanna's virtues. I don't know about you, Tate, but I'm tired from that ride. I believe I'll go and take a nap myself, while you round up your wayward wife."

"Throw some wood in the kitchen stove, Pete," Tate instructed, leading the mare to the barn door. "Timmy, you go with your brother. I'm going to take a ride and see if I can scout up Johanna before that rain cloud moves any closer."

"You'll hafta saddle up again, Pa," Pete told him.

Tate slid the bridle back on the mare. "No, I'll ride bareback, son. I won't be gone long. How about puttin' off your nap for a while, Bessie, and keepin' an eye on the boys for me till I come back?"

"I wonder sometimes if Tate and the boys wouldn't have been better off staying in Ohio, Selena." Johanna lifted the teacup to her lips and sipped the sweet brew. It was the second cup she'd accepted, and from the looks of the sky to the west, it had better be the last.

Selena pushed the porch swing into motion again, the bouquet of violets brushing her nose as she sniffed their fragrance. "I think Tate's better off right where he is, Johanna. He's a man in a million, you know. And I think he's aware of how fortunate he was to find you."

"We get along all right," Johanna said, placing the teacup carefully on its saucer.

Selena laughed aloud. "If the way he looks at you is any indication, I'd say you get along just fine."

Johanna's smile was wistful. "I didn't think I'd ever be

so head over heels. I thought—'' She stopped, biting her lip.

"You thought Joseph Brittles had broken your heart when you were sixteen years old and you'd never get over the sorrow of it, didn't you?"

"That was a long time ago. Sometimes I forget he ever existed," Johanna said quietly.

"I fear he left you with a lasting remembrance of his presence in your life, though." Selena bent forward, her eyes soft as she looked at the young woman who sat on her porch steps. "I was so fearful for you, Johanna. I thought you'd never get over the misery you lived through in those days."

"You knew?"

Selena nodded. "I suspected you were going to have a child. I have rather a sixth sense about those things. In fact, I'd be willing to guess that you're in the family way right now, my dear." She laughed aloud at Johanna's look of surprise, and then sobered as she continued. "I figured out that you'd lost your baby ten years ago, Jo, and I knew your father wouldn't let me do a thing to help. You were so young, I wasn't really surprised. Those things happen…but this time will be different."

"I thought no one knew," Johanna whispered, turning her head aside, unwilling to meet Selena's gaze.

"I doubt anyone else did." Selena stood, leaving the swing to rock behind her as she settled on the top step, next to the young woman. "I'm going to tell you something that only one other person in Belle Haven knows about, Jo. I was left at the altar when I was nineteen years old. The young man hauled buggy and ran off, leaving me to carry his child."

"You had your baby all alone? Where…?"

Selena's whisper was fraught with sadness. "I gave my little girl away, the day she was born. I've never seen her since. I never will."

Johanna's eyes filled with tears, and she reached to grasp Selena's hands. "And you never married? He never came back?"

Selena shook her head. "No, I left Grand Rapids and moved here to live with my aunt. My parents couldn't stand the disgrace. Then, when Aunt Millie died, I just stayed on, and when they needed a postmaster in Belle Haven, I applied for the position." She smiled, a bittersweet movement of her lips that reflected the sorrow in her eyes. "It isn't often that a woman like you or me can find a man willing to overlook our past."

"Tate knows about my baby," Johanna said. "Does August Shrader... Have you told him, Selena?"

She nodded. "Yes, and he says he loves me no matter what happened to me twenty years ago." She squeezed Johanna's hand. "We're going to be married next month. It will be announced in church next Sunday."

Johanna's heart lightened at the news. This day had been one of discovery, one of fulfillment. One of secrets shared. "You're right, Selena. I'm going to have a baby." Her laughter gurgled as she reached to hug her friend. "I only figured it out myself lately. I don't know how you could tell."

"You have a look about you, Johanna. Sometimes I just know things about people. August says I'm perceptive. I knew the first time he walked me home from Sunday church that I would marry him one day. I think he's my soul mate."

"I've never heard that term before," Johanna said, savoring the sound of the phrase. "You know, I worried that Tate should have married Bessie instead of me. She's so good with the boys, and so beautiful, and the Lord knows she wants him badly enough. But I think maybe Tate and I were meant to be together—maybe we're soul mates too."

"Speaking of soul mates, I think I see yours coming up

the road, riding bareback on one of his new horses." Selena stood and waved at Tate as he brought his mare to a stop by her gate.

"She's here, Tate!" Selena called cheerfully. "I'll bet you thought she'd played hooky, being gone so long."

Johanna met her husband's gaze as he sat astride the bay mare, his eyes dark, his face somber. "I'm coming," she sang out, turning to hug Selena quickly. "I think he's upset with me," she whispered.

Selena returned the hug and chuckled. "Maybe, but I'll warrant you can handle him."

Johanna walked quickly down the path to the gate, passing through to where Tate waited. "Were you concerned about me? I should have left you a note, I suppose."

Tate offered her his hand and stuck out his foot for her to hike up on, lifting her to sit behind him on the mare's back, her skirts pulling taut, almost to her knees. His hand lifted in a salute to Selena, then he turned the mare in a tight circle, heading back the way he had come.

"Tate, are you angry?" Johanna hung on for dear life to his waist, wrapping her arms around him as she slid precariously on the mare's sleek back.

"What do you think?" he asked, his voice harsh, his callused hand reaching back to grasp her leg, tugging it forward to hug his thigh. He repeated the movement on the other side. "Ride up tight behind me."

"I think it's going to rain," Johanna ventured, wary of his anger.

"I wouldn't be a bit surprised. You'd be in a bad way walking home in it, wouldn't you?" He nudged the horse into a trot, and Johanna clung tighter. Then, as the first sprinkles fell, the horse broke into an easy lope, as if she scented the promise of hay and a handful of oats awaiting her in the barn.

By the time they rode through the barn door, Tate ducking to miss hitting his head, the rain had begun to come down in a soft shower. Johanna slid to the floor, shaking her skirts and brushing at her hair.

Tate picked up a feed sack and rubbed at the horse, drying her quickly. "Why's your hair hanging loose?" he asked gruffly, eyeing her over the horse's back.

Johanna tossed her head. "I felt like taking it down."

"The boys were worried that you'd run off, Jo." He rubbed down one back leg and then, moving to her side of the horse, tended to the other.

She was silent, watching him. "And what did you think, Tate?" she asked finally.

He glanced up, admiring the feminine grace of her, hair flying as she shook her head, bending low to run her fingers through the long golden tresses. "I think Johanna Montgomery would never run away from me. She'd stay and give as good as she got. I married well this time, Jo."

She stood erect, a halo of tangled locks about her head, her blue eyes dark with a passion she did not attempt to hide. "I'll never hurt you the way Belinda did, Tate." Her fingers lifted to trace the scar that ridged his cheek. "Bessie told me how this happened, that Belinda did it."

"Bessie talks too much." He shook his head, reaching up to snatch her hand, bringing it to his lips. He spoke against her palm, his words rueful. "I should have told you myself, honey. But I just couldn't."

"Whyever not, Tate?"

"It was going to involve a lot of explaining when I finally got around to it," he said in a soft flurry of words, as if he must blurt out his explanations before he thought better of it. "To start with, there were some folks in town who looked at me afterwards—after Belinda died—like they thought I'd been responsible for her death. And I guess I was, when it comes right down to it."

Johanna shook her head, then spoke, unable to remain silent in the face of his self-condemnation. "I doubt you could have stopped her, Tate. I'll bet she felt guilty for hurting you so badly.''

"Not nearly as guilty as I felt."

"She was unhappy, Tate. You couldn't be held responsible for that. We're all accountable for our own happiness. We have to find it where we can, and from the sounds of it, Belinda didn't bother much looking.''

"She was a far sight from happy, honey. I just don't know how I inspired such hatred in her. And I didn't want to admit that anyone could detest me the way she did, I suppose. The worst part of it is, I'll never know if her drowning was an accident that day, or if she threw herself into the river on purpose. And I've lived with that guilt ever since it happened. I guess I've felt like this scar she gave me is my penance for making her life so miserable.''

"Penance? Hardly! We only do penance for sins committed, and you never set out to do anything but good for Belinda. Besides…'' Johanna's fingers escaped his grasp and ran lightly over the scar again. "I think it makes you look kind of mysterious and—oh, maybe dashing and dangerous.'' Her words splintered into laughter as she caught sight of his disbelieving grimace.

And then his frown dissolved into a crooked smile as he beheld the woman he'd married. She'd shattered his gloom, and he relished her ability to lighten his darkness. "You wait right there, Mrs. Montgomery, while I put this horse away. I'll tend to you in just a minute.'' His eyes swept over her as he spoke, his agile fingers making quick work of buckling a halter on the mare.

Quickly he led the bay to her stall, his gaze barely faltering from its feminine target as he worked.

"Maybe I'd better run to the house and get some supper put together,'' Johanna said, peering out the door through the spring shower.

"Maybe you'd better stay right here and deal with your husband,'' Tate said, his long arm capturing her and pulling her from view of the house. "Get on up that ladder," he said, pushing her toward the steps leading to the hayloft.

"Whatever for, Mr. Montgomery?" she asked innocently.

"This time there'll be no room for excuses, Johanna. There's no Bessie across the hallway, no Timmy with a bellyache, and no supper to cook. That bunch in the house are on their own for the next little while. You and I have a score to settle."

She laughed, glancing at him over her shoulder, a luxurious sense of security enveloping her. His dark eyes spoke a silent message, their gray depths darkening even as she watched. And then he was pressing against her as she climbed, his hands sliding beneath her skirts to clasp her calves, slipping to above her knees and then to her ankles again. She slowed her progress, enjoying the seduction of his touch, and he nudged her upward, easing her over the edge onto the wide planked floor of the loft.

There he lifted her, carrying her several feet, to fall with her against a fragrant pile of hay from their last harvest. "The day we hauled this stuff to the barn, I thought about making love to you up here," he said against her ear.

She shivered at his words, at the damp pressure of his mouth as it moved against her throat. He clasped her tightly, rolling her beneath himself, and she opened her legs to welcome his weight against her body. Lowering his head, he brushed his mouth across her throat, his teeth touching her skin, where the top button of her dress gaped open.

"I'm so hungry for you, sweetheart," he whispered, his voice a groan as he suckled at the tender flesh. His fingers made a path for his mouth to follow, opening buttons, folding back the fabric of her dress, tugging down the beribboned edge of her chemise until he found the prize he sought.

Her hands lifted to his head, her fingers tangling in his

dark hair. "Tate...I was jealous of Bessie," she confessed, needing to wipe her mind clean of the blemish.

"Bessie is... I'll only say you had no reason, honey," he told her, his cheek resting against the swell of her breast. "If I'd wanted her, I could have had her years ago, before I married Belinda. I suppose I owe her for being so good to my boys, but I never wanted her. Not the way I want you, Johanna. The way I've wanted you since the morning I saw you walking across the meadow with a frown on your face and the sunlight in your hair."

"You wanted me then?" she asked, her eyes alight with pleasure at that piece of news.

"Yup!" He chuckled, the sound muffled against her breast. "Since the moment I saw you. I talked you into our bargain, but I hoped from the beginning I'd not be held to it for very long."

"This wasn't part of it," she reminded him. "In fact, if I remember right, you said you didn't want a woman in your bed."

"No, sweetheart. I said I didn't want an unwilling woman in my bed. All I had to do was get you to be willing."

"It didn't take you too long, did it?" she asked, tugging at a stray lock, eliciting a grunt from him as he lifted to tower over her.

"It seemed like forever," he vowed. "And let me tell you, these past two weeks have seemed like forever. Can we forget all the things we said, that night we quarreled? I'm sorry I didn't tell you what you wanted to know a long time ago, Jo. And I'm sorry I haven't explained my plans to you better. It wasn't fair to expect you to sit back and let me run the show without asking questions. Please trust me, Jo."

"I do," she said simply, and just that easily she did. "I love you, Tate Montgomery." She wiggled against him, her eyes closing as the familiar rush of desire caught her unawares. So quickly he could fan the flames, so easily her heart was moved by his words of need, and so readily she willed him to woo her with his touch.

"I've needed you for days, Jo."

He lifted over her, and she opened her eyes, her lids heavy, as she gazed at him in the dim light of the hayloft. Husky, with a seductive lilt, her words coaxed him. "Well, far be it from me to make you wait any longer, Montgomery."

"What do you suppose Pa and Miss Johanna are doing in the barn, Aunt Bessie?" Pete asked, peering through the window.

Bessie stirred the pan of oatmeal on the stove, refusing to look to where the boy's attention had been focused for the past half hour or so. "Probably doing the chores," she said sharply.

"I don't like oatmeal for supper," Timmy whined. "Miss Johanna fixed it once, and Pa didn't like it, either."

"Well, tonight you'll eat oatmeal," Bessie told them, stirring more vigorously. "I have to pack my bag after supper and get my things together."

"Are you leavin' tomorrow?" Pete asked, turning from the window.

"Yes!" Barely suppressing a shudder of distaste, Bessie looked around the comfortable kitchen. "I'm looking forward to my nice running water, turning on a faucet instead of having to pump every drop that comes into the house."

"Miss Johanna doesn't mind," Pete said idly, moving to sit at the table as he awaited his meal.

"Well, maybe she's a better woman than I am, then." Bessie's laugh was scornful.

"She don't make kites, but she's a good mama," Timmy chirped. "She loves us."

"She's not your mama," Bessie said adamantly.

"Yeah, she is," Pete told her. "We don't call her that, but she's still our mama."

Bessie sniffed, lifting the pan and carrying it to the table where the boys waited. "Sit down on that chair right, Timmy. Push your bowl over here, Pete." Silently, she ladled the thick porridge and poured yellow cream into each dish. She scattered sugar over the steaming mounds and pushed them before the waiting children.

"There now," she said, giving one last glance out the window through the gathering darkness, toward the open barn door. "Eat your oatmeal."

Chapter Twenty

The sewing room had changed, with no trace of her mother remaining. Standing in the doorway, Johanna was aware only of the scent of Bessie Swenson, the memory of the woman's flamboyant, stylish wardrobe and the trilling laughter with which she'd bedazzled the males of this household.

"Out you go, Aunt Bessie," Johanna muttered beneath her breath, marching into the room Bessie had occupied for two weeks. Her mouth set in a victorious grin, her sleeves rolled up to her elbows, Johanna set about putting it to rights. Sweeping vigorously, she had managed to set up quite a cloud of dust when Tate poked his head in the doorway.

"Spring-cleaning?" he asked, tipping his hat back with one finger.

Johanna shook her head. "Just trying to get this room cleaned up and aired out."

"Why don't we take that rug out to the clothesline and I'll beat it for you?" Tate offered.

Johanna looked up at him. "Far be it from me to turn down an offer like that. It could use a good dose of fresh air, anyway."

Tate's lips curved in a knowing grin. "I'd forgotten

about Bessie and her perfume. Smells good for a while, bu
over the long run I'm kinda partial to that soap you use.'

Johanna flushed at his backhanded compliment. Since th
encounter in the hayloft, she'd sensed a new awareness i
Tate's glances, an element of intimacy in his remarks. Al
most as if he were gifting her with the courting she'd neve
received from his hand, he'd teased her, touching her wit
a gentle hand as he encountered her in the house. His fin
gers had caressed her shoulder, rested against her waist
brushed a wayward strand of hair from her cheek.

He'd told her the chicken soup was tasty and backed up
the claim by eating two bowls of it at supper Monday eve
ning. He'd watched her ready herself for bed and told he
that her hair looked like sunlight shining through clove
honey. She'd paused in her brushing to turn an incredulou
look in his direction, gaining a chuckle of glee for her ef
fort. He'd kissed her with decorum and curled against he
back through the long night hours, leaving her to wonde
at his restraint.

In all, he'd managed to set her mind in a whirl, fillin
her thoughts with small touches of his caring, allowing hi
lazy little compliments to surround her over the past tw
days.

Now he stepped within the room, filling its limited spac
with his presence, taking the broom from Johanna's hand
and leaning it against the wall. "I'm going to lift the en
of the bed, and I want you to roll the rug, Jo. Then we'r
gonna haul it to the yard and maybe set Pete to work wit
the rug beater."

"Thought you offered to do it," she reminded him.

He shrugged, flexing the powerful muscles of his shoul
ders. "Might do Pete good to lend a hand. Build him som
muscles." He bent, lifting the weight of the bed with a
easy movement, waiting as she did his bidding, steppin
high to allow her access to the rug beneath his feet. Sh
straightened, nudging the rolled carpet with her foot.

"Think you can handle it by yourself, Mr. Montgomery?" she asked. "Or shall I give you a hand?"

"I can manage, ma'am. What else do you need done up here?"

She looked around. "I'll strip off the bed and wash the bedding and polish the furniture. The floor could use a mopping before you put the rug back down, I suppose." She tossed him a questioning look. "Don't you have any work to do today?"

"There's always something to do on a farm, Johanna. You know that. We've got six or seven new calves in the pasture since Bessie came, and a few more of those cows look like they're about due to drop. I need to take a ride over to Jonas Cooney's place to ask him to give me a hand right soon. Before the end of the week I'll give the springhouse a coat of whitewash, and the corncrib has a couple of broken slats on the far wall I need to replace."

Johanna measured him with a wary eye. "Then why on earth are you in here, messing with my work, when you've got a pile of your own to tend to?"

His grin was provocative as he lifted the rolled-up carpet to his shoulder. "Maybe I just like the way you smell, Mrs. Montgomery." He leaned to sniff loudly and appreciatively at her neck, nudging her against the wall. The carpet whacked loudly against the open door, and Johanna pushed at Tate, palms against his chest.

"Get that thing out of here before you knock everything helter-skelter." Her eyes shining with delight at his foolishness, she followed him out into the hallway. "Send Timmy up, will you? He can drag the bedding down to the washroom for me."

"Yes, ma'am." He was down the stairs and heading for the back door as she watched, and her gaze softened as she allowed it the liberty of feasting on Tate Montgomery's backside. He was a fine figure of a man, all long, ropy muscles and firm flesh, a man in the prime of life.

"And he's all mine, Bessie Swenson," Johanna said softly. "All mine!"

The new calves were enchanting, scampering about the pasture with long legs aspraddle, leaning at odd angles to nurse from their patient mothers, exhibiting a penchant for suckling on unwary fingers, should a human hand be held temptingly near. That particular tendency was going to be a lifeline for one small black-and-white heifer, Johanna thought, coaxing the stubborn creature toward the bucket she held between her knees.

The calf had been abandoned in the pasture when her mother didn't survive the birthing, something that just happened once in a while, according to Johanna's father. A tight-lipped Tate had brought the newborn to the barn and wiped her clean, delivering her into Johanna's hands for feeding. Now Pete urged the baby forward, helping to hold the stubborn calf in place.

Johanna coaxed her with soft entreaties, pushing the hard head into the pail of milk, holding her fingers beneath the surface for the heifer to encounter. A warm mouth enveloped her index finger, and Johanna grinned.

"That's the way, baby. You've got it now."

The calf snorted and jerked back, milk running from her mouth and nose. Then a long tongue lapped at the residue of milk, and the calf perked up.

Johanna repeated the process, and once more the heifer suckled her finger, managing to swallow a good portion of the creamy offering in the effort.

"I didn't know that's how you did it," Pete exclaimed, fascinated by the process. "You're a good mama, even for the baby cows."

Johanna's laughter rang out. "I'm afraid I'm not much of a mama at all, Pete. This little gal won't need me for long. She'll catch on fast."

Pete's chin stuck out defensively. "You're our mama,

Me and Timmy already told Aunt Bessie you were. And Pa promised us a long time ago you were gonna be our new mother.''

Johanna straightened on the milking stool, her expression a blend of wonder and disbelief. "You told Aunt Bessie…''

Pete nodded. "Yeah, we did. She was kinda poutin' the other night when she had to fix our supper.''

"And you told her I was your mama,'' Johanna repeated slowly.

Pete looked up quickly. "That was all right, wasn't it? Me and Timmy think you're a good mama for us.''

"Oh, yes!'' Johanna's fingers rubbed against the broad forehead of the calf. The newborn was dipping her head repeatedly into the pail, sniffling and snorting at the contents and Johanna took pity on her, reminding the creature again how to suckle the milk. She bent low, brushing her face against the animal's head. "Oh, yes,'' she repeated, her heart filling with joy as she savored Pete's declaration.

"You sure cleaned the bejabbers out of that bedroom, Jo.'' Tate slid his suspenders over his shoulders, his fingers busy at the buttons of his shirt as he watched his wife remove her stockings.

She glanced up at him from her perch on the side of the bed. "You may have set a dangerous precedent, helping me with it,'' she told him. "I thought I'd tackle the parlor next.''

"Not tomorrow. I've got a dozen things lined up outdoors.'' Turning to the washstand, Tate soaped his hands, then scrubbed at his face and neck. He rinsed off quickly, then soaped up a washrag and ran it under his arms and down their length to his wrists, a nightly ritual Johanna enjoyed watching.

"I can do most all of it alone,'' she said, rising from the bed, ridding herself of the dress she'd worn all day. She piled it in a basket atop the rest of her soiled clothing behind the screen and remained there, stripping off her underclothes, adding them to the pile.

"Pete says I'm his mama." Unbidden, the words fell in a rush from her lips. She waited for his reply, clutching her nightgown to her bosom in the shelter of the screen.

"Pete said that?" Hushed and surprised, his words were accompanied by the man himself, lifting the flimsy barrier of the screen to one side as he faced her in the dim light. His gaze was intent on her face. A towel dangling from one hand, the other holding the edge of the screen, lest it topple over.

She nodded. "He and Timmy told Bessie I was their mama."

"They did?" Tate smiled broadly. "How about that!"

"Tate! I'm getting undressed," Johanna protested, waving with one hand to shoo him from her private corner of the room.

His brow cocked teasingly, and he nudged the screen over a bit more, making room for himself in front of her. "I'd be glad to help," he offered, his fingers tangling in the gown she held, wrestling it easily from her grasp. He took in her bare shoulders. Then, skipping over her front parts, he peered over her shoulder, clearing his throat and raising one eyebrow as he considered her lack of covering. "In fact, looks to me like you've already done the job."

"Tate!" Her muted squeal was diminished by the presence of his mouth as he bent to silence her protest. And then she was enclosed in the cage of his embrace, a willing prisoner. She rose to her tiptoes, sliding up over the firm surface of his body, relishing the sensation of crisp, curling hair and ridged muscles caressing her breasts.

He lifted her easily, swinging her around and heading for the wide bed. Gently, he lowered her, tugging the sheet and quilt from beneath her, placing her in the center of the mattress. His gaze hot with a passion he made no attempt to conceal, he stripped from his trousers and drawers. And then he was upon her, spreading her knees as he knelt there, his big hands urgent as he explored the surface of her flesh.

His palms ran over the flare of her hips, the curve of her waist, the rounding of her shoulder, filling themselves with the plush softness of her breasts. He was intrigued, enchanted, by her body, as if he had just discovered the wonder of her.

"I've about gone crazy without you, Johanna." He'd intended to woo her gently, coaxing her with tender touches and entreating her response, but the reality of her welcoming arms and the sinuous movement of her body against his was his undoing. He lifted her hips and eased himself against her, his eyes closing at the pure pleasure of their joining.

And then he was lost, caught up in the joyous response of the woman he'd taken with such haste. Her soft cries of entreaty urging him, he bent to her, his hands and mouth claiming her flesh and molding it to his purpose, his kisses feeding her desire. She lifted against him, her soft, keening cry of fulfillment a symphony in her ears as he spilled his seed within her.

"I'm gonna smuch you into the mattress," he whispered against her cheek, his eyes closed, his nostrils flaring as he gasped for breath.

She shook her head, unwilling to allow his escape, her arms twined around his neck, her legs holding him captive. And he allowed it. He basked in it, this sensation of being cradled in the depths of Johanna's body, of loving her.

"I love you, Jo." He spoke the words without hesitation, uttering them from the depths of his being, his mouth brushing damp kisses across her face. And then he repeated the phrase, slowly, as if he must imprint the words upon her.

It was more than she'd hoped for, this pledge of love from Tate Montgomery. He'd been bold in his expectations of her, taking hold and running her farm. He'd been brash in his dealings, riding roughshod over her concerns, bringing home the bull and expecting her to be thrilled with the purchase. He'd beguiled his way into her heart with his care of her, then claimed her body with tender touches and gentle wooing.

And through it all, he'd won equal amounts of her love and anger. They'd have a time sorting out their differences, she decided, she and this strong man she'd married. But she could not deny the welling up of passion within her as she held him in her embrace.

"I thought you might never come to that," she told him.

"Loving you? How could I help it?" he asked with a chuckle. "You're everything I ever wanted in a woman, Jo."

"I'm plain, and I'll probably never have a striped taffeta dress to my name."

"What the hell does that have to do with anything?" he blurted out, rolling with her until they lay facing each other. "You almost had one, anyway. It's under the bed, in a package from the Sears catalog. But I decided we'd better send it back. I don't think it's gonna fit you for a while."

"Not going to fit?" she squeaked. "What dress?"

He held her fast. "I'll show you later on. Right now we need to talk about your looks."

"My looks?" Her eyes widened at his foolishness.

"Yeah. I want to tell you, you're a long way from plain, with that long, sunshiny mane of yours and those big blue eyes and the prettiest, roundest, softest..." His index finger drew a line from her throat to the center of her left breast, and his drawled assessment of her charms came to a halt.

His mouth touched the spot his finger had so neatly drawn his attention to, and his murmur of praise was muffled against her flesh. "Pete was right," he said after a moment. "You're a good mama."

"Tate!" Her squeal was a mixture of delight and chagrin. "What are you talking about?"

"I'll just bet that baby of ours is gonna love this bosom of yours about as much as I do," he said, peering up at her with a smug grin.

"What baby?" She drew back, but he was quick, and her retreat ended almost before it began.

His long arms held her against him, and he slid up to face her, nose to nose. "You know what baby, Johanna. The one we made in this bed a couple of months ago. When were you gonna tell me?"

"Pretty soon," she quibbled. "I just actually realized it myself over the last little while."

"Are you happy about it?"

Was that a worry line she noticed creasing his forehead? Was it really so important to him that she be pleased about this baby?

"Johanna, it'll be different this time. I'll be here. You know that, don't you?" Low and soothing, as if he must allay any fears she possessed, his words spread a quilt of comfort over her.

"You're the first person who's ever hung around for the long haul," she said quietly, one finger lifting to smooth away the crease that had deepened as he spoke. "My mama couldn't help dying, but I think I took it as a personal thing. I was really angry with her for a while, along with missing her so badly I could hardly stand it. And then there was Joseph."

"He wasn't worthy of you, Jo. Any man who would leave a woman to carry his child on her own isn't worth the powder it'd take to blow him away."

"Yes, well, even that baby..." She drew a shuddering breath.

"That poor little mite missed out, honey." His hand brushed against a tear that slid down her cheek. "You're gonna be a wonderful mama."

She smiled at him, blinking against a salty deluge that would not be denied. "And then my pa. He just didn't care.

Not only about me, but about anything, once my mama passed on. I felt like there'd never be anyone...just for me.''

"I'm here, and I'm not going anywhere." It was a simple statement, and his eyes narrowed as he held her face ready for his kiss of promise. His lips were firm, brushing against her mouth as if he sought just the right place to imprint his vow. "I'll never leave you, Johanna. I'm a man who believes in forever, especially when it comes to you."

She clung to him, and his hand slipped to her back, his fingers spread wide as he held her closely. "Jo? I have something to show you, something I made."

She nuzzled against his cheek. "Now?"

His chuckle rumbled as he shifted against her. "Yeah, I think now would be a good time. We need to be alone for this, and I can't guarantee much privacy in the light of day around here."

She roused, scooting back to sit against the headboard, tugging the sheet to cover her breasts. "All right, Mr. Montgomery, show me."

He grinned ruefully. "I'm afraid this involves getting some clothes on, sweetheart. Maybe your nightgown and that flannel robe of yours." Swinging his long legs over the side of the bed, he reached for his discarded trousers and slid into them.

"Are you sure this is a good idea?" The whereabouts of her gown was in question, but unless she was mistaken, it was clear over in the corner, where he'd interrupted her earlier.

His eyes lit with a glimmer of understanding. "I'll get it for you."

It landed in her lap, a balled-up mass of fabric, and she quickly pulled it over her head, tending to the buttons before she slid to the side of the bed. Standing, she allowed it to fall around her, distracted by the knowledge that Tate's eyes were on her every move.

"You do have a pretty pair of...ankles."

"Tate!" It was a subdued wail of dismay as she turned to find her robe. "Where are we going?" she asked, determined to get his late-night adventuring done with.

"Outside." His grin faded, and he opened the bedroom door, waiting for her to precede him.

"All right." At this point she'd be willing to follow the man anywhere, she decided, even when most folks were sound asleep.

They left the house in silence, the moon lighting the yard and the meadow beyond. Tate took her hand and led her in the other direction, toward the hillside where the graves of Fred and Mary Patterson were marked by hewn pieces of granite. In the pale glow of moon and stars, they lifted toward the sky, small markers barely visible from the house.

Tate's arm was around her shoulders as they walked, and Johanna felt the familiar fullness in her chest when they approached the small graveyard. And yet there was a difference, a lightening of the load she'd carried for so long. As if this man had taken part of her burden upon himself, and in the sharing had eased her grief.

"Look, Jo. There, by the baby's grave." He halted her just yards from their goal and stood behind her, his arms around her, firm beneath her breasts as he held her against the warmth of his body.

And ahead of her stood a graceful wooden slab of hickory, marking the grave of a baby who had been mourned only by his mother, up until now.

"What does it say?" There was lettering on it. She could see that the surface was cut, engraved with a series of letters, indiscernible in the dim glow of moonlight.

"It says 'Beloved Son.' Just that, Jo. If you want more, I can carve something else on it."

"When did you make it, Tate? Was it that piece you showed me the other day?"

His head nodded, brushing against her hair. "Yeah. I finished it last night and put it into the ground this afternoon. It sanded up real nice, Jo. I put a finish on it and set it up with concrete so it won't budge."

"What if the boys ask?"

He leaned to kiss her cheek. "We'll tell them the truth, if it's all right with you. Just that once, a long time ago, a baby was born and died, and his mama remembers him."

She waited for the terrible pain to descend. But found only the warmth of his embrace filling her with joy. She rubbed her face against her arm. "It doesn't hurt like it used to, Tate."

"It'll hurt less as time goes on, honey. It's easier when someone shares the sorrow."

She shuddered, visualizing what her future had contained before Tate Montgomery entered her life. Turning in his arms, she curled against him, secure in his embrace, tucking her face against his throat, inhaling the male scent of him.

"I love you." She rose on tiptoe, tilting her chin to capture his mouth, sealing her vow with a blending of lips.

His hands slid up to cradle her face, and he tipped his head to one side, allowing the moonlight to shed its glow, illuminating her. "And I love you. Have you forgiven me for the bull, sweetheart?" His grin was rueful, but the hesitation he offered as he awaited her reply was telling.

She nodded, her own smile an answer. "I trust you, Tate. That's the bottom line. I wouldn't have gotten so bent out of shape if you'd told me first."

"Bent out of shape? You were madder than a wet hen, honey."

"I suppose I was, at that," she conceded. "Don't ever pull another stunt like that, Tate Montgomery."

"From now on I'll know better, Jo. I've never had a partner before, you know."

"Well, you've got one now, mister."

"Yeah." He hugged her against him, quickly, firmly, as

if he were sealing their bargain anew. And then whispered against her ear a proposal so blatant, so filled with promise, it elicited a smothered gasp of disbelief as she pushed against him, sputtering her protest.

"All night? You're crazy, do you know that?"

He turned her, his arm pinning her to his side, her feet skimming the ground as he hauled her down the sloping hillside. Behind them, the moon caressed the barren hilltop, softening the edges of the markers that guarded the graves, lending a silvery glow, as if the heavens were gathering up the grief inherent in such a place, leaving only peace behind.

Epilogue

⟡⟡⟡

Selena Phillips was a beautiful bride, and her matron of honor was equally lovely, wearing a striped taffeta dress that had been let out at the waist for the occasion. Leah Ibsen and the barber, Jacob Nelson, walked the same aisle two months later, on the hottest Saturday in July, providing the residents of Belle Haven another opportunity to celebrate.

Three weddings in one year, one gentleman had been heard to remark, as if such a thing were unheard-of. The town was growing by leaps and bounds, what with the new babies being born. And from the looks of it, Tate Montgomery's wife would be providing him with another mouth to feed.

The summer provided a bumper crop of corn, Tate's new seed proving to be dandy. The apples were ripening up, the transparents bringing in a tidy amount for Johanna's bank account. She'd hired on a boy to help pick, and Mr. Turner had taken every bushel he could get. Tate had not allowed her to climb a ladder, and she'd contented herself with gathering up the windfalls and watching.

They'd tried their hand at cider-making and ordered in some jugs to hold product. Tate predicted a real future in cider, once the trees were full-grown and they could figure out a better process of making the tart drink.

It was while the Baldwins and snows were at their peak that Johanna left the orchard one hot late-September afternoon to climb the stairs to the big bedroom on the second floor of the farmhouse. And it was there that Tate found her a little later, garbed in her nightgown in the middle of the day.

He'd cast one look in her direction and known that the months of waiting were almost at an end. But it was nightfall before the tiny, perfect form of his daughter was placed in his hands.

Merry Johanna Montgomery, named for her grandmother, but with the name spelled to reflect the promise of the joy she would bring. The first of four children Johanna would bear her husband, a living harbinger of happiness yet to come.

* * * * *

Harlequin Historicals presents an exciting medieval collection

THE KNIGHTS OF CHRISTMAS

With bestselling authors

Suzanne
BARCLAY

Margaret
MOORE

Debborah
SIMMONS

Available in October
wherever Harlequin Historicals are sold.

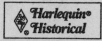

WELCOME TO *Love Inspired* ™

A brand-new series of contemporary inspirational love stories.

Join men and women as they learn valuable lessons about facing the challenges of today's world and about life, love and faith.

Look for:

Promises
by Roger Elwood

A Will and a Wedding
by Lois Richer

An Old-Fashioned Love
by Arlene James

Available in retail outlets
in October 1997.

LIFT YOUR SPIRITS AND GLADDEN YOUR HEART with *Love Inspired* ™!

Steeple
Hill™

LI1197

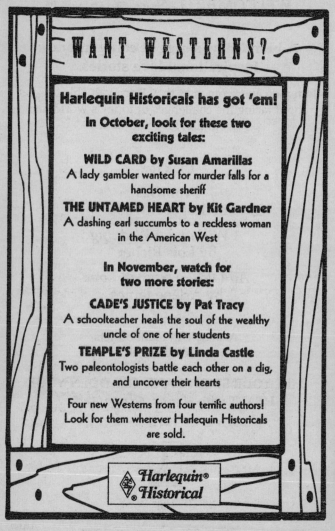

WANT WESTERNS?

Harlequin Historicals has got 'em!

In October, look for these two
exciting tales:

WILD CARD by Susan Amarillas
A lady gambler wanted for murder falls for a
handsome sheriff

THE UNTAMED HEART by Kit Gardner
A dashing earl succumbs to a reckless woman
in the American West

In November, watch for
two more stories:

CADE'S JUSTICE by Pat Tracy
A schoolteacher heals the soul of the wealthy
uncle of one of her students

TEMPLE'S PRIZE by Linda Castle
Two paleontologists battle each other on a dig,
and uncover their hearts

Four new Westerns from four terrific authors!
Look for them wherever Harlequin Historicals
are sold.

Harlequin®
Historical

DELTA JUSTICE

**A family dynasty of law and order
is shattered by a mysterious crime
of passion.**

Don't miss the second Delta Justice book
as the mystery unfolds in:

Letters, Lies and Alibis
by Sandy Steen

Rancher Travis Hardin is determined to right a
sixty-year wrong and wreak vengeance on the Delacroix.
But he hadn't intended to fall in love doing it. Was his
desire for Shelby greater than his need to destroy her
family?

Lawyer Shelby Delacroix never does anything halfway.
She is passionate about life, her work...and Travis. Lost
in a romantic haze, Shelby encourages him to join her in
unearthing the Delacroix family secrets. Little does she
suspect that Travis is keeping a few secrets of his own....

**Available in October
wherever Harlequin books are sold.**

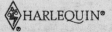

CHRISTMAS MIRACLES

**really can happen, and Christmas
dreams can come true!**

BETTY NEELS,
Carole Mortimer and Rebecca Winters
bring you the magic of Christmas in this wonderful
holiday collection of romantic stories intertwined
with Christmas dreams come true.

Join three of your favorite romance authors as they
celebrate the festive season in their own special style!

Available in November at your favorite retail store.

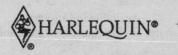
HARLEQUIN®